RAVEN ONE

RAVEN ONE

CAPT KEVIN P. MILLER
USN (RET.)

Braveship
BOOKS

Aura Libertatis Spirat

RAVEN ONE

Copyright © 2014, 2015 by Kevin P. Miller

Cover Copyright © 2017 by ZamajK

Second Edition

Braveship Books

www.braveshipbooks.com

Aura Libertatis Spirat

This book was edited by Linda Wasserman, owner of Pelican Press Pensacola:

Pelican Press Pensacola

PO Box 7084

Pensacola, FL 32534

850-206-4608

http://www.pelicanpresspensacola.com

Cover Design by ZamajK, 99Designs

Back cover photo courtesy of *Rusty Buggy*

Map courtesy of University of Texas Libraries (Public Domain Resources)

Book layout by Alexandru Diaconescu

www.steadfast-typesetting.eu

ISBN-13: 978-1-939398-22-2

Printed in the United States of America

*To Terry, who once had
the toughest job in the Navy*

ACKNOWLEDGMENTS

Not long after I retired from the Navy, my friend Captain Dave Wooten suggested I write a book. Though flattered I demurred, claiming that my career experience and "war stories" were not particularly noteworthy in comparison to several of my friends. He said, "No, you have stories." He was right—I do have some stories, and memories.

My goal in writing Raven One is to answer the question I have often been asked: *What is it like?* This novel, I hope, serves to answer that question, and while it is compelling and entertaining for those who are familiar with the world of carrier aviation, it is written primarily for those who are not. Readers of *Raven One* are going to experience a deployment as part of a strike-fighter squadron. Not all deployments, however, are the same. Each of the several I made in my career was different, and the scenes in *Raven One* are not necessarily autobiographical nor are the characters based on actual people with whom I served. That said, I spent years of my life on carriers and each extended deployment took me to the Middle East. The memories of the flight decks, the ready rooms, the bunkrooms, the wardrooms, the training hops, and daily interaction with the finest men and women I'll ever work with remain vivid.

Before they lead a strike, fighter pilots get a "sanity check" from their seniors and fellow pilots to ensure success. I wish to thank CAPT Chuck "CAP" Nash USN (Ret.) for his invaluable observations on squadron culture, CAPT Rich Thayer USN (Ret.) for his keen thoughts on leadership decision making, and CAPT Kevin "KC" Albright USN (Ret.) for his thorough editing and content suggestions, as well as his observations on leadership. RDML Greg (and Mrs. Liz) Nosal USN (Ret.) were instrumental and enthusiastic in the editing process and storyline improvement, as were CAPT Will Dossel USN (Ret.) and LCDR George Walsh, USNR (Ret.). CAPT Don Gabrielson USN provided vital feedback and suggestions on surface combat and descriptive prose, and CDR Gordon "Dart" Fogg USN (Ret.) was instrumental in explaining modern close air support procedures with which I was not familiar. LCDR Gillian V. Jaeger, MSC USN (Ret.) was also helpful with her excellent observations and suggestions. CAPT George Galdorisi USN (Ret.) and CDR Ward Carroll USN

(Ret.), both prolific and accomplished writers in this genre, freely offered solid suggestions and were encouraging to me when the publishing process got me down, as was CAPT Tom Schneider, MC, USN (Ret.) who added sage advice about his experience with modern publishing. Thank you shipmates, one and all. My brother-in-law retired NYPD Lieutenant John Dove, also an accomplished professional writer, provided much appreciated suggestions, observations and encouragement. Throughout the years of writing and refining, my wife Terry — herself a veteran of those deployments but from the perspective of the spouse back home — and my late mother Margaret, also a career Navy wife, provided timely observations and edits in company with the love and support both of them have shown me all my life. I love you!

When *Raven One* was in need of an editor, I found a superb one in Linda Wasserman of Pelican Press Pensacola. Linda, another Navy wife and mother, had very little background in naval aviation and had not edited a military action-adventure novel such as this one. Once we set out on this journey I did not know what to expect, but soon realized Linda's exceptional literary knowledge and remarkable attention to detail was vital to make a good manuscript great. We discussed every sentence and did not move on until we found the right combination of words to convey the intended message with precision and flair. Readers of *Raven One* owe Linda a debt of gratitude, and, had she chosen another avenue for her life, would have made a fine fighter pilot.

Many thanks to Jeff Edwards and the superb authors at Stealth Books for their belief and support. Great to be aboard.

I never flew a perfect flight, and suspect most (honest) pilots haven't either. While we all strived for perfection, flaws were identified and corrected. If readers find flaws with *Raven One*, I take full responsibility.

Okay, reader. Are you ready to strap in and head up north?

GLOSSARY OF JARGON AND ACRONYMS

1MC — ships public address system

5MC — flight deck loudspeaker system

20mm — Twenty millimeter cannon round, the size of an FA-18 and CIWS bullet, also known as "twenty mike-mike"

AAA — Anti-Aircraft-Artillery; Pronounced "Triple-A"

Afterburner — FA-18 engine setting that provides extra power by igniting raw fuel creating a controlled overpressure. Also known as "burner," "blower," "max," or "light the cans."

Air Boss — Officer in Primary Flight Control (ship's control tower) responsible for aircraft operations on deck out to five miles from ship.

AMRAAM — Advanced Medium Range Air-to-Air Missile (AIM-120)

Angels — altitude in thousands of feet. "Angels six" = 6,000 feet

AOM — All Officers Meeting

AOR — Area of Responsibility

APM — All Pilots Meeting

ARG — Amphibious Ready Group

ATFLIR — Advanced Targeting Forward Looking Infra-Red. IR targeting sensor placed on fuselage mounted missile station.

Bandit — confirmed enemy airborne contact; also known as "'hostile."

Bingo — emergency fuel state divert from ship to shore base

Bogey unknown airborne contact

Bolter — tailhook flies past or skips over arresting wires, requiring a go-around for another attempt.

BRA — Bearing, Range, Altitude

CAG — Carrier Air Wing Commander; formerly Commander, Air Group

CAOC — Combined Air Operations Center

CAP — Combat Air Patrol

CAS — Close Air Support

Cat — catapult

CATM — Captive Air Training Missile

CATCC — Carrier Air Traffic Control Center

CENTCOM — U.S. Central Command

Charlie — come down and land now. "Signal Charlie"

Cherubs — altitude in hundreds of feet. "Cherubs three" = 300 feet

CIWS — Close-in Weapons System; surface ship 20mm gun primarily for terminal airborne threats

CO — Commanding Officer; in aviation squadrons known as "skipper;" on ships, "Captain."

COD — Carrier On-Board Delivery. The C-2 *Greyhound* logistics aircraft is known as "the COD."

Commodore — functional wing commander, shore based; supplies aircraft, pilots and maintenance personnel to air wings as required.

CPA — Closest Point of Approach

CVIC — Aircraft Carrier Intelligence Center

CVW — Carrier Air Wing

DCAG — Deputy Carrier Air Wing Commander

Delta — hold, delay. "Delta six" means delay 6 minutes

Dhow — small boat typical of southwest Asia region

Flag officer — admirals *or* generals…but typically a navy term for admiral

FLIR — Forward Looking Infra-Red. Targeting pod that detects heat contrasts. Aka ATFLIR.

Fox — radio call associated with firing of air-to-air missile with type. "Fox-2" = *Sidewinder*.

Fragged — as planned or previously assigned. "Proceed as fragged."

g — the force of gravity. "4 g's" is four times the force of gravity.

GCC — Gulf Cooperation Council (Saudi Arabia, Kuwait, Bahrain, Qatar, Oman, United Arab Emirates)

GOO — Gulf of Oman

GPS — Global Positioning System

Gunner — squadron ordnance officer; typically a Chief Warrant Officer specially trained in weapons handling and loading.

HARM — High Speed Anti-Radiation Missile (AGM-88) used to home in on radar energy

Hawkeye — popular name for E-2C Early Warning aircraft, also known as the *Hummer*

Helo — helicopter

Hornet — popular name for FA-18C Strike Fighter

HS — Helicopter Anti-Submarine Squadron

HUD — Head-Up Display. Glass display in front of FA-18 pilot that depicts aircraft and weapons delivery information.

IED — Improvised Explosive Device

IP — Initial Point

IRGC — Islamic Revolutionary Guard Corps

IRIAF — Islamic Republic of Iran Air Force

JDAM — Joint Direct Attack Munition – GPS guidance kit placed on a general purpose bomb body. Also known as GBU (Guided Bomb Unit).

JO — Junior Officer - lieutenant (O-3) and below

JTAC — Joint Tactical Air Controller (formerly FAC – Forward Air Controller)

Knot — nautical mile per hour. One nautical mile is 2,000 yards or 6,000 feet.

LEX — Leading Edge Extension. Narrow part of FA-18 wing leading to the nose of the aircraft.

LGB — Laser Guided Bomb – laser guidance kit placed on a general purpose bomb body. Also known as GBU (Guided Bomb Unit).

LSO — Landing Signal Officer, also known as "Paddles."

Marshal — designated holding airspace prior to landing; also name of landing sequence controller.

Maverick — popular name for AGM-65 infra-red or laser guided air-to-ground missile

Military — Military Rated Thrust, the maximum engine power without selecting afterburner.

Mother — radio reference for the aircraft carrier

MOVLAS — Manually Operated Visual Landing Aid System – LSO depiction of pilot position on glideslope – typically used for pitching deck operations

NAVCENT — Central Command (CENTCOM) Naval component commander…three-star flag officer

NFO — Naval Flight Officer

Ninety-Nine — radio broadcast call used to gain attention; i.e. "listen up"

Nugget — first cruise pilot

NVGs — Night Vision Goggles

OPSO — Operations Officer

Plug — take fuel from tanker

Prowler — popular name for EA-6B Electronic Warfare Attack aircraft

RAS — Refueling at Sea, also known as Underway Replenishment, or UNREP

RWR — Radar Warning Receiver. Cockpit display of threat radars.

Rocket One — another term for Skipper in a tailhook squadron. *Rocket Two* is the XO, and so forth down to *Rocket Last*, the most junior pilot. A variation is the using the squadron callsign, such as *Raven One*.

ROE — Rules of Engagement

RPG — Rocket Propelled Grenade

SAM — Surface-to-air missile

SAR — Search and Rescue (CSAR is *Combat* Search and Rescue)

Seahawk — popular name for MH-60 series multi-mission helicopter

Sidewinder — popular name for AIM-9 infrared heat seeking air-to-air missile

SINS — Shipboard Inertial Navigation System

Strike — tactical airspace controller/coordinator in vicinity of ship

SUCAP — Surface Combat Air Patrol

Super Hornet — popular name for upgraded FA-18E/F single seat or two-place Strike Fighter with increased range and payload; also known as *"Rhino"*

Texaco — nickname for a tanker aircraft, typically S-3B

TLAM — Tomahawk Land Attack Missile; long range cruise missile launched from surface ships and submarines

TOPGUN — Navy Fighter Weapons School, Fallon, NV

Trap — arrested landing

VAQ — Fixed Wing Electronic Attack squadron

VAW — Fixed Wing Early Warning squadron

VFA — Fixed Wing Fighter Attack squadron

Viking — popular name for S-3B Sea Surveillance aircraft, also known as the *Hoover*

VMFA — Fixed Wing Marine Corps Fighter Attack squadron

VS — Fixed Wing Sea Control squadron (formerly Air-Antisubmarine squadron)

Winchester — out of ordnance

Wire — A 1.25" diameter steel cable stretched across carrier landing area to arrest tailhook aircraft, also known as "the cable" or "cross deck pendant."

XO — Executive Officer

CVW-4 *Tomahawk* call letters AH *Alpha Hotel*

Squadron	Nickname	side number	Callsign	type aircraft	ready room #
VFA-91	Spartans	(100)	"Spartan"	FA-18F	RR 8
VMFA-262	Moonshadows	(200)	"Red River"	FA-18C	RR 6
VFA-47	Buccaneers	(300)	"Cutlass"	FA-18C	RR 3
VFA-64	Ravens	(400)	"Raven"	FA-18C	RR 7
VAQ-146	Sea Owls	(500)	"Rickshaw"	EA-6B	RR 1
VAW-111	Knight Riders	(600)	"Knight"	E-2C	RR 2
VS-36	Bloodhounds	(700)	"Redeye"	S-3B	RR 5
HS-12	Golden Angels	(610)	"Switchblade"	SH-60F	RR 4

Strike-Fighter Squadron SIX FOUR (VFA-64) Officers

CDR Steve Lassiter Commanding Officer *Cajun*
CDR Bill Patrick Executive Officer *Saint*
LCDR Jim Wilson Operations Officer *Flip*
LCDR Mike Hopper Maintenance Officer *Weed*
LCDR Walt Morningstar Administrative Officer *Clam*
LCDR Ted Randall Maint. Material Control Officer *Ted*
LT Sam Cutter Strike Fighter Tactics Instructor *Blade*
LT Mike Van Booven Safety Officer/LSO *Dutch*
LT Kristin Teel Training Officer *Olive*
LT Zach Offenhausen Quality Assurance Officer/LSO *Smoke*
LT Nicholas Nguyen AV/ARM Division Officer *Little Nicky*
LT Ramer Howard Airframe Division Officer *Prince*
LT Tony Larocca Line Division Officer *Guido*
LT Melanie Hinton Personnel Officer *Psycho*
LTJG Josh Fagan Schedules Officer *Nttty*
LTJG Bob Jasper NATOPS Officer/LSO *Sponge Bob*
ENS Anita Jackson Material Control Officer *Anita*
CWO4 Gene Humphries Ordnance Officer *Gunner*

"Most of us, most of the time, live in blissful ignorance of what a small elite, heroic group of Americans are doing for us night and day. As we speak, all over the globe, American Sailors and Submariners and Aviators are doing something very dangerous. People say, 'Well, it can't be too dangerous because there are no wrecks.' But the reason we don't have more accidents is that these are superb professionals; the fact that they master the dangers does not mean the dangers aren't real.

Right now, somewhere around the world, young men are landing aircraft on the pitching decks of aircraft carriers – at night! You can't pay people to do that; they do it out of love of country, of adventure, of the challenge. We all benefit from it, and the very fact that we don't have to think about it tells you how superbly they're doing their job — living on the edge of danger so the rest of us need not think about, let alone experience, danger."

George Will commenting after the loss of the
Space Shuttle Challenger, January, 1986

Part I

Lord, guard and guide the men who fly
Through the great spaces in the sky,
Be with them always in the air,
In dark'ning storm and sunlight fair.
Oh hear us when we lift our prayer,
For those in peril in the air.

Navy Hymn Alternate Verse

CHAPTER 1

The formation wheeled right, steadied on a heading of 165, and accelerated into the cold darkness. With Mosul just off to the left, the pilot selected the target bullseye on his navigation display.

Penetrating Iraqi airspace, the four FA-18 *Hornets* led a package of aircraft *going downtown* on night one. The pilot shifted the position of his back and legs in a vain attempt to relieve the strain of being strapped into his seat for the last two hours. He had at least another two hours ahead.

Three miles below was "friendly" Kurd territory, but from this height it seemed dark and foreboding. He checked fuel, checked his position off the lead, and scanned the horizon for threats. His eyes, though, always came back to the mesmerizing confusion of moving lights on the far horizon: the lights of Baghdad.

"Ninety-nine *Buckshot, armstrong.*" The voice of the strike leader was calm.

The pilot raised the MASTER ARM switch to ARM. Pulling the trigger now would send off a radar-guided missile to find and kill its assigned target. The radar cursor bounced back and forth across the display like a metronome, but the display showed nothing ahead, nothing yet for the pilot or his wingmen to kill. *Where are you? Come on up! Come up, you dickheads, and fight!*

The lights of Baghdad loomed larger.

Breathing through his mouth, the pilot realized his throat was bone dry. His eyes tracked the occasional flashes of cruise missile impacts throughout the metro area, which he could see in its entirety through the windscreen. The flashes grew larger as they neared the city.

All around Baghdad, ordered rows of lights lifted slowly and silently from dozens of locations to fill the sky above the city. Some gracefully turned this way and that before they reached their apex and died out. These great tentacles of AAA, almost elegant in their beauty when viewed through the night vision goggles, formed gnarled fingers of light as they, too, looked for something to kill. They wanted to swat down some piece—any piece—of American aluminum so that it made a flaming, cartwheeling plunge toward a fiery impact on the desert floor.

The pilot imagined, if he had to eject, the gunners pointing at his parachute and the raging mob below waiting to beat him senseless—or worse. *This is the Cradle of Civilization.* The pilot couldn't help but think of the irony as he neared this web of death at nearly 10 miles a minute.

"*Brooms, Excalibur*, picture bullseye, single group cold, low."

"*Broom* Four One, declare."

He looked right with a start. His NVG field of view was filled with a *Hornet* centerline fuel tank and underside coming right at him. Seconds from midair collision, he instinctively pushed nose down. After he managed to recover, he looked up to his left and saw the aircraft stop its leftward slide and come back above him to take station. *Did I miss a call? Or did he?*

"*Brooms, Excalibur*, single group bullseye three-five-zero for ten, hot, climbing. Hostile, repeat, hostile."

Fighters! The Iraqis are coming up! Forgetting his near midair but keeping a wary eye on his wingman, the pilot ran his radar elevation down. A blip immediately appeared, and, with a flick of his thumb, he locked it.

The suppression element miles behind him fired their high-speed, anti-radiation missiles. As the missiles flew above the *Buckshot* formation, they resembled supersonic sparklers rocketing along unseen tracks, blazing forward to home in on enemy radar emitters and destroy them. That gave the pilots an opportunity to maneuver into a position to fire on the enemy "bandits." The bandits were coming right at him right now. *Yes! Yes, they're coming! We're gonna splash these guys!*

As he approached the target area, the radio came alive with calls of AAA and radar spikes, check turns and threat locations. For a few seconds, he noticed the contrast between the radio activity and the silent light show in front of them, especially as the impacts of the Tomahawks occurred with a greater frequency and the AAA arcs rose to their altitude. He could make out specks of radiance far to the south—formations of carrier strike aircraft coming up from the Persian Gulf. *Right on time*, the pilot thought. The slowly rotating tentacles of light grew closer.

He squeezed the trigger. With a lurch, a missile fell from the aircraft and ignited into a giant sun that sprinted ahead with a deep rumbling.

WHOOOMMmmm!

Even as the flash momentarily blinded him, he could see through his goggles that the missile seemed to run like a cheetah after its target. He saw another missile come off his wingman's aircraft and watched it rise into the star-filled sky toward its target.

Without warning, but accompanied by a muffled boom, he was jolted in his seat by something that slammed into his jet from behind. The airplane rolled right. Full left stick was useless to stop the roll. His headphones erupted into the cries of his airplane's death throes, recorded by an impassive female voice: *Flight Controls. Flight Controls. Engine Right. Engine Right.*

Warning and caution lights, too many to comprehend and too many of them red, popped up on the digital displays and lighted panels. As the rotations got tighter and tighter, he saw that the scattered lights on the ground below were also spinning in his windscreen.

"Get out!" he heard someone call over the radio.

Yes, get out! he thought, at the same time he sensed his airspeed increasing. He tore the goggles from his helmet, dropped them on the console and found the handle between his legs. He grasped the handle with his right hand and grabbed his right wrist with his left as he was trained to do. With his back against the seat and elbows in, he pulled.

The pressure and cold of the 500-knot airstream roared into his cockpit void and gripped him hard as the canopy exploded off the airplane. For a moment, he wondered if the seat was going to ignite, but then was compressed into it as the rocket he was sitting on blasted him into space with deafening and painful force as the slipstream violently wrenched helmet and mask from his head. Legs and arms flailing, he tumbled through the darkness...

When Lieutenant Commander Jim Wilson opened his eyes in the early morning shadows, the first thing he saw was the rack above him in stateroom 02-54-1-L aboard USS *Valley Forge*, a carrier en route to combat in the Persian Gulf. Breathing deeply, he realized the ejection had been a dream. *Just a dream.* But as he slowed his breathing, he actually considered it a flashback to what could have happened to him that March night in 2003. *Don't fool yourself. It can happen next month, or even next week over Iraq.* Then, just as suddenly, he berated himself. *Stop thinking like this.*

He looked at the clock: 5:52. Reveille in eight minutes, but he could go right back to sleep. Since he had a night hop scheduled, he could not break his 12-hour "crew day" by beginning his day too early, despite the fact that one could never escape "work" at sea.

He remembered yesterday's hop in the Gulf of Aden, a functional test hop on a clear, blue day, one of those days when he still couldn't believe they paid him to fly. He was the last aircraft to trap, and after shutting his jet down on the bow, he had taken a favorite route toward the carrier's "island," the towering six-story superstructure that housed the bridge that allowed him to enjoy the sunshine. As he had trudged down the flight deck in 40 pounds of custom flight gear, he had taken in the scene and wondered if this would be one of the last times he would ever experience it. *It may be the last time this cruise...may be the last time ever,* he had thought. He was conscious of the fact that once the cruise ended—some five months from now according to the schedule—he may not come back here on a deployed aircraft carrier again. *Possibly by the Navy's choice—probably by my own.* He thought of the exhilaration of flying off the ship, being up on the "roof" and experiencing what only a handful of humans can even imagine. Experiencing life on a warship on the other side of the world—a reason to stay. And, at times, in his innermost thoughts, a guilty desire for combat, a reality which was now little more than 1,000 miles over the horizon, and getting closer with each passing minute.

A dread began to creep inside, bringing him back to the realization of what waited him later that morning and every morning, a reason he would resign his commission. *Five more months,* he thought, as he turned over and closed his eyes.

Chapter 2

At thirty-five years old, "Flip" Wilson was at the pinnacle of his flying prowess. As a *Hornet* pilot of some 3,000 hours, he had been in the cockpit each year of the twelve since flight school and was a decorated combat veteran. Approaching the end of his tour in the *Ravens* of Strike Fighter Squadron Sixty Four, Wilson was the Operations Officer responsible for both training the squadron pilots for any contingency and producing a daily flight schedule. Below him in rank were three more department heads and a gaggle of junior officer pilots. And, as mandated by the Navy's career managers, he had a desk job awaiting him after this cruise.

The *Ravens* consisted of 15 pilots, a small number of maintenance officers, a dozen chief petty officers, and some 160 sailors who maintained the 11 aircraft and performed various functions that allowed the operation to run without hiccup. The *Ravens* flew the multi-mission FA-18 *Hornet* strike-fighters, and were equally at home with anything from air-to-air fighter sweeps and combat air patrols to air-to-surface bombing and defense suppression missions with an array of weaponry each pilot mastered. VFA-64 was commanded by Commander Steve "Cajun" Lassiter, an easygoing former Tulane linebacker with a thick moustache and a shock of dark hair. He was known as the "CO" or Skipper to those inside the squadron. The second in command, the executive officer, or XO, was a sour-faced martinet. Commander William "Saint" Patrick was responsible for all squadron administrative functions and in line to succeed the CO. Patrick was a slender man of medium height with a thinning hairline he combed to perfection. Unlike any other air wing pilot, he wore his flight suit only from brief to debriefing a flight. Once the debrief ended, he changed into a khaki uniform within minutes.

Four hours later, Wilson rolled his six-foot frame out of his rack. *What is today? Day 25 of a six-month cruise?* He did the math as he stumbled to the sink... *No, day 21. Three weeks. With 21 more weeks to go.* And he knew almost every one of those days would run together, a reason the crew called their time on-station "Groundhog Day."

Wilson thought of Saint immediately as he ran a razor under the water. *What bullshit crisis is it going to be today? Dental readiness report? Scratched tile on the deck?* He didn't technically work for Saint, but because the XO was a heartbeat from command and well-connected at the wing staff—and a senior officer—you didn't mess with him. *Yes, sir. Yes, sir. Three bags full.* Wilson shaved in silence and switched his thoughts to his upcoming day.

At nearly 1,100 feet long, *Valley Forge* was one of the largest warships afloat, a *Nimitz* class nuclear-powered aircraft carrier, one of twelve U.S. Navy aircraft carriers. Below deck, *Happy Valley,* as the crew referred to her, was a fluorescent world of overhead pipes, electrical cables, and steel bulkheads with strange number and letter combinations. Damage control equipment was spaced at intervals and oval openings, called "knee knockers," were cut into the steel frames. Yellow battle lanterns hung above the openings. The air smelled of fresh paint and machine oil, accented by sweat-soaked flight gear and the odor of jet fuel. The ship was a maze of right angles that provided a heart-pumping workout comprised of 18 decks of ladders—from bilge to tower. She now plowed through the Indian Ocean on her way to the location the Washington leadership had deemed she was needed: the northern Persian Gulf where she could launch close air support missions to support American forces on the ground in Iraq, hundreds of miles inland. For this purpose she was at her full combat load-out of over 100,000 tons.

The *Ravens* lived in Ready Room 7, located aft one deck beneath the flight deck's arresting wires. Ready 7 was situated between Ready 8, which housed the *Spartans,* who made up the two-seat FA-18F *Super Hornet* squadron, and the Marine squadron, and Ready 6, which housed the *Moonshadows* who flew older *Hornets* like the *Ravens.* Despite the common bond of service and having some individual friends in the *Spartans,* Wilson and most of VFA-64 liked and hung out with the marines, who shared the same airframe. The marines also joined in with the rest of the wing with their collective disdain for the arrogant and imperious *Spartans* of VFA-91 and their brand-new *Super Hornet* jets. With not a little scorn, most of them referred to the *Spartans* as "the girls next door."

Located amidships in Ready 3, the remaining *Hornet* squadron aboard *Valley Forge* was the *Buccaneers* of VFA-47. Like the *Ravens,* they also flew the FA-18C, and the two squadrons were known as "sister squadrons." These two squadrons were the only two of the eight aboard that were mirror images of each other, all reporting to the Commander of Carrier Air Wing Four, known as the CAG.

As "sisters," friendly, and sometimes not-so-friendly, competition was a part of their daily lives. The *Ravens*—from the Skipper down to the airman swabbing a passageway—wanted to outfly, outbomb, and generally outperform the *Bucs* in every area, and vice versa. In conversation, each squadron regarded the other as "Brand X."

Before going to lunch, Wilson opened the rear door of the ready room. His eyes immediately focused on the back of the XO's head in his front-row seat. The room was quiet now as most of the pilots were at lunch up forward. The squadron colors were blue and black, and each chair had a blue cover with black trim. The design depicted the squadron emblem—a black raven silhouette, wings outstretched as if swooping in for the kill. The image was simple, yet menacing, and a familiar tradition in carrier aviation over four major wars. Behind their backs, however, many in Carrier Air Wing Four and the fleet sarcastically referred to VFA-64 as the *Crows*.

Here it comes, Wilson thought. He grabbed a cup of water and made his way between the two groups of high-backed leather chairs to his own front-row seat.

"Hey, Olive," he said to the duty officer. Lieutenant Kristen "Olive" Teel wore khakis and sat at the duty officer console. Behind her was a status board with the day's flight schedule, each pilot's name written in grease pencil in bold capital letters.

Olive was nearly six feet tall, her slender body bordering on anorexia. The combination of her close-set eyes and long, dark hair pulled back into a tight bun made her a dead ringer for Popeye's girlfriend Olive Oyl, but without the squeaky voice. A no-nonsense woman of few words and fewer emotions, she participated on the periphery of any ready room hijinks only when avoiding it would call attention to herself. "Morning, sir," she replied to her department head, as she kept her eyes down and made a notation on the status board.

Wilson sat down in his chair in the front row, next to the Skipper's. He checked for something in the large drawer under his chair. He then sat back with his legs outstretched, took a breath, and waited. His wait lasted only a few seconds.

"Mister Wilson, I see you've not initialed the message board today," Saint said from across the aisle. He did not bother to look up.

"No, sir."

"An oversight?"

"No, sir. Haven't read them yet," Wilson said. He stood up and took a few steps, eyes locked on his XO.

Still looking down, Saint continued. "Do you know Strike-Fight Wing took all of our 2,000-pound practice bombs for noncombat expenditure and gave them to Air Wing Eight?"

"No, sir."

"It's right here," Saint replied, lifting the message board a few inches toward Wilson. Wilson noticed that a gaggle of JOs had arrived. *Oh, great!* Wilson thought. The XO continued with his quiz.

"Why did you not know? Actually, the more important question is, why did they take them?"

"The Wing did not contact me, sir. I'll e-mail them and find out." The JOs had stopped next to Wilson. Aware that he was in a serious exchange with his XO, they didn't dare interrupt. Saint noticed them, too…and liked having an audience.

"You're the OPSO of this squadron—for the next several months—and you're supposed to know these things before they happen. Had you reviewed this message board first thing this morning instead of rolling in here at 1030, you would have known about this before I did. You would have also had the chance to call the Wing and leave a message to find out *what the fuck. And* you could have had them e-mail you back to give the CO a full report. There could have been an answer in your mailbox *right now.*" For the first time, he raised his eyes to stare at Wilson. He couldn't have planned the moment for greater effect.

The JOs kept their eyes downcast, embarrassed to be part of the public dressing down of a senior officer and too discomfited to leave. From her perch on the SDO desk, Olive feigned inattention, but she was listening. Wilson's countenance remained rock steady.

"No excuse, sir. I'll find out."

"Thank you, Mr. Wilson. That will be all." Saint returned his attention to the message board, oblivious to the fact that the East Coast would not arrive at work to respond to Wilson's query for several hours.

"Yes, sir." Wilson responded. He managed to maintain control and repress his rage as he took his seat. *Company man,* he thought, scolding himself as he felt the JOs' eyes on him.

An hour later, Wilson's roommate, Lieutenant Commander Mike "Weed" Hopper, entered their stateroom. He found Wilson at the computer in PT gear. Weed took the measure of his roommate.

"Hey, man."

"Hmm," Wilson grunted without turning his head.

Weed clicked the light on above his desk. "Olive told me what happened."

"Hmm."

Hopper was the squadron Maintenance Officer, one place below Wilson in the *Raven* pecking order. Tall, with red hair, he possessed a big smile that matched his sense of humor. The *Ravens* were fortunate that these two department heads were friends, as they both had to work together to make the squadron flight schedule work.

"Five more months, my friend," Weed said with frown.

"Roger that," Wilson replied, and then added, "I can stand on my head for five months."

"He grabbed me earlier, too. Said there were *too many* boot marks on four-oh-two and the troops needed to be more careful. Imagine that— too many boot marks on a deployed fleet *Hornet*."

"Where is the skipper?" Wilson asked.

"He went to the wardroom with some JOs. C'mon man, let's do the same."

Wilson donned his flight suit and began to lace his boots. *Five more months.* He took stock of his situation. One thousand miles north kids were getting their legs blown off with IEDs on a daily basis. And that didn't even take into account the misery of living day-to-day in the 110-degree talcum-sand hell of Anbar Province…for a full year.

Compared to that, putting up with humiliation from known prick "Saint Patrick" is a small sacrifice. The bigger one is being away from Mary and the kids. Combat flying over Iraq would be a relief, and short of that, the routine flight schedule offered an almost daily respite from the XO. Wilson knew if he wanted to be a squadron CO, he would have to take it. All he had to do was *take it* for the remainder of this cruise. The question was whether or not his pride and vanity would let him.

Maybe I don't want it, he thought as he pulled tight on the laces.

CHAPTER 3

In her stateroom that evening, Olive wound down from a long day at the duty desk. She forced herself to e-mail her mother a birthday greeting full of the emoticon hearts and flowers her mother loved. The head cheerleader at Vanderbilt in the late 1970's, her mother was a Knoxville socialite, still stunning at age fifty. The hair, the teeth, the heels—Camille Bennett had it all. She also attended every important community event. Junior League. Democratic Party fundraisers. Garden Club tea parties. With one son in Vanderbilt medical school, and the other as Sigma Nu president at Ole Miss, no one could match her.

Olive's mother left her father, Ted Teel, when Olive was a small child—probably because she couldn't stand to hear *"Camille Teel!"* from her squealing sorority sisters one more day. She didn't mind Ted's six-figure salary at the prestigious downtown law firm of Smith, Teel and Martin, but that was adequate only until 50ish investment banker Mike Bennett came into her life with *seven* figures. Her mother was pregnant within a year, and Olive suddenly had a distant middle-aged stepfather to go along with her absent father.

From the time Olive was born, Camille wanted to use her as a dress-up doll, a role Olive fought for as long as she could remember. Olive could play the piano and had learned about white gloves and party manners at the cotillion. She could even navigate the make-up counter at Lord and Taylor, and her statuesque height and athletic prowess caught everyone's attention. But Olive knew how to draw boundaries; for example, she eschewed the cheerleader culture.

She liked the guys—but wanted to be around them on her terms, not as an arm piece—or piece of anything. Her mother cried when Olive was accepted into the Naval Academy and rarely visited. When she did visit on the yard, radiant in her navy-colored suit and stilettos, she would scoff under her breath and say, "Kristin, must you wear those mannish Oxfords?" Then she would spy a boy and whisper, "There's a cute one! Unbutton a few buttons and go up to him. Go on." Olive shook her head at the thought of it.

Camille cried again when Olive was accepted to flight school. "You *marry* a pilot, not become one!" Olive was a huge disappointment to her mother, and always had been. The calluses of emotional defense she had developed from childhood were the foundation of the reserved personality she still maintained. Even now, whenever one of her Junior League friends asked about Olive, her mother politely said, "Kristin flies for the Air Force," and quickly changed the subject. Camille could not have identified an FA-18 *Hornet* to save her life.

Just as Olive hit "send" on the e-mail, her roommate, "Psycho," burst through the door.

"Hey, how was duty?" Psycho asked. Without bothering to listen to Olive's answer, she undid her hair and began peeling off her flight suit.

"Fine. How was midrats?"

"Awesome! Sat with a bunch of *Moonshadows*. You know Lester and Crunch? They crack me up every time! Smoke was there...Dutch...Sponge.... good time." Lifting her t-shirt over her head, she added, "You should go up there. They are probably still there."

"No thanks. Writing my mother on her birthday."

"Awww...Happy Birthday, Mrs. Teel!"

Olive waved off the reference to Mrs. Teel—Psycho didn't know and never listened—and then admired her roommate's shape for just a moment as she changed. Psycho had *curves*—curves Olive wished she had. She had had boyfriends in the past, but with her insecurities made it a point to catch them eyeing a full sweater or tight pair of jeans on other girls and then blew up at them. Because she had been hurt before, she now dismissed all men (*boys*) as incorrigible pigs—a belief she had thrown up to act as another layer of defense.

However, she was alone—and didn't like it.

With her pajama bottoms on, Psycho maneuvered into her top and began buttoning the buttons.

"Hey, what do you have tomorrow?"

"A night intercept hop with the skipper," Olive replied. "How about you?"

"A day dick-around with Smoke."

Olive glanced over and saw a flash of Psycho's perfect breast before the last button was buttoned. *I may need to get me some of those*, she thought.

Psycho flung on a robe, stepped into her flip flops, and opened the door to visit the female head down the passageway. "B-R-B!" she called out airily as she left.

Olive smiled to herself. *Psycho*, she thought, *if Mom could overlook the fact you "fly for the Air Force," she would love to have you as her daughter.*

CHAPTER 4

The ethos of fighter squadron life is competition. Against other squadrons and outside groups, between squadronmates, and even against oneself. The competition is daily and relentless, and, once at sea, there is no escape from it. Landing grades, boarding rate, interval timing, bombing accuracy, air-to-air training engagements won, aircraft system test scores, flight hours per month, career night vision goggle hours, career traps, night traps per month (high and low), squadron flight qualifications, ground jobs held (high and low), combat sorties, combat drops, strike/flight Air Medals, and squadron competitive ranking... In fact, practically every area of their lives—including beers consumed on liberty, facial hair quality, stock portfolio knowledge, video game victories, coolness of car, and hotness of girlfriend—become legitimate areas of competition for the aviators in a fleet carrier squadron.

For a pilot, and for some more than others, each flight is one big pass/fail test. However, each flight also includes dozens of little tests, some institutionalized but many self-administered. These tests allow the pilot to measure his performance against others but most importantly against himself in order to do one thing—get better. The pilots live with a constant undercurrent of anxiety; in no way do they want to embarrass the squadron or themselves. It is not surprising that the overwhelming majority are first-born perfectionists.

Even killing time in the ready room turns into evaluation and critique sessions as they watch their air wing buddies on the closed-circuit flight deck TV, called the Pilot Landing Aid Television or PLAT. The eyes of every pilot of every experience level are drawn to the PLAT whenever it is on. The pilots check the weather outside or how the aircraft are parked on the deck or "spotted," but more often than not, they just want to watch the minute-by-minute drama of carrier aviation. At night, the PLAT is genuine entertainment in its own right, depending on the weather conditions, with the ready room "cowboys" able to monitor the side numbers and recognize the voices—and voice inflections—of their fellow air wing pilots and naval flight officers as they struggle to make their approaches. Like everything else, the landings always create an environment for stiff competition between squadrons and individuals. A missed trap bolter for "the girls next door" is almost always good; a bolter for a trusted squadronmate is the source of feelings of sympathy, or even of personal disappointment—however, for a rival squadronmate, not so much.

Despite the fact most of it is healthy, competition is ever present in a fighter squadron, and it is magnified by the hours spent going over every aspect of a flight in an effort to improve—to attain perfection. To this end, constructive criticism is a daily occurrence for a pilot of any rank, and every flaw—personal and professional—is identified. Most can handle the feedback, but those who can't are easy targets of ready room mockery until they succumb to a certain amount of humility. And if they refuse, squadron life is brutal for these loners. With so many healthy, if not huge, egos in close quarters, the near constant competition acts as a control mechanism to keep the egos of certain ones in check. Therefore, since no one can be number one in everything with so many overachievers looking over one's shoulder, the competitive atmosphere allows everyone to stake a claim someplace.

CHAPTER 5

As the sun set the following evening the ship began to pick up some appreciable movement from the long Indian Ocean swell. Wilson noted this as unusual in the IO. These waters off the Arabian Peninsula were often calm and sunny throughout the year. If seas were heavy at any time, it was during the winter months, when squall lines with heavy thunderstorms and occasional sand storms were not uncommon.

From his stateroom desk, Wilson checked the flight schedule: the XO and Sponge Bob were on the "pinky" recovery, followed by the Skipper leading a practice intercept hop with Olive. *Glad I'm not out there tonight*, he thought. Night carrier aviation was difficult enough without a pitching deck. He surmised the weather was deteriorating, and realized he had not been outside the whole day.

He clicked on the PLAT…the ceiling was down from earlier and the deck was slick from a passing rain cloud. The *Hornets* on the bow were preparing to launch and the camera showed one taxiing out of its Cat 2 parking spot. Wilson watched it taxi aft past the bow jet blast deflectors, take a 45-degree right turn to clear the aircraft parked amidships, and then turn left down the angle to the "waist" cats. The camera showed a close-up of the aircraft…side number *406*. Wilson clicked up two channels for the air ops status board: *406* was Sponge Bob's aircraft, and the XO was in *402*. He clicked again and checked the weather. Low broken-variable-overcast clouds, three miles visibility in rain, with occasional lowering to 500 feet overcast and one mile with lightning, freezing level at 14,000 feet and high gusty winds.

Not a good night at all.

Wilson wondered about the thought processes of the captain on the bridge, the admiral in flag plot, and the CAG in his office. *They've got all the information I've got, and more,* he thought, *and these guys are still taxiing to the cats.* He saw Sponge Bob on Cat 4, with the *Viking* tanker next to him on Cat 3. Ten minutes to launch.

The sound of an E-2 on Cat 2, two decks above, caused him to switch again to the PLAT. The screen was obscured by water droplets from another rain cloud as the *"Hummer"* extended its wings at a measured pace while its big turboprops kicked up clouds of spray behind it. *Clackety, clackety, CLACKETY, CLACK-ETY, clackety, clackety* sounded overhead as the "shuttle," the above-deck catapult launching mechanism, was retracted aft for hook-up. Underneath the shuttle and below the metal catapult track, two large pistons, the size of a small car, moved into launch position. Once the aircraft was connected to the shuttle, and on signal, superheated high-pressure steam exploded into the piston cylinders to propel the aircraft forward to reach flying speed. The pilots likened it to being flung out of a slingshot.

Wilson exited his stateroom and headed for Ready 7. As he strode aft on the passageway, the noise of the *Hummer*, although at idle one deck above, surrounded him. He heard the familiar "thunk" as the catapult was placed in tension. That was followed by the increased engine reverberation as the aircraft props changed pitch at full power for launch. *Are they really going to shoot these guys?* he wondered. *They are going to have a tough time getting back aboard in these conditions.*

He made a right turn, then a left, as he continued aft to the ready room. He had to cover his ears as the familiar, yet annoying, din from the jet blast deflector pumps and the aircraft at full power pounded into his brain. A thud above and behind signaled the firing of the catapult, and the swift movement of the shuttle made a *zziiiiipp* sound as it moved forward pulling the E-2 with it. The sound of the E-2 engines also faded away at the instant a *THUNK* was felt forward on the bow: the sound of the catapult slamming into the water brake as it flung the *Hummer* into the air.

Just then a loud *CLACK, CLACK, CLACK* passed from inside the ship on his right side as the shuttle roared along the track. It stopped with a booming *THUNK* that rattled the ship's frames. This was followed by a faint whistle sound as the S-3 tanker was launched off the waist. *They're gonna do it.* Wilson smiled and shook his head as he stepped over a knee-knocker.

Halfway to the ready room he steadied himself as the ship took a starboard roll. Right after it stopped, the grim-faced Deputy CAG and his Operations Officer, whom he knew as "Bucket," passed him in a hurry.

"Sir," Wilson said. The DCAG passed with a barely audible acknowledgement and turned outboard toward the island ladder, shoulders hunched and head down.

As he trailed his boss, Bucket raised his eyebrows at Wilson to convey his thoughts: *I don't know what's going on.*

Wilson wondered where they were headed. *The bridge? The tower? Who knows where?* He walked past the S-3 and helo ready rooms, pushing off a bulkhead to steady himself as the ship took a roll. *It's getting worse.*

When he entered the ready room, Wilson's eyes were drawn to the Skipper, who was conducting his brief in the front of the ready room. Olive, two *Buccaneer* pilots and two aircrew from the *Sea Owls* listened intently. If Cajun Lassiter was concerned about the conditions his squadron pilots—and he—would face that night, he didn't show it. *Too professional for that.* But Wilson knew he would brief the aircrew on every contingency and would further brief Olive on pitching deck LSO calls and other heavy weather techniques he had picked up over 17 years of carrier flying.

LT Ramer Howard, known in the squadron as "Prince Charming," both for his dark good looks and as a sarcastic reference to his disagreeable personality, sat in his khakis at the duty desk. The blank look on his face belied the question they all had as the roar of a jet at full power filled the room. The Skipper raised his voice an octave to be heard above it. It was a *Super Hornet* in tension on Cat 3, and on the PLAT Wilson could see light rain falling from the low clouds that extended to the horizon. With a dull thud, the *Rhino* screamed down the deck and kicked up billowing clouds of water drops in its exhaust. The familiar sound of the water brake reverberated through the ship and the *Super Hornet's* WHOOSH served as evidence it had cleared the deck—airborne over 500 feet forward. Wilson glanced at Prince Charming, but his face remained blank.

"Wanna get some food?" Weed asked.

"Yeah, let's do it," Wilson replied.

JOs Psycho, Smoke, and Guido had just left the ready room, also on their way to the forward wardroom. Before he reached the door, the sound of a strike-fighter in tension caused Wilson to return to the PLAT, with Weed right behind him. They could make out Sponge Bob's salute to the catapult observer, which was followed by the usual 10-second wait. When the cat fired, the *Hornet* thundered down the catapult track and into the air, another wake of wind-driven spray behind it.

The pilots proceeded out of the ready room and forward along the passageway. "Gonna be a varsity night," Weed began.

"Yes, it is," his roommate responded. "What's been happening down here?"

"Deputy CAG called about 45 minutes ago. The Skipper talked to him, and I discerned that DCAG wanted to know about Sponge Bob. Skipper said he was a solid pilot. If it were me, I would have asked about the XO instead!"

Wilson decided to keep the fact that he agreed with Weed to himself. "How are your guys doing up there?" he asked, as he glanced at Weed over his left shoulder.

"Drenched and loving it," Weed chuckled. "Guys are fighting to go topside so they can get some sea salt on their shoulders."

"Yeah…think that's what Sponge is thinking right now?" Wilson dead-panned.

"He looked confident as he walked, but the XO was real tense, more than usual."

After they walked a distance of two football fields over a series of frame knee-knockers, they came to the "dirty shirt" wardroom, which was located below and between the bow catapults. Cat 2 was still firing, and the sound of the shuttle roared through the wardroom overhead. The tremendous crash that came from the water brake, located on the extreme forward part of the flight deck some 200 feet away, shook everything in the room that was not bolted down. The pilots were used to the noises and the shaking and paid little attention—unless there was something unusual about them. Tonight, they noted the increased movement of the ship, well forward of its center of gravity.

Wilson and Weed picked up their trays, drinking glasses and silverware as they got into the already long buffet line. The junior officers were about ten ahead. Everyone in line wore a flight suit.

Wilson had experienced severe pitching deck conditions several times off the Virginia Capes and once near the Azores, but not out here in the IO. Regardless of where it was, the great 100,000-ton ship could bob like a cork in heavy seas. In fact, right now, the ship was creaking as the bow rose and fell in the deep swells. It pitched up and down, often accompanied by what the seamen called a Dutch Roll, a roll induced by the pitching oscillations. Pitching and rolling decks were difficult enough, but the seas could also heave the whole ship, lifting it up and down in the water.

All this was a recipe for a poor boarding rate, which meant lengthy recoveries, stressed aircraft components, and tension with everyone involved with flight operations exacerbated by the fact that each plane had limited airborne fuel. USS *Valley Forge* just signed up for it.

The two sat down next to the *Raven* junior officers. Each squadron had staked out their own "unofficial" table where they—as the trained creatures of habit that they were—almost always gathered for a meal. The *Raven* table was all the way forward on the port side.

"Anyone care to go flying tonight?" Wilson asked the group as they joined them.

"No, thank you," Psycho answered. Her voice carried throughout the room as she continued. "I flew last night and twice at night in the Red Sea. Think I'm covered for at least tonight."

"JOs complaining about flying at night," Weed said, shaking his head in feigned disgust. "Can we count on you for a full moon night? Waxing gibbous at least?"

"That would be nice—if you must fly me at night at all!" she giggled. Nugget pilot Lieutenant Melanie "Psycho" Hinton was an anomaly. The daughter of an admiral, she was blessed with California surfer-girl good looks. But she didn't act like she knew it, and she could keep up with any of the guys. Her loud and obnoxious commentary—on any subject—earned her the call sign Psycho, which stood for "Please Shut Your Cake Hole."

"It was clear and a million in the Red Sea, and last night was fairly pink, as I remember," Wilson interjected. "You'll just have to take it up with the schedules officer."

"He gives you the schedule to sign!" Psycho cried, her eyes wide in mock indignation, enjoying the attention.

"I just sign what Nttty gives me," Wilson said with a smirk as he reached for his salad plate, which slid to the left as the ship took a roll. "Nttty" was Lieutenant Junior Grade Josh Fagan, the Schedules Officer, who, after one memorable multiplane intercept hop, was christened with his call sign Nttty—"Not Time To Talk Yet."

"So does the CO. Take it up with him," Weed added.

Psycho also caught her plate in midslide and sighed. "Should have known the hinge-heads would band together in support of the front office. Next time I'll just take it up with my good friend, Nttty. Thank you, sir."

"Good answer," Weed mumbled, through a mouthful of food.

SLAP!

A swell slammed hard against the bow and rattled the dishes. The group heard the water gurgle down the hull.

"It's serious out there," Guido muttered into his food as he took a big gulp of fried rice.

Smoke agreed. "Yeah, they've gotta be thinking about canceling the night events."

Just then the loud *WHOOOMMMmmm* of a jet on a bolter filled the wardroom. The aviators exchanged knowing glances as the jet climbed back into the pattern. *The first of many bolters this recovery*, Wilson thought. He turned to Smoke, one of the squadron landing signal officers, and asked, "Were you guys working manual recoveries earlier?"

"NO!" Psycho howled and slammed her hand on the table. "I had a sweet OK going and then the deck pitched down—or came up—and I caught an ace on the fly. They gave me a "fair." They said that was a gift because the ship did a little dance in close, but not so much that I couldn't have made a better correction. I mean, it's either a pitching deck OK or not! They should have rigged the MOVLAS, the *bastards*."

Sensing an opening, Smoke chided her. "Was the deck down, or did it come up?"

Psycho's eyes narrowed as she shook her head at him. "You A-holes stick together, don't you? I thought squadron blood might be thicker than LSO water. Guess not."

"Well," Smoke said, and grinned at her. "We have two senior aviators here who are charged with advising the commanding officer as to proper procedure, given the operating conditions we face. So what was it? Up or down?" Smoke folded his hands in front of him and held her gaze.

"It was UP!" Psycho shot back, fire in her eyes. "As in '*Shut up!*'"

"All right! I'm sorry." Smoke smiled and extended his hands in front of him. "Just wanted to get that straight!" His eyes remained on her as he mouthed *"LSO water?"* with a quizzical look.

"What did you get, Paddles?" Wilson asked Smoke, instantly wishing he hadn't. Pausing for effect, the LSO suppressed a grin. "OK three, sir."

"SEE!" Psycho exploded, her food barely staying in her mouth. "It's good-old-boy collusion out there!"

Wilson saw the Skipper and Olive duck into the room carrying plates of food. It was an hour and ten minutes before their launch, just enough time to eat a rushed meal before man-up. Lassiter found a few spots at the table and placed his tray across from Wilson.

"Hey, Skipper."

"Flip," Lassiter greeted him over a *WHOOOMMMmmm* from above—the sound of another *Hornet* on a bolter.

"What's the story on your event, sir?" Weed asked him.

Lassiter exhaled. "Nothing yet, we'll walk on time. My guess is they will make a decision in the next hour. CAG is recovering on this event."

Weed grinned. "Maybe that was him going around."

"Hope not," Lassiter said and smiled.

"I'm sure Paddles will no-count it for a pitching deck," Psycho chimed in, as she shot Smoke a look.

"As they should," Smoke retorted with a confident grin. "Paddles always does the right thing." Psycho responded to that with her most feminine sniff.

Wilson watched the exchange and figured there might be something going on between Smoke and Psycho. Lassiter shoveled another spoonful of rice into his mouth. He kept his eyes down, as if lost in concentration about his upcoming flight, and acted oblivious to the flirting between his junior officers. Wilson knew, however, the skipper was paying attention and was probably on to them.

"Smoke" was the call sign of Lieutenant Zach Offenhausen, a blond pretty boy of supreme confidence who, in fact, *was* a California surfer and had been a motocross champion in his teen years. Now a second-cruise JO, he aspired to TOPGUN training once the deployment ended. Both Smoke and Psycho—despite the fact that she never shut up in social situations—were good officers and solid pilots. Fraternization was one way to destroy that good standing. Here they were, attractive young single adults, working and eating together day after day for months—and, from what it looked like, maybe even sleeping together.

Wilson got up from the table and said, "Excuse me, sir," to the CO. Weed did the same, followed by Smoke and Psycho. Lassiter waved and nodded and swallowed a final mouthful. He and Olive picked up their trays, took them to deposit in the scullery, and hurried back to the ready room. They wanted to walk on time.

In the passageway, the JOs and Weed continued aft while Wilson ducked below to his stateroom to check for e-mail from home. The darkened room was illuminated only by the screen saver of his laptop. A note from Mary awaited him.

Dear James,

Derrick rode the bike this morning without training wheels! He did great! I just ran behind him a little and then he took off on his own. He went to the end of the cul-de-sac and turned around. I was praying he could do it. When he got back to the house though he crashed—into the Hopper's car! Karen had just pulled up and we were standing by the car cheering him on as he rode toward us. He tried to turn away but hit the left front and fell off. He skinned his elbow and cried a little. No damage to the car, but Karen felt awful. Derrick was over it after a band-aid and a kiss. Just another day as a navy wife.

Oh, great...

Brittany was so cute yesterday in her new winter boots. She drew a picture of herself wearing them just for you, which I'll send to you soon with some goodies. I miss you, my love.

He looked at Mary's picture on his desk and daydreamed for a few moments. The photo, taken at the Strike-Fighter Ball, was sensational. It caught her beautiful face, her dazzling smile, which generated more wattage than all the sequins on her dress. He dreamed of her feminine shape. Thirty-three years old...and she had not changed since college.

Click, click...weeEEEEeeoowww!

The sound of a *Viking* recovery above brought him back to his O2 level stateroom and the realization that holding Mary was over five months away. With the *Viking* aboard, the recovery must be nearing completion. He checked the schedule again and verified his CATCC watch for the next recovery, fifty minutes from now.

Wilson composed a quick note to Mary and headed aft to the ready room.

CHAPTER 6

Thirty minutes later, Wilson walked into Air Ops, amidships on the O3 level. The cool, dark room was illuminated by a few small overhead lights over the work desks. The desks and two rows of Naugahyde-covered benches faced the event status boards.

Wilson was the first CATCC rep to arrive, and he took a spot on the back row. Commander Marty O'Shaunessy, the Air Ops Officer and a career naval flight officer, was hunched over his desk talking on the phone, his usual pose. Wilson knew O'Shaunessy was having a miserable night with this weather. He also knew that, as the sun sank below the horizon, the misery was going to get worse.

Wilson studied the acronyms and numbers on the status monitors for the information he needed. XO and Sponge Bob were checked into *marshal*, the aircraft holding pattern aft of the ship, at 12,000 and 13,000 feet, respectively. XO had 8,000 pounds of fuel, Sponge only 7,100. And that information was five minutes old. *If the launch goes on time, Sponge should get here with a little over 4.0.* That 4,000 pounds gave him two passes before he would need to be directed to the tanker overhead.

The ship was working "blue water ops" as normal, as if there were no divert fields in the area, but Wilson sought them out on the status monitors anyway. He needed to find a location in Oman where a divert aircraft, which required a climb and descent through icing conditions in order to make an instrument approach to an unfamiliar field at night, could land as safely as possible in the wind and rain. The ship was definitely where the pilots wanted to recover tonight… if the deck would cooperate. Wilson recalled a salty instructor pilot describe the cause of an aircraft mishap as a "box," where the sides are closed, one by one, by poor decisions and conditions. He thought tonight's operations had the construction of such a box well underway.

Wilson caught the eye of LT Mike Metz, the Assistant Air Ops Officer, and gave him a nod to join him. Metz glanced at O'Shaunessy, then got up and walked the few steps to the bench where Wilson was seated.

"Hey, Flip."

"Hey, how's it going?" Wilson asked in a low tone. "Are we going to continue?"

"Yes, sir. The weather should be improving with frontal passage. The Captain wants to fly, too."

"Great," Wilson muttered as he looked at the status board. "How was the last recovery?"

Metz glanced again at O'Shaunessy. "Took forever. The commander got reamed by the Captain for having too many tankers airborne. We had three sweet tankers and needed to tank four guys almost simultaneously, so we needed them. Hey, did you see that *Cutlass* bolter?"

Wilson shook his head. "Who was the pilot?"

"I think they call her Betty. It was *really* long. She went to the tanker but had to climb through some clag to find him, and she finally plugged with about 1,500 pounds. When she got back here, it looked like she trapped hard… She was determined not to go back up there again."

"I can relate." Wilson realized he was keeping Metz too long. "Hey, thanks, man. You have a great recovery."

"You, too, sir," the lieutenant said with a smile and returned to his seat.

Wilson nodded. He was right. Air Ops was *the place* to be at night, especially a night like this. Dozens of decisions were being made that affected the human drama of operating high performance aircraft in the close vicinity of the ship. And, for the most part, that drama centered around fuel states. Airplanes could recover aboard a carrier only if they had a certain amount of fuel. The typical requirement was half of a full load; that amount would not overstress a 17-ton *Hornet* airframe as it smashed into the deck at the rate of 700 feet-per-minute. During the descent, the plane looked as if it were suspended a few feet above the flight deck and then dropped. At the moment of the "drop," the plane's tailhook grabbed one of the steel cables stretched across the deck and wrestled the jet to a halt, slowing it from over 140 miles per hour to zero within the distance of little more than a football field.

The hook sometimes skipped over the wires, or the pilot came across the ramp too high and landed long. Either circumstance resulted in a "bolter." Therefore, landing called for full power on each touchdown to ensure the aircraft could get airborne if necessary. Until it did, its hook clawed at the nonskid surface and kicked up a dazzling spray of sparks. The jet then zoomed off the end of the angled deck and struggled back into the air for a downwind turn and another approach.

Sometimes the pilot would get a "wave-off" signal from the LSO due to a poor approach or due to the deck status. Pilots liked recovering with "max-trap" fuel in these conditions. More fuel meant more options, more chances to get aboard. All aircrew sweated fuel when operating around the ship, but "blue water ops" at night, especially with a pitching deck, put everyone on edge. Sometimes pilots cheated, bringing an extra 100-200 extra pounds of fuel aboard; that extra fuel equaled one or two more minutes airborne if they needed it for another pass, to rendezvous on the tanker, or to make the divert field, even if they had to fly on fumes. That was certainly better than flaming out and ejecting 10 miles short. The fuel gauge was, indeed, the most important instrument in the cockpit at times like these.

More pilots dropped in next to Wilson in the peanut gallery: squadron department heads and COs and XOs from the other squadrons were all there to act as subject matter experts, if the need arose. He exchanged greetings or nods with most of those who caught his eye, but they were all there, like Wilson, to assess the situation facing their pilots that evening. CDR Randy "Big Unit" Johnson, the *Buccaneer*'s Executive Officer, sat down next to Wilson. Johnson shared the same name as the flame-throwing major league hurler, stood at six-foot-four, and had a bone-crushing handshake he had developed from regular workouts in the foc'sle weight room. He possessed the good looks of a movie star—with his thick, dark hair, brown eyes, square jaw and cleft chin—he was one of the nicest guys in the wing and a solid carrier pilot.

"Flip, ready for another fun-filled night of stupid human tricks?"

"Yes, sir!" Wilson responded, and then added, "How's Betty doing? Heard about her long bolter."

"She saw the elephant on that one. She said she had a ball, but she could sense the deck pitch down—it just slid out from under her. She knew she was going to bolter and just held what she had, but the deck seemed to fall further and further away. She saw nothing but water and lit the cans just as she touched down. My understanding is that she was pretty far up there."

"Yes, sir, my gunner saw it from the de-arming hole. His eyes were big."

"Yeah," Johnson chuckled. "I'll bet he could see *Betty's* eyes a mile away when she was abeam on downwind! After she trapped, she came into the ready room in her gear muttering 'Holy shit! Ho-ly *shit!*' "

Wilson laughed, having been there before.

Johnson continued. "You know, it always amazes me… Here we are in the middle of friggin' nowhere, flying in these varsity conditions, which is pretty dangerous when you think about it. Yet, we go to the ready room, watch the PLAT and *crack up* laughing as our friends risk their lives! No one else on earth has any idea this little drama is happening. And only about 50-60 people aboard are intimately involved in it right now. That means *only* about one percent of the crew has a clue about how screwed up this is."

Wilson smiled and nodded. "Yes, sir."

"And we howl laughing and critique the finest pilots in the world doing their best under tremendous stress with very little margin for error." The Big Unit shook his head. "And before long, it will be our turn again."

"I promise I won't laugh at you, sir," Wilson said with a straight face.

"Bull*shit!*" Johnson whispered and smiled. "We heard the *Raven* ready room howl from a hund'erd frames away when Betty boltered!"

"I swear I wasn't there, sir!"

A loud roar filled the space and made further conversation difficult. A *Hornet* in tension was at full power on Catapult 3 above them. Two white cones of fire leapt from the tailpipes and licked at the jet blast deflector, the brilliant light washing out the camera. The sound inside Air Ops became a deep, vibrant, continuous boom. They watched the pilot select external lights—*ON*—and the pulsing aircraft glow illuminated the deck around him. That was the signal he was ready. Wilson watched the LED display on the clock: 17:59:49…50…51…. The *Hornet* remained stuck to the deck, burning fuel at a prodigious rate. A familiar pop and zipper sound started the *Hornet* down the track, its afterburner exhaust tearing at the deck. Wilson kept his eyes on the PLAT as the *Hornet* got to the end and went airborne. Another *THUNK* of the Cat 3 water brake shook the ship's frames down to the keel.

Ding ding, ding ding. The sound of four bells played over the 1MC loudspeaker, signifying 1800 hours. *Valley Forge* prided itself on "launching on the bells."

Another *Hornet* roared off Cat 2. Olive's husky voice sounded over the departure frequency. "Four-one-two airborne." Wilson watched her aircraft on the PLAT, and with a positive rate of climb, she deselected burner to save fuel to remain aloft for the planned 90 minutes. The skipper launched off the waist one minute later, and Wilson recorded their times in a log book. Seven more jets to go. Wilson had to steady himself as he wrote. The ship was still moving appreciably in the heavy seas.

The marshal frequency radio crackled over the loudspeaker as the first returning aircraft began its approach: "*Marshal, Spartan* one-zero-three commencing out of angels six, state seven-point-eight."

"Roger, one-zero-three, check-in approach on button fifteen."

"One-zero-three, switching fifteen."

CHAPTER 7

The recovery commenced. Each minute, as one aircraft, with the hook down for landing, pulled power and pushed the nose over, another pilot or aircrew entered a precision realm of absolute concentration. Airspeed, heading, and rate of descent were monitored to maintain position in an exact sequence as the aircraft lined up behind the ship. More than anything else, the fuel state of each aircraft dominated everyone's thinking.

The instrument scan, the voice calls, the procedures were rote, all trained into each pilot to become second nature, even to Sponge Bob at the beginning of this, his first deployment. Also common to all the aircrew was a level of tension that, at times, bordered on fear. Wilson knew tonight was going to be one of those bordering-on-fear nights; everyone faced low overcast with sporadic rain, a pitching deck, and unfamiliar divert fields that were over 200 miles away.

At sea, away from the cultural lighting of shore, an overcast sky at night blocks out even the moral support starlight can offer. With no discernible horizon, the sea and the sky become a whole. *Black.* Inside-of-a-basketball black. Nights like these bring out the inner demons harbored within each pilot. *Cold cat shots. Ramp strikes. Total electrical failures.*

Those who bolter or receive low state wave-offs are given vectors to a tanker located overhead in the gloom. Those pilots, sometimes near a state of desperation, must try to find it without becoming disoriented, without losing control of the aircraft, and without letting a moment's inattention cause them to collide with the tanker.

Pilots who experience brake failure on deck must make a frantic pull of the ejection handle before the aircraft goes over the side. The seat blasts them out of the cockpit and then blasts them again into a parachute. They have no more than a second after the disorientation of the opening shock (*OOMPH!*) to get their wits about them and to prepare for water entry.

Inflate! Pull at the toggles. *Raft!* Reach for the release.

Immersed in frigid seawater, they struggle to get free of the chute, conscious of the great ship parting the waves mere feet away. As the wake breaks over their heads, they get tossed about, get sucked under, gag constantly and spit out mouthful after mouthful of salt water. They must feel for their raft in the blackness, as icy cold numbs their fingers. Above all else, they hope the plane guard helo sees them and puts a swimmer in the water *now. Please, God, help me!*

It gets worse. If a pilot can't get aboard or tank, he may be directed to divert ashore. This requires that he transit alone over miles and miles of open ocean. If disaster strikes then, and the jet is no longer flyable, the pilot makes a desperate *Mayday!* call, giving his range and bearing before he ejects into black nothingness and a shivering cold descent. Added to that is the dreaded knowledge that *no human being is within 100 miles!* And even if a rescue helo is sent immediately, it won't get on scene for nearly an hour, and the pilot is in the cold water that whole time, fighting shock and hypothermia. They hope to muster the strength to signal for the helo if it, by miracle, finds the "needle in the haystack" of the black and limitless sea.

Wilson and the others were well aware of the sudden and violent ways aviators could meet their end. Episodes like this were quite rare. The Navy, as a whole, often went many years between such incidents. Their training was superb and they knew how to handle any situation placed before them. But the nightmares did happen on occasion, and deep in their minds—in the darker than night place where the demons lived—they knew that some gloomy night fate could choose them.

The external lights of a *Hornet* at full power came on, a signal to the deck crew the pilot was ready for launch. In the corner of the screen, however, Wilson noted the squadron troubleshooter with wands crossed over his head, the signal for suspend. He watched the Cat crew go through the suspend procedures and heard the Mini Boss make the radio call.

"Two-one-zero, you're suspended."

"Roger," the pilot replied. Another first-cruise aviator, he kept his left arm locked in order to hold the throttles forward until given the signal to throttle back.

A groan went up from O'Shaunessy as he reached for the phone once more.

"Two-one-zero, we didn't see a rudder wipe out. Let's try it again," the Mini-Boss radioed.

"Yes, sir," the young marine pilot answered.

O'Shaunessy turned to the peanut gallery, his eyes searching for any pilot with a high and tight representing the Marine *Hornet* squadron. *"Red River* rep, you catch that from the Boss?"

"Yes, sir, he'll be debriefed," the major responded.

"Good, and you can apologize to the *Spartan* rep sitting next to you if we don't catch one-oh-three," said O'Shaunessy as he glared at the major. Just then his phone buzzed, and he turned to answer it. "Roger," he spoke into the receiver, and raised his voice for all to hear. "Take one-oh-three over the top."

With a sheepish expression the major whispered, *"Sorry, man!"* to the *Spartan* pilot who sat next to him, who then took it as an opportunity to extract payment from the *Moonshadows.*

"I think, when we get to port, a beer for the one-zero-three aircrew will make amends, *and* a beer for me having to stay here in this pressure cooker longer than I should have, *and* a beer for the maintenance department for keeping one-oh-three airborne on this shitty night, *and* for the CO for general purposes. Hell, just buy the whole squadron a beer, and we'll call it even."

"We ain't *that* sorry!" the marine chuckled.

The PLAT screen shifted to the approach view and looked aft into space. Three aircraft showed on the screen as twinkling bundles of light set against the black. Two FA-18s followed 103, which was the largest bundle. They were all three to the left of the crosshairs, the lines in the middle of the screen that signified heading and glide slope. The ship was now on a 115 heading in the never-ending quest to put the winds down the angle.

As the pilots in Air Ops suspected, after what they had seen on the screen, the voice of the approach controller came over the radio loudspeaker with new coordinates: "One-zero-three, discontinue approach, maintain angels one-point-two, fly heading one-one-zero."

"One-oh-three, roger, one-one-zero."

As the *Hornet* on Cat 4 was placed in tension, Wilson heard the sardonic voice of "Saint Patrick" as he commenced his approach. "Four-zero-two commencing."

"Roger, *Raven* four-zero-two, take speed two-seven-five, say state."

"Two hundred pounds less than when you asked me *two minutes ago,*" Saint replied. Wilson cringed at the unprofessional sarcasm in his XO's voice.

When he heard this exchange, O'Shaunessy, whose attention had been on the situation regarding the deck status, turned his head and said to no one, "Who the fuck's in four-oh-two?" He answered his own question by looking at the status board. He shook his head in disgust when he read "PATRICK" and turned to search for a *Raven* flight suit patch among the pilots seated behind him.

"If your XO would make proper voice calls, we wouldn't have to ask him for his state."

All Wilson could do was acknowledge him with a chastened "Yes, sir."

"*And* give him a speed change because he can't hit his marshal point on time," O'Shaunessy added. The room was silent except for the clipped radio exchanges from the final approach controllers and pilots.

The Big Unit leaned over to Wilson and whispered "*Bad hair day...*" Wilson nodded but wondered if he was talking about O'Shaunessy or his XO.

The marshal controller queried the *Raven* XO a second time. "Four-zero-two, say state."

Wearily, Saint responded, "Six-point-*one.*"

Next, Wilson's ear was attuned to Sponge Bob's voice over marshal frequency as he began his approach. "Four-zero-six commencing out of angels thirteen, state five-two."

"Roger, four-zero-six, five-point-two."

Wilson did some fuel calculations in his head. Sponge had enough for a few looks at the deck before he hit tank state. The ship had two tankers overhead, a *Rhino* with 6,000 pounds to give and a *Viking* with 4,000. Outside the wind blew at 36 knots down the angled deck, most of it natural as the ship was making nothing more than bare steerageway. Glancing at the PLAT, Wilson saw a flash on the horizon. Thunder in all quadrants, varsity pitching deck, rain and dark, with the nearest *open* unfamiliar divert field 250 miles away. *Why do we do these things to ourselves?* He turned his attention to the *Hornet* above the crosshairs on the PLAT.

"Two-zero-one, three quarter mile, call the ball."

"Two-zero-one, *Hornet* ball, four-eight."

"Roger, ball, workin' thirty-five knots, MOVLAS." Wilson recognized the voice of Lieutenant Commander Russ "Shakey" McDevitt. He was the new Air Wing Four LSO who had reported aboard just before cruise.

Conversation stopped as everyone in Air Ops looked toward the PLAT. The first aircraft of the recovery, *Red River 201*, flown by a marine captain on his second cruise, was coming in. The light cluster grew larger and the external strobe lights on the *Hornet* blinked every half second as the aircraft approached the ship at over 140 knots.

"You're goin' *a lit-tle* high," Shakey said in his characteristic LSO bedroom voice. Wilson thought *201* looked *way* high, but Shakey was going to talk him down. He added a pitching deck call. "Deck's movin' a little, you're high...coming down. You're a *lit-tle* fast."

Wilson felt the ship take a lurch and saw the crosshairs drop suddenly on the PLAT. As the *Hornet* reached the wave-off decision point, Shakey finally made the decision by squeezing the "pickle" switch. "Wave-off, pitching deck," he radioed. At once Wilson saw the *Hornet* add power and disappear out of the top of the screen as it passed over the deck, much of the sound penetrating the flight deck into Air Ops.

"Oh for two," The Big Unit said softly.

CHAPTER 8

Wilson's guys were next. Saint was at one mile, and despite the deck motion, appeared low and lined up left, as he was for most of the approach. Wilson shook his head imperceptibly. *He just accepts being off*, he thought.

"Four-zero-two, slightly below glide path, slightly left of course, three quarter mile, call the ball."

"Four-oh-two *Hornet* ball, five-one."

"Roger, ball, thirty-five knots."

After the "ball" is called, radio communications are limited to the LSO only, and at that signal, the dozen pilots in Air Ops also ceased their whispered conversations. Instead, they watched the light cluster loom larger in the glide slope crosshairs. Saint was holding left, and Shakey, on the LSO platform, saw it, too, and coaxed him back to centerline. "You're lined up a *lit-tle* left...Lined up left...Deck's movin' a little. You're on glide path."

Wilson saw Saint correct for line up, and as he did, he carried too much power and drove himself high. Wilson thought, for sure, his XO would bolter, but suddenly the aircraft took a lunge to the deck.

"ATTITUDE! PO-WER!" *Raven 402* slammed into the deck hard, and the sound of the *Hornet* at full power, straining against the number one arresting wire, filled Air Ops.

"*Saint* wasn't going around," murmured The Big Unit. Wilson heard him, but kept his eyes on his XO in the landing area. As the arresting wire was pulled back, the arresting hook was retracted too early and fouled the wire between the hook and the fuselage underside. Wilson knew why it happened...Saint raised the hook before the yellow shirt signaled him.

The PLAT showed the *Hornet* stop and drop the hook to the deck. The hook runner, a sailor with a long steel crowbar, ran underneath the aircraft and pulled the cable clear of the hook, which was then raised again. Once untangled, the *Hornet* advanced the throttles to taxi forward and get clear of the landing area. The jet's exhaust blasted the water on the flight deck into another cloud that tumbled aft. The PLAT switched to Sponge Bob, the undercarriage of *402* visible as it taxied forward over the camera.

"Four-zero-six, on and on, three quarter mile, call the ball."

"Four-zero-six, *Hornet* ball, four-oh."

"Roger, ball *Hornet*, deck's movin' a little, you're on glide slope."

Wilson watched the deck status light indication flashing foul in the top of the screen as Sponge drew closer. *"It's gonna be close..."* he said to no one in particular. Shakey continued to guide the pilots with his calming voice, as if there were no worries. "You're on glide slope...*onnn* glide slope," he called to Sponge, keeping a careful eye on him but conscious that the deck was still foul since *402* had not yet cleared the landing area. Seconds from the decision point, the deck motion subsided for a moment. With the deck still foul, though, Shakey had to wave him off.

"Wave-off, foul deck," paddles called, just as the deck went clear.

Damn, Wilson thought. His XO caused the wave-off by retracting his hook too early and not waiting for the yellow shirt signal.

O'Shaunessy turned to him. *"Raven* rep, your flight lead shit-in-the-gear caused that."

Wilson nodded and said, "Yes, sir." O'Shaunessy kept his narrow eyes on him for a count and turned away. While Commander O'Shaunessy could be a dickhead, he was at least *fair*, taking on peers like The Big Unit to his face, or Saint behind his back, as well as lower ranking squadron department heads. The Irishman always looked pissed off, and who could blame him? He had to orchestrate the tension of carrier recoveries night after night after night, while the captain up there watched his every move and ripped into him when the airborne ballet was less than perfect. If air wing pilots were fouling up *his* pattern, they were going to know it, and *screw 'em* if they didn't like it.

Wilson looked at the status board with a grim face. This recovery was not going well, and no wonder! Varsity pitching deck, high gusty winds, rain and thunder in all quadrants, barely enough gas airborne on a dark night...and the divert fields practically out of reach, the best one of them closed.

Spartan 104 then trapped on a lucky four wire, and CATCC came on the radio to Sponge: "Four-zero-six, turn left to downwind. Fly heading three-five-zero. Report abeam."

"Four-zero-six," answered Sponge.

Wilson thought that Sponge Bob sounded cool. Despite his relative inexperience as an aviator, and despite a baby face that resembled the cartoon character, he could handle this. *Maybe this experience will be good for him*, thought Wilson. *He needs to add a few lines to that face.* CATCC was sending more aircraft to waiting tankers overhead. O'Shaunessy called to launch the alert 15 tanker, a *Super Hornet.* "Tell 'em I need it in ten minutes," he said.

Ding ding, ding ding...ding. The 1MC bells sounded again...1830. Wilson turned his attention to a *Hawkeye* lined up left on the PLAT and watched it settle on a one wire and roll out on centerline. The familiar *whooumm* of the turboprops at full power penetrated the space. That sound was followed by a deep *whhaaa* as the prop pitch reacted to the throttle setting on deck. Now, there were three *Hornets* and a *Viking* left to recover, and Sponge was first in line.

On departure frequency, Wilson heard "*Cutlass* three-zero-five, report plugged and receiving."

"Three-oh-five, *wilco.*"

Wilson glanced at The Big Unit, whose eyes remained locked on the PLAT. Both watched the flickering strobes of Sponge on final at three miles, but Wilson knew he, too, had to be listening to the departure frequency transmissions and thinking about the young *Buccaneer* pilot struggling behind the basket overhead.

All the aviators in the room had been there. In their minds, they climbed off the bolter with the pilot, raised the gear, switched frequencies to receive instructions, activated the radar and commanded it to automatically acquire the assigned aircraft. Even as their eyes joined the pilot's eyes in search of the tanker, the idea of being in a low-state aircraft far from land lurked in the corners of their minds...

There it is! That cluster of lights at 2 o'clock high. The pilot levels off at 2,000 feet and holds 250 knots, on altitude, controls the closure, and gets on bearing line. The pressure is on to join up and plug on the first try. As the pilot draws near, the flashing strobe lights illuminate the outline of the tanker, and the basket suddenly extends out of the refueling store. With his left hand, the pilot reaches down from the throttle and extends his refueling probe. With his left foot, he feeds in some bottom rudder to align the fuselages. Stabilized on the tanker's left wing, he sees the tanker pilot make a circle with his flashlight—the signal to plug.

The pilot slides into position and, with no horizon to reference, attempts to line the probe up behind the basket. Rigid with concentration, and "*squeezing the black out of the stick,*" the pilot attempts to anticipate the movements of the basket, which is constantly buffeted in the airstream. He adds a little power to ease forward, misses low, pulls a bit to back out, and lines up again for another stab. *Hurry back*, stabilize, now easy, *easy...* He takes a lunge with throttle and stick to slam the probe into the basket. The hose buckles from the impact before the take-up reel returns tension. The pilot pulls some power, but not so much that he backs out. As he maintains that position on the tanker, he watches the status light on the store, willing it to go from amber to green.

Green. Good flow. Life blood enters the aircraft. *Time* enters the aircraft. A split-second glance at the fuel page on the multifunction display, followed quickly by another glance, confirms the increase in fuel. *Yes, yes.* Even as his eyes scan for the first hint of relative movement on the tanker, he relaxes a bit and exhales deeply, his mouth open against the mask's microphone. Another chance, more time to live.

Air Ops let out a collective sigh of relief when the *Cutlass* came up on the radio. "Three-oh-five, plugged and receiving."

"Roger, three-zero-five, take three-point-oh."

"Three-oh-five."

Wilson heard The Big Unit murmur. "Oh, thank you, thank you, thank you."

"Four-zero-six, two miles, going slightly below glide path."

"Four-zero-six."

O'Shaunessy assigned one of the tankers, *Spartan 102*, to keep their eyes on—or "hawk"— Sponge. As Wilson watched the PLAT, he could see the familiar strobes of the *Super Hornet* high in the screen. They crossed from right to left across the screen as the tanker passed behind the ship and into a position to catch Sponge if he needed their services. The final controller called to Sponge with "Four-zero-six, on glide path, slightly right of course, one mile," and followed that with "Four-zero-six, on and on three quarter mile, call the ball."

"Four-zero-six, *Hornet* ball, two-seven."

"Roger, ball, workin' thirty-six knots, slightly axial."

O'Shaunessy turned to Wilson with an amused look and, referring to Sponge's *below tank* fuel state, said, "At least he's honest."

"Yes, sir," Wilson said and smiled. He appreciated the small break in the tension and stood up to take full advantage of it. He heard Shakey assure Sponge of his position on glide slope just as the PLAT crosshairs moved up, then down. The screen displayed a sudden pitch of the ship's deck, one they also felt in their stomachs. The chance of catching Sponge on this pass was very low.

O'Shaunessy picked up the phone. "If he doesn't get aboard, send him to one-oh-two for two-point-five."

C'mon, Wilson thought, trying to control the motion of the ship. *Settle down.* Sponge was in close. *Maybe he can make it...*

"Wave off, pitching deck," Shakey said as he depressed the pickle switch. Sponge added full power and maintained his proper landing attitude as he flew away.

"Dammit!" O'Shaunessy sighed, and spoke to CATCC. "Tank him."

Seconds later, they heard approach call to Sponge. "Four-zero-six, your signal is tank, clean up, take angels one-point-two, *Texaco* is at two o'clock, angels two, report him in sight."

"Visual," Sponge responded.

"Four-zero-six, roger, take angels two and switch departure button two."

"Four-zero-six, angels two, button two."

After a short lull in the action, and while he was chatting with The Big Unit, Wilson heard Sponge's voice on the overhead speaker.

"One-zero-two, there's a heavy stream of fuel coming out of the basket."

Wilson's head snapped to the status board and looked at Sponge's fuel state...2.5 two minutes ago. He then looked at O'Shaunessy, but he appeared not to have heard the transmission.

"Roger, we'll recycle," the tanker pilot answered.

"Commander?" Wilson called to O'Shaunessy, who turned to him and cocked his head.

"I just heard four-oh-six say there's a heavy stream of fuel coming out of the basket."

O'Shaunessy whipped around and picked up the phone. "Get me a status on four-oh-six."

Sponge watched the basket retract into the refueling store and glanced at his fuel: 2,300 pounds. Roughly, he had 20 minutes. A wisp of cloud flew past; then they were in the clouds. He edged closer to the tanker to keep the position light on the red wingtip of *102* in view.

The *Spartan* tanker pilot pushed down to get out of the clouds, and Sponge saw a minor stream of fuel emitting from the back of the store as the small generator prop on the store turned. Minor, yet *disconcerting.* He hoped it was just residual fuel from an earlier stream and, for an instant, when the basket started to move out of the store, he thought all was well. When it opened, however, a solid flow of fuel billowed into the airstream.

"Still streamin' heavy," Sponge radioed. His breathing was deep, and he squeezed tighter on the stick. Departure control called to him. "Four-zero-six, update state."

'Two-point-three," Sponge replied.

The tension in Air Ops ratcheted up as the focus shifted to *406*. O'Shaunessy rubbed his forehead. "What's the status on three-oh-five?" he asked Metz. The room was quiet except for the sound that came from the air conditioning vents overhead.

"Still on one-zero-seven, sir." At that moment the radio crackled. "Three-oh-five, tank complete."

"Get him aboard!" O'Shaunessy shouted and looked at the status board. "What's the story on one-oh-seven?"

"He's dry, sir, four-point-oh," Metz answered, his voice almost an apology.

"*Fuck!* Get him back here, *now!*"

CHAPTER 9

Wilson figured Sponge was good for 25 minutes airborne at low altitude—if he "hung on the blades" at a max conserve power setting. The two desired outcomes of flying an approach to the ship with gear and flaps down or joining up on a hoped-for tanker for a desperate "drink" would burn up more gas. He estimated Sponge really had 20 minutes before a third outcome was required: controlled ejection.

Wilson got O'Shaunessy's attention. "Sir, he's got about 20 minutes."

"I know… He's been doing good, hasn't he?" Wilson interpreted his question to be about Sponge's ability behind the ship.

"Yes, sir, if the deck cooperates, he'll get aboard."

Sponge remained on *102*, fuel still streaming from the basket. He edged closer to see if he could plug anyway and noted a heavier flow than he first thought. The flow was solid, as if the basket was engaged and fuel was being pumped into an invisible aircraft. If he attempted to plug now, he risked getting the windscreen covered with fuel that could then be ingested into the right engine. That could cause problems he didn't even want to imagine. When a bolt of lightning from a nearby squall exploded off their right wing, Sponge made up his mind.

"One-zero-two, recommend you stow the basket."

"Concur," *102* replied. He retracted the basket almost immediately.

When the prop was secured, Sponge radioed, "Good stow." After a moment, he added, "Departure, four-zero-six detaching," as he deflected the stick to the left.

"What's the story on one-twelve?" O'Shaunessy said to no one, then picked up the phone and asked the Air Boss the same question.

Wilson heard Sponge ask the question. "Departure, tanker posit?"

"Four-zero-six, we have no sweet tankers airborne. Launching alert *Texaco, Spartan* one-zero-five in five mikes. Your signal is max conserve. Say your angels?"

"Four-zero-six is at angels two."

"Roger, four-zero-six, take low holding."

"Four-zero-six…Ah, you want me to go to angels *eight?*"

"Affirm, four-zero-six."

With alarm, Wilson shouted from the back row. "Sir! *Commander O'Shaunessy!*"

Half expecting a vocal blast from the Commander, Wilson noticed that O'Shaunessy was shaken as he put down the receiver. He turned to Wilson as if to a friend who has a solution to his dilemma. "Yeah?"

"Sir, Departure told just told four-oh-six to take angels eight. Recommend you keep him down low so he doesn't chew up gas in the climb."

"Concur…because we're gonna barricade him."

Wilson stared at O'Shaunessy, not comprehending what he had heard. "*Sir?*"

"He's at barricade fuel. We're gonna catch the tankers and rig the barricade." O'Shaunessy saw the look of astonishment on Wilson's face and added, "Captain just made the call." His eyes remained locked on Wilson, as if to convey he understood but was powerless to overrule the Captain.

Wilson took a breath. "Sir, this is a night pitching deck barricade with a nugget pilot. My recommendation is to bring him aboard. He's got two more looks right now."

"What if we don't catch him?"

"Then a controlled ejection alongside."

"I thought you said he was good behind the boat."

"He is for a nugget, but why take the risk in these conditions?"

The Big Unit interjected, "Marty, I would recommend that for any pilot in these conditions."

O'Shaunessy studied both of their faces. "It's from the bridge. As soon as we get this *Bloodhound* aboard, we rig the barricade." He turned to Metz and gave more orders. "Get four-oh-six ten miles aft, max conserve."

"Yes, sir," Metz answered and picked up the phone.

Wilson got up and went to a J-dial phone circuit to call the CAG office. The Ops officer, known as Bucket, answered.

"Yes sir, Flip here in Air Ops. Four-zero-six is low state and the tankers are dry or sour. They're riggin' the barricade."

"Yeah, we just got the word. I'm tryin' to find CAG… We'll be right there."

"I'm tryin' to find my XO."

"Is your skipper airborne?"

"Yes, sir...my recommendation is to trap Sponge now or fly alongside and eject."

"OK, Flip, got it, thanks," Bucket said as he hung up. Wilson went back to his place next to XO Johnson, aware that the eyes of the other aviators were on him. Wilson dialed Ready 7 and Prince Charming answered. "Ready Seven, Lieutenant Howard."

"Prince, Flip, where's the XO?"

"He hasn't come in yet."

"Find him and get him to Air Ops *now!*" Wilson ordered.

"Yes, sir."

"Tell him they're gonna barricade Sponge."

"Holy shit!"

"Find Dutch and Smoke, maybe they can help the LSOs up there. Break out the premishap plan."

"Aye, aye, sir. Dutch is up there waving now," Prince said.

Wilson realized he was powerless to do anything. The Captain had decided to barricade Sponge, and that was that. He looked at Commander O'Shaunessy hunched over his desk with the phone receiver in one ear. He saw the PLAT crosshairs moving slowly relative to the S-3 on glide slope. Cajun is airborne. CAG isn't here. XO isn't here. Even if they were, he realized, they couldn't overturn the Captain's decision. The book says when a *Hornet* gets to 2.0 at night, you barricade him. The captain was nothing if by the book. *Rig the barricade! Yes, sir! Aye, aye, sir!*

The barricade was a nylon web net made of heavy-duty nylon bands that hung down vertically from a steel cable rigged across the landing area. It was held up by two great stanchions that lifted it some 20 feet above the deck. This allowed the aircraft to make a normal carrier approach with the barricade net stopping the aircraft. Typically, the arrestment ended with significant damage, and the pilot had no option to eject once the aircraft was caught. The pilot shut down the engines on LSO command as the aircraft crossed the ramp, which further reduced the scant 10-foot hook-to-ramp clearance. The aircraft had to roll into the net with little drift—drift would cause the aircraft and the net to veer over the side or into the jets parked alongside the foul line. Too high was disaster. If the top loading strap were to snag the hook or landing gear, the aircraft would be slammed to the deck with back-breaking force, and the fiery wreckage would slide down the angle and into the water. And once inside a certain point subjectively determined by the LSO, there was no way to wave-off.

It was rare for the Navy to barricade an airplane, maybe once a decade. And when it happened, it was an event felt throughout the fleet. *Hey, did ya hear Valley Forge barricaded a Hornet last night?*

I can't believe we are doing this, thought Wilson. *Night, dog-squeeze weather, pitching deck barricade! If all works well, if the barricade is rigged in time, if the deck steadies out, if we don't steam into a squall, if Shakey or Stretch give him the right sugar calls, if Sponge flies a solid pass, everything will be fine.* Just trap him! *He has one, maybe two looks. If he doesn't get aboard, then eject alongside.*

Wilson wondered if Sponge knew what was happening. He got up from the bench to review the NATOPS manual for barricade procedures when he saw his XO standing at the entrance to the room. Still in his flight gear, Saint scowled at him and cocked his head in a motion to come over. Saint then led them into the back office.

"Yes, sir," said Wilson.

"Mister Wilson, *what the hell* is going on?"

"Sponge couldn't plug because the tanker was sour, fuel streaming from the hose. The other tanker was dry from tanking all the bolters and wave-offs. They're gonna barricade Sponge."

"Did you recommend that?"

"No, sir…the Captain made the call. I recommended they trap him normally in these conditions. He's got two looks."

"And if not aboard he's out of gas. Then what?"

"Controlled ejection alongside," Wilson replied, keeping his face expressionless as he held the XO's gaze.

Saint looked down at the deck with tight lips steadying himself on a desk as the ship took a roll. The overhead creaked under the strain. He snapped his head up, eyes narrow with contempt.

"I expected more from my Operations Officer."

"*Sir?*"

"Why is that nugget out there in these conditions? I expect my Ops Officer to write a schedule that reflects the expected weather. But I don't expect him to then go and countermand an order of a Captain more than twice his seniority! *Unsat.*"

Wilson felt his upper body tighten.

"Sir, the Skipper signed the schedule almost 24 hours ago—before we knew what we would be facing tonight, before we knew we would be over 200 miles from *any* divert. Any senior officer in Air Wing Four could have broken the chain today with a recommendation to stop flying." He paused and lowered his voice. "Any flight lead could have ensured his wingman came down with sufficient fuel for any contingency instead of showing up here at minimum fuel. Any flight lead could have sent his lower-state wingman down first. And any pilot could have gotten out of the gear clean so his wingman could trap."

The XO's eyes narrowed even more, and he forcibly exhaled through his nose. Wilson knew right away he had overstepped several boundaries. Back-talk to commanders, even when justified, was never career-enhancing. He waited for the blast. When Saint just glared at him, apparently unsure of how to counter, Wilson decided to change course.

"I didn't countermand anything, sir. I made a recommendation. Sponge has to fly a solid pass, and if he doesn't hit the barricade clean, he probably doesn't get a chance to punch if he needs to. My recommendation is made and noted. Our squadronmate is in trouble, and I made a call. Now I have to get back—unless you want to take over, sir."

At that moment the familiar sound of an S-3 catching an arresting wire filled the space, and through the armored steel of the flight deck, they heard the muffled voice of the Boss on the loudspeaker. "Rig the jet barricade. We've got a low-state *Raven*! Ready Cat 3 for the alert *Texaco*! Get movin'!"

The overhead fluorescent light shone down on the *Raven* pilots as they looked at each other, unyielding and firm. Either one apologizing for the exchange was unthinkable.

"Get up there," Saint finally said.

At least he kept his eyes on me, Wilson thought, before his thoughts turned back to Sponge. As soon as he returned to his place next to The Big Unit, but before he could sit down, O'Shaunessy motioned Wilson over to the console and handed him the radio handset. "Tell Jasper we're gonna barricade him in about five minutes. Do you guys have a procedure for that?"

CHAPTER 10

Sponge breathed deeply as he flew away from the ship eight miles aft. *Two thousand pounds... I've got a little over 20 minutes at this fuel flow.* He wondered why they were vectoring him out here and keeping him at angels two. When he looked over his left shoulder, he could make out a cluster of lights in the distance...*Valley Forge*...and home. He desperately wanted to be aboard her. A bolt of lightning flashed nearby and for an instant the ship was illuminated in a bluish light, before darkness surrounded it again. During Sponge's short aviation career, he had already become accustomed to being at low fuel states. Judging from their ready room conversations, the old guys like Flip and Weed loathed them as much as he did. *Sweating fuel* was part of life when a *Hornet* pilot was at sea.

So this is my night in the barrel, he thought, a sea story he could tell at the O-Club just like the heavies did when they held court there. Each story, it seemed, involved a black night, a tanker, and a low-state trap. However, if this was his rite of passage, he would gladly decline. *Damn XO!* Sponge had seen Saint's aircraft taxi over the foul line just before Sponge got the wave-off on the first pass. If Saint had gotten out of the gear sooner, Sponge would probably be aboard right now, drinking a cup of water in the ready room. He *was* thirsty, so he pulled out the plastic canteen from the left pocket of his g-suit and unscrewed the top. He then popped a fitting on his oxygen mask so he could drink.

Just as he took a gulp, the approach controller's voice filled his headset. "Four-zero-six, fly heading two-one-five. Take angels one-point-two. Stand by for your rep."

Sponge screwed down the canteen top and shoved it back against the left console. After fumbling for the mask, he brought it to his face and keyed the mike. "Four-zero-six."

"Four-zero-six, rep," Wilson called to him.

"Go ahead," Sponge replied, glad to hear Wilson's familiar voice. He then adjusted the mask against his face.

"Four-zero-six, the airborne tankers are dry or sour. We're starting one up on deck but still haven't been able to get him airborne. We're rigging the barricade."

Rigging the barricade. Sponge sat motionless as the message sank in.

"Four-zero-six, you copy?"

"Affirm" Sponge responded. "I'm still headin' away from mother."

"Roger, Sponge. Mark your father with state."

"I'm on the two-six-five for niner, one-point-niner."

"Roger, we're gonna hook you in soon, but first I'm goin' to go over the barricade checklist... Do you have any ordnance?"

"Negative."

"Roger, OK... We're gonna punch off the drop tanks. See anything underneath you?"

Sponge dipped his wing to the left, looked below, and saw nothing but black. "Negative," he said.

"Roger, then emergency jett your tanks. Big switch on the upper left...hold it in till they're gone. Let me know when you've done it."

Sponge placed his left thumb on the switch, looked at the tank under his left wing, and pushed. He heard a *ka-chunk* and felt a twitch as small explosive cartridges pushed away the empty 300-gallon drop tanks from stations on the wing and fuselage. He watched the left drop fall and disappear into the darkness.

"I'm clean."

"Roger, Sponge," Wilson answered.

The final controller followed immediately and said, "Four-zero-six, turn left fly heading zero-five-zero."

"Four-zero-six, left to zero-five-zero," responded Sponge.

Wilson proceeded with the checklist.

"Sponge, Paddles is going to come up in a bit and give you the barricade brief, but as you get lower in fuel, remember, no negative g. You have a fuel low light yet?"

"Not yet."

"OK, but when you do, the airplane still flies. Just don't horse it around."

The amber color of the master caution light suddenly illuminated the cockpit. The impassioned voice of the aural warning tone, which the pilots called *Trailer Trash Tammy*, sounded a warning in Sponge's headset. *"Fuel low. Fuel low."*

Sponge's eyes went to the FUEL LO caution on the left multi-function display. "Jus' got the fuel low."

"Roger that. Net's goin' up." Wilson regretted his last comment. The barricade was actually still in its locker, despite the high activity of the crew in the landing area. They were busy making preparations so they could run it across the flight deck. "I should'a been straight with him," he said under his breath to The Big Unit.

The Commander replied, "He doesn't need to know. Just tell him everything's fine here."

CHAPTER 11

"WHAT?" Lieutenant Commander Russell "Shakey" McDevitt exclaimed to the LSO phone talker on the platform. *"Barricade?"*

"Yes, sir," the young sailor replied. Shakey saw the look of concern the sailor couldn't hide as he relayed the message. "After this *Rhino,* they gonna rig it for four-zero-six!"

Shakey looked aft at the blinking lights of the *Super Hornet* some five miles away. "Who's in four-oh-six again?"

"Jasper," a young LSO sang out, at the same time Dutch said, "It's Sponge."

Sponge, Shakey thought, and immediately his mind spat out a trend analysis: *Sponge tends to get overpowered and drive himself high in close and overcorrect to an early wire. He responds to calls, a solid nugget, trainable.*

Shakey then turned his attention to the aircraft at one mile. The rain started to pick up again.

As Shakey, with Dutch backing him up, worked to get the *Rhino* aboard, he fought to keep from thinking of the barricade approach he would wave less than 10 minutes from now. Mercifully, the deck cooperated with the *Spartan,* and it flew a solid pass. Shakey then walked over to call the tower, picked up the receiver, and dialed.

The call was answered after the first ring. "Air Boss."

"Boss, Shakey. Are we really going to barricade this guy?"

"Yeah, he couldn't plug. We've got an alert tanker, and we're shootin' him now. But we need to get four-oh-six aboard. How's Jasper been lately?"

"He's doin' good, sir. Tends to be overpowered."

"A few extra for the wife and kids. Nothin' wrong with that!" he said, in an attempt to lighten the mood. Then the Boss turned serious. "Can he handle this?"

"Yes, sir. We'll get him aboard." Shakey hoped he was right.

"You ready for this?"

"Yes, sir. We've got it."

"Good job, Paddles. We're workin' a 28,000 gross… Gotta go."

"Yes, sir" Shakey said as he hung up.

Seconds later the Boss came over the 5MC. "On the flight deck, we've got a low-state *Hornet* comin' in. *Rig the barricade*. Rig the jet barricade for *Raven* four-zero-six."

Shakey looked at Dutch, who was still stunned by the news. "You good to go?" he asked.

Dutch looked toward the horizon and back toward Shakey. "Yep, I'm right behind you—unless, of course, you want Stretch up here."

"No, his eyes aren't night adapted. You back me up."

"Roger that," Dutch replied, and grabbed a radio handset to listen to the CATCC controlling his sqadronmate.

Shakey still couldn't believe this was happening. He reached up to rub the tension out of his neck. The pain felt like an ice pick digging into the base of his skull. When the phone rang, which was barely audible over the wind and the roar of the *Rhino* engines up forward, one of the LSOs answered and turned to Shakey. "It's CAG."

Shakey walked over toward the console and took the receiver. "Lieutenant Commander McDevitt, sir."

"Paddles, CAG. Can we get this guy aboard?"

Shakey looked at the dozens of sailors swarming into the landing area to rig the barricade, their shouts audible above the din of the flight deck. "Yes, sir, but I would prefer, and even recommend, a normal arrest. When is that tanker gonna get launched?"

"They're workin' on it," CAG said, and then added, "Paddles, the Captain made the call. It's going to be a barricade, but if Jasper is not where you want him, pickle him and try again. If he's not there the next pass, don't take him out of parameters. If he flames out, he ejects, and we'll pick him up. Don't think you have to save the world here."

"Yes, sir, thanks CAG," Shakey said.

"You can do it, Paddles!" CAG said as he hung up.

Shakey took a few steps to the LSO console and picked up the radio transceiver. He felt the eyes of every LSO on the team focus on him as he moved toward the platform wind barricade. As he pressed his back against it to minimize his exposure to the elements, he opened his gouge book, his LSO platform "Cliff Notes," and quickly scanned the barricade brief.

I must convey confidence. Smile, he thought, and keyed the mike. "Four-zero-six, Paddles!"

"Go ahead," Sponge replied.

"Hey, Sponge, we're going to rig the barricade for this next pass. I know you've been workin' hard out there. You flew some solid approaches, but the deck just didn' cooperate. I'm going to go over the brief with you... Ah, let's see... What's yer configuration, approach speed and gross weight?"

"I'm slick. Just punched off the tanks...estimating one-thirty knots and twenty-seven K."

"Roger that," Shakey said as he proceeded with the brief. "Deck's movin' a little, and I'll be givin' ya calls to back up what I'm showin' ya on the MOVLAS. Don't chase the deck. We're workin' thirty-five knots right now. Line-up is going to be *real* important, so keep that in your scan. We don't want any drift at touchdown."

He took a breath and continued with the checklist.

"Fly it on speed, and fly the ball I'm showing ya. Now, I'll be talking to you the whole way—advisory calls early, imperative calls in close." Shakey took another breath. "You can't execute your own wave-off in close. Jus' follow my calls, and, at the proper point, I'm going to give you a *cut*. When I do, shut down the engines and you'll roll into the barricade. Keep the throttle under control. Don't get overpowered and drive yourself high. If you do, I'll be talking to you. Big corrections early, *smaaall* corrections in close. Got it?"

"Roger, sir."

"One more thing, the ship's moving, and it's gonna generate a Dutch Roll...Fly your needles, and don't chase line-up at range. After the ball call, it's meatball, line-up angle of attack." Shakey paused to let it sink in.

"Roger," Sponge replied.

"Any questions?"

"Negative."

Shakey was encouraged by the confidence in Sponge's voice. He knew he held Sponge's life in his hands.

CATCC jumped in. "Four-zero-six, turn right zero-eight-zero to intercept the final bearing one-one-six."

"Four-zero-six," Sponge said. His mouth was parched with fear as he reached down to set the course line.

"Bingo! Bingo!" sounded *Tammy*, warning Sponge again of his emergency fuel situation.

Sponge had never been this low on fuel in a *Hornet*. Breathing through his mouth, Sponge thought he could hear his heartbeat. Even under his mask, he could smell a metallic odor emanating from his person. Adrenaline. *Fear.* The realization surprised him. *You can smell your own fear,* he thought, and fought to keep himself under control. *It's bad enough to be on fumes at night. But this is a night pitching deck barricade!*

Turning back to the ship, he double-checked the course-line, touched the hook handle to ensure it was down, and fiddled with the HUD intensity. He had any number of minor cockpit tasks to distract him. *Night, pitching deck barricade in the middle of fucking nowhere!* After his moment of self-pity, he realized he was the only pilot in the airplane. *You can do this,* he told himself.

As he removed his kneeboard and set it in the map case for a possible ejection, CATCC called again. "Four-zero-six, dirty up."

"Four-zero-six," Sponge acknowledged as he slapped the gear handle down and moved the flap switch to half. The aircraft ballooned with the increased lift, and the landing gear caused a dull roar behind him as it extended into the airstream. He countered the increased lift with a nose down bunt and retrimmed the aircraft. He tried to concentrate on flying the airplane so he would not think about the barricade.

A few moments later, though, he glanced at the ship to see if he could see it.

CHAPTER 12

"Tower, one-zero-five, we just lost nose wheel steering."

"*WHAT?! Dammit!! Mother-f...!*" Marty O'Shaunessy was not having a good recovery. He needed the alert tanker to launch immediately to get more gas in the air, and instead he gets this. He shook his head in disgust and grabbed for the phone.

"Roger, one-zero-five. Stand by," the Boss said.

Wilson heard O'Shaunessy plead with the Boss. "Can you put a tractor and tow bar on him? Push him to the Cat! We need that gas airborne!" Wilson knew there was no time even for that desperation measure, maybe not even time for 105 to taxi to the catapult normally.

Sponge was expected at the ramp in minutes.

"*Fuck!*" O'Shaunessy said, as he slammed down the receiver.

When Air Ops next heard the flight deck loudspeaker through the deck, it was the Air Boss. "C'mon! We've got a *Hornet* at five miles! *Chop! Chop!*" Things were obviously not going well on the roof.

The Boss was not happy with the barricade progress. The nylon netting was laid out on deck and was attached to the two barricade stanchions embedded into the deck. However, the heavy strands were tangled and bunched together, and some of the plates were not yet in position. The Flight Deck Officer and Bos'n were everywhere. They shouted orders, grabbed sailors, jumped over nylon straps, and checked the connections to the stanchions. While Shakey and the other LSOs watched, they were joined on the platform by a new LSO. It was Stretch.

"Are we havin' fun, guys?" he said with a grin. Stretch was a perpetual optimist.

"Hey, glad yer here," Shakey answered. "We're set. Just briefed him. He's about one-point-five now... See him out there?"

"Yeah...I'm not night adapted, so you and Dutch wave him. You've been doing great out here tonight. And remember, if he's not set up, pickle him early."

"Roger that," Shakey said.

The Air Boss exploded again on the 5MC microphone. "All right, get out of there! Raise the barricade on signal!"

From the platform they heard more shouting as dozens of sailors scurried away into the catwalks and behind the island. Moments later, the Flight Deck Bos'n gave the signal and watched as the barricade assembly rose into the air, carried aloft by the two large stanchions.

In the subdued Air Ops space, Wilson and the others watched the barricade ascend, its heavy vertical nylon straps fluttering in the wind, into the PLAT's field of view. In the distance, on the left side of the picture was Sponge, represented by the pulsing external lights of an FA-18. Saint was still there in Air Ops and still in his flight gear. He sat off to the side and concentrated on the PLAT.

A radio call from CATCC broke the silence. "Four-zero-six, lock-on six miles, say your needles."

"Fly up and left," Sponge replied.

"Concur, fly your needles," the controller commanded. Wilson recognized the approach controller's voice and thought, *They've got their best guy controlling him.*

"Four-zero-six, update state."

"One-point-two."

Damn, Sponge is cool tonight, Wilson thought as he returned to his place. *At least cooler than I feel right now with all these eyes on me. And Saint over there adding zero value.* Wilson wished Saint would just leave and watch from the ready room. Was he here because he cared about Sponge, or was he thinking about having to answer questions at the mishap board? That meeting would surely be convened tomorrow morning, no matter what happened right now.

"Four-zero-six, four and a half miles, right of course correcting. Mother's in a starboard turn. Expected final bearing one-two-six."

"Four-zero-six... Jus' got a *fuel hot.*"

"Roger, four-zero-six, right of course and correcting. Turn right to zero-niner-five to intercept final."

"Four-zero-six, zero-nine-five."

On the platform with Dutch standing behind him, Shakey held the headset to his left ear. He had his right arm tucked under his left elbow and looked aft into space. As he watched, the lights of Sponge's Hornet and those of the escort ship behind the carrier drift left. *We're in a fucking turn!* he realized. He listened to the exchange between Flip, CATCC and Sponge and was impressed by the calm in their voices. He felt anything but calm, but maintained a stoic exterior. The dull tension at the base of his skull spread to his shoulders and was intensified by the isolated raindrops that splattered on his back and head.

His mouth felt like cotton, but he had to sound confident on the radio. *Fight it!* he thought.

He took a deep breath, glanced at the wind speed indication, and willed his voice to be calm as he keyed the mic. "Workin' *thirty-four* knots...Barricade's up." He exhaled deeply and put the handset down to rub his shoulder. A bolt of lightning flashed from somewhere behind him.

"How ya doin', Shakey?" Stretch asked.

"I've got it...Just picked a bad day to quit sniffin' glue!"

The tension broken, Dutch chimed in, "Yeah, I've never waved a barricade either, but I did stay at a Holiday Inn Express last night." Although it was somewhat forced, the officers on the platform laughed. It was a welcome relief from the strain of the recovery.

A radio call from the final controller brought them all back to the task at hand. "Four-zero-six, approaching glidepath. Slightly right of course correcting. Expected final bearing, one-two-eight."

"Four-zero-six."

Stretch shouted over gusting winds to the controlling LSO. "Shakey, after the ball call, jump in early. Lip-lock him the whole way down if you have to."

"Roger that!"

To minimize the danger to the others on the platform, Stretch shouted, "Guys, let's clear the platform. Primary and backup LSOs, myself and the phone talker stay. Rest of you guys go below and hang out in Ready 8 until he's aboard. Sorry." Four of the LSOs nodded and walked to the catwalk ladders.

The J-Dial circuit buzzed, and Stretch answered it. "Lieutenant Commander Armstrong, sir."

"Stretch, Boss... Captain wants you to call him."

"Yes, sir," Stretch answered. He killed the connection and then dialed the Captain's chair on the bridge. After one ring, the Captain picked up the receiver and growled, "Cap'n."

"Lieutenant Commander Armstrong on the platform, sir."

"Paddles, time to stop screwing around and get this guy aboard. *Now!* Got it?"

"Yes, sir," Stretch said, then swallowed. "Will we have winds down the angle? Because..."

Before Stretch could finish the Captain boomed. "I'LL TAKE CARE OF THE WINDS! *Now you do your job!*" The Captain slammed the receiver down.

Stretch looked aft into the dark. He had received blasts from the Captain in the course of predeployment training. His temper was legendary, and over time Stretch had built up a mental layer of protection. *Same shit, different day,* he thought, trying to reassure himself about tonight's display of temper.

"Stretch, who was that?" Shakey shouted to him.

Stretch smiled. "It was the Boss. Says barricade's set. Actual weight 27,000. The bridge is workin' on the winds. We're good to go!"

CHAPTER 13

Sponge concentrated on his instruments but took a peek at the ship off to the right of his HUD. He was curious... *Will I be able to see the barricade from three and a half miles?* When he looked over his nose, he saw nothing but the outline of the landing area, the drop lights, and the tower sodium vapors...a cluster of yellow lights surrounded by black.

One thousand pounds of fuel remaining...this is it.

"Four-zero-six. You're on course, approaching glide path," the controller said.

"Four-zero-six."

He watched the glide slope indication steadily descend from the top of his HUD. He focused on obtaining the best possible start to the approach and let everything else—the fuel quantity, the aircraft cautions, the weather, the barricade stretched across the deck—become secondary to flying a night carrier approach. The tension left him as he entered a mental realm that took all his attention.

Most pilots made use of this type of compartmentalization. It allowed him to sit still in the ejection seat, with his hands making tiny corrections to the stick and throttles. His eyes rapidly scanned his HUD instrumentation, primarily centered on the needles. As he approached the glide path inside three miles, he pushed the nose over and pulled some power, and then reset it to hold the steep 800-foot per minute rate of descent.

"Four-zero-six, up and on glide path, begin descent," said the CATCC contoller.

Sponge keyed the mike. "Four-zero-six."

"Four-zero-six, going below, below glide path, two-point-five miles."

Sponge corrected with deft movements of the throttle and stick. Once the plane was back on the four-degree glide slope, he reset power. This steep approach angle, where he was just able to see the ship over the nose, gave him the impression of peering down into a void from the opening of a well. He could see he was lined up right of course and nudged the stick to the left. Suddenly, the needles jumped left. *The ship must be in a turn,* he thought, a fact confirmed right away by CATCC.

"Mother's in a starboard turn, turn left five."

"Four-zero-*six*," Sponge replied, with some exasperation.

Here, on the pass of my life, the ship jinks on me—inside *three miles*. He quickly put the thought out of his mind and concentrated on the HUD display. He slid his velocity vector to the left then recorrected once on course.

The sound of raindrops increased and beat on the canopy in great sheets. The rain also reflected light from the ship as it streaked aft on the smeared windscreen. The white noise of the rain added to his tension and caused his breathing to deepen and his hands to tighten on the controls. He worked hard to stay on glide slope and on centerline. Through the sheets of rain attacking his windscreen at over 150 miles per hour, he looked out at the ship and sensed he was lined up left, but the needles showed him on-and-on. *Trust the needles!* he reminded himself. His fuel indicator showed 930 pounds.

"Four-zero-six, on and on, one-point-five miles."

"Four-zero-six," Sponge acknowledged, and then he saw it.

The barricade was raised perpendicular to the landing area and looked almost like a solid swath of amber as it reflected the floodlight from the tower. It felt like a dive-bombing run, a dive-bombing run into the side of a chalky yellow cliff spread across the deck. He fought the urge to stare at it. The rain subsided a bit as he concentrated on maintaining glide slope, but his breathing rate picked up speed.

On the platform, the LSOs watched in grim silence as *406* approached. The wind velocity increased to 38 knots, and the plane guard destroyer aft on the invisible horizon seemed to float in space, up and down with the changing pitch of *Valley Forge's* deck.

"Barricade set two-seven, *Hornet!* Clear deck!" The phone talker shouted for all to hear.

Dutch glanced back into the landing area out of habit to ensure it was clear and was mesmerized by the barricade, where the high winds buffeted the thick nylon strands. Through the strands he could see shadows on the island weather deck galleries. Dozens of sailors were gathered there to watch the approach from the aptly named, "Vulture's Row."

"Roger, clear deck," he said, and immediately returned his attention to the familiar FA-18 light pattern manifested by *406*.

Shakey picked up the handle of the visual landing aid system and showed Sponge a centered ball. The rain was coming down harder now, pelting them in their exposed position. They both straddled the coaming, with one leg each placed on the flight deck. *We're probably going right into a squall*, thought Shakey.

Subconsciously, he pulled the collar of his flight suit up to cover his neck. Dutch, right next to him, cared much less about the weather than the fact that his squadronmate Sponge was in that jet.

Dutch saw Sponge drift left, as did CATCC. "Four-zero-six, one mile, drifting left of course, on glide path."

"Four-zero-six."

"Four-zero-six, slightly left of course, on glide path, three quarter mile, call the ball."

"Four-zero-six, *Hornet* ball, point-niner." Sponge sounded calm.

Shakey did, too, when he responded. *"Roger ball, Hornet,* working thirty-seven knots down the angle. Deck's movin' a little, yer *ooon* glide slope."

Dutch sensed the escort ship on the horizon slide left. "Ship's turnin' right!" he shouted to Shakey, who immediately informed Sponge.

"Ship's in a turn, come left...on glide slope...*come left*...yer goin' high...on center line."

"Talk to him!" Stretch called out.

Shakey keyed the handset microphone and held it depressed while he raised the MOVLAS handle higher. "Yer high! *Easy* with it."

Sponge made an aggressive correction, just as the ramp pitched down. He was uneasy with his steep view of the deck and felt as if he were right on top of it— and already past the cut point. He lost the ball due to the barricade stanchion and his eyes became glued to the deck and the bewitching movement of the barricade strands. *I'm going to hit the top loading strap!* he thought. Reflexively, he pulled power and bunted the nose down, dangerously steepening his rate of descent.

On the platform, Shakey and the others immediately sensed disaster. The *Hornet* was high and fast, and at a quarter mile Shakey *heard* the strike fighter pull power to correct. The deck was coming up now, fast, and Sponge was in danger of overcorrecting and flying through glide slope. If he did, he could impale himself on the *ramp*, the opposite of hitting the top loading strap of the barricade.

"*Pickle him!*" Stretch screamed.

Shakey squeezed the wave-off switch and shoved the handle to the bottom. "Wave off! *Wave off!*" Within the next couple of seconds, the rate of collision between Sponge and the ramp or Sponge and the barricade picked up considerably. *He must have been way back on the power!* thought Shakey as he screamed, "*BURNER! BURNER! BURNER!*"

Dutch and Stretch shouted the same into their handsets. As a result, they saw the afterburners stage and the white burner plume leap from the tailpipes as the engine pitch changed to a booming roar. The *Hornet* continued to settle and the ramp continued to rise, with the red glow from the wave-off lights now reflecting off the bottom of the aircraft. Sponge had stopped his rate of descent and was now safe from collision with the ramp. The LSOs, however, were horrified as they watched the plane head for the top loading strap.

If Sponge hit the strap, the aircraft would smash violently onto the deck. The potential results were ominous: Sponge might be knocked out; the ejection mechanism might be crunched; the aircraft might explode into a mass of twisted metal and fire; or the wreckage, whatever its condition, might slide off the angle into the dark sea.

Shakey froze as he focused on Sponge's hook point, time seeming to slow as the *Hornet* thundered over them. *Oh, God, please,* he prayed, and turned his body left.

Dutch shouted, "Holy *shiiit!"*

Traveling at over 130 knots, the hook point nicked the top loading strap. The hit started an undulating motion that quickly moved from the heavy steel cable to the stanchions. At that instant the burner plume passed over the barricade and shook it violently, the plume igniting a small grease fire at the top of two nylon bundles.

The LSOs, stunned by what they had just witnessed, watched the small fire struggle with the wind and rain. Sponge climbed out ahead of the ship at a steep angle, burner cans still white.

Dutch had the presence of mind to call *"Out of burner!"* That would help preserve what remained of Sponge's fuel.

"Clean up," added Stretch.

I can't believe it didn't break! Shakey thought, as the Boss yelled over the 5MC for sailors to put out the fire on top of the barricade.

Sponge was still climbing ahead of the ship, and CATCC directed him back for another pass. "Four-zero-six, take angels one-point-two. When level, turn to the downwind three-zero-five."

Shakey knew Sponge didn't have the gas to turn downwind for even a four-mile hook-in to final.

As the crash and salvage tractor drove out to the centerline to douse the small flames still flickering on the loading strap, he took matters into his own hands. "Four-zero-six, Paddles contact. *Turn downwind now.* Level off at cherubs six."

"What're you doing?" Stretch cried.

"He doesn't have the fuel. We've gotta get him back here now! Watch him, guys!"

CHAPTER 14

Sponge breathed heavily through his mouth and fought the urge to remove his mask. *Holy shit!* he thought. He had pulled the throttles out of burner when Dutch called to him, but what did Shakey want? *Level off and turn downwind?! Another first! A night pitching deck barricade out of a day visual pattern!* A look at his fuel, though, confirmed Shakey was right. *Five hundred pounds left!*

He pushed the nose over and banked left. To keep from becoming disoriented, he concentrated his attention on the instruments. In less than three minutes he was either going to be on that ship or in the water next to it. Sponge took a series of deep breaths to remain calm. *One step at a time.*

A sudden bolt of lightning in the downwind turn made Sponge flinch. His shoulders ached. They had been under strain for the last 40 minutes, ever since he had pushed out of marshal. And he could smell the adrenaline; the smell was stronger than ever, and it seemed to seep right out of his skin. *Concentrate!*

Shakey called to him again. "Cherubs six, no lower."

Sponge was concentrating so hard to maintain his tight turn, he didn't even answer. He was at 800 feet, and would descend to six once on downwind. As he leveled off, he took a glance at the ship, which looked about level with him to his left. He saw one helo close on the starboard quarter and another nearby. He almost wished the ship would just tell him to punch out. The rain was picking up too, another unwelcome sensory.

"Damn, this sucks!" he shouted into his mask.

Wilson and the others in Air Ops watched the raindrops bounce on the deck in front of the PLAT camera embedded in the centerline. Wilson was incensed. He couldn't believe that, after witnessing the near catastrophe, the ship was going to attempt another barricade recovery. *What else can go wrong tonight?* he thought.

O'Shaunessy, who had lost the bubble, was on the phone to somebody but overwhelmed by the crushing demands put on him by the Captain, the elements, the scheduled track, and the air wing tankers. And Shakey had now turned

Sponge downwind for a day pattern on a shitty night like this! Saint just stood off to the left and watched the PLAT. He offered no answers whatsoever.

"Sir?" Wilson called to O'Shaunessy.

"Yeah?" When O'Shaunessy looked over his shoulder, Wilson saw the deep circles under his eyes.

Wilson glanced at Saint, who still stared at the PLAT. Damn, he wished the Skipper were here now, but for the moment he was the only *Raven* representative thinking about Sponge's well being. He leaned forward on the bench.

"Recommend a controlled ejection alongside, sir." Wilson said in a measured tone, eyes locked on O'Shaunessy.

Saint "woke up" with a start. "Negative!" he exclaimed. "Barricade him! Mister Wilson, I've got it."

Despite the in extremis condition of *406*, O'Shaunessy and the others were astonished by this public display. After a moment, the Air Ops Officer looked to Wilson and said, almost apologetically, "He outranks you."

Wilson sat still and said nothing, but he felt his blood pressure rising. The silence was broken by Shakey as he talked to the lone *Hornet* abeam. "Sponge, nice job on that one, the ship jinked for winds, but you did a good job of getting that good start. You're real light, so keep that right hand under control and make easy glide slope corrections with power. We're gonna get 'cha this time… We've got a little raindrop here, so check windshield air… What's yer DME?"

"One-point-four," Sponge replied.

"Roger that, turn in level, dirty up. CATCC, say final bearing."

The approach controller, monitoring everything, was on top of it. "Final bearing one-three-seven."

"Roger that. Sponge, you have *bullseye* needles?"

"Affirm."

"OK, use them to help get set up. We'll show you a ball when you get in the window."

"Roger, *Paddles.*"

As Sponge prepared his airplane for approach, however disjointed this one might be, his training took over and he became calm. He went through the checklist by memory: gear – DOWN; flaps – HALF; antiskid – OFF; hook – DOWN; harness – LOCKED. His hand touched each handle and knob to ensure they were all set as required. Keeping a good instrument scan and flying the ball was something Sponge could do. And, in his mind, he had resolved to wave off if one of the engines rolled back due to fuel starvation. He would then take a cut away from the ship—portside—and eject when abeam. He could do that, too.

Shakey also had a newfound confidence. Stretch, the senior partner, was letting him wave, not because Stretch wanted to avoid waving but because his vision was still not night adapted and because Shakey was handling this pitching deck MOVLAS recovery quite well. As *406* appeared and moved across the ship's longitudinal axis, Shakey picked up the handle and showed Sponge a slightly low indication. The steady rain pelted him and Dutch as all eyes looked aft toward Sponge. *Please help me, God,* Shakey whispered into the rain as the wind swirled around him.

"Two-seven *Hornet,* clear deck!" the phone talker called out.

"Roger, two-seven *Hornet, clear deck!"* Shakey bellowed back.

In Air Ops, The Big Unit leaned over and murmured to Wilson. "You made the right call. You're on record."

Wilson said nothing, but his eyes followed Sponge as his aircraft came into view on the right side of the screen. *Shakey is doing good,* he thought, *taking charge out there.* Wilson knew only prayers could help them now. *Our Father, who art in heaven...*

"Four-zero-six, got a ball?" Shakey called over the radio.

"Four-zero-six, *Hornet* ball, point-four," Sponge answered.

"*Ro-ger* ball, thirty-nine knots down the angle, workin' a little low... You're low and lined up left, come right...Come right...Approaching centerline, back to the left, you're on glide slope...*Ooonn* glide slope."

The ship heaved up and rolled right. Air Ops was silent, save for the radio transmissions from the platform. Throughout the ship all eyes were on the PLAT crosshairs, and hundreds of prayers were asked of God to help the young pilot.

"Deck's movin' a little. You're on glide slope, on course. *Oooonn* glide slope...a lit-tle power, a little right for lineup."

Sponge lost the ball behind the stanchion and cried, *"Clara!"*

"Roger, clara, you're on glide slope, going a *little* high, easy with it...power back on..."

"Ball!" Sponge sang out again.

"Right for line-up!" Dutch called. The deck steadied out a bit...they were committed.

Wilson saw the *Hornet* behind the barricade correct the drift. *C'mon!* he thought.

Shakey kept the calls coming as Sponge approached the ramp. "Roger ball, a little power...Now cut! *CUT! CUT! CUT!"*

"Right for line up!" Dutch added.

With that, the *Hornet* fell out of the sky, slamming on the right main-mount, followed by the left main and nose. A twisting motion sent the airframe into the barricade, which enveloped the aircraft in webbing, water and debris.

The LSOs saw the hook catch a wire somewhere in the maze of confusion, and the stress and strain of the arrestment was too much for the overstressed right main. As the main suddenly collapsed, the whole jumble slid down the deck into the centerline PLAT camera, where the wreckage and right wing dragging on deck kicked up a shower of sparks as it veered to the starboard side of the landing area.

On the PLAT image, Wilson saw Sponge's white helmet move in the cockpit. Sponge then opened the canopy as crash and salvage sailors swarmed the nose, some of them employing foam on a small fire underneath the aircraft. A booming cheer in Air Ops released a torrent of tension and anxiety. Wilson's air wing shipmates all patted him on the back.

"You got him!" The Big Unit said as he grabbed Wilson's shoulders. Wilson offered a weak smile in return, feeling he had done pitifully little. Wilson's eyes met Saint's scowl before the commander wheeled and left for the ready room.

***

Sponge had never wanted so much to get out of an airplane. Leaning to the right, his hands raced over the Koch fittings and seat manual release handle that secured him in order to get free of the cockpit. He opened the canopy normally and flipped off a bayonet fitting to let his mask dangle to one side. Instead of breathing fresh air, he gagged on a cloud of CO_2 from the crash crew's attack on the aircraft. He then got splashed by firefighting foam, supposedly pointed at the fire coming from somewhere by the right intake. The foam spotted his helmet visor and obscured his vision as the rain caused it to run down the front.

A hooded sailor wearing a silver fire retardant suit, a chief by the sound of his gravelly voice, climbed up on the leading edge extension. He yelled, over the chaos, to Sponge, "You okay, sir?"

"Yeah! I'm okay!"

"Nice goin', Lieutenant! Let's go!"

Sponge pulled himself up and over the canopy sill. The chief and three other sailors grabbed at him as he tumbled down to the deck. He got covered in foam, and some of it splashed into his mouth. Just as he got to his feet and tried to spit out the foam, they began to both pull and push him from the wreckage. Still spitting foam, he trudged 50 feet toward a throng of sailors.

"Sir, you have to get in the stretcher!" a sailor yelled. He pulled Sponge toward a wire mesh stretcher on the flight deck.

"I'm fine!"

"Sir, orders. Get in!"

"Lieutenant, it's procedure. *Get in*." added another unfamiliar sailor.

Sponge tilted his head up and saw an older sailor under the cranial and goggles next to him— maybe an officer, a medical type. He decided not to fight. *I've had enough fighting for one night. I'll let someone else take care of me.*

"Lie down here, sir. You'll be OK," the first sailor said.

Sponge got in the stretcher and the medical department sailors strapped him in. Now on his back, Sponge faced the rain and had to squint his eyes to shield them from the raindrops. He heard the sound of helicopter rotor blades getting louder and louder. *Is that guy going to land on top of me?* The straps were cinched down to keep him in place, and he couldn't move his arms. White smoke was still pouring from underneath *406*, the Air Boss was yelling orders over the 5MC he didn't understand, and rain was pelting his face. Sponge couldn't see well and that scared him. A sailor, or maybe the old medical guy, stood over him and talked into a portable phone. "Pull down my visor!" he yelled, but no one heard him over the din. Then someone bumped the stretcher, which sent a sharp pain into his left thigh.

Sponge snapped. The tension of the past five hours—beginning with the XO's bullshit brief, followed by launching in awful weather, dodging the embedded thunderstorms during the hop, marshaling in the clag, and finally ending with his night-in-the-barrel foul decks, sour tankers, jinking ships and a pitching deck barricade—turned to rage in an instant. *Everyone on this ship* really is *trying to kill me!* he thought.

Lieutenant Junior Grade Robert K. Jasper, United States Navy, drenched and immobile, had had enough. He took a deep breath, tensed his body and exploded with a roar he was certain could be heard by the plane guard destroyer across the waves.

"Get me outta here! *Now! RIGHT Fucking NOW!!*"

CHAPTER 15

From the desk chair in his stateroom, Wilson watched the E-2 grow larger in the PLAT crosshairs. When it touched down and rolled out on centerline, the nose gear tires, in a blur, rushed up and over the embedded flight deck camera.

With his legs stretched out in front of him and his hands folded on his lap, Wilson sat alone in the stateroom to escape, for a moment, the pressure-filled aftermath of the barricade. Cajun and Olive had diverted with most of the older *Hornets* to Thumrait to be out of the way while the crash crew removed *406* from the angle and swept the deck for debris. Making the deck ready for recovery took almost an hour, and Wilson was surprised that the ship then recovered the remainder of those airborne, the *Rhinos* and big-wing aircraft. At least the deck had settled down and the wind had subsided.

Valley Forge had lucked out. A busted *Hornet* and a bunch of jets on the beach was a small price to pay for the decision to fly tonight. And it was a foregone conclusion that the Captain was going to recover what he could after clearing off the deck. The conditions had improved and everyone got aboard with no fodded engines—as far as he knew.

As he watched the *Hummer* fold its wings and taxi to its parking spot abeam the island, Wilson realized the night's ordeal was basically over. But for Wilson, it was just beginning.

And everyone's okay. Nerves may be shot, but everyone has all their fingers and toes, and we're all breathing. Amazing. Wilson tilted his head back and yawned as he fought the urge to crawl into his rack and forget this night had even happened. *This is going to be a long deployment.*

The squadron, VFA-64, however, was not okay. Sponge's plane, *406* was likely down for the cruise, and might never fly again. Sponge Bob was in sick bay for who knew how long, and no one knew what kind of pilot would emerge when he was discharged. Would he bounce back, or would he lose the confidence the squadron had spent the past year building into him?

Word of Wilson's exchange with the XO was, no doubt, a major topic right now at midnight rations, or midrats. *Summarily relieved of CATCC watch.* Wilson replayed the image of Saint's face as he relieved him. His own face, as well as his ears, flushed with blood as he fought to contain the flood of emotions that spread through his whole body—a mixture of rage, humiliation, and fear for Sponge's life.

Should I have gotten up and left? No, he thought. *I did the right thing.* Leaving CATCC—with the eyes of all those witnesses on him under the crushing silence of embarrassment—would have been an act of capitulation. It had been bad enough just sitting there. He knew that issue was also being dissected at midrats, and he could imagine the discourse. "Man, if it were me, I would have said, 'I stand relieved,' and shoved the book in his gut on the way out." Wilson slouched low in his chair staring at the gray locker in front of him, lost in his thoughts. *Can I get through the next five months?*

The door opened and Weed entered. He had just returned from the flight deck where he had accompanied the Maintenance Master Chief and airframe mechanics to assess the damage to *406*. The Air Department had placed it, slumped over as it was on one wing, out of the way on the starboard shelf. Still wearing his float-coat, Weed dropped his cranial on his chair and began to rummage through a drawer.

"Hey, man."

"Hey," Wilson replied. "What's the verdict?"

"Class Alpha mishap, no question. Right motor is toast, right wingtip launcher all but torn off, leading and trailing edge flaps worn down, right wingfold mechanism AFU. Of course, the right main is shot and the nose gear probably stressed, and foam covers the aircraft, including everything inside the cockpit. Nothing a year in the depot can't fix. And Station 8 is ground down with big divots in the deck. You seen Sponge?"

"Yeah, about 30 minutes ago in sick bay. A different Sponge—*pissed* like I've never seen him. They took him down there and made him remain on his back while they cut away his gear and flight suit. They then pronounced him fit to pee in the bottle and said they are going to keep him overnight."

"Does he get a shot of medicinal brandy?" Weed said, as he continued digging through the drawer.

"Not sure if Doc goes for that."

"You mean he's a gin guy?" Weed found the package of AA batteries. "Well, the boys in the Ranch will hook him up before long."

"Yeah," Wilson mumbled, his stare steady on the locker as his thoughts returned to his role as Operations Officer. "All of Sponge's gear is gone. Do the PRs have enough to outfit him?"

Weed placed the fresh batteries inside his utility flashlight. "I'm sure, between us and brand X, we can throw something together."

"I want to fly him within 48 hours. Thinking tomorrow we can get the MIR and human factors investigations well underway."

"Who's gonna do the human factors board for the XO?"

Wilson shot a glance at Weed, then looked back to the locker.

"You okay, OPSO?"

"Yeah, just need to sulk for another 20 minutes."

Weed looked at his exhausted and humiliated roommate. He knew what had happened in CATCC and knew Wilson *knew* that he knew. There were few secrets in the air wing, and a scene like what happened in CATCC tonight flew through the ship. He asked the question anyway to get Wilson to unload. "What happened?"

Wilson pursed his lips and said nothing.

"Just tell me, for crying out loud."

Wilson opened his mouth but couldn't vocalize anything. How does an experienced aviator like him, a *prideful* man like him talk about the *disgrace*, the *shame* of being relieved of CATCC watch? Finally, he was able to get it out.

"After Sponge nicked the top loading strap with fumes remaining, I'm thinking, 'Fuck it! Punch out now—and live! Break the chain.' I made a recommendation and Saint goes ballistic, adding no value." Wilson felt like he was whining.

"I'da done the same." Weed said.

"Well, better not, or you'll be relieved, too."

"Saint isn't qualified to carry your helmet bag."

Both pilots knew about Saint Patrick's carrier bona fides. As a junior officer, he had made one deployment, and, as a department head, was in a squadron that had a long turnaround between deployments. Saint had rotated out before they went across the pond.

Weed shook his head and resumed, "Three hundred and ten career traps. *Smoke* has more than that. And XO has never been CATCC watch on cruise in his life, not even this cruise. Hey, why don't you schedule him for one?"

Wilson allowed a faint smile. "Because I care about you guys."

Unfazed, Weed continued. "Saint knows paperwork though! *That's* the way to command. Admiral's aide, staff weenie, War College, Pentagon Joint Staff. Punch tickets and visit a cockpit once in a while, a long while. Having the right last name helps, too."

Wilson appreciated the comments of his indignant roommate. If he wouldn't—or couldn't—unburden himself, Weed would do it for him.

"And then a middle-management job as XO/CO... Let's send Saint to the *Ravens.* They are due to be brutalized. I mean, how much damage can one incompetent commander do in one tour?"

"*The horror, the horror.*"

"Yep. *Where do we get such men* indeed?" Weed got up and clapped his hands to end the bull session. "Been to the ready room?"

"Uhhmm...to help Prince with the initial mishap report. XO made the call to Norfolk."

"C'mon, man. Let's go to the ready room and help Dutch write up the follow-on message. Then we can go to midrats and get a slider."

Wilson lifted himself up in the chair and exhaled. "Those things can kill you, ya know."

"Yep, but since we are surrounded by machinery, tons of ordnance and jet fuel below us, teenagers everywhere, homicidal maniac XOs, the raging sea outside and hostile countries over the horizon, I'll take my chances. And I'll have mine with cheese."

"You forgot the nuclear water we drink."

"Which makes great bug juice and mixes well with scotch...or so I'm told."

CHAPTER 16

Riiinnnngggg.

Wilson jerked his head up from the pillow and stumbled toward the phone. He glanced at the LED digits of his clock: *7:12.* He had been asleep five hours. Light from the passageway filtered into the stateroom from under the door and through a grate on the bulkhead.

He cleared his throat and picked up the receiver. "Lieutenant Commander Wilson, sir."

"Flip, Nicky at the duty desk...XO just called an APM."

Wilson stood motionless as he let the message sink in. *An APM? Called by the XO?*

"Flip," Nicky continued, "it's for zero-seven-thirty."

Wilson exhaled. "Roger, we're on our way," he said and hung up the phone. "Get up...APM," he said to his roommate in a frustrated undertone.

Weed groaned into his pillow, but he began to stir. "What the fuck?"

"XO called an APM. Fifteen minutes."

The Maintenance Officer tossed his covers off and rolled his body over the bunk. He braced himself with one foot on the frame of the lower bunk and eased to the floor in one familiar motion. Wilson turned on the water and filled the sink to shave.

"Any idea what this is about?" Weed asked.

"No...and the CO's not here. Not good."

"When are they coming back?" Weed asked as he put on a fresh, black squadron t-shirt.

"Around 1500," Wilson said as he lathered. "Just one recovery today for the Thumrait birds. Then a RAS."

"So, with Cajun gone, the XO can play Skipper for a day." Weed pulled on his flight suit.

"Yep...not good."

At a hurried pace, the two pilots finished dressing, laced their boots and brushed their teeth. Wilson quickly checked his e-mail and saw a note from Mary. It would have to wait.

With only five minutes to go before the meeting, they headed toward the ready room. Most of that time was spent navigating 700 feet of ladders, passageways, hatches, and knee-knockers. They ascended a ladder in quick steps, pulling themselves up with their arms. At the top, they swung their legs into the passageway and darted left, crouching low under the Cat 2 track, and then onto the portside O-3 level "main drag" passageway.

Wilson acknowledged passing sailors with a nod and reflexively lifted his boots high over the knee-knockers. He was lost in his thoughts, and his thoughts were gloomy. *Why is the XO calling an APM? And why now, rousting everyone with only 20 minutes notice?*

Aviators, who were night owls by nature, ignored reveille and rarely went to breakfast. Their days were, therefore, skewed between a midmorning wake-up to a bedtime where they hit the rack long after midnight. These 16- to 17-hour days included one hop, maybe two (with hours of briefs and debriefs), all manner of meetings, assigned duties, and myriad admin functions relating to the pilot's "ground job." For Wilson, this meant a late night every night as he and Nttty, the Schedules Officer, wrote and refined the flight schedule for the following day. Although they could also find time for movies, exercise, video games, and e-mail home, everyone was always at and available for "work."

Wilson continued aft as the ship swayed back and forth on the swells. It was rare for an XO to call an All Pilots Meeting. The overall squadron leadership of pilots and flight policy was the unquestioned province of the Skipper, while the XO was charged with admin duties relating to personnel and work spaces. *Depending on his message, what Saint is doing—with the CO off the ship and after the night the squadron just experienced—could be insubordinate. And, with the hours we keep, such short notice certainly shows contempt toward us,* he thought.

Wilson recalled the first time he had met Saint, last year at the O-Club while Saint was still in refresher training. Cajun had introduced them. Without making eye contact with Wilson, Saint had given him a tight-lipped, perfunctory nod and a quick handshake. Saint then took a sip of beer and turned his attention back to Cajun. Wilson received the message loud and clear: *You are an underling, nothing more.* Since that meeting, Wilson had found that Saint's ignoring him had not been personal. Commander Patrick treated the whole squadron that way.

Weed and Wilson got to the ready room with three minutes to spare. Wilson was surprised to hear music blaring from the stereo. The bleary-eyed JOs were either seated or getting a cup of coffee, and all but Nicky were in flight suits. Bubbly Psycho bebopped between the chairs, mouthing the words to the song: *"Shake it like a po-la-roid pic-cha."*

Wilson poured a cup and strode up the aisle to his chair in the front row. "Anything from the beach?" he asked Nicky.

"No, sir, but both jets reported safe-on-deck last night."

Wilson glanced at the status board; LASSITER and TEEL were the only *Raven* sorties listed, their mission a fly-on at 1500.

As the 1MC sounded the first of seven bells signifying 0730, the XO walked in. He entered from the front door that connected to Maintenance Control. Dressed in his khaki uniform with full ribbons, he placed his notebook inside his footstool and turned to Nicky. "Turn that shit off. What if CAG comes in?"

"Yes, sir!" Nicky wheeled in his chair to comply. As the ready room became quiet, the remaining pilots started to move to their seats. Wilson spotted Sponge Bob as he entered from the back door and took the seat nearest to the door. It was obvious he did not want to call attention to himself. He was also dressed in khakis and stoically acknowledged the nods and smiles many of his squadronmates sent his way.

Saint looked at Wilson and bulged his eyes to convey his impatience to start. Wilson turned to the group and said, "Okay guys, attention to APM. Take your seats." Wilson took stock of the room as he returned to his own seat. Satisfied, he faced forward, but sensed the XO was looking at him.

Wilson met his eyes, and Saint asked, "Do you have anything to pass on the schedule?"

"No, sir."

Saint exhaled in apparent disgust and took the floor. He stood directly on top of the *Raven* emblem embedded in the deck tile, an act that violated an unwritten squadron rule.

"All right...I've called you here because we had a mishap last night, preventable like most mishaps are. I realize the CO is off the ship, but we have to talk about this now, while it's fresh in our minds. We may not get another opportunity before transiting Hormuz. People, we are America's first team right now. Next week we will be in combat over Iraq, and, in my view, it is likely we'll be involved in combat with Iran at some time during this deployment. Pakistan is also heating up, as is Afghanistan—which we will probably see at some point during the cruise. We have got to be prepared for any contingency, and we must know the procedures for any tasking in the CENTCOM Area of Responsibility."

Combat with Iran? Wilson thought and dismissed the XO's dramatics.

All eyes were on Saint as he continued. "Last night VFA-64 lost a significant portion of the combat power we took with us from Norfolk, provided and entrusted to us by the taxpayers. Four-oh-six is a class Alpha mishap that may never fly again, but it was not shot down and it delivered nothing against the enemies of freedom. Right now, it just clutters up Hangar Bay 3, and it will become a daily reminder to CAG that the *Ravens* weren't ready when it counted."

Wilson could feel the tension building. He stole quick glance at Weed, who sat with his hands folded, his eyes focused on something on the tile floor.

"We had a full workup with which to train and to be on the step when we enter a combat situation. We cannot and *will not* regress now. *Basics*, people…from launch to recovery, they have got to become second nature, and they must be executed *without flaw*."

The front door of the ready room burst open, and Gunner Humphries emerged from Maintenance Control wearing a float-coat, his cranial perched atop his head. Gunner froze as he realized he was interrupting an APM. For a second, no one moved, and Saint glared at him from a few feet away. Embarrassed and caught off guard—but sensing the tension in the room, Gunner, the squadron joker, blurted out a salty verse learned from his younger days:

> Get a woman, get a woman, get a woman if you can.
> If you can't get a woman, get a fat young man!

As the room exploded into laughter, Gunner turned on his heels and exited the way he had entered. The deep, stress-releasing howling was welcome by everyone—except the XO.

"*SILENCE!*" he bellowed, now incensed.

The room went silent at once. The tension returned as fast as it had disappeared.

"That's what I'm talking about!" Saint began. He snapped his fingers at Nicky to place the Do-Not-Disturb sign on the door. "We can't even get the room secure for a meeting!" His face was flushed with fury.

"Here it is, people. The Skipper is *kicking my ass* because of the lackadaisical attitude of this ready room. Sleeping all morning. Playing video games all night. Complacency in the brief. Bolters, like we had last night. Poor interval and not maintaining proper airspeed on the approach. Your job is to land the airplane safely, not to slam it into the deck. And when you get a wave-off, you do it now!"

With that, Sponge got up and exited through the back door. Saint shouted, "Sit down, Lieutenant!" but Sponge ignored him. The XO, seething, turned to Wilson.

"Mister Wilson, Lieutenant Jasper is in hack until further notice."

"Aye, aye, sir," Wilson replied, eyes downcast.

"In his khakis and out of his rack."

"Aye, aye, sir."

Saint surveyed the room to assess the mood. The pilots were tight lipped and sullen. Few looked at him.

"This is *nothing*, people. We are in a dangerous business, and the slightest inattention to detail can be fatal. Our job is to execute the plan given to us by the admiral's staff and by CAG. We *do not* question their actions."

Wilson realized it was now his turn.

"When a decision is made by a senior officer responsible for any evolution, you do not question it. When we are airborne, the ship owns us. And when they need the advice of a squadron rep, they will ask."

The pilots sat still, taking it, but they could not wait to leave. Wilson felt the eyes of the JOs, *his* JOs, watching him. He did not bolt out like Sponge, but he mentally condemned himself. *Company man, that's me.*

"The CO is disappointed with our performance so far. My job is to ensure that the CO looks good and that VFA-64 is ready in every respect. So, let's turn it around, *now*. Any questions?"

The room was silent. Nobody believed Cajun had chartered the XO to *fix* the ready room, much less confide in him. Nevertheless, Saint looked at every pilot to ensure his message was received.

"Good. Dismissed."

The JOs got up and headed for the back door. Wilson wanted to follow them, but he knew he would not get the chance.

"Mister Wilson," Saint motioned him over.

"Yes, sir."

"I understand the pressure you must have been under in CATCC last night—with a low-state nugget pilot in the pattern. Commander Johnson spoke to me and said you did a good job working the situation. Receiving praise from an officer of his caliber is commendable, and mitigates the momentary lapse in judgment regarding your call to have him eject alongside. We'll just call this a learning point in your department head training. As far as I'm concerned, the matter is closed." To Wilson, Saint looked more compassionate and understanding than he had ever seen him.

"Yes, sir."

"What happened last night is between us. No need for the CO to know."

Between us and the entire air wing, Wilson thought. "Yes, sir," he replied as he fought to keep emotion from his face. Wilson kept his eyes on the XO, but he sensed Nicky listening over Saint's shoulder.

"That is all," Saint said as he turned to his chair.

CHAPTER 17

A few minutes later, Wilson was forward on the O-2 level. He knocked on the door of the JO's bunkroom.

"Enter," answered a voice. Wilson recognized it as Guido's.

Wilson entered the six-man bunkroom. The furnishings consisted of three top and bottom metal racks behind blue curtains, six metal built-in desks, and sets of drawers along each bulkhead. Everything was painted gray. Two sinks and mirrors occupied the other bulkhead, and towels and robes hung on hooks nearby. Fluorescent desk lamps from two open desks provided some subdued lighting. A small TV was rigged in a corner of the overhead for viewing in what passed as the common area, a space little more than 8 by 8 feet. Guido and Sponge were seated, Sponge at his desk with his jaw set.

"Hey, Flip," Guido said. Sponge remained motionless.

"*Guido,*" Wilson replied, and then added in a low tone, "How about taking a walk topside?"

"Yes, sir," Guido replied, grabbed a pair of sunglasses from his desk, and exited the stateroom.

Sponge did not move as Wilson pulled up a chair. Sponge kept his eyes forward.

"I've never met anyone that flew a barricade pass," Wilson began.

"Paddles graded it an OK, little right wing down to land—*crash,*" Sponge hissed. Wilson did not recognize the junior officer before him. The old Sponge Bob was gone. He needed to get him back.

"That was a night pitching deck barricade," Wilson continued, "...on fumes, after essentially a day pattern in varsity conditions. Damn impressive flying."

"The jet's trashed."

"Screw the jet," Wilson responded, with a casual wave. "They'll send us another one."

Sponge didn't answer. Wilson kept his eyes on him and began.

"You've now been in this squadron one year. You've made the entire workup: Fallon, the Key West det, probably 250 hours of hard-core tactical flying—everything the Navy says a *Hornet* pilot needs to go on cruise a full-up round.

Now we're on cruise, and in two days, we're going through Hormuz and will enter the Gulf. Two days after that, you will probably be in an aircraft with green bombs under the wings on your way up to Baghdad."

Sponge's eyes remained down.

Wilson continued, "There are Marines and soldiers down there who are going to need us—that are going to need *you*. You know any Marines in the box these days?"

"My college suitemate… He's an infantry Marine in Anbar," Sponge replied.

"Well, you never know, he may need you one day. And it doesn't matter, really, if it's him, does it? Whoever calls us in wants fused ordnance on target, and you and I have to deliver it—on target, on time. That's our job. That's what we've been trained to do. You ready to go up there?"

Wilson saw Sponge's jaw tighten.

"Sponge, you are a hell of a pilot, and you did good last night. I doubt anyone else on this ship has flown a barricade, much less night pitching deck. When the pressure was on, you came through."

Sponge looked at Wilson. "I just crashed a jet, my flight gear is *literally* in tatters, the squadron XO blames me in public and puts me in *hack* when I refuse to 'sit down' for more humiliation. I've got to write my statements for the mishap board, the JAG investigation, the human factors board, and who knows what else. Oh, yeah, my girlfriend knows—already, knows it's me! I just got an e-mail from her. Which one of my air wing buds sent *that* news home? She's freakin' that *I* didn't let her know—not that I've had a spare *minute* the past thirteen and a half hours."

"Should'a married her," Wilson deadpanned, "and, as a wife, she'd get an official call. And at least a *chance* at $400 grand in life insurance."

Sponge shot him a look at first and then sensed the humor. A wan smile crossed his face in response to Wilson's barb.

"Sponge, you'll be ready to go soon. We'll scrounge up some flight gear, hack will end, and you'll be on the flight schedule before you know it. Take today to do your statements, write to your girlfriend and your family, and blow off some steam with the guys. Guido and them will bring you food. In 48 hours, though, we're in the Gulf. We're gonna need your game face."

Sponge held Wilson's gaze. "You've got it, Flip."

"Good man."

"One thing though," Sponge added.

"Go."

"I don't want to fly with the XO again this cruise."

Wilson listened to his words and thought for a few seconds.

"I mean it. I flew with him a lot on workups; he's my fighter section lead. He gives a shitty brief, and then he shits on you in the debrief when things go bad—which they often do. Know what we did last night? We were supposed to do 2v2 intercepts with the *Bucs*. XO calls their Skipper before the brief and bags out with some BS excuse about the weather and my training requirements. So we brief breakup and rendezvous training for me, like I'm back in flight school. We did *six* of 'em—him in the lead the whole time and me chewing up my gas. There was *no* discussion of the weather, the diverts, pitching deck procedures, how many incoming and off-going tankers airborne. Flip, *I* should be the lead for *him*. No more. I'm done."

Leaning forward in his chair with his elbows on his knees, Wilson stroked his chin. "That's a tall order. I can minimize your time together, but it's a long cruise. Once we draft it, the CO can still tweak the sked, and you could be paired with Saint."

"Flip, I need a break from the XO." Sponge looked almost desperate.

"I'll keep you apart in the short term—no promises about the entire cruise."

"Thank you, sir."

"What are you going to do first?"

"Honestly, sleep. Too keyed up last night."

"Good. We'll find you some flight gear and bring it down for fit later. Don't expect to fly tomorrow or the next day, so do the admin stuff you need."

"Yes, sir. Thanks, Flip."

"No worries," Wilson replied as he got up to leave.

CHAPTER 18

"He did *what?*" Cajun exploded, both angry and dumbfounded. His eyes narrowed on Wilson.

"Yes, sir, he called it early this morning." Giving up the XO gave Wilson the perverse pleasure he had wanted all day.

"What did he say?" Cajun asked with disgust, as he got ready to study the flight schedule. With the JOs at dinner up forward and Nicky out of earshot at the duty desk, the ready room was more or less deserted.

"He said we're entering a combat zone, and we've got to be at the top of our game. Need to look good around the ship, brief everything, and fly the brief." Cajun knew Wilson was telling the truth, but sensed there was more. The fact that Saint had called the APM was transgression enough, but Cajun wanted to know if he had done anything else over the line.

"Flip...everything."

Wilson drew a breath. "Sir, he said you've been kicking his ass about the 'lackadaisical attitude' of the ready room. Sleeping till lunch, the video games. He also implied that Sponge gooned the approach, and that's what led to the foul-deck wave-off and the low-fuel barricade. Sponge got up and bolted out the back with the XO shouting for him to stop. When he didn't, XO put Sponge in hack. I visited Sponge a few hours ago and he's pissed—no longer the happy-go-lucky Sponge. Skipper, Sponge flew a night barricade in *varsity* conditions. The jet's broke, but he did well."

Cajun looked away with his jaw clenched. "What happened in CATCC last night?" he asked. Wilson told him. As the CO stared at the bulkhead, his jaw tightened even more.

In his mind, Cajun summed up the results of the past 24 hours. *Raven 406* in a heap below with such catastrophic damage she would probably never fly again. One of his nugget pilots banished to his stateroom with who-knows-what damage to his confidence. His Operations Officer and, by extension, VFA-64 publicly humiliated in front of the senior pilots in the Wing. His own authority usurped by the XO. He could hardly comprehend it all. Less than one month into the deployment, and just days before commencing the combat operations

76

they trained all year for, the *Ravens* were in the shitter as the scuttlebutt topic of *Valley Forge*, and soon the Atlantic Fleet—once the e-mails started flying, which they surely had. He would visit Sponge, free him, and put him back on the flight schedule. Beginning the process of rehabilitating him as an aviator was all important. *Get back on the horse.* He would also need to have a "come-to-Jesus" with Saint and visit CAG. But first, he needed to repair the damage to Wilson.

"Flip, I believe you handled the situation in CATCC well," he said softly. "It takes two years to build a jet, but 25 to place a 'Sponge' in a squadron. You made a call, a *recommendation*, and your logic was sound. I want you to know I'm always confident when you're in CATCC." Wilson knew the CO was much too professional to bad-mouth his XO in front of a subordinate, but the message was clear.

"Thank you, sir," Wilson replied.

Cajun turned to depart and over his shoulder said, "All Officers Meeting, followed by APM tomorrow."

"Yes, sir."

When he reached the ready room door, he turned again and added, "Put me with Sponge on the next event, preferably a 1v1 with him leading." Cajun winked with the trace of a smile.

"Aye, aye, Skipper," Wilson said, relieved that Cajun was back aboard.

CHAPTER 19

Wilson stepped out onto the well of the catwalk ladder and looked down through the grating. Some 50 feet below, the ship made huge waves as it pushed through the Gulf of Oman. He climbed up a few steps to the starboard catwalk to assess the weather: clear, sunny, warm, gentle wind. Considering the speed the ship was making, Wilson was surprised by the wind and figured it around 20 knots...and out of the south since the ship was headed north by west. He walked aft and found the small ladder that led to the flight deck. He kept his head down, climbed the steps and crouched low in order to step over the deck edge coaming and onto the deck. Still ducking, he moved under a *Hornet* horizontal stabilator and moved along the aircraft, avoiding obstacles such as tie-downs, trailing edge flaps, and the external fuel tanks hanging on the wings. The engine turbine blades turned freely in the breeze. Their steady chatter created the ever-present wind chime of the flight deck.

He had eaten lunch only a short time ago, but this was the first time he had been outside that day. Across the deck he saw a squadron maintenance crew working on an aircraft; to his left a plane captain stood in a *Hornet* cockpit as he polished the windscreen. Dozens of joggers ran up and down the 1,000-foot flight deck as they followed a deformed racetrack pattern that avoided parked aircraft and yellow flight deck tractors. He spied Smoke and Lieutenant "Blade" Cutter, the squadron strike fighter tactics instructor, moving in long strides—down the deck and with the wind. A leisurely no-fly day on the flight deck.

He walked aft behind a *Raven* jet; his trained eye scanned its skin for signs of corrosion. When he found an area between two aircraft where he could stand with an unobstructed view of the horizon, he looked across the Strait of Hormuz. Miles to starboard—Wilson estimated over 20 miles—he saw the shadow of a ridgeline. Just visible in the distance. *Iran.*

Each time he had been to the Gulf, Wilson was struck by the desolate and forbidding landscape. To him, the entire Arabian Peninsula was simply inhospitable. Centuries of crushing heat and simoon winds had baked and eroded the land into one of the most continuous bodies of sand in the world. When he looked at the charts in the ready room, Wilson noted one could go *hundreds and hundreds* of miles and see nothing but sand dunes. Called The Empty Quarter, this inland sea of sand was so barren that the borders of Saudi Arabia, United Arab Emirates, and Oman were not distinguishable. From Aden all the way up to Baghdad, the terrain, and everything on it, was a light shade of sand marked with occasional patches of tan. Even the towns were tan; the only things not tan or sand were the black asphalt roads and the blue gulf along the coast. Flying over Arabia was like flying over a giant horizon-to-horizon *sandbox*, which is what three generations of American military personnel called the U.S. Central Command Area of Responsibility.

As he surveyed Iran in the distance, Wilson reflected on the times he was high over the Persian Gulf at night. To the south and west, the countries of the Gulf Cooperation Council were illuminated with bright clusters of lights in the cities and settlements. Natural gas flare stacks flickered and burned off at the well heads at oil fields ashore and on platforms dotting the Gulf. Desert roads in the middle of nowhere were lighted as if the roads were in a large city. Far to the south the modern metropolises of Dubai and Abu Dhabi shone brightly, and further up the Gulf, the cities of Doha, Manama, Dhahran and Kuwait City glowed—evidence not only of life but of prosperity. In this part of the world, light meant money, and under the sandy desert of the Arabian Peninsula, the former nomadic peoples of the region sat on a pile of it.

To the east and north it was another matter. Aided by the fact that the Iranian coastline was mountainous, and to a great extent devoid of humans for some 400 miles—from Bandar Abbas to the Bushier/Kharg Island complex—Iran gave the impression of being dark and foreboding. Even well inland, there were few lights to signify settlements. Basra in Iraq seemed to have a greater degree of lighting than a comparable Iranian town. Wilson found the Iraq/Iran comparison a perplexing metaphor—free enterprise on one side and essentially a command economy on the other, with both dominated by a religion that oversaw every aspect of its believers' lives. Despite their similarities, the two peoples regarded each other with deep suspicion, and in the case of the sheikdoms, fear of their powerful and populous Shiite neighbor to the north. They disagreed about much, even the name of the body of water that separated them. *Persian* Gulf. *Arabian* Gulf. To be fair, it could not be said that the GCC sheikdoms were *free*, but when he could actually view the paradox in the light patterns he saw whenever he flew high over the Gulf at night, he found it fascinating.

All around *Valley Forge* merchant ships plied the strait, visual proof that 30% of the world's crude oil passed through this vital strategic waterway. Behind the ship, and all the way to the horizon, a line of black-hulled oil tankers rode high in the water as the Indian Ocean funneled them into the Gulf to pick up loads of crude from Dhahran or Kharg Island--or maybe from Iraq. Far to the south, he could make out the white superstructure of a very large crude carrier, its hull obscured by the horizon.

One mile to port, a full tanker rode low in the water and pushed the sea before it as it lumbered into the open ocean with another 100,000-ton load of crude. Wilson scanned the deck and peered into the bridge—no sign of human life. In all his years of observing merchant ships on the high seas, even when he flew right over them, he never saw sailors on deck. For a moment Wilson wondered where the tanker was headed, and thought of Norfolk. He then noted the flag flying from the mast; it appeared to be Japanese.

Further to port, the mountainous and seemingly deserted coastline of Oman was visible, a landscape dominated by dull sandy browns and grays, with a touch of olive drab vegetation, but mostly a light beige color, or coffee with cream, which was the primary shade of the whole Arabian Peninsula. Wilson walked further up the angled deck to get a better view. Merchant ships dotted the horizon; *Valley Forge* was passing a blue-hulled containership that had shipping containers stacked high over all available deck space to bridge level. The officers on the carrier's bridge had much to contend with while avoiding traffic in these restricted waters. Their efforts were compounded by dozens of speedboats crisscrossing the narrowest part of the strait between Iran and Oman. *Smugglers.*

Wilson got to the end of the angled deck and stood there to watch the speedboats bound north and south over the waves. They left thin, white wakes as they weaved between the large merchants heading either east or west in this portion of the strait. Carpets, gold, knock-off clothing, watches, CD's, and who knows what else stashed in those fiberglass hulls… He surmised some of the boats were *boghammars*, the ubiquitous Iranian Revolutionary Guard speedboats with small arms and RPGs used to harass shipping. *Modern day pirates following centuries of tradition in this God-forsaken place. The vessels change shape, but the business stays the same*, he thought.

From his perch at the end of the angled deck, Wilson saw *Valley Forge's* bow cut into the Strait of Hormuz, the sea flaring out into a large wave that emanated from the hull and crashed over itself, leaving a frothy white blanket on the water as the ship sped past. He thought of how American Navy ships, and the waters they visited, had changed over the ages. The Navy's mission, however, remained the same: prompt and sustained combat operations at sea.

CHAPTER 20

Wilson went below to his stateroom. The first thing he looked at was his laptop. As he had hoped, a new e-mail, a long one from Mary, waited for him.

Dear James,

I miss you very, very much and so do Derrick and Brittany. When I heard about the crash the other day, I was just sick about it. Stephanie told me Bob was the pilot and is okay. I'm so glad he's okay, but what happened? She said it was at night with rain and lightning. Why don't you just stop when it's bad outside? Can you advise the Skipper to stop flying? Bob's girlfriend Meagan just flipped out – she comes across as this sweet-as-she-can-be sorority girl, but when Billie Lassiter called to tell her about the crash, she just blew up and snapped at Billie because Billie didn't know the answers to all her questions. She wanted Bob to come home and when Billie said that was not going to happen, she went off about how dumb the Navy was and why is an aircraft carrier involved with a land war – a war she hates, etc. She called back to apologize to Billie the next day, saying she's new to this and loves Bob so much. Billie is a saint, having to put up with this chick – who is not even a wife yet! I used to wish they had gotten married before the cruise, but now I'm not so sure. She said the pressure of him being gone <u>one month</u> *is getting to her. I say she doesn't know the half of it.*

Wilson saw where this was going, and, with the AOM in twenty minutes, he knew better than to continue reading. Yet, he couldn't help himself.

Sometimes I just don't know why you go on these cruises. Isn't it enough that you've already been on four cruises? And each one was a combat cruise, even before 9-11. I counted last week – in our nine years of marriage, you've been gone almost four years, counting the cruises, workups, and detachments. When you return in May, you'll have been gone 20 of the last 36 months. Haven't you – we – given enough to our country? I'm proud of you, James, and I know you are a good pilot and do a great job of teaching the new guys and keeping them out of trouble. You are now, and always will be, my hero! But does it always have to be you? Can't someone else step up? Unless they do, all I can see is more of the same for years to come.

After you leave VFA-64, you'll get that admiral's aide job you want, and after we move to Washington, you'll be working all day. And once again, you'll be gone on travel with the admiral, and I'll be stuck in a new and expensive town, not knowing anyone, with two little kids. Then you'll get command, and we'll move again back here, or to Lemoore, or Japan, and like everything else, it will probably be "get here right now." When the war started, you flew back here to join the squadron. Then I drove from Fallon across the country by myself with a two-year-old, found a house, and moved us in while you did shock-and-awe over Baghdad on CNN. I am not going to do that again.

James, I look at Billie Lassiter and think, do I want that? Not only does she take care of her own houseful alone, but she has to put up with bitchy wives – and now girlfriends – as she leads our support group. She does it with a smile, and I do admire her because she is doing it with no help because your XO doesn't have a wife. But I'm not sure that I can do it or want to do it.

And after command, there will more moves into key 12 hour-a-day jobs and then CAG, with more deployments, and then admiral... The point is, we'll never see you. Your kids will grow up and graduate from college, and you won't be there. Do all of us have to pay the price?

Wilson inhaled deep and exhaled long. Mary must have had this building up inside her for months or years. She was not prone to emotional outbursts in e-mails or letters. Sponge's mishap must have been the catalyst. The next part hit him hard.

It kills me that you have missed so much of Derrick and Brit growing up. You are a wonderful father and have so much fun with them – when you are home. They miss you, Derrick especially. He's enjoying first grade and he's really doing well. Many of the dads in his class (and one mom – ugh) are Navy and deployed, but when they have parent events like the Thanksgiving pageant, it's so nice to see the dads there. Derrick said he wished you could have seen him. (He was the Pilgrim leader.) By the time this cruise is over, you will have missed Thanksgiving, Christmas, and then Easter...all the big family holidays, not to mention my family reunion in August while you were on workups. In fact, you have missed half of Brittany's life. It is not fair to the kids that their father is gone so much of the time – by choice.

James, I need you too. Not only to help with them but as a woman. I knew you were a Navy pilot when I met you, and I went into this marriage with my eyes open, but after nine years the reality is I have a part-time husband. I want a full-time husband at home and in my bed. I'm lonely, and a future Navy career means more loneliness. Haven't I supported you through your service to our country? I love you for that and America owes you and everyone out there everything. You, and I, have given so much. Can't someone else step up and save the world? You have lived your dream, and every time you go out, you come back with more medals. At what point is enough, enough? Is it worth sacrificing your family?

This is not an ultimatum. I know we've got five more months ahead of us. But you need to know what it's like for me, and I want you to give this serious thought. With your talents I know you can get a good job that will allow us to live as a family. Lots of our friends are airline pilots, and your brother has a good job in Chesapeake. You can fly for the naval reserves, can't you? That seems like a good balance. You've done much more than your share, and have nothing to be ashamed of. Come back to me, James.

I love you so much, and pray for you every day.

Love always,

Mary

Wilson sat back and propped up his chin with his fingers, reeling from her words. He stared at Mary's Strike Fighter Ball picture, a photo taken about four years earlier. He thought of their years together as he studied her face and her gorgeous smile. *She has not changed from the day I first laid eyes on her,* he thought.

Or had she? She *was* older, and in his mind's eye, he studied the face of the woman who dropped him off at Oceana four weeks ago. It was a long morning, the culmination of what to Wilson always felt like the countdown to a death sentence. It began two weeks before each deployment. Two weeks to go. Ten days to go. Four days. Tomorrow. Two hours. Fifteen minutes. Wilson remembered standing next to the hangar gate in his flight suit as he watched Mary pull the minivan out of the parking lot that morning. His heart begged her to look at him and wave one last time. Instead, she drove off without a glance. *That* face, discounting the puffiness around her eyes as she had hugged and kissed him goodbye moments earlier, had lines in it. Lines he and his profession had put there over the years.

Then he remembered the glimpse through the tinted back window of little Derrick from his car seat. As Mary made the turn onto 1st Street, Derrick lifted his hand to wave. Wilson fought to keep his composure as they faded from view. Then he turned to salute the gate sentry and walked toward the hangar to get ready for the flight that would begin his fifth deployment. And Mary was right. It was a deployment he *wanted* to be part of.

"Damn," he whispered, as he pushed himself out of the chair to go to the ready room.

CHAPTER 21

Zydeco, the kind of music Cajun loved, blared from the stereo speakers as Wilson entered Ready Room 7. Most of the officers were in their seats, but several gathered around the water cooler. Gunner held court with the JOs in the back and sipped on a glass of red bug juice that complemented his red flight deck jersey. The pilots were in flight suits except for khaki-clad Psycho at the duty desk. The XO drank his coffee hunched over the message board with his green pen, oblivious to the laughing and banter around him.

Four bells over the 1MC signified 1400, and Wilson stood to face the group. "Okay, guys, seats. Attention to AOM." Psycho killed the music and the room came to order.

In a familiar routine, each officer with a message to pass addressed the group, followed by the XO. Then, it was time for the CO to have the last word. Typically, the ground pounders were excused at this point, while the pilots remained to repeat the ritual in order to cover pilot-specific issues, but as he stood before his squadron officers, Cajun's message was one the CO wanted all of them to hear.

"Okay, guys, welcome, or welcome back, to the Persian Gulf," said Cajun. "In forty-eight hours we'll be up in *carrier box four* and fly our first OIF hops into Iraq. We are going to spend the next four or five months flying combat missions—long ones—day and night in support of our troops. First we go to Iraq, then to Afghanistan later in the cruise. Here's the bottom line… For the foreseeable future we are here to answer *their* tasking and the tasking of National Command Authority. That's one main reason we are here. The guys on the ground are going to need us sooner or later, and we have to be on station with fused ordnance available, and we must deliver it when and where they want it. After a while, the kill box geography, and most everything else, will become routine. You'll know the procedures by heart, and even the controller's voices will become familiar to you. However, it is *not* routine for the guys on the ground. They are in a firefight, or they got hit by an IED or they see the bad guys planting one. For them it's very, very personal, and when they need 'fast mover' support, they need it *right now*. They are in combat—and so are you.

85

"If you, *all* of you, do not have your game face on right now, you are late. If you have not made a Gulf divert chart that includes the divert fields inside Iraq, make it. And if you do not know the JDAM max release airspeed, are confused about how to preflight your expendables and set a program, do not know the Mk 80 series frag patterns in diameter and altitude, are not intimately familiar with your survival radio, have not preflighted the items in your survival vest in months, learn it or do it. Any one of dozens of small details can bite you if they drop out of your scan. So, you've got 24 hours to get your act together. Ask yourself where your deficiencies are and use this time wisely.

"Last cruise we drilled around a lot in the box and didn't drop much. I admit it was hard to stay focused week after week as we lugged bombs north only to bring them home. This time, though—if what *Ike* and *Enterprise* have done recently is a guide—we are dropping plenty. If we find an IED, we aren't screwing around. If there are some bad guys holed up in a hut, *level it* once you are given the 'cleared hot.' Remember, though, if there is a doubt *there is no doubt*—don't drop. Work with the controllers, but unless you are 100 percent sure of the target, don't drop on a hunch. Bring them back. The last thing we need is to give CNN and Al Jazeera incidents to fill their air.

"The other main reason we are here, and have been at least since 1979, is to deter Iran. We are not at war with Iran, but Iran certainly is not friendly to us or to the GCC countries in the Gulf. Those countries are scared to death of Iran, not only because of Iran's military capability but also because of the exportation of Shia Islam and revolution to their populations. Anything more is above my pay grade. The bottom line is maintain a 12-mile standoff and don't thump Iranian oil platforms, dhows, *boghammars*, or Iranian P-3s. They have rights in these waters, too. If you see an Iranian unit, tell the ship and stand by for tasking. This is a rough neighborhood, but believe me, they are more afraid of you and your intentions, so it's smart to give everyone a wide berth out here. The overwhelming majority of Iranian people hate their government and the ayatollahs are afraid of the people and repress them. The Iranians are looking for a reason to fight us and unify their population in order to take the heat off themselves. Let's not give them a reason by doing something dumb.

"One more thing. We must guard against complacency *every single day*. We can hurt ourselves on this ship dozens of ways in *peacetime*, not just during combat ops. This affects everyone in this squadron, and we are all susceptible to it. When each day becomes like Groundhog Day and you lose respect for this environment, and if you pilots get into the mindset that another kill box hop is just a routine cross-country with bombs, you have got to step back and *compartmentalize* why you are out here."

Wilson immediately thought of Mary's e-mail, but willed himself to concentrate.

"We saw the other night that this can be an unforgiving business. Weather, the deck, tankers…the situation can go south real fast. Sponge found himself in a box, not because he placed himself there, but because of the way one event built upon another. Sponge, your recovery on a night pitching deck barricade was a fine piece of flying under extreme pressure. None of us here have done what you did, and I'm not willing to say I would have done any better. The airplane *is* broken—but we'll fix it. As soon as we can, we'll get you back in the air, and I hope that is tomorrow."

What a great leader, Wilson thought. He stole a glance at Saint who listened with eyes down. Regardless of the Aircraft Mishap Board outcome, Cajun knew enough to absolve Sponge of responsibility for *406* in public and, by extension, disagreeing with Saint in public. Wilson wondered if Cajun had already had a one-way conversation with his XO behind closed doors.

"Okay, anybody have anything for me?" asked Cajun, ready to wrap it up. No one did.

He clapped his hands and said, "Okay, ready, *break.*"

"QUOTH THE RAVEN!" the room responded in unison.

Wilson got up and projected his voice over the sudden disorder. "Okay, pounders, excused. Pilots, back in yer seats in five minutes." Psycho turned and pushed the play button, and the high-spirited sound of accordions and washboards once again filled Ready Room 7.

CHAPTER 22

A few minutes later, Wilson called the room to order. The pilots went around the room again, this time with their pilot-specific discussion items. When it was his turn, Wilson stood up to go through a PowerPoint presentation on flying in the Gulf. "Okay, guys, this is the gouge, so listen up. The Skipper just got our minds right about flying here. Now, I want to give you a brief on how CAG Ops is going to build the Air Plan and what a typical fly day is going to be like over here.

"First, stand off. NAVCENT gets their ass kicked if we even get close to territorial airspace, so know where you are and don't press the limit. Even if you know you are safe according to your system, realize that if you fly right at a limit, you are going to set off alarms inside the host nation's airspace. Especially if you get close to Iran.

"Also, we need to follow the standard routes into Iraq, and those are basically along the al-Faw Peninsula with altitude deconfliction. They are *not* over Iran. If you are going to be off, be off to the west." Wilson stomped his foot to emphasize the importance of the point, and several pilots nodded. He changed to the next slide.

"The action right now is in Diyala, north and east of Baghdad, southeast of Baghdad around Salman Pak, and in Mosul. The Marines out of al-Asad have Anbar. Chances are you won't go there this cruise—but you may—so be ready. Get ready to be strapped into the seat for eight hours at a time, and the hours are going to accumulate. The guys on *Enterprise* were getting 70-80 hours a month. If you want to bag flight time and traps, you've come to the right place. For those of you who haven't experienced it, 80 hours a month kicks your ass.

"You heard the CO. Get ready.

"We are loaded for bear each hop," said Wilson, as he shifted gears, "but we have to adopt the mindset that we do *not* want to drop. Our job is to support the guys on the ground who are in a battle for the hearts and minds. When we drop, even if we're on target and are killing bad guys, it doesn't help us with the populace if we break windows and make babies cry. We have got to determine through our own assessment of the tactical situation—through the voice inflection of the JTAC and through the passdown of the flights ahead of you—whether it's right to drop. Remember, the bad guys *want* you to drop, that's why they are holed up next to mosques and in the middle of neighborhoods. Ask the JTACs to declare *troops in contact*, and if they report TIC, support 'em with fire. If the JTAC can get the bad guys to hole up or to cease fire by calling you in to make some noise, that's mission success. So, we have to assess the situation and assess when it's smart to release, and it's going to be *you knuckleheads* who are gonna make this call on the spot. Remember, you do *not* want to be on CNN by making the wrong call.

"So, triple-check the coordinates, use a run-in that minimizes collateral damage and your exposure to the threat, listen to the JTAC. If he wants you to hit something in the middle of a city, question him. Have him declare TIC, see if he's taking fire. Like the CO said, if you need to drop or strafe to support these guys, *do it.* But there should be no doubt. We cannot make a mistake."

Wilson reminded them to make area divert charts and to study the terrain around Diyala and along the Tigris to Mosul. When he finished, Cajun looked over his shoulder at the group, pointed toward Wilson and cracked, "What *he* said!"

"*QUOTH THE RAVEN!*" boomed the pilots inside Ready 7.

After dinner, Wilson went down to the "clean-shirt" wardroom and was grateful there was no one using the satellite phone to call home. It was early afternoon in Virginia Beach, and Wilson hoped Mary was home and in the mood to talk. She had been distraught when she wrote the e-mail, and he knew the stress of facing another holiday season alone was what was really bothering her. He dialed the number and took a deep breath. After two rings she answered.

"Hey, baby," Wilson said softly.

"James?"

"Yeah...anybody else callin' you baby?" he chuckled.

She giggled. "No! No one else! How are you? I'm glad you called!"

"Doin' good. Just finished dinner." Wilson sensed by her voice she was having a good day.

"Did you get my e-mail from last night?" she asked. Wilson didn't expect it to come up so soon in the conversation. He paused and answered flatly.

"Yeah."

Wilson could also sense, from thousands of miles away, the wave of emotion that swept over Mary as she broke down.

"Oh, James, I'm *so* very sorry! Please forgive me!" In an instant she was sobbing.

"Baby, don't cry, it's okay."

"As soon as I sent, it I wanted it back!" He heard her sniff. "It's just that with you gone *another* Christmas and the disposal broken..."

"The disposal's broken?"

"Yes, but I handled it. It's okay, but, James, I *don't* want you to worry about that or the kids or me."

"Well, I always *worry*," he replied.

"I know you love us and worry about us, but you are over there flying that airplane, and I want you to concentrate on that." She gasped a little for breath. "I don't want to distract you from your job."

"I can..." The short delay in the satellite transmission made the conversation stilted.

"I don't want you to *crash...*" Mary blurted. Wilson imagined her shoulders heaving as she spoke.

"I'm not gonna crash. Have I crashed yet?" he joked weakly. Mary ignored it and passed her message to him in a stream of consciousness.

"I need you to come home to me after this cruise is over, not before. You are in my prayers every day, and I know you are a good pilot. Billie tells me Steve thinks the world of you. The new guys need you to get them home safely. But right now, I know why you are there, because those Army and Marine kids on the ground need you. You are my knight in shining armor!"

"We'll be okay. We're ready." He sensed she had regained some of her composure, but he needed to find out more. "What's wrong, Mary?"

"James, nothing is wrong. We're okay. Please concentrate on your flying. I'm okay, really, and I don't want you to be distracted. We'll talk when you return home."

"I won't be distracted. We're prepared, and we have the best equipment and best training. Bob did a great job flying his airplane; everyone involved did a good job to get him aboard. We'll fix the airplane."

"Is the airplane broken?"

"It's fine. Just needs some minor repairs," Wilson lied.

Mary exhaled. "I miss you already. Five more months?"

"No, only four months and three weeks."

"Oh, great."

Now that he knew the emotional storm had passed, Wilson desperately wanted to hear her laugh. "Did you say we'll talk when I get back?"

"Yes."

"*First* thing?"

"Well," Mary coyly replied, "maybe not the *first* thing!"

They continued to talk about the kids and her holiday plans until Wilson noticed one of the marine pilots waiting to use the phone.

"I gotta go, baby. I know you support me out here, and it's okay to blow off steam. I can take it."

"I promise I won't do that again, James. We're fine here, surrounded by friends and family. Get another medal, will ya."

"Medal of Honor this time?"

"If it will keep you home, yes."

"Okay, I'll work on it," Wilson said, smiling.

"I love you very much."

"I love you, too."

"Bye, baby."

"Bye."

Part II

OH, East is East, and West is West, and never the twain shall meet,
Till Earth and Sky stand presently at God's great Judgment Seat;
But there is neither East nor West, Border, nor Breed, nor Birth,
When two strong men stand face to face, tho' they come from the ends of the earth!

The Ballad of East and West by Rudyard Kipling

CHAPTER 23

Wilson looked over at his wingman, Smoke, inside his *Hornet* in tension on Cat 1. Seconds prior to launch, Smoke's head was back against the headrest, left arm locked against the throttles at full power. All around Smoke's aircraft, *Raven 410*, the troubleshooters and catapult crewmen held thumbs up aloft to signify ready. The catapult officer, topside on this clear blue day, had returned Smoke's salute seconds earlier and was in a crouch pointing toward the bow. The green-shirted crewman in the catwalk looked left and right, arms raised, and then dropped his arms and depressed the FIRE button on the console in front of him.

As the catapult fired, Wilson saw Smoke's body compress, due to the sudden forward motion. It then seemed to bounce in the cockpit as the 44,000 pound aircraft was slung down the track by the shuttle attached to the nose gear. The aircraft accelerated from zero to 180 knots with an instantaneous 3 g-force that drove him further into his seat and caused the stabilators to deflect down to lift the aircraft up on the climb out. Wilson saw the burner cans stage open with yellow fire halfway down the track as Smoke selected afterburner. In a fraction of a second, the aircraft departed the ship, accompanied by a sharp *Boom* as the catapult shuttle crashed into the water brake at the end of the stroke. Two seconds from the first motion, Smoke's bomb-laden *Hornet* was airborne 60 feet above the peaceful waters of the Gulf, accelerating as the pilot gently picked up the nose and turned right, away from the ship, while raising the gear and flaps, then reversing his turn to the left to parallel the ship's course.

A *Prowler* roared past on Wilson's left off Cat 3. The pilot banked left, cleaning up and climbing into a mirror image of Smoke's flight path. As both aircraft receded from view off the bow, Wilson grew impatient to launch. He wanted to minimize the distance building each second between him and his wingman.

The catapult crew now focused their attention on him, and at the instant the yellow shirt gave him the "take tension" signal, Wilson brought the throttles to military as the engines thundered to life behind him. On signal he lifted the launch bar switch to "UP." In rote sequence, he extended the flight control stick to full travel in a deliberate motion forward... back... left... right.... Simultaneously, he pushed the rudder pedals to their limits with each leg and kept his eyes on the engine instruments.

Satisfied, Wilson turned to the catapult officer, made eye contact, and popped a jaunty salute before he, too, placed his head back in the head rest and braced for launch. Off to his right he saw the catapult officer return his salute and make his final checks of the aircraft and the cat track. Leaning into the 25-knot wind, he then looked forward, touched the deck with his hand, and pointed to the bow on one knee. Remaining motionless but taut, with his left arm locked and pushing the throttles forward to ensure they didn't come back to idle during the stroke, Wilson's eyes shifted left. He saw the green-shirted crewman with arms raised look up and down the track, then lower his arms.

Unseen and instantaneous force pinned Wilson's shoulders back into the seat. His oxygen mask pushed tight against his face and caused his eyes to squint behind the helmet visor. The FA-18 seemed to bounce down the deck as it accelerated to flying speed, and like Smoke moments earlier, Wilson shoved the throttles past the military stop into burner. He heard the shuttle increase speed and saw the bow rush up to meet him. The 3 g's against his body felt good as he hurtled down the track, and the airspeed box in the HUD rapidly scrolled above three figures. With an abrupt lurch forward, the g-force disappeared and a deafening boom sounded below as the shuttle slammed into the water brake beneath him.

At that, Wilson was also thrown into the sky above the glassy blue-green Persian Gulf. His right hand dropped to take the stick and command his own gentle climb and turn to the right. His left slapped up the gear and the flaps in a practiced motion. Still in burner, he rolled back left to parallel the course and bunted the nose to level at 500 feet. With the radar on, he pushed the weapon select switch forward to sweep for contacts, as an instructor had taught him years ago: *Get the radar searching ASAP, like you are going to kill something.*

Wilson's radar detected something about five miles ahead, and he bumped the castle switch to lock it. An aircraft heading northwest at angels five closing at 150 knots. *Must be Smoke*, he thought. Minutes later, as he closed on the left bearing line, the bright afternoon sun illuminated the black *Raven* insignia on the vertical stab and confirmed his assumption.

Earlier, they had briefed to join northwest of the ship, but Smoke knew Wilson was next off the bow and had slowed his acceleration to allow his flight lead to catch up. Smoke had, thereby, expedited the join-up and had minimized the time needed to get to the tanker south of Baghdad. None of this was discussed on the radio. After two years of turnaround training and combat flying together in VFA-64, Wilson and his favorite JO wingman were at the point they could anticipate each other's thoughts.

Wilson crept up to Smoke in a shallow climb. He inspected *410*'s left side and, in a graceful maneuver, slid under to repeat the procedure on the right. He then pushed up next to Smoke, who had been looking over his shoulder, waiting for him. Using hand signals Wilson took the lead, led them through a frequency change, and checked the drop tank fuel transfer. Then, with an open-palm hand signal, he pushed Smoke out into a more comfortable formation for the long flight north.

Wilson prepared them to test their decoy expendables. "Stand by for confetti checks...from lead."

Wilson's left thumb rocked forward and back on the chaff/flare switch, expending one bundle of chaff and one flare. His headset clicked as they were released, and even in the bright sunlight, he could see the flash from the flare reflected off his left drop tank. He looked over at Smoke 400 feet away, and soon saw the metallic fibers of the chaff bundle blooming, followed by the dazzling yellow flare as it ejected from below his aircraft, and rapidly fell behind.

"Good checks," Wilson said. Satisfied the go/no-go criteria from their brief were met, he added, "Lead's fenced, eleven-eight."

"Two's fenced, eleven-four," Smoke replied.

With both aircraft now combat ready, there was no need for Dutch. He had launched a few minutes after Wilson and was there to serve as the airborne spare if one of the two primary *Ravens* was not fully mission capable for the assigned combat mission. Dutch was now free to go on an alternate mission for the ship, such as sea surface search around the strike group ships. He would look for contacts of interest like dhows or unusual watercraft and would recover on the next recovery.

Wilson called to him on squadron tactical. "Dutch, we're fenced and outbound."

"Roger that. Have fun," he replied.

Wilson clicked his mike twice in acknowledgement as they continued north and into combat.

CHAPTER 24

The "Surge," which had begun in earnest earlier in the year, was paying big dividends for the Commander, Multi-National Force Iraq. The strategy of trying to limit the Iraqi footprint of the Multi-National Force—by garrisoning the troops in fire base enclaves, making only high-speed patrols through towns, and by treating IEDs as a law enforcement problem—had failed in 2005 and 2006. The Iraqi people, fed up with the violence but unsure of the American commitment, withheld their allegiance until they could be confident of U.S. resolve. They did not want to back the loser in the struggle with the Al-Qaeda insurgents.

The surge strategy—enter a town, clear it of insurgents, stay to ensure the personal security of the inhabitants, and support the fledgling government and Iraqi security forces—involved heavy firepower up front. If people were observed digging alongside a highway in the wee hours, they were taken out immediately. If mortar fire was observed from an urban dwelling, it was obliterated with a 500-pound bomb.

Nowhere were the results more striking then in al-Anbar province, known for years as "the Wild, Wild West" to the Marines responsible for that area. Through the coalition's aggressive destruction of insurgents and the engagement of the tribal sheiks by mid-grade officers, the formerly restive region came to trust and to communicate intelligence to the Americans. The officers were schooled in classic counter-insurgency tactics which suggested that by working with the coalition Anbar could have a better future than that which al-Qaeda offered.

The "Anbar Awakening" was a success story many Americans were aware of by late 2007, but Iraq was not a place where one political solution or one counter-insurgency model fit all provinces. Several pockets of resistance remained north and south along the Tigris River, and it was likely Wilson and his wingman would find evidence of one of those pockets on this flight.

They continued northwest and climbed above 30,000 feet in their transit of Kuwait. As they talked to air traffic controllers at various stations in Kuwait, in

Iraq, or in AWACS aircraft, they noticed the occasional detached accent of a Brit ex-pat controller. Wilson selected his mission computer destination for *Padres,* the aerial refueling track. It was located southeast of Baghdad, 345 miles away from their present position, or about 50 minutes away. They were scheduled, or "fragged" to be on station 30 minutes later. Wilson set his fuel flow to burn 2,800 pounds per hour per engine and engaged the autopilot.

Below to his right, about 10 miles away, were the twin oil pipeline terminals Al Basrah and Khawr Al Amaya, thin angular man-made "islands" set on the blue Gulf and connected to Iraqi oilfields by underwater pipelines. Wilson observed one tanker at each terminal: a large, traditional, black-hulled crude carrier with white superstructure at one and another of similar design, but smaller and painted bright orange at the other. He locked up the larger vessel on the radar and slewed his infrared aiming diamond on it. The crude carrier showed up as a ghostly white image on his digital display, the wisps of its mooring lines visible on the infrared display because of the midday heat.

The two terminals dispensed the economic lifeblood of Iraq to eager customers from around the world. Wilson knew that SEAL teams lived on the platforms in austere conditions, and in triple-digit temperatures, to provide security. Off his left nose, he saw one of the strike group frigates, stationary in the water, but within close visual range of the platforms ready to serve as another layer of defense for the vital terminals. Further off his left side, and to the south, numerous oil platforms, some Saudi and others Kuwaiti, dotted the Gulf. He craned his neck to the right and behind in order to study Iran's Kharg Island oil complex. Some 40 miles distant, the island had several bright flare stacks scattered about the sandy terrain. Nearby more tankers stood off from the island.

The nose of Wilson's *Hornet* passed over Bubiyan Island, a large plug of barren land dividing the al-Faw Peninsula from the mainland of Kuwait. A small vessel was transiting up the Shatt-al-Arab waterway, the confluence of the Tigris and Euphrates rivers. This narrow ribbon of brown water, less than a half mile across, separated Iraq from Iran.

Wilson shot a glance at Smoke, flying in loose tac-wing formation, and in the distance saw the large metropolis of Kuwait City, with the distinctive Kuwait Towers dominating the northern shore. The city blocks were tightly packed into irregular geometric shapes that all converged on the north of the city and the Grand Mosque. Outside of the great city were only small scattered settlements.

Wilson's daydreaming was interrupted by the radio hand-offs from controller to controller.

"*Nail* four-one, contact Basra Control on Red one-five," the controller said, using the call sign assigned by the Combined Air Operations Center, or CAOC, for this mission.

Wilson responded, "Roger, *Nails* switching Red one-five," and in a command intended for Smoke, added, "Go button six."

He punched in preset button six, waited several seconds, and then keyed the mike. "*Nail* check."

"Two," Smoke replied.

Wilson then called the new controller. "Basra, *Nail* four-one flight with you enroute *Padres* at flight level three-five-zero."

"*Nail* four-one, Basra center. Radar contact, cleared direct *Padres*," answered the voice, which had a definitive Iraqi accent.

"*Nail* four-one."

Crossing into Iraq, Wilson noted the range to *Exxon 55*, the aerial fueling tanker orbiting at *Padres* for their fragged mission give of 8,000 pounds. With over 300 miles to go at 435 knots ground speed, they had almost 45 minutes of cruising ahead of them.

Although he had flown through this narrow band of airspace between Kuwait and Iran dozens of times in his career, Wilson was once again struck by the landscape below. He scanned the desert floor of northern Kuwait both with his eyes and aircraft sensors for scars left over from Desert Storm some 17 years earlier. Scattered over the entire region, which was pockmarked with craters from coalition bombs, were long berms with irregular breeches that marked former Iraqi fighting positions and bunkers.

Wilson could only imagine the terror of the Iraqi boys who had lived for months on the cold, winter "moonscape," as they faced the daily onslaught from above. Death came suddenly and with little warning through many means: iron bombs, LGBs, *Rockeye*, artillery, rockets, *Mavericks*, *Hellfires*, 20 or 30 millimeter, 105 millimeter. Mere *movement* in the open likely meant death, the stuff of their regular nightmares...

Outside on a cold, clear February night, three scared, hungry and chilled conscripts from Saddam City share a cigarette after relieving themselves. Enjoying the moon and stars and thinking of home, they are grateful to be out of that wretched bunker, ignoring their sergeant's warning about lingering outside. The three soldiers watch the gunners to the east shoot their 57mm into the air and cheer them on to find a mark among the formations of invisible jets high above, the sound of which bathes the air in a low-frequency rumble. An American bomb flashes on the horizon, and they time the seconds until they hear the muffled *Wump…8 kilometers? 10?*

Without warning, the guttural roar of a fighter pulling out of a dive rips through the air just above. Wordlessly and in unison, they bolt for the bunker like scared rabbits, wide-eyed with fear, not by conscious thought but by instinctive terror, knowing what it could mean. *They saw us!*

Exhorting each other to run for their lives, they hear an almost imperceptible "crack" over the noise of their boots and the rattle of their canteens under their winter coats. Gasping lungfuls of heavy desert air and searching for the bunker, they sprint wildly with gripping fear through the sand and the darkness toward the soft glow of light from the bunker entrance, hoping that they or their bunker are not targeted.

Only 30 meters to go! Keep pumping! Then a sound, a high-pitched whistle close above them, registers louder and louder in their brains, *dozens* then *hundreds* of whistles slowly melding into one terrifying *shriek* as the boys whimper for their mothers. A sparkling flash to the left, accompanied by a sharp *POP*, causes them to hunch over by reflex and as a second and third *FLASH! POP!* hit near them, they throw themselves headlong (*Mama!*) into the dirt as reality registers in their consciousness. *Cluster bombs!* They claw at the land in a vain attempt to pull themselves into the sun-baked dirt as the whistling becomes a piercing din, and lethal bomblets pepper the ground all around them causing the earth to erupt in a deafening cacophony of horror and death.

And after the last fragment comes to rest, calm…as the low rumble of jet aircraft permeates the stillness of the now lifeless desert floor.

Wilson imagined what it must have been like for those kids almost 20 years ago.

Time and wind-driven sand had eroded the earthen fortifications and covered the vehicle hulks—and the bodies. Desert Storm—the "Mother of all Battles." Wilson glanced at Smoke, where he should be in stepped up tac-wing, the same formation American fighters had been using to enter Iraqi airspace almost daily since the long ago winter of 1991. The battle was still not over, morphing, over time, into this routine Iraqi Freedom patrol.

CHAPTER 25

An asphalt road, running from east to west, formed a distinctive black-on-sand visual cue of the Kuwait-Iraq border. Berms and lines of other man-made objects ran parallel to either side of the road. A great oilfield straddled the border, dominated by features of Iraq's Ar Rumaylah complex: storage tanks, pipelines, various earthworks and the ever-present flare stacks. The stacks blazed through the midday haze and sent dark gray smoke aloft, where the prevailing winds carried it to the northeast. Underneath the smoke were large swaths of black, oil-stained sand. From Wilson's vantage point five miles above, the swaths looked like giant ink spills on the desert floor. Though far from human settlements, environmental considerations were not high priorities on this bleak landscape.

Wilson shifted in his seat. Yesterday, Shakey and Dutch had dropped two GPS-guided Joint Direct Attack Munitions apiece on an insurgent stronghold in western Diyala north of Baghdad. They were the first weapons CVW-4 had released in a week, and the Air Force had done some "good work," too. Before he had walked, he learned the *Spartans* and *Moonshadows* had released on targets in Diyala that morning. Wilson's two-plane "section" carried a mixed load of two 500-pound JDAM and two LGBs split between them. Each also carried several hundred rounds of 20mm. Wilson wished he had a *Maverick* missile to shoot at a vehicle or something moving. He had never had the opportunity to shoot one before. Positioning himself more comfortably, he settled in for the next 200 miles to *Padres*.

After 15 minutes of looking at the brown countryside of southern Iraq, the airspace controller broke the silence. "*Nail* four-one, switch up *Exxon* five-five on Violet three."

Wilson keyed the mike and replied, "*Nail* four-one, roger. Switching *Exxon* five-five on Violet three. *Nails* go."

"Two," Smoke acknowledged.

His radar swept back and forth in the 80-mile scale. Wilson picked up a contact in the top half of his display and bumped the castle switch to the right. The cursor went to the contact and locked it, showing an airborne contact 10 degrees left of the nose at 24,000 feet heading east. On the left display his FLIR showed the bogey as a white image, which to Wilson's trained eye was a KC-135 *Stratotanker*, call sign *Exxon 55*. In his HUD was displayed a course to intercept, but Wilson ignored it, knowing that the tanker would begin the racetrack turn to the west before long.

Minutes later, when the tanker turned, Wilson set an intercept course to the northwest, listening to two *Buccaneers* line up behind *Exxon 55* for a long drink. Through his FLIR, he discerned two white dots behind the tanker. Raising his head, he could see with his naked eye a small dash set against a lone cumulonimbus cloud 30 miles away on the northern horizon, with two tiny dots behind it.

The boom operator called to one of the *Hornets*. "Three-zero-seven, that was 7,200."

"Three-zero-seven, roger." Wilson recognized the voice of one of the VFA-47 JOs.

Sliding closer, Wilson positioned them on the tanker's left wing, using geometry to close the distance. Inside 10 miles he could discern the tanker aspect, and hoped they would hold this heading to affect an expeditious join up. He wasn't in too much of a hurry. The second jet had just plugged, and 8,000 pounds took eight minutes.

Soon Wilson joined up on the left wing of the gray *707* airframe using visual cues, while *Cutlass 310* was still plugged in on the boom. Smoke drew in closer in a loose cruise, and using hand signals, informed Wilson of his fuel state—5.7. Wilson gave a thumbs up and passed his own state—5.9— with an open hand (five) followed by four horizontal fingers (nine).

As *310* backed out with a small puff of fuel vapor over his fuselage, the basket swung like a mace in the relative wind before it steadied. The boomer radioed *310* that he had taken 9,000 pounds, and *310* crossed under to the outside of his own wingman.

Wilson called, "*Exxon* five-five, *Nail* four-one flight joined on your left wing as fragged, nose cold, switches safe." He took a glance over his left shoulder at Smoke, who nodded an acknowledgement.

"Roger, *Nails*, cleared precontact," the boom operator replied.

"Roger, precontact," Wilson answered. He then reached down with his left hand to extend the air refueling probe, which extended into the airstream from his right nose.

In a practiced motion, he dropped his right wing and pulled a bit of power, gliding back to a position behind the boom. For a few moments, the five aircraft flew as one at 300 knots. However, as Wilson drew closer to the basket, the

Buccaneer section banked right and opened away from the formation at a measured clip. Wilson noticed their weapons were still secured under their wings,
weapons they would take home with them on the one-hour return flight to the
ship.

When he lined up the probe five feet behind the basket and stabilized, he
could make out the face of the boom operator. The "boomer" wore sunglasses
and headphones as he watched Wilson from a window on the bottom of the
fuselage.

"Precontact," Wilson transmitted.

"Cleared contact," the boomer replied.

The tanker then began a right turn to remain on the track, and Wilson com-
pensated by matching the roll and adding a bit of power. As his probe inched
closer to the basket, Wilson maneuvered his aircraft with tight deflections of the
stick. Satisfied with the angle, Wilson added a little power and flew his probe
into the basket, then took a bit off to cause the six-foot hose to bend a little, but
not too much.

"Contact."

Fuel flowed into the aircraft while they completed the turn to the right and
rolled wings level. Wilson concentrated to keep the probe engaged with the
basket. For the next eight minutes he maintained this position by holding the
aircraft within an area no more than three feet square, down and to the left of the
tanker. Fuel transferred through this connection filling his internal tanks and
centerline drop. Wilson made his corrections to stay engaged almost by reflex.
This allowed his mind to speculate on where, and for what purpose, *Falcon*, or
the CAOC airborne coordination controllers, would send them once refueling
was complete.

Once transfer was complete, he was careful to get aligned with the end of
the rigid steel boom as he slid aft to unplug. The basket came off the probe with
a little whip motion and then steadied out into the relative airstream. Wilson
waved thanks to the boomer and retracted the probe, sliding over to the tanker's
right wing.

"Four-zero-seven. That's 8,400."

"Roger, eight-point-four," Wilson replied and scribbled *8.4* on his kneeboard
card.

While Smoke went through the same procedure, Wilson was able to relax a
bit on the right wing and study the tanker. Painted a dark shade of gray with
a black nose, it had four fat turbofan engines on the wings. At the top of the
tail the word "MISSISSIPPI" was spelled with large interlocking "Ss," the style

common to the state's promotional literature. Wilson knew this Air National Guard refueling squadron was based at Key Field in Meridian, just across town from where Wilson had gone to flight school 12 years earlier. He pulled acute to the cockpit, some 60 feet away, and saw that the copilot was looking at him. The pilot next to him then popped his head into view. When another face appeared in the window behind the copilot, Wilson gave them a thumbs-up, which the three Air Guard aircrew returned. The copilot pointed at the ordnance under the *Hornet's* wing and slammed his right fist into his left palm, then bared his teeth and flexed two clenched fists in front of his face. The message was unmistakable, and Wilson nodded an acknowledgment.

CHAPTER 26

Despite the ever-present haze, it was a nice day over central Iraq. Wilson slid back and looked below at a town hard along the Tigris River. The town consisted of packed brown rectangular structures set within a crosshatched street pattern amid larger streets that funneled out from a central square near the river. The whole scene resembled a huge spider web. Wilson checked his digital moving map—Az Zubaydiyah. From this altitude everything appeared as an earth tone: the buildings, the streets, the surrounding fields, even the river. Though he was rather familiar with the topography and the landmarks of Iraq, this town was one he had never worked.

Five minutes later Smoke was complete and joined Wilson on his right wing. Once Smoke was stabilized, Wilson waved to the still fascinated copilot, whom Wilson surmised had not seen many Navy fighters. As they took a gentle cut away and opened distance from the tanker, Wilson activated his radar and was careful to keep his head on a swivel to watch for nearby tanker traffic.

After they exchanged their new fuel states by hand signal, Wilson tapped his helmet and showed Smoke one then two fingers with his right hand. Smoke nodded.

Wilson switched up Button 12 on his radio, waited a few seconds, and then transmitted. "*Falcon, Nail* four-one and flight off *Exxon* five-five at *Padres* with you as fragged."

After a long pause, *Falcon* replied, "*Nail* four-one, roger. Proceed to eighty-nine ALPHA, ten to thirteen K. Keypads eight and nine hot all altitudes. Switch *Bowstring* on Indigo five."

"*Nail* four-one, roger. Proceed to eighty-nine ALPHA, ten to thirteen K. Eight and nine hot. Switching *Bowstring* on Indigo five. *Nails* go!"

"Two," Smoke said into his mask.

The airspace over Iraq was crowded with aircraft of all types. While the controlling agencies provided traffic calls as best they could, pilots were wise to look outside the cockpit. Wilson descended them down under 20,000 feet, sweeping in front of his flight path, as well as across the horizon, for other aircraft. The previous week, north of Baghdad, he and a *Predator* UAV had had a close call, close enough for Wilson to see the *Hellfire* missile it was carrying under its left wing.

He was pleased they were currently heading to a position in Diyala, where Shakey and Dutch had dropped their JDAM the day before. Leaving the Tigris behind, they glided north in a lazy descent, Smoke following on his wing. Both pilots moved their heads from side to side, pausing for a second on one "piece" of sky at a time and focusing their eyes for movement at range, scanning more for traffic than ground threats.

Wilson examined the surface below, a mixture of desert wasteland and anemic-looking irrigated fields in small slapdash rectangle shapes, canals feeding what meager water was available to them and the occasional village. Under 15,000 feet and able to see better through the desert haze, Wilson began to pick up color in the fields, an olive drab green. He spotted a lone vehicle, a sedan, moving on a road at a normal speed toward a village, resumed his scan, and keyed the mike to contact *Bowstring*, the terminal area controller.

"*Bowstring, Nail* four-one flight checking in mission one-three-one, one Mk 38 JDAM and one GBU-12 each plus twenty mike-mike, ATFLIR. Playtime zero plus four-five. Sitrep."

"Roger, *Nail*, proceed to eighty-nine ALPHA, cleared to roam north and south. Quiet now."

"*Nail* four-one, roger."

The two *Ravens* cruised at a max endurance fuel setting in an area 75 miles northeast of Baghdad, which was obscured from their view by the haze. Wilson edged to the western border of their assigned area, which paralleled the north/south road from Baghdad to Mosul, a notorious insurgent corridor that included the town of Tikrit. As *Bowstring* had said, it was quiet, or so it seemed from altitude. The minutes ticked off one at a time, and he shifted uncomfortably in the seat he had strapped himself into three hours ago.

They flew in a 30-mile racetrack up and down, as Wilson scanned for puffs of dust on the surface or palls of smoke. He was reminded of a pilot's axiom: *Flying is hours and hours of boredom interrupted by moments of sheer terror*. Nothing was going on down there, and Wilson, hoping to hit something today, was ashamed to realize that the satisfaction he derived from releasing a weapon was to a great extent dependent on American kids first getting ambushed by the enemy.

Wilson called to Smoke on his aux radio. "Lead's seven-point-oh."

"Two's six-point-seven."

Heading south and initiating an easy climb, Wilson informed *Bowstring* that they were departing for *Padres* and more fuel. *Bowstring* answered, "*Nail* four-one, standby. We've got a mission for you. Contact *Bowser* on Yellow Fourteen."

Wilson bunted the nose, pulled a handful of power, and turned away from Smoke as he rogered a response. With the *Exxon* refueling track some 80 miles away, Wilson figured they could squeeze 15 minutes before departing for a drink. He looked up the UHF radio frequency for Yellow 14 on his kneeboard package and entered it into the radio keypad.

"*Nail* check."

"Two," Smoke replied.

"*Bowser, Nail* four-one flight checking in mission one-three-one as fragged with two Mk 38 JDAM, two GBU-12 and twenty mike-mike. Standing by for nine-line."

Bowser was the call sign of a Joint Terminal Attack Controller, a young soldier on the ground who needed help. By the sound of his voice, Wilson guessed he was a southern kid in his early 20s, and anxious.

"Rog' that *Nail*, copy all. We're in Balad Ruz on Highway 82. Got a sit'ation here, where y'all at?"

Wilson checked his sector chart and made a calculation. *Bowser* was 25 miles to the east. Smoke was to his right in combat spread. To get them moving east, Wilson keyed the mike and said, "Tac right—go," as he rolled the aircraft on its right side and pulled across the horizon toward Smoke.

"Two," his wingman replied. Wilson went back to *Bowser* on his primary radio.

"Be there in about four minutes *Bowser*, and we'll have about ten minutes on-station for you. Need us sooner?"

"Ahh…yeah…need you *NOW, Nails,* for a show o' force. Lemme know when you have the town."

Wilson keyed aux and said, "Gate," as he shoved the throttles to burner and unloaded for knots. Out of the turn Smoke matched him as their indicated airspeed increased rapidly, still in spread but now to Wilson's left.

"Roger, *Bowser*, be there in 2.5 minutes for a show of force, wilco."

Wilson wondered what lay in store for them in Balad Ruz. Was *Bowser* and his squad facing some angry townspeople, or did they get hit by a roadside bomb? Through the haze, he followed Highway 82 toward the town, located about 50 miles from the Iranian border. The town was in the middle of an agricultural area characterized by small, rectangular fields and ditches, some partially flooded by recent winter storms.

In the air-to-ground mode, Wilson selected "GUN" to ready his 20 mm cannon. He called "Tapes on... *armstrong*" to Smoke on aux, then lifted his own Master Arm switch to ARM and energized the video tape recorder.

"*Nails,* need you to thump this town, low and loud."

Sensing the rising tension in *Bowser's* voice, Wilson nevertheless asked for more details. "*Bowser,* what heading do you want us on?"

"*Nails,* don' matter, any head'n will do. Do you see the town?"

Through the milky haze the town, another packed jumble of small, boxy structures surrounded by disorganized fields, came into view south of the highway. Wilson called to *Bowser* that he had it in sight.

"Roger, *Nail,* we're near a small minaret on the southwest part o' town. Jus' took a mortar. How far you out?"

"One minute, *Bowser.* Looking for you," Wilson assured him. He told Smoke to take high cover and continued down in a shallow dive to the deck. In his mind he recited the low-altitude training dive rules: *15 for 750.* The airplane intakes were moaning at high speed, and he looked at his fuel: 5.4. With the ground rushing up at a steady pace, and a large bird whizzing past his left side, he realized he was no longer bored.

CHAPTER 27

Taking a cut to the right to set up a southwest-northeast run over the city in order to put the low afternoon sun at his back, he leveled off at 200 feet and scanned the fields in rapid motion for signs of small arms or MANPADS. There were single trees here and there, and he saw a stand of trees to the south.

Bowser's excited call filled his ears. "Gotcha in sight, *Nail!* Bring it!"

At treetop height over the fields, Wilson approached the low wall that surrounded the town at over 500 knots, a high transonic airspeed that would rattle the windows but not break them. When he saw *Bowser's* minaret, he made a quick jink away from it, then rolled out to fly over the center of town at 200 feet. Smoke, 5,000 feet above, watched for threat fire.

The town appeared quiet as he approached. A few people walked along the dusty streets and alleyways and cars were parked here and there, but very little moved. Color in the form of green date palms and various Arabic signs dotted the cityscape, a light brown hodgepodge of row houses and courtyard walls, everything cut at right angles by east-west streets and north-south alleys. An Iraqi flag flew from a modest building to his right.

At this speed the people could not hear Wilson approach until his was right on top of them. He noticed a man flinch on the sidewalk as the jet thundered past, and a second later he caught a glimpse of an *abaya*-clad woman trudging down an alley with a small child dressed in a nightgown. Wilson threw up a wing and jinked right a few degrees to look for telltale flashes of small arms fire and MANPADS launches. A brown blur of rooftops covered with water tanks, antennae and satellite dishes whizzed underneath him. Another minaret, this one larger, passed down his left wing. More people were outside in this part of town, and as they saw him approach, they darted inside buildings and alleys. He rolled up on his left wing and looked down, just in time to see the face of a boy, mouth agape, looking up in wonder from a courtyard below.

He traversed the town in less than 10 seconds, and at the eastern wall pulled up and to the left. He traded airspeed for altitude and punched out some flares as he looked over his left shoulder for threats.

"I'm high at your left eight, six clear," Smoke called.

Wilson replied, "Visual, six clear," and continued up.

"Fuckin' sweet! I mean nice job, *Nail.* That's jus' what we need. We were startin' ta' get some trouble down here. I've got 'nuther mission for you, right now!"

Wilson had about five minutes of fuel before he had to bingo to *Exxon.* "Make it quick, *Bowser.* We've got five minutes of playtime."

"Yes, sir, this will be a talk-on. See the road 'long the town's southern border? See where it kinks?"

Wilson saw it and replied, "Affirm." He leveled off at 8,000 feet in a shallow bank north of Balad Ruz.

"OK, that corner is bisected by a dirt road that leads southeast, connectin' with the corner of a parallel road, 'bout a mile."

"Nail, four-one contact."

"OK, using that measure of distance, 'bout two thirds of the way down from the city and to the north of the dirt road is a maroon sedan parked in the field. Need ya t' hit that with a GBU on a zero-niner-zero run in. You've got friendlies to the north in town."

"Nail, four-one, roger. What's in the car?"

"We filled it with a bad-guy arms cache and IED explosives. The car belonged to an insurgent we captured, and his friends are pissed, 'specially his ol' lady!"

"Roger that…looking."

Wilson extended to the west, and slewed his FLIR on the road south of town, running the aiming diamond to the kink in the road. He was now at bingo fuel, but could stay a few minutes more for *Bowser.* He widened his field of view, took a guess at the distance, and narrowed his FLIR picture. A white smudge stood out in the display, likely the "hot" infrared image of a car left out in the midday sun. Wilson kept his turn in and was now flying east and closing the "smudge." Several seconds later the smudge began to take on the shape of a sedan. He overbanked and pulled his nose down to put the aiming diamond image in his HUD. It showed a vehicle in the distance, the maroon color discernible—but barely—against the dark green field.

"Nail, four-one, *captured,"* Wilson said and took a fleeting look at Smoke, who joined to the inside in tac-wing. "Switches set, *armstrong,"* he relayed on aux while pulling up to level off.

"Two has contact, visual, roger, *armstrong."*

The mission computer calculated a heading and a time to release the 500-pound, laser-guided bomb: …14 seconds, 13 seconds, 12 seconds…. Wilson triple-checked his switches: weapon – SELECTED; laser – ARMED; tape – ON. He monitored the greenish FLIR imagery and slewed the aiming diamond with small corrections to keep the diamond centered on the target. It was now easily identifiable on the FLIR as a compact sedan with the hood open.

"*Bowser, Nails* are five seconds, wings level," Wilson called.

"*Nails*, gotcha in sight. Yer cleared hot," *Bowser* responded.

"Roger, cleared."

In the last few seconds before release, Wilson "sweetened" the computed solution and saw no life around the vehicle. With three seconds left, he placed his right thumb on the pickle switch and pushed.

The 500-pound weapon left the aircraft with a familiar twitch from the sudden release. He looked over his shoulder at Smoke, flying a little above on his right side in time to see Smoke's LGB release and fall away, wings extended. He turned his attention to the FLIR and looked at the time of fall countdown …10 seconds, 9 seconds… then returned his focus to the diamond to prevent drifting off the car.

At one second to impact, a white dash shot from the top of the display and into the sedan, causing the display to burst into images of explosive flash and smoke. Wilson selected "WIDE" field of view and rolled up to his left in time to see Smoke's weapon enter the maelstrom of smoke and fire. It detonated with a white concentric shock wave that expanded in rapid fashion away from the explosion. One huge secondary explosion, then another, caused additional shock waves to ripple away like high-speed rings. Wilson saw tumbling fragments thrown into the air, leaving thin smoke trails above the dark roiling cloud. Debris pelted the field hard enough to kick up small dust clouds all around the sedan's former location.

"*Nails–SHACK!* A hun'rd over a hun'rd!" In the background, Wilson overheard one of *Bowsers'* mates exclaim, "*Fuckin' –A!*" to his buddy as they watched the scene.

"Roger that, *Bowser*. We are bingo for the tanker. You guys take care."

"*Nail*, are you guys done for the day? Can you all come back?"

Wilson answered, "We've gotta get a drink, but we've each got a JDAM and bullets left." After a pause, he added, "We'll let *Falcon* Control work it out." He reached down and marked his position over Balad-Ruz.

"*Nail*, four-one, roger. Think we are the only game in town today. Hope t' talk t' y'all later."

"Roger that, *Bowser*, we'll expedite. *Nails*, switch *Bowstring* on Indigo five, go."

"Two," Smoke replied.

"Switches safe, camera off," Wilson added on aux.

"Two."

CHAPTER 28

The *Raven* pilots worked their way back through the controlling agencies to the *Exxon* tanker, now 60 miles away. As they climbed to the tanker track over eastern Iraq, the landscape below was again transformed through the haze into an overall beige patina. Wilson surveyed the scene and unclipped his oxygen mask bayonet fitting and took a drink from the plastic flask he kept in his g-suit pocket. The haze reminded him of the smog that so often covered the Los Angeles basin. He set the power to rendezvous on the tanker with 3,000 pounds of fuel, and checked the bingo to Al Asad as he clipped his mask back into place.

Nail 42 broke the silence. "There's hope for those Army guys—they swear like Marines." Smoke was close enough to see Wilson's white helmet move up and down in the affirmative as he searched the sky for *Exxon*. Minutes later they joined on the same Mississippi tanker they had tanked from earlier. The boom was all theirs, and both pilots plugged and took on fuel in turn. Although they could have topped off with more, Wilson directed Smoke to take 10,000 pounds to shave some time tanking and to get back to *Bowser* in a hurry. In a little over 20 minutes they completed their tanking. While Smoke was still in the basket, Wilson was coordinating their next mission...back to Diyala and *Bowstring* control. Ten minutes later they were enroute to *Bowser*.

"*Bowser, Nail* four-one, flight of two, checking in with one JDAM and twenty mike-mike each, play time 0+40." Wilson saw the outline of Balad Ruz, just visible through the haze, in his HUD field of view.

"Rog' that, *Nail* four-one, welcome back! Y'all ready t' copy nine-line?"

"Go ahead."

"OK, head t' Wizards...and stand by for brief."

Bowser read off a standardized close air support targeting checklist. It consisted of nine lines in sequence, each line corresponding to a piece of information required to build the tactical picture with a minimum of transmissions. These nine lines would give the aviators all the information they needed to release their weapon on target at the precise second required. This precision also served to avoid fratricide and the targeting of noncombatants.

After half a minute, *Bowser* keyed his mike.

"Nail four-one, nine-line as follows…

"…Wizards…

"…Zero-sev'n-five…

"…Six-point-four…

"…One-three-two…

"…building, insurgent stronghold…"

Bowser read the detailed latitude/longitude info for the JDAM, and continued.

"…not applicable…

"…southwest three thousand…

"…egress north back t' Wizards…

"…advise when ready to copy amplifying remarks, over."

Wilson finished scribbling the nine-line into his kneeboard CAS card and answered, "Ready to copy remarks."

"Rog-o, *Nails*, need jus' one JDAM fer now. Restriction for collateral damage is a mosque west one thousand…troops in contact. Time on target when able." The JTAC sounded nervous.

Wilson hit his countdown timer. *Bowser's* assignment to the *Nails:* leave the initial point *Wizards* on a heading of 075, and 6.4 miles later, hit an insurgent building at an elevation of 132 feet with a single JDAM. *Bowser* and his squad were southwest at 3000 meters, and a mosque was west at 1000 meters. Once the weapon was delivered, the *Nails* were to come off north and return to Wizards for more tasking. From what Wilson could see, and from the inflection of *Bowser's* voice, they needed fire support *now*.

Wilson answered, "Roger…about five minutes." *Bowser* asked him to read back line six, and Wilson complied. The contract was set.

Wilson directed Smoke to take high cover. He then set his own destination for the target and readied himself for a busy five minutes filled with mental time-distance-heading calculations, triple checking the lat/long entered into the computer, and verifying the numbers with his wingman. He selected his JDAM on Station 2, and set a course line of 075 from Wizards. He maneuvered west of town at 7,000 feet, over open fields, and saw no movement below him. As he approached the run-in, he pushed the throttles to burner and pulled to the northeast.

"*Nail* four-one, IP inbound."

"Rog-o *Nail*, continue."

Upon reaching a tactical air speed, Wilson pulled it out of burner and lined up on his steering. The town floated under his nose ahead of him. On his FLIR he saw a clutter of square shapes—buildings—and as he drew closer, he was able to break them out on the north/south streets. He selected his tape ON and noted 25 seconds to release.

"*Nail* four-one, wings level."

"Cleared hot, *Nail*"

"*Nail* four-one"

Wilson lifted the master arm switch to ARM and continued at high speed toward the town.

Smoke called to him. "Got a puff to the southwest. Maybe near *Bowser's* posit…Yep, there's an impact flash."

Wilson looked over his right leading edge extension and saw two small smoke clouds wafting up from a nondescript neighborhood. He was well above small arms fire, but was concerned about hand-held SAM launches, even though no firings had been reported in this area for some time. With seconds to release, he concentrated on the release cue and accelerated. *Bowser* seemed like a guy who wouldn't mind a JDAM a bit early. The airplane jumped as another 500 pounds of ordnance, guided by satellite signals all the way to the target, fell earthward to the precise point *Bowser* wanted it to hit.

Wilson went to military power and rolled up on his left wing to egress north and watch the impact. The FLIR showed a car approach the targeted building; in anticipation he looked over his left shoulder to watch the weapon impact. He saw a massive explosion in the middle of the city, the shock wave raising a concentric cloud of dust above the structures around the building covered in smoke. Secondary explosions shot out of the burning building, and projectiles rammed into the houses across the street. One missile-like projectile flew crazily over the houses and landed in a dirt field north of the highway. The driver of the car he saw before impact reversed down the street in a panic. Wilson was surprised it was still running. A raging column of flame and black smoke towered over the targeted building.

Wilson was transfixed by the scene until the radio crackled. "*Nails*, we gettin' mortared! Gotta move, out!"

Wilson overheard a soldier in the background shout, "*Andy, let's go!*"

"Roger, *Bowser*, we're standing by."

With his wingman in trail, Wilson orbited northwest of the city, the pall of black smoke showing no signs of abating. To the southwest he also saw a tight group of small puffs caused by mortars. *Bowser* must be in that area.

Wilson called to Smoke. "Let's make some noise south to north. Follow me after I come off."

"Roger!"

To keep the insurgents' heads down, Wilson commanded Smoke to take trail as he led them from the south over the narrow part of the city in another show of force. With airspeed increasing, he descended in a left-hand turn to begin his run. Approaching the city, he popped out chaff and flares and initiated jinking in three dimensions. From the secondary explosions he saw, Wilson figured they had just hit an even larger weapons cache than the one they had destroyed in the sedan. The throttles were at full power, showing 550 knots indicated, as Wilson flew over the city and pulled up to the left to watch Smoke begin his run.

Wilson made a call to *Bowser*. No answer.

After Smoke's run, Wilson overflew the town again, higher and slower. He and Smoke were in a perfect wagon-wheel orbit, which would allow one of them to pounce on a pop-up contact while the other maintained a position to provide support.

"*Nail* four-one, y'all up?" It was *Bowser*.

"Go ahead, *Bowser!*"

"We got a vee-hicle, a white SUV, movin' outta town on Highway 82. Movin' west now. Bad guys in there."

Smoke called a tally. "*Nail* four-two has a white SUV passing the northwest corner of the city on the highway." Without warning, a bright flare separated from the SUV and climbed into the sky leaving a gray corkscrew trail of smoke.

"SAM at your left seven! Break left! Flares!" Smoke cried.

Wilson saw the launch and turned hard into it. He sensed, though, he was not the target because the missile veered low and behind him well before the rocket motor burned out. He expended some flares and kept an eye on the SUV, which continued to barrel west away from town.

Smoke called to *Bowser*. "*Bowser*, *Nail* four-two, that guy just launched a MANPAD at *Nail* four-one. Request clearance to engage with twenty mike-mike."

"You're cleared, *Nail* four-two. Take that mo-fo out!"

"*Nail* four-two's in hot."

Wilson watched Smoke roll in on the white truck. Although it sped away from the town, it was now completely in the open and stood out in contrast to the black asphalt road that stretched across the desert. Smoke extended a little to the south to get a better run in, and when he turned back, the SUV was still moving west at high speed. It was going to be a 90-degree crossing shot for Smoke, and Wilson took up a position in trail. Wilson selected GUN, and armed up.

Smoke bore in on the SUV and kept his eyes padlocked on it from two miles away. Wilson saw a car on the highway heading east and called it to Smoke.

"I've got it... *Nail* four-two's in hot on the SUV," replied Smoke.

"*Nail* flight, *Bowser*. I've lost y'all. Engage at pilot discretion."

"Roger, *Bowser*, engaging."

Wilson watched Smoke in his strafing run. Once the eastbound vehicle passed the SUV, a faint white trail of vapor emerged from Smoke's aircraft. Wilson saw the tracers as they flew toward the insurgent truck.

Dust kicked up along the highway 50 yards in front of the SUV, and one ricochet spun into the far field with a wild trajectory. Smoke had calculated too much lead and missed.

The bullet impacts stitched across the highway, however, and startled the driver. In what must have been a panicked state, the driver slammed on the brakes and turned south onto a side road. Wilson saw right away that the insurgents were trapped.

The dirt road ran between two partially flooded fields in flat farmland— about three miles west of Balad Ruz. Despite the fact he was driving an SUV, the driver couldn't change course to turn left or right through the muddy fields. The only chance the insurgents had was for the driver to drive straight ahead and limit Wilson's firing window by closing the range and making him aim steep.

Wilson watched the SUV come right at him, trailing a cloud of dust. Although the target was moving, all he had to do was aim short and walk the rounds up to the vehicle, or let it drive into the bullets. He felt as if he were rolling in on a strafe target run-in line, with Smoke, on a local training mission back home over the Dare County target range in eastern North Carolina. He keyed the mike.

"Lead's in hot," he said with a calm voice. *Oh, yeah!* he thought and rolled left.

His g-suit squeezed him and the horizon tilted as he overbanked and looked out of the top of his canopy at the SUV. He pulled his nose to a point on the road ahead of the vehicle. For Wilson, the situation was ideal: Against the landscape, the vehicle appeared to be a white dot moving toward him. The brown cloud of dust it kicked up behind was proof of the driver's desperate attempt to avoid another strafing attack. Wilson stabilized in a shallow dive; pulled some power; placed his gunsight "pipper," in front of the SUV; and watched the range ring unwind on the reticle.

As the truck and the fighter drew closer, Wilson wondered if the insurgents could see him. A faint muzzle flash from the passenger side of the vehicle answered that question. Wilson squeezed the red trigger on the stick with his right index finger and held it for *three...long...seconds.*

A cloud of white gun gas formed above the nose of the aircraft as 20-millimeter rounds flew out of the six-barrel cannon. The deep *BURRRRRRRRP* sounded similar to the noise of a large chain saw. Wilson noted the tracers explode away from his aircraft at supersonic speeds, but he kept his concentration on the green pipper, the "death dot," in front of the white truck. His hand clenched the stick hard as he pushed forward a hair to keep a tight bullet grouping; he released some pressure to "walk" the rounds up and then back down the road. The first rounds of the bullet stream kicked up the dirt in front of the truck. They were followed by bright impact flashes that ripped open the vehicle and churned the dirt around it into a brown cloud. Approaching 500 feet, Wilson yanked the stick up and rolled left, looking down to check his work.

Below he saw the burning truck. Peppered with huge holes and missing jagged chunks of its body, the vehicle had emerged from the confusion of dirt and metal and careened into a field, splashing water as it came to a halt. The road behind it was pockmarked with bullet impacts. As Wilson whizzed past the smoking vehicle, and as it receded into the distance, he saw no further motion on the dirt road.

"Good grief! You Winchester now?" Smoke asked on aux. He then added, "I can see your nose glowing from here! Sierra Hotel!"

Wilson ignored him and called to their JTAC. "*Bowser*, the white SUV is neutralized and burning approximately three miles west of your position. We've got one JDAM and a few bullets left for you."

"Way t' go, *Nail*! Those a-holes been screwin' with us for days! Nice shootin', sir!"

"Roger that, *Bowser*. Happy to help. We'll orbit high for now. Have 'bout twenty mikes left. Where you from, *Bowser*?"

"Hardeeville, South Carolina, sir! Goin' home in two weeks, too. In time for the Super Bowl!"

"I know Hardeeville... You guys okay down there?"

"Yes, sir, we're good. Happens ever' now and again. An' next time you're in Hardeeville, we got some good home cookin' restaurants, too. Not just that fast food on the highway."

"Roger that, and safe trip home, soldier. You're a damn good JTAC," Wilson replied.

"Thanks, sir. Great hits today."

CHAPTER 29

One hour later, Wilson and Smoke were headed back to the ship, having tanked a third time. Wilson made mission reports to the CAOC in Qatar and to the ship via E-2 radio relay. *Nail 41* flight had completed an eventful Iraqi Freedom patrol, and the ship would want to hear all about it ASAP.

As he and Smoke transited to the southeast in silence, Wilson thought about the white SUV. The insurgents had never had a chance once they made the turn onto the dirt road, not that they had had a much better one on the main road. *Who was in that vehicle? Iranians?* They had taken a shot at him with a MANPAD. *Where could they have gotten that but from Iran?* Wilson could not get the image of the SUV—coming right at him—out of his head. With a cool demeanor, he had placed his 20-mm aiming reticle on it and shot the truck to pieces in one massive burst. They had been trapped; it was as if he had been holding them in his hand and had shot them point blank. *They didn't have a chance. Was it* murder? They had shot at him twice, including the potshot the passenger took at him seconds before he died. *Was the weapon an AK? Another gift from Iran?*

Over the course of his career, Wilson had dropped bombs and shot anti-radiation missiles against fixed targets. Enemy buildings. A bridge. A radar in a field. Maybe enemy personnel had been inside…maybe not. Regardless, Wilson had always slept well afterwards. But an hour ago, he had seen human beings in that truck, human beings that Wilson had reduced to lifeless, and probably unrecognizable, bodies. *That guy took a shot at me. This is war,* he thought. They were *clearly* enemies, but they were humans, nonetheless, with human reflexes and emotions. He tried to imagine what it must have been like to be inside the SUV and to see his aircraft looming larger, unable to turn left or right to avoid the bullets that were only seconds away. Wilson could only guess about how close the AK bullets had gotten to his jet…the guy who took the shots must have been a bad mother or scared to death.

Weren't they all scared kids in a foreign land, like *Bowser* and his squad, thinking about home? Like those Iraqi soldiers freezing in their bunkers? *Maybe so, but these guys were fighting in the shadows, behind civilians, and not in uniform.*

Getting in the SUV and making a run for it was as stupid as it was suicidal, Wilson rationalized to himself. *The world now has two, three, or four fewer terrorist insurgents to cause mayhem and murder—here or anywhere.*

The sun was just above the horizon, and Wilson watched it over his right shoulder, his dark visor sitting on top of his helmet. Smoke's aircraft formed a sharp silhouette against the bright western sky as he flew a loose cruise formation next to Wilson.

From altitude the desert sunsets were often spectacular. Airborne particles turned the horizon a deep red, and sunlight from the now orange ball illuminated the bottom of stratus clouds over 100 miles away, the sky transitioning to a yellow band, then deep blue. Above them, several miles away in the blue, he saw an airliner heading southeast with twinkling anti-collision lights. The setting sun turned its four long contrails into platinum. Wilson wondered, *Where is it going? Dubai? India?* He thought of the wealthy passengers sipping cocktails in first-class comfort, oblivious to the combat below them. He studied the aircraft a little longer and identified it as an *Airbus.*

As Wilson contemplated the western sky, his thoughts turned to Mary. *Can she see this same sun right now?* He realized today was a Sunday. Eight time zones away—maybe she was packing the kids in the van for church. *They have no idea what just happened here,* he thought, and he was glad that was so. He would keep it that way. *And tomorrow is New Year's Eve back home. Out here, it's just another fly day.*

On the surface, the desert floor was a dim grayish blue in the twilight. Scattered lights shone here and there and the wispy outline of a river—*Tigris or Euphrates?*—meandered to the Gulf. A large cluster of lights from Basra loomed ahead off the nose, and oilfield flare stacks were visible to the west. Another 30 minutes to the ship… Wilson adjusted the cockpit lighting and checked his fuel.

Soon Wilson's mind drifted back to Balad Ruz. He reached up and turned the rear view mirror down toward him. His eyes reflected back over his oxygen mask; the eyes of a hunter… the eyes of a trained killer.

That day, combat became personal for James "Flip" Wilson.

Mary awoke the next morning to the sound of the *Virginian-Pilot* hitting the driveway while it was still dark. With so much on her mind, she hadn't slept well. Her parents were coming down from Baltimore to spend New Year's with her, and her plan was to put them up in her room. She still had to clean the bathroom, pull sheets off the bed, do the wash, move her things into Derrick's room (for three days), vacuum the house, and go to the grocery store. She then had to make something for when they arrived and get ready to go out with some of the squadron girls to a New Year's Eve party in Lago Mar. When she thought about that...the outfit, the shoes, the small nub of her favorite lipstick left on her dressing table...she wondered, *Is that enough for tonight?* She looked at the clock: 5:55 a.m. *Ugh!*

After she fixed breakfast and dressed the kids, she threw on a sweatshirt and looked in the mirror, groaning at what she saw. *I hope no one sees me at Safeway.* She made a mental note to get nacho chips. *Dad is going to watch a lot of football tomorrow.*

Damp winter cold greeted her as she opened the door and loaded the kids into the minivan. Fumbling with Brittany's car seat, she saw the paper at the end of the driveway.

"Derrick, please get the newspaper."

At once he spun around and sprinted to retrieve it. *He sprints everywhere,* she thought. *How does he get the energy, and how can I bottle it?*

"Here it is, Mommy!" Derrick said as he proudly handed her the newspaper. Still struggling with Brittany, she kissed him, asked him to get into his car seat, and tossed the paper onto the floor of the vehicle under Brittany's feet. Inside, in the "News in Brief" section on Page Six, was a wire service story:

U.S planes bomb al-Qaeda safe haven east of Baghdad

BAGHDAD, Dec 30 (Reuters) – U.S. warplanes bombed a suspected al Qaeda safe haven east of Baghdad, a U.S. Air Force spokesperson announced, the latest in a series of strikes aimed at disrupting the Sunni Islamist group's operations.

The operation, which began Saturday night and continued through Sunday, involved B-1 bombers and F/A-18 jets. It targeted Balad Ruz, an area 50 miles east of Baghdad.

"This particular mission targeted an area where al-Qaeda laid obstacles in the way of improvised explosive devices and took up safe haven at the same time. They also used the land to send fighters into Baghdad," the Air Force spokesperson said in the statement. Several houses booby-trapped with explosives were destroyed in the air strikes. Six U.S. soldiers were killed in Diyala province north of Baghdad at the start of the offensive when the house they were searching blew up and collapsed on top of them.

A U.S. military spokesperson said 117 militants, including 82 characterized as "high-value targets" were killed in the operation, including three fleeing in a vehicle that was destroyed by machine gun rounds from an F/A-18 jet fighter.

Upon returning from the store, Mary received a cell phone call from her mother as her parents traveled along Interstate 95. With the phone in the crook of her neck, she removed Brittany from the car seat and scooped up the newspaper, still in its wrapper, and deposited it in the garage recycling bin, never to be read. It dawned on Mary that she had forgotten the nacho chips, and she asked her mother to pick up a bag on the way.

CHAPTER 30

The January sun shone brightly on *Valley Forge* moored at Jebel Ali. In the company of containerships and other merchants, the carrier dominated the main UAE seaport south of Dubai. The piers were covered with loading cranes, warehouses, thousands of containers, and all manner of modern port equipment. The whole area hummed with constant activity. The carrier was there on a port visit to provide liberty to the crew in Dubai, the region's mega-trade center to the north. Sailors dressed in civilian slacks and collared shirts departed the ship via two brows, officer and enlisted, and stepped into busses for the 30-minute drive to the city.

Taking care to avoid their male squadronmates, Olive and Psycho got off the ship as soon as they could. Olive was fascinated by Dubai. She watched its spectacular skyline, a sharp gray outline against the white sky, loom up through the morning haze. In a dozen directions huge skyscrapers alternated with construction cranes.

When she had visited the city on the last cruise, she had marveled at its variety: the soaring buildings and opulent hotels with lush gardens; cars everywhere on the roads but the traffic did not choke them; locals in both traditional Arab garb and western clothing. So far, this visit was no different. The signs were in English and Arabic. A woman on the sidewalk, dressed in a black *abaya*, dragged a small child in shorts and a Mickey Mouse t-shirt behind her. Two Arab men held hands while they walked by an electronics store. A western man in a stylish business suit talked on his cell phone. To Olive it was a land of contrasts—ancient tribal customs blended with 21st century modernity.

And then there were the sights, sounds, and smells of money—everywhere. On every visit she found a new world-class building or complex to gawk at from inside the plush, air-conditioned motor coach.

Psycho was on her first trip to Dubai, the first time she had set foot in Asia. She either dozed during the bus ride or became otherwise lost on her cell phone. About halfway to Dubai, Olive noticed Psycho crack her eyes open, survey the scene, and close them again as she murmured, "I can't wait to get some sun."

Olive looked away. *Yeah, it will be nice to relax by the pool*, she thought. *I wonder when I should bring Psycho in on my little plan for this evening.*

An hour after they departed the ship, they were checked into the luxurious Regency Plaza Hotel in the Deira district of Dubai. Now fully awake, Psycho's eyed darted everywhere as they stepped into the lavish lobby. Indian bellhops carried their luggage past middle-aged Arab men in flowing dark robes—a sign of money—and past both Asian and western women in chic business suits and heels. The American officers, easily identified by their "liberty uniforms" of cotton slacks and polo shirts, couldn't take their eyes off the other women in the lobby. As they admired the hairstyles and makeup, they determined that's what they wanted to wear and *feel like* again—if only for their few days on liberty.

After checking into their $400-a-night room, they skipped lunch and went straight to the rooftop pool. *"Yes!"* Psycho said when she learned it was "Women Only." Less than 20 minutes after they checked in, they were lounging under the hot Arab sun in their swimsuits.

Olive smoothed sun block on her long legs. *Ahhh. I'm off the ship. I have a cool drink. I'm sitting by the pool.* Only 18 hours ago she had recovered aboard *Happy Valley* on a glorious full-moon night in the southern part of the Persian Gulf, the glittering lights of the coastline and diamonds-on-velvet lights of oil rigs and shipping scattered about the dark waters adding to the beauty. *Yep, I'm getting paid for this,* she thought.

She looked around her. Who among the dozen European women sunning themselves would suspect Olive and Psycho were combat-experienced fighter pilots? Through her oversized Dolce sunglasses Olive spied on the others, some-what unnerved by an older woman with close-cropped blonde hair lying topless across the way, adding more rays to her leathery brown skin. Olive dismissed her. *Fine,* she thought. *Tomorrow she can deal with melanoma, and tomorrow I can deal with the ship. Up here she's a woman without a care in the world—like me.*

Psycho rolled over and unhooked her bikini top before dozing again. Olive just lay there sunning, her mind wandering.

"Hey, I need your help tonight."

"Wha…" Psycho answered. She was half asleep with her head turned away. After shifting slightly, she said, "What's the plan?"

"Karaoke. There's this place the air wing goes to every time. I'm going to sing."

Psycho spun her head toward Olive. "You sing? *Cool!* Are you good?"

"Okay. My mother pushed me—in all kinds of ways—but I can sing."

"Yes! What are you going to sing?"

"You'll see. I need you to help me get ready. I have a dress and some shoes. Tonight I want to be 'Kristin' for a change."

"You've been holding out on me!" Psycho boomed as she rolled over onto her back.

Horrified, Olive whispered, *"What are you doing?"* She was surprised the pool boy did not appear to notice Psycho's bare chest.

"Just giving the girls some sun. It will be good for them. When else can I this cruise?"

"But that guy over there!"

"The Filipino kid? He's gay. How else do you think he got this job? Look." Psycho lifted her arm, and the boy jumped up immediately and began to walk toward them. Stunned, Olive watched him approach. None of the other women seated around the pool seemed to take notice.

"Yes, miss!" The pool boy gave Psycho a huge smile.

"Hi." Psycho smiled back and said, "Could you please bring me a towel?"

"Yes, miss!" he responded as he smiled again and bowed.

Staring at his nametag, Psycho asked him, "What is your name?"

"Homobono, miss."

*"Homo-*bono... What a lovely name!"

"Yes, miss. Thank you, miss!"

The boy spun to retrieve a towel, and Psycho turned to Olive with a smug smile. "Ha," she giggled, "he has the perfect name, too. And he didn't look at my boobs once." Psycho then shimmied her back into the lounge chair for full effect.

Olive realized that, despite the fact she was older and a more experienced pilot than Psycho, up here in the glorified air of Dubai, her junior roommate was, in fact, the flight lead. She settled back into her own chair and thought, *Yes, Psycho will be the perfect "wingman" for tonight.*

CHAPTER 31

With a surgeon's steady hand Psycho placed the false eyelash on Olive's left eyelid. *"Ohhh,* girlfriend, they are gonna be creamin' their jeans when they see you up there."

Next to the bathroom counter covered in make-up and hair products, Psycho worked on her roommate while she sat on the toilet seat.

"And I *love* your dress. Where have you been hiding it?"

"In my locker...been there the whole time." Olive said, eyes closed while Psycho applied the finishing touches.

"You've been planning this..."

"Yes."

"Are the hajis going to freak when they see you in it?"

"No, I've seen local women wear minidresses here. So long as the shoulders are covered and there's not too much cleavage—not that I have to worry about that. Hey, why don't you go get yourself a minidress at the boutique downstairs."

"Nope, I'm the wingman tonight. This is *your* run through the target-rich environment of Carrier Air Wing Four. I have skinny jeans and a cami top, a jacket, and some heels to dress it up. The best outfit to kick in the balls of any dickhead who hits on me. But tonight I won't have to worry about that because they will be rolling in on *you*."

"Hardly."

Psycho pulled a handful of Olive's hair into the curling iron. "Who are you going for tonight?"

Olive thought for a moment. "I don't know. Maybe Crusher, if he's there."

"Ohh, I'd love those big Marine Corps arms around me! Look, I'm going to find him and keep him occupied before you come out so that hobitch from the *Knights* doesn't get close to him. Don't even need a reason to kick *her* in her balls."

"He can have her."

"No! Listen, *fighter-goddess*, you told me to never give up in a guns situation. You haven't even turned at the merge, and you offer your throat to that skank. Here's what we do... I sweep the bandits ahead of you and then you

126

schwoopenhousen in for the kill. That dress, those shoes, *those legs*…you have a full weapons load out, and I want to see them expended!"

"Thanks, wingee."

"And this voice of yours…it's the siren song. You want me to spend the night in the lobby?"

"No!" Olive turned her head in protest. "*Oww!*" she then cried as Psycho's grasp pulled on her hair clamped to the iron.

"*Relax!* I know you are a nice southern girl. How are you going to snag him?"

"I don't know. We'll see what happens."

"Just unbutton an extra button and laugh at their stupid jokes. Works every time."

"That's not me, and I need every button I can."

"For *once*, Olive, can you not be an officer and a gentlewoman? Look, right now, there is no wash-khaki material within miles of us. You've got silk and lace tonight, and if you don't know how to use them with these guys 5,000 miles away from the Oceana groupie-sluts, you are *never* gonna get laid."

Olive stared ahead and said nothing in an awkward silence.

"I'm sorry," Psycho muttered. Unspoken between them was what they both knew. Olive was *plain*, and while the makeup and clothes helped at the margins, they had their limits. And her businesslike personality didn't help matters.

"It's okay. I'm going out of my comfort zone for tonight. I'm glad you are here to help me."

"Me, too!"

The officers turned some heads as they clicked through the hotel lobby. Psycho stuffed wads of dirhams into the hand of every bellman who held a door open for them. The bellmen figured the tall woman in the short dark dress was a famous movie star accompanied by her personal assistant. After the women stepped into a waiting cab, the bellmen argued among themselves in Hindi as to who she was.

It was a cool but pleasant evening in Dubai as the cab departed the hotel and entered the wide boulevard. "The Highlander my good man! How many doo-dahs?" Psycho asked the driver.

"Thirty-five dirham," the Pakistani driver replied.

"Thirty-five!" Psycho exploded. "No, no, twenty."

"No, no! Thirty-five, but for pretty ladies, thirty."

"Thank you, but do you know who this is? Ms. Jolie is going to be upset and may not make her next movie here. Twenty-five," Psycho said as she playfully flinched from Olive's jab to her side.

The driver inspected Olive through the rearview mirror as he navigated the traffic through the canyon of tall buildings. His dark eyes burned a hole in hers before she turned away.

"Twenty-five and Ms. Jolie gives a big tip if you get us there in 10 minutes." Psycho could not be stopped, and was picking up the bargaining thing quite well. Olive rolled her eyes.

"Okay, okay. Twenty-five and big tip, I get you there safe and fast."

"Thank you, sir," Psycho replied. She then turned to Olive and added, "Ms. Jolie, everything will be fine ma'am, and you won't have to worry your pretty little citizen-of-the-world head." Psycho was having too much fun to stop.

"Would you shut up?" Olive muttered as she suppressed a smile.

"I have been to the United States," the driver said suddenly. The women froze.

"Where?" Olive asked, sensing the jig was up and attempting to salvage what little dignity she could.

"Orlando. Disney World. I took my wife and son. Very nice place."

The women did not know what to say. Olive wondered how a third-world cabbie could afford that, and even converse with them in English. Maybe he was pulling *their* legs.

"Disney World *is* very nice," Olive volunteered.

"I've never been," Psycho added wistfully.

Minutes later they pulled up to the Highlander nightclub and Psycho put two 20 dirham bills in the driver's hand, the promised big tip for their Ugly American conduct. When she turned toward the entrance, Olive spotted some air wing guys walking up to the door.

"Hide me!" she ordered Psycho under her breath.

"Here," Psycho said as she pulled her coat up and wrapped it around herself and Olive. "Guys see two women huddling under a coat in front of a Middle Eastern nightspot, and they don't give it a second thought."

Once the men disappeared inside, they entered and Olive took the lead, moving fast to another hiding spot near the stage, not making eye contact with any of the Americans there. A favorite watering hole for Brit expats and American sailors on liberty, the Highlander boasted wood paneling, velvet seating, Fosters beer and flashing lights. A disco ball hung over the stage. A Filipino ensemble, three young men with guitars and a keyboard accompanied by two women singing and swaying in tube tops, performed a remarkably accurate "Dancing Queen" on the cramped stage.

Dozens of *Happy Valley* aviators, identified by their clean-cut appearance and American denim, dominated the tables and dance floor. Most of them nursed a Fosters bottle. None, however, were dressed as glamorously as Olive was. If she did not stay out of sight, she would be noticed before she wanted to be, but not as Olive. *No one* would think that the *Amazon* with wild, dark locks in the black minidress was Lieutenant "Olive" Teel from VFA-64.

Still hiding near the stage, Olive and Psycho surveyed the crowd. "Tally-ho on Crusher, left eleven," Psycho said. "Good, there's *slut-bitch* working a gaggle of *Rickshaws* over there."

Olive then spotted a group of *Ravens*: Sponge Bob, Little Nicky, Blade *and* Crusher were talking with some marines. Suddenly, a group of three tall young women entered, flowing blonde hair, sleek outfits...they were clearly not from the ship. The air wing guys locked on immediately. This was big game.

"Oh, oh. Brit flight attendants. Or Aussies," Olive surmised. Turning to Psycho she briefed her wingman." Okay, *wing-girl*. Get over to Crusher and keep his attention away from those flying baristas while I get on stage. After I'm done, meet me back here. We will then bolt to a pub I know downtown, one with leather, scotch, and Brit guys."

"Why? This is…"

"Never leave your wingman, girlie. Besides, I want to leave *him* wanting more, and I'm not going to be pawed and ogled by the rest of these assholes all night. Trust me on this one."

"Okay, fine, I've got your 6 o'clock," Psycho said. She inspected Olive. "Hey, you look *incredible* and your legs go on *forever!*"

"Let's hope he's a leg guy," Olive deadpanned as she nervously assessed the performers on stage.

"They *all* will be after they see you." Touching Olive's arm, Psycho added, "Have fun with this, Okay?"

"Okay, now go." As Olive shooed Psycho away, she took a moment to get into full combat mode. She had planned this "coming out" for months: the outfit, the song, the Highlander, the right moment on the stage. Now, even though she tottered a bit on her fresh-out-of-the-box stilettos, she was ready.

And despite the pounding adrenalin, she felt a calm confidence spread through her.

She *did* look good. If only Camille could see this... The thought of her mother reminded Olive of Camille's recital stage coaching tips: *One foot in front of the other, suck in your tummy, shoulders back, chin up.* Never forgetting she was an officer 24/7/365, Olive checked her outfit again and was satisfied it did not cross the line of *too* much.

After speaking to a stagehand, Olive went back to observing the crowd. Three JOs from the *Spartans* took the stage to perform a Black Eyed Peas favorite. By playing with her hair and laughing at whatever he said, Psycho had successfully cornered Crusher. The flight attendants were completely surrounded by air wing JOs and were not a factor. *Perfect.*

After a momentary lull, the DJ's Filipino accent boomed over the speakers. "An' now, ladies and gem'men, please welcome, *Miss Kristin!"*

Smile! Olive thought again of her mother as she took the first step.

Olive walked up and tried to gauge the hushed crowd but could not with the blinding and hot spotlight on her, hearing the whispers as the air wing tried to figure out who this creature *was.* Unfazed, she grabbed the microphone.

CHAPTER 32

The following day Wilson and the others who had remained behind for duty departed the ship and headed to the rented squadron hotel room, the *admin*, which the first wave of *Raven* officers had set up the day before. Wilson enjoyed Dubai, but even with this first Gulf port call of the deployment, he'd been there and done that. Dubai would be here for several more nights before they got underway again, and, no doubt, for several more visits this cruise.

Once off the bus, he and Dutch took a cab to the hotel, admired two Asian women employees in fashionable business suits in the lobby, took an elevator to the 15th floor and found their way to the *admin*. This room, which they had each chipped in for during the port visit, served as a base from which the officers could relax, explore Dubai and, in many cases, spend the night after an evening on the town. When they entered the room, a familiar sight, no matter where the *Ravens* set up shop, met their eyes.

Sleeping bodies were sprawled across couches and chairs. Some still wore clothes from the night before; one, with his head back and mouth agape, slept on a chair wearing nothing but boxers; and yet another had rolled up in a ball under the desk and covered himself with a sheet stripped from the bed. At first, Wilson couldn't place the sheet-covered body but soon identified him as Blade.

Empty Fosters beer cans littered the room. Pieces of open luggage and other detritus from the previous night's activity were strewn about or heaped up on the floor. Room service items cluttered every furniture surface. The curtain to the sliding glass door was open, and sunlight streamed into all corners of the room except into the brains of the "dead bodies" sleeping it off. The squadron drinking flag with the *Raven* emblem was still flying in proud defiance above them, despite being held aloft by only two of three rings.

Wilson and Dutch walked into the adjoining bedroom. Wilson identified five bodies in the darkened room, two each on the double beds and one on the floor under a blanket. Everything smelled of beer. One of Wilson's sleeping squadronmates stirred to see who was there. It was Sponge Bob. "Hi, OPSO," he croaked.

Dutch was quick to roll in on his hungover LSO trainee. "Sponge, did we get a little *large* last night?"

"Yeeesssss…" he groaned.

"And your impression of Dubai?"

"Needs more water," Sponge said, rolling over and hoping Dutch would go away.

"No, *you* need more water. Did you take your aspirin?"

"Noooo."

"Man, I told you to take a preemptive aspirin and hydrate. You never listen."

"Yes, Dad," came the muffled reply from Sponge, face down in his pillow.

One of the "dead bodies" spoke up from the other bed. "Dutch, shut the fuck up or leave, or both." It was Stretch.

"Paddles, is that *you?*" Dutch replied, feigning hurt. "I'm a brother, know the secret handshake, two mike clicks on the ball and all that." Dutch relished any attention, and, despite his low tone, his voice boomed throughout the suite.

"But today you're a dick," Stretch answered.

Sponge added, "*Today* he's a dick?"

"LSO, dick, Dutch, all the same thing." Clam spoke from under a bedspread.

"Hi, Admin O!" Dutch replied with an exaggerated cheer. "XO was just asking for you before we left the ship. I'm sure there's a dental readiness report that AIRLANT needs right away, or tomorrow's plan of the day to be chopped by you. 'Where's Lieutenant Commander Morningstar? Where's Lieutenant Commander Morningstar?' "

"Eat me, Dutch," Clam mumbled, motionless under the bedspread.

"Glad to see you doing so well, sir! And it's a beautiful day in this neighborhood—this exotic desert country! Say, any of you guys wanna get up and *drink?*"

In unison, and with their heads pounding, the *Raven* officers pummeled him with obscenities and ordered him to leave. Wilson took it all in with a knowing smile. Same morning-after scene, different port.

As Wilson went back to the living room, the door of the *admin* opened. Weed entered, saw Wilson, and said, "My brother, how're things *bak sheep?*"

"Fine, where's the skipper?" Wilson asked.

"CAG rounded up all the COs and XOs to play golf at Dubai Creek. They left at eight…Cajun was *huge* last night, booming till 0400. I don't know how he does it."

"XO was still aboard when we left. Where were you guys last night?"

"The Highlander, and it was amazing. The whole air wing was there." Now, from across the room, voices of the veterans from the previous evening's activities, joined in.

"They had this Filipino karaoke band with this *smokin'* hot lead singer chick. They were real good, and the place was rockin'," Blade said as he got up from the floor. "Then they opened it up for volunteers, and Killer, Hondo, and Wanda from the *Spartans* took the stage and did *Pump It*. They were damn good. Killer had the rhyme down, and Wanda did this dead-on Fergie impersonation. Even the Filipino chick was impressed."

Little Nicky took over. "Then from out of nowhere comes Olive. She's in this black minidress with stiletto heels, hair flowing, makeup. I mean, she looks *good*—for *Olive*. We'd been there for hours, but hadn't seen her all night. Then she takes the stage and does *Zombie*. Flip, I'm tellin' ya, nobody moved. We were captivated. She can sing, and she knew how to move on stage. *Incredible*."

Prince Charming rolled over and added, "She belted it, especially that last part. You would have sworn it was off the CD."

Nicky continued. "She finishes, and the place goes *nuts*. I mean *our Olive* owned that place, and now the Filipino girl thinks she's out of a job."

"Where has she been keeping this?" Wilson chuckled.

"That's what the CO said," Nicky replied. "So we're yelling at the *Spartans*, 'You got served!' And we're trying to find Olive, and she disappeared. Gone."

"Where'd she go?"

"Dunno. I guess back to her *admin*...She and Psycho went in on a cathouse someplace."

"I knew under that zoombag and hair bun was a hammer," Dutch chimed in.

"Still a head case though," someone shouted from the other room.

CHAPTER 33

Wilson slid into the hotel pool with Dutch and Nttty. They had all gone shopping that morning for polo shirts and CDs and now had a plan to relax in the company of friends. They headed toward the swim-up bar, ordered a Fosters and surveyed the scene. Several groups of air wing officers were lounging about, some playing full contact water basketball. The first wave of *Ravens* was back in the fight.

Wilson sipped on his beer at the shaded bar, truly enjoying the warm water that covered him from the waist down. He was seated next to two *Buccaneer* department heads, Gramps, their maintenance officer, and Rip, the administrative officer. The Filipino bartender eyed Wilson warily, but he ignored it.

"Wonder what the poor people are doing today," Gramps thought out loud as the three lieutenant commanders surveyed the pool scene. Nttty had made his way to the other side of the pool to make friends with two bikini-clad flight attendants, while Dutch hung on the edge in an effort to be noticed by them.

"They have the duty *bak sheep*," Rip answered as he pulled on his beer.

Wilson had gotten used to the fact that when he was surrounded by pilots, the conversation always came back to flying. He hardly noticed that, even in this resort setting where they wanted to decompress from shipboard life, they couldn't help talking about it.

"Been anyplace interesting lately?" Rip asked Wilson.

"Lots of stuff in Diyala and Salman Pak. Haven't been to Mosul yet. How about you?"

"Had an interesting hop in Al-Amarrah the other night. We were working with a Shadow UAV along the river and found some guys planting an IED on the road north of town. The JTAC talked us on the target and we each dropped a LGB. We were watching them dig on our FLIRs…oblivious… diggin' all the way till impact." Rip shook his head in wonder. "Can't believe they didn't hear us."

"I had a hilarious hop up around Mosul last week." Gramps added, while looking at Wilson. "It involved your XO."

"Oh, great!" Wilson exhaled in mock embarrassment. He looked forward to hearing the story, but he still cringed at the thought.

Keeping his voice low, the *Buccaneer* pilot began. "Me and Dog checked in with *War Eagle*, a JTAC we worked with a few weeks ago who was really good, so I was looking forward to workin' with him again. We switched up the freq' and I hear *War Eagle* talkin' with Saint.

"'Shotgun flight, acknowledge nine-line.'

"'Can you clarify the target?' Saint asks.

"*War Eagle* gives him the lat/long and says, 'Target is open field west of the hamlet.'

"Saint says, 'Still not clear on the target. All I see is a field.'

"*War Eagle* wants a bomb to go off on the field because his colonel is telling the hajis that, as colonel, he can make one go boom on command. *War Eagle* imagines the Army colonel looking over his shoulder as he talks with the locals. 'Now, I will summon *fire* from the *heavens*...uh, Sergeant, bomb...now!'

"Saint repeats, 'There is nothing in the field.'

"*War Eagle* says, 'I need a bomb in the field NOW.'

"'Where in the field? What quadrant?'

"*War Eagle* is cool, and says, 'Anywhere in the field you want. Go ahead. Just need a bomb in the field ASAP. You're cleared hot. Come on in.'

"Saint, still pressing, asks, 'What's in the field? Troops in the open?'

"*War Eagle* grabs the lifeline Saint has offered and says, 'Yes, sir, troops in the open. Yeah, we're in contact with a whole *division* of al-Qaeda. Cleared hot.'

"'I don't see any troops on my FLIR,' Saint counters.

"*War Eagle*, his ass now gettin' ripped by his colonel, says, 'Shotgun, do you have the field west of the village, south of the tree line bordered by a north/south road to the west?'

"'Affirm,' Saint says.

"'Roger, *Shotgun*, bomb that field with any weapon in any delivery. You are cleared hot.'

"I mean, I take a look at Dog on my wing and he's got his mask off he's cracking up so bad. I've never seen him laugh that hard." Gramps was on a roll.

"'Roger, *War Eagle*... What *crop* is in the field?'

"And *War Eagle* loses it! 'SIR - just bomb the fuckin' field! NOW!'"

Gramps realized his voice was carrying too far and too loud. He looked around him with a half-apology on his face as he reduced his howls to a snicker. Rip tried to suppress his laughter, but failed miserably, Wilson noticed the bartender looked at them with a disapproving frown. *What's his problem?* he thought. *Or is it just me?*

"Saint is upset and says, 'Hey, soldier, watch the language on the radio. Do you *know* who this is?'

"*War Eagle* swallows it and says, 'Sorry, sir, it's a soybean field.'

"There's a pause, and then this gruff voice comes on and says, 'Shotgun flight, this is Colonel Johnson of the 2nd battalion, 16th Infantry, 1ˢᵗ Division' … I dunno … *Royal Armored Fusiliers*, whatever. 'If you fast movers can put a weapon on the field we've requested, do it!'

" 'Roger, sir,' says Saint.

" '*Much obliged*,' the colonel responds, his voice dripping with sarcasm."

Rip was wracked by convulsive laughter, and his eyes were glassy slits. Wilson had to grab him to keep him from falling off his stool. Wilson had gamely smiled through the embarrassment his XO had caused the squadron, but, for the most part, he just looked down and shook his head.

Rip was still laughing. "Was he a radio colonel or full bird?"

"He sounded like the real deal to me—he sounded like fuckin' Patton!" Gramps' answer elicited another roar from Rip.

"There's one thing I want to know. Did he ever hit the field?" Wilson asked.

"Oh, yeah," Gramps said, as he finished the story. "He drops a LGB right in the *middle* of the field."

"*War Eagle* says, 'Good hit, sir.'

" 'Roger, bomb impact assessment please?' Saint asks, and *War Eagle* tells him 100 over 100, anything to get him out of there!"

"How do you paint a soybean field on the side of a jet?" Rip asked, with a chuckle. He was rewarded with a guffaw from Gramps.

Wilson groaned and looked across the pool. The flight attendants were now surrounded by a gaggle of *Raven* pilots who had tired of "basketball." He was grateful Gramps hadn't told the story with the JOs around, but by now, no doubt, the details of this flight had made it to the bunkroom. He made a mental note to find out who the wingman was for the flight when he got back to the ship.

"Your boys bagged a few over there," Gramps said as he looked at the girls across the pool.

Wilson nodded. "In the process. Looks like it will be another big night at the Highlander."

Chapter 34

One week later, Wilson returned from a night hop, deposited his flight gear in the paraloft, and plopped down in his ready room seat to watch the PLAT recovery of the last event. The CO was flying with Blade on an intercept hop against the *Spartans*, and Weed was out doing a night sea surface search around the strike group. Guido was at the duty desk watching "The Office" on the ship's closed-circuit TV.

A copy of *Navy Times* was on the skipper's footstool. Wilson picked it up and thumbed through the pages: articles about pay raises, new uniform standards, the usual stuff. He then came across a familiar section highlighted with photos of American personnel who had lost their lives in recent weeks in Iraq and Afghanistan. Most of the time the photos were formal poses, but he often found a boot camp photo of a 19-year-old Marine in dress uniform or a candid shot of a soldier. On occasion he came across a photo of a young woman, a girl really, or a senior officer. They were almost always young—too young.

When he scanned the photos in this issue, he found the photo of an Army major. Age 35. His own age. He wondered if the major had a family at home. Chances are he did.

The photo next to the major was of a young man in his early 20s. Clean shaven and wearing cammies, he had big, dark eyes, a full mouth and a square jawline. Just under the cap Wilson could make out bushy eyebrows. Something caused Wilson to dwell on this soldier. He looked at the name: Spec. Donnie Anderson.

He studied the photo again. Anderson. *Anderson. Andy, let's go! Was Andy short for Anderson? Was this "Bowser" from Balad Ruz?* He stared at the photo of the fallen soldier. No unit, no hometown. *Specialist? What the hell is that? Are JTACs Specialists? Balad Ruz was three weeks ago—would the* Times *publish a photo so soon, even if he lost his life the day after we worked with him?*

Driven by the need to know, Wilson got up and logged on to the classified computer at the back of the ready room. He would contact the Air Wing rep on the CAOC staff in Doha, a naval flight officer on temporary duty from the *Spartans*.

Subject: JTAC track down
  Hey, Biscuit, Flip.
  I was working with a JTAC around Balad Ruz on New Year's Eve; his call sign is "Bowser." We were Nail 41 flight that day. Don't know what unit he's with but he did a good job and other guys in the wing have talked about him. Said he's from Hardeeville, South Carolina. He may have rotated home but I want to send him an attaboy through his CO. Can you ask the JTAC guys there to track him down; name, unit and contact info? Thanks man.
  It's dark out here, you aren't missing anything. They have cold beer where you're at?
  Thanks again,
  Flip

He hit send and went back to his seat to watch the recovery. An hour later, after the uneventful recoveries of his squadronmates, he returned to the computer to check for an answer from Biscuit. One was waiting for him.

Subject: RE: JTAC track down
  Flip, we tracked him down but bad news. "Bowser" was hit and killed two days after your hop with him. He entered a booby-trapped house in Balad Ruz after some of his buddies were hit inside. The hajis waited for rescuers to enter before they set off the bigger charge.
  Apparently "Bowser" was the first to go to their aid. The house collapsed and he was killed. The only one though...another guy lost a foot.
  His name was Spec. Donnie Anderson and he was from Hardeeville, SC. He was 20. He was a good JTAC; had a great mission effectiveness record.
  Sorry, Flip,
  Biscuit

Wilson felt his body going numb as he stared at the screen. *Bowser*—Specialist Anderson—was 20 years old, just days from going home to watch the playoffs. He was so excited to be going home to watch football "live," as well as to leave that hellhole town. Wilson thought of Bowser's photo in *Navy Times*: the square jaw, the distinctive features. *Such a good-looking guy. Did he have a wife or girlfriend? Did he ever get to experience the love of a woman?* he wondered. *Whatever he experienced, his life was too short.* Wilson's throat tightened, and he swallowed hard.

That night in his rack Wilson's mind drifted back to *Bowser* in Balad Ruz. *Just a kid. Twenty!* Though they had never met, fate had brought them together at a moment in time to fight a common enemy. Wilson wondered, *Why am I alive and why is Bowser dead? Why is any of that fair? So young, so much to live for...*

In the darkness, he was surprised by a tear that escaped his left eye and dampened the pillow.

Chapter 35

"Flip, XO wants to see you in his stateroom."

Wilson looked up at Olive. She waited behind the duty desk, her face as expressionless as usual, for his acknowledgement. "Thanks. Did he say what it's about?" Wilson asked.

"No, sir."

Wilson placed the message board on his chair and walked to the sink with his coffee cup. He gave it a quick rinse it and hung it on the wooden peg above the sink that said "OPSO." In place, the cup blended in with all the others emblazoned with *Raven* logos and individual call signs.

Stepping out of the ready room and into the starboard passageway, he strode toward the XO's stateroom up forward. He made his way, as if on autopilot, past the knee-knockers and through the sailors inspecting damage control gear, his mind trying to figure out what the XO wanted. Halfway there he realized it was pointless.

Commander Patrick's stateroom was aft of the Cat 1 jet blast deflector on the starboard side. Next to him was the stateroom of the Spartan's XO. Commanders bunked alone in individual staterooms on the O-3 level, but Wilson disliked this part of the ship. The XOs lived on a very public passageway and right under the deafening catapult. During launch operations, conversation in the staterooms was impossible. Quiet is a relative term on a carrier, of course, but he liked his O-2 level quarters. He would certainly miss them if he stayed in and was promoted to squadron command.

Unlike other squadron stateroom doors, the XO's door was bare—except for a placard that read KNOCK TWICE THEN ENTER. Wilson rapped twice, paused, and opened the door. He stepped inside and said, "Yes, sir."

Saint sat sideways at his desk, scribbling in an open notebook on his lap. He wore his usual khaki uniform with full ribbons, the only officer aboard to do so. Without looking up, he motioned to the couch and said, "Mister Wilson, good morning. Please have a seat." Wilson did as he was told and took a place in the middle of the couch with both feet on the floor, hands folded.

Saint pored over the notebook and said nothing, his familiar and unnerving tactic. Wilson looked around the room for anything new, any window into the soul of his executive officer. The room was not only immaculate, but devoid of personal effects, as if he had just moved in yesterday. The television displayed the Ship's Inertial Navigation System (SINS) screen, a series of numbers showing the ship's position, course and speed. His desk held nothing but a plain coffee cup that stored pens and pencils. On a hook near the sink hung the XO's blue bathrobe, emblazoned with a gold naval academy crest. The robe was the only item of sentiment Wilson could find.

"Mister Wilson, I'm looking at the Navy Relief Society contributions by department. The Administrative and Safety Departments are at 100 percent, Maintenance is 77 percent, and the Operations Department is 50 percent. The squadron goal I set last fall was 100 percent for all departments. Do you recall my discussion on this at an AOM?" The XO's voice was calm and measured.

"Yes, sir."

"Then why is the Operations Department so deficient in meeting this squadron goal?" For the first time Saint lifted his eyes to look directly at Wilson. He waited for an answer.

Wilson kept his eyes on his executive officer. "Sir, may I ask who has not contributed yet?" He regretted adding the word *yet*.

"Certainly, and I like your modifier 'yet.' Let's see… Airman Ayala and Petty Officer First Class Johnson. Your other two sailors made modest contributions."

He once again waited for Wilson to answer.

"I have no excuses, sir. I will ask Ayala and YN1 Johnson about it."

"Very well…I look forward to your answer after lunch." Saint made a mark on the notebook spreadsheet.

"Sir, Ayala is on night check and doesn't report 'til 1830. I'll…"

Saint jerked his head up, eyes wide under his thin eyebrows. With his mouth slightly open, he held Wilson's gaze for several seconds. "I look *forward*… to your answer after lunch," he responded with a cold stare, struggling to keep his fury in check.

"Yes, sir," Wilson said meekly, his eyes locked on Saint.

"Very well," Saint replied, the fire gone from his face as fast as it had appeared. Drawing a deep breath, he then launched into a new subject.

"You are leaving the squadron soon. Why don't you have orders?"

"I'm still working with the detailer, sir."

"What does he tell you?" Saint asked, with a hint of a smile.

"Washington, War College, Joint staff duty—the usual career path." Wilson lowered his defenses a bit.

"The CO tells me you are dragging your heels. What do you want?"

Wilson realized his answer had to be the truth.

"I'd like to stay in the Norfolk area. My family needs a break."

"Yes, the family. Isn't it always so… You have four kids?"

"Two, sir."

"Two. Are they young?"

"They are," Wilson responded, his defenses going back up. To know the answers to these questions, Saint only needed to take a basic interest in his people.

Saint looked off at the bulkhead in thought. He turned back to Wilson. "Are you going to resign?"

Wilson fought to remain calm. "No, sir." The answer was technically true, but he had been giving the idea a lot of thought lately.

"Mr. Wilson, despite your many years of service and family sacrifice, the Navy needs fine young black officers like you to stay for a career."

So there it is, thought Wilson, Saint's motivation for this talk. Officer retention figures, especially minority officer retention figures, drew great scrutiny in Washington. Wilson saw right through it…*Saint doesn't care about me as a person. I am just one of his statistics. Can't have a minority officer resign under his watch.*

"XO, does the Navy want me, an officer who happens to be black, to command a squadron, or an air wing…or a ship?"

Saint hesitated for a second and looked down, then recovered. "Yes, of course, but you won't get there if you continue to underperform or if you fail to meet established squadron goals. You can't do that to get to the next level. In addition, you must obtain every possible qualification. There are lots of officers with records like yours who didn't screen for command last year. You can't just coast along, depending on…"

"On what, sir?" Wilson asked, feigning ignorance.

Saint knew he was losing control. "To screen these days you have to go the extra yard."

"XO, I have every qualification available to me in this squadron—from functional check flight pilot to Strike Fighter Tactics Instructor. In fact, I have more qualifications than you and the CO, sir. There's no syllabus training hop I can't instruct, much less fly. What further qualifications do I lack?"

"We've established that your ground job performance needs significant improvement, that you are not meeting squadron goals." Saint was beginning to lose his temper.

"Yes, sir, I've not met the personal goal you set for the squadron, and I'll address that by encouraging my sailors to contribute something. I will do everything short of *compelling* them to contribute to the Navy Relief Society. Will do, sir. But I would still like to know.... Is there a Navy-wide performance standard I'm not meeting? One that directly affects the combat readiness of this deployed strike fighter squadron?"

"Mr. Wilson, I will remind you to watch your tone."

"A little too uppity, sir?"

"Dammit, Wilson!" Saint thundered, as he rose to his feet. "Get the hell out!"

Wilson, also enraged, sprang to his feet and took a step toward the senior pilot, who flinched ever so slightly. "XO, I'm a naval officer and *Hornet* pilot who happens to be black. Nobody *gave* my wings to me. I earned them myself. The airplane does not care who's flying it, male, female, black or white. The Navy does not need quotas. It needs warriors to stay for command, and I am a warrior. If I do resign, this meeting will feature prominently in my letter."

"DISMISSED!" Saint roared back, inches from Wilson's nose. Wilson stepped to the door, and as he passed through, Saint added, "And take that chip on your shoulder with you!"

Wilson closed the door with a firm grip. When he turned to head forward, he met the eyes of the Spartan's XO who had opened his door half expecting to break up a fight. Trembling with anger, Wilson passed Dutch without acknowledging he was there. "Hey, Flip," said Dutch and stopped to watch his department head bound forward. Finally, Wilson realized someone had addressed him. He stopped and turned to see a bewildered Dutch about five frames back. He then saw Saint appear from his athwartship passageway. Their eyes met, and Wilson spun for his stateroom. Dutch looked at Wilson and then at his XO. *What just happened?* he wondered.

Wilson burst into his stateroom to find Weed typing on a laptop. "Kimo sabe," Weed greeted him, without taking his eyes off the screen. When Wilson answered only by yanking open a drawer, Weed knew something was wrong. "What happened?"

Wilson unzipped his flight suit and worked open the laces of his boots. "Oh, just a come-around with the XO. Seems my department's Navy Relief numbers are short of the squadron goal."

"Bummer. Should we call a stand-down to address the problem?"

"Yes, we should," Wilson answered. "Your department is only at 77 percent, but the OPS department is making you look good. We're last at 50. Admin is at 100 and the one-person Safety Department is also at 100. We're both on his shit list, but at least you aren't last." Wilson slipped out of his flight suit and put on his black gym shorts.

"Thanks for the heads up and for making me look good. What else?"

Wilson bent over to tie one of his sneakers. "Well, we then had a counseling session. Seems the Navy needs black officers to stay, which it does. What I got from Saint, though, was that he doesn't particularly care for black *commanding* officers, but he wants me to 'please stay' for the retention numbers." Wilson pulled the laces tight.

Weed looked at Wilson as he worked the other shoe. "I may have over-stepped," Wilson added.

"Whad'ya mean? He throw you out of the room?"

"Yes."

"Oh..."

"I will not be placed in a box!" Wilson continued, still furious. "I'm a Navy fighter pilot. I am not a *black* Navy fighter pilot. I've only had to deal with two guys in my whole career who judged me for my color. You know, one guy in flight school, and now the XO."

"Master Chief Morgan?" Weed added.

"Oh, yeah, okay. Three guys in 13 years."

"Not a bad track record."

"Concur! The Navy's been great to me every step of the way, and I've had it a lot easier than my dad did in his day, with the race riots and everything else. At least here you get promoted on merit. You work hard, play by the rules, and compete. I love that."

"Why don't more African Americans come through the front door?"

"*Hell if I know!* I'm tellin' 'em all the time! I go to friggin' Norfolk State, family gatherings. I'm spreadin' the word, tellin' the homeboys they got nothin' on my posse. Brothers are joining and they have bright futures, but not many go air."

"Why're you so fuckin' pissed off?"

Wilson stopped and looked at Weed, who was giving him a wry smile. *Weed is right. I am furious—but why?* Wilson already knew, everyone knew, the XO was an arrogant bastard...and he had still let him get under his skin, especially with the "chip on your shoulder" crack. Was he angry that Saint treated him like a number, a quota, instead of a key member of the squadron, even a person? Did that surprise him? Was he angry that it did? Was he angry with the Navy and the sacrifices it demanded of Mary? He looked forward to his run so he could think.

Weed then added a typical Weed comment. "It could be worse, you know. If you were a woman, the XO could be after you!"

Shaking his head in disgust, Wilson turned for the door. "Man, you are one sick puppy!"

"I'm thinking Tyra Banks with a big—ah—Adam's apple."

"I'm outta here," Wilson said, still smiling in spite of himself.

"Where ya goin'?" Weed asked.

"Topside for a run."

"It's 30 knots up there."

"Perfect," Wilson replied.

CHAPTER 36

"Lead's air speed, angels on the left." Prince transmitted from a mile abeam.

"Two's speed 'n' angels on the right," Wilson replied.

"Take a cut away," Prince ordered.

"Two," Wilson acknowledged.

With that, both pilots pushed the throttles to military and banked away from each other for the last of three engagements they had briefed for this good deal flight, a 1v1 air combat maneuvering training sortie. This was Wilson's favorite part of the hop: the neutral setup where both aircraft extend away from each other to build separation and then, on signal, turn back toward one another. The track the airplanes flew on this maneuver resembled a butterfly wing, hence the name, "butterfly set."

Wilson steadied out on a heading of 210 and scribbled some notes on his kneeboard card, with a drawing of a God's-eye picture of the two aircraft heading 180, and taking cuts away from each other. He drew a circle to depict the sun ahead of them and wrote the number "60" to indicate 60 degrees up.

Prince was leading because he needed the hop for his flight-lead-under-training syllabus. After 15 months in the squadron, it was time for Prince to become a *section leader*, the flight lead of two aircraft. Wilson was disappointed with Prince's performance on this qualification flight. It began with the brief, when Prince did not know the ship had moved south during the night. His perfunctory preflight briefing was nothing more than satisfactory, and his performance on this flight, so far, was *unsatisfactory*.

In both his offensive and defensive setups Prince had mismanaged his air speed and lift vector. In the first, Prince allowed Wilson to escape when he began the engagement behind him in a firing position. In the next setup, when beginning from a defensive position, Prince was unable to shake Wilson from shooting him with a tracking guns shot. Although Wilson possessed 2,000 more FA-18 hours than Prince, and was a *TOPGUN* graduate, he was upset. "*C'mon, Prince, pull!*" he had muttered as Prince arced above him and let up on the pressure. Wilson liked to win an engagement as much as anyone, but it was as if Prince had been just going through the motions, not challenging Wilson or himself. The two pilots were not friends and there was a clear superior/subordinate relationship, but as Operations Officer Wilson wanted and *needed* Prince to qualify as section lead to allow more flight scheduling options. After the last fight, as they climbed to altitude, Wilson had radioed a simple comment to him on how to improve his lift-vector placement. Prince had answered with a glum "*Roger.*"

An overnight cold front had left behind a gorgeous winter sky, clear and crisp, and the visibility was unlimited from horizon to horizon, rare anytime in the Gulf. From 18,000 feet, Wilson had a clear view of the Saudi coast, with Dhahran off his nose and Bahrain just to the left. Offshore were numerous oil rigs, and the two dominant colors were the blue of the Gulf and the beige of the Arabian land mass. He could see the frontal clouds far to the east over Iran. Wilson loved moments like this: high over the water in a single-seat jet with a sparring partner to bump heads with and log some great training. He remembered how a friend once described air combat training: *the sport of kings.*

Even if Prince would not give him a good fight, Wilson was ready...no, *eager...* to kick his ass if he again ignored his advice. *No holds barred, full up air combat maneuvering,* he thought. *This day is too perfect and the fuel too short to waste.* Brimming with anticipation, he looked at Prince over his left shoulder some three miles away.

Thirty seconds later Prince broke the silence. "Turnin' in, tapes on, fight's on."

At the "*f*" in "fight's on," Wilson slammed the throttles to afterburner and snapped the *Hornet* over on the left wing in one motion, pulling hard across the horizon in a slightly nose-low energy sustaining pull. "Tapes on, fight's on," he responded.

Keeping sight of Prince through the top of his canopy, Wilson pulled hard across the horizon and put the "dot" of Prince's airplane in the middle of the HUD. The radar locked on and formed a box around the jet 2.5 miles away. Wilson pulled tighter and was on the inside position as they accelerated to the merge. The aircraft were now pointed at each other with air speed building to over 900 knots of closure. By the geometry, Wilson could see a right-to-right pass forming as they approached like knights in a jousting match.

"Right-to-right," Prince radioed.

"Right-to-right," Wilson responded, as he pulled the throttles out of burner.

A 1v1 fight with a modern forward-quarter missile threat aircraft like the *Hornet* calls for a one-circle or *pressure* fight to stay close and deny the opponent the forward quarter missile, often a heat-seeker like the *Sidewinder*. In like-performing aircraft the initial move inside was vital to gain angles that allowed one to position the opponent out in front of the canopy, or even to take a gun shot if one presented itself. Such fights often degenerated into slow-speed scissors, or "knife fights," as the aircraft kept close. They also often ended up with both aircraft groveling at slow speed just above the 5,000-foot "hard deck," which simulated the ground. Wilson knew he had to pressure Prince, and noted the sun up and to the right. If he pulled hard across Prince's tail and into the oblique, after 180 degrees of turn he could be inside his turning circle and lost in the sun above him, able to pounce once Prince lost sight. Wilson decided on this strategy in an instant. In essence, he would be toying with Prince instead of pulling hard into him and going for the jugular.

As they drew closer, Prince drifted right on Wilson's windscreen. The norm was to pass close aboard, 500 feet, but Prince did not correct this drift. The added distance meant *turning room* for the pilot who was willing to "bite" and take advantage of an early turn to get angles, and Wilson wasn't going to pass up free angles. *You give me room, I'm gonna take it,* he thought. With Prince's *Hornet* growing and lateral separation building greater than 500 feet, Wilson took a sharp breath—*Hookkk!*—while tightening his muscles, relit the burner cans and pulled hard into Prince.

Wilson snatched the jet up and to the right at the instant a force of 6.5 times his body weight pushed and squeezed every square inch of him. At the same time, a cloud of white condensation formed on top of the aircraft as he flew into and above Prince's flight path. Straining to keep sight of Prince over his right shoulder, he sensed the horizon elevate and go perpendicular on the canopy.

To Wilson's surprise, Prince held his lift vector on as he went up with Wilson. *Well, well,* Wilson thought, as he watched the outline of the *Hornet* going up a mile away. *Prince is showing some aggressiveness.*

Wilson sensed his sun strategy was now superseded by Prince's nose-high move. He kept his left arm locked against throttles, pushing them against the burner stop as he pulled the nose through the vertical and to the horizon. He rolled into Prince with a boot full of rudder to knuckle his own aircraft down and inside the younger pilot. The horizon rolled underneath Wilson as he reached the apex of his modified loop and put the top of his canopy, his lift vector, on Prince. The dark silhouette of Prince's *Hornet* zoomed past less than 500 feet away. Wilson dug his nose down to regain needed air speed, ruddered the jet to the left and kept the top of his airplane facing Prince in a nose-low pirouette.

The extensive training the two pilots had been through allowed them to maneuver by instinct, each managing air speed and angles to get behind the other and into a firing position. If one of them allowed too much separation, the other would fire a missile shot. If the other got too close, the "knife fight inside a phone booth" could lead to a position change at best—or a raking guns shot at worst. They rolled and pulled in three dimensions, the background changing from water to sky to water, as they craned their necks to full extension in an effort to keep sight.

With his experience, Wilson got every angle he could with his available air speed, and moved Prince forward on his canopy. After less than a minute, they were passing 10,000 feet in a rolling scissors, with Prince going up and Wilson coming down, building knots. Prince fell off right, and Wilson had the energy to loop—if he remained patient and resisted the desire to keep pushing Prince around the sky. Wilson got off the g and let the aircraft ride the burner cans into a loop, a graceful pull into the vertical that stopped his downrange travel. His purpose was to flush Prince out in front and underneath.

For an instant, the two pilots saw each other in the cockpit as they passed on the horizon, their visor-covered eyes padlocked on their opponent, mouths gasping for air in short, deep breaths against the pressure. *Hold it! Hold it!* Wilson said to himself as he watched Prince descend and gain air speed. He fought the urge to overbank and allowed the optimum separation to build. Wilson slowed below 100 knots and let his nose track down to the horizon. About a mile below, sharply set against the blue Gulf, he saw condensation stream off the wingtips of Prince's gray fighter as Prince pulled to meet Wilson once again. As Wilson's nose fell through the horizon, he mashed down on the weapons select switch. The familiar *Sidewinder* growl sent a greeting through his headset. One second later, the growl changed to a high-pitched *Scrrreeeeeee!* as the seeker-head locked on to Prince's engine heat. Wilson squeezed the trigger.

"Fox-2," he radioed to Prince.

"Out of burner, chaff, flares," Prince replied.

"Continue," Wilson answered.

Sensing Prince had little air speed to counter, Wilson closed the space between them. He pulled up at the bottom of the loop and turned to align his fuselage with Prince, who was only 2,000 feet above the hard deck. Selecting GUN on the control stick with his right thumb, Wilson rendezvoused on the inside of Prince's turn. Prince appeared to be motionless in the sky, doing little to throw off Wilson's impending shot.

"*C'mon, Prince!*" Wilson shouted into his mask as he pulled the green pipper to the back of the nugget's aircraft. Prince was arcing again, not pulling down and into him, not making his aircraft skinny. In essence, he had rolled over and exposed his neck for the kill. He had given up. From 1,000 feet away, Wilson pulled the throttles to idle and squeezed the trigger.

"Guns, *knock it off!*" Wilson transmitted his disgust along with his words.

"Lead, knock it off, *joker*," Prince replied.

Wilson saw that he, too, was a few hundred pounds below joker fuel as he maneuvered to join on his flight lead. Both aircraft accelerated to 300 knots and began a long climb to high altitude. The pilots routinely climbed to *bladeland*, as they called it, in an effort to "hang on the blades," or to conserve every drop of fuel they could as their jet turbine blades turned in the cold, thin air. They would need it for the recovery 35 minutes hence.

Wilson slid into position on Prince's right side and inspected Prince's aircraft for popped panels, fluid leaks, or anything out of the ordinary. He glided below the *Hornet* to check the bottom of the aircraft and then moved to the left side, bottom and top. Satisfied, he drew forward to where Prince was waiting for him to take the lead so Prince could inspect Wilson's fighter using the same procedure. When the checks were completed, Prince resumed the lead. Via hand signals they learned that each aircraft had roughly 6,000 pounds left.

Wilson eased away from Prince as they leveled off at 28,000 feet, turning left and to the east as they drew too close to the Saudi coast. *Dammit, Prince!* he thought. *Not getting it is one thing, but not trying is something else.* Wilson scribbled notes, mixed with arrows and symbols, on his kneeboard card. First, he recorded his recollection of how the fight ended and followed that with notes about the initial nose-high move they took at the first merge and how that became a rolling scissors. He wrote ARC at a point in the engagement where Prince arced to lose angles, and recorded his estimation of his *Sidewinder* shot range. Once on deck, they would review their video tapes before the debrief. Wilson knew it would not be a smooth one. He hoped Prince could end the hop on a positive note by managing their fuel before leading them into the break. The post-flight debrief was not going to be easy.

CHAPTER 37

The formation steadied up on a heading of 060, with Wilson 400 feet away in loose cruise. Wilson looked down as a heavily laden southbound tanker plied the textured blue surface below. It left a wide wake behind, as the load of hundreds of thousands of tons of crude began its long voyage to Japan, or Europe…or Houston. Forty miles to the north he could make out *Valley Forge,* escorted by the guided-missile destroyer, *Stout.* Though they were at a max endurance fuel setting, the two *Hornets* cruised along at 250 knots indicated air speed. Wilson checked the winds at altitude: 125 knots on the tail, cooking right along after the frontal passage. He looked about the sky for other traffic and scanned his radar in range-while-search mode. *Clear.*

Wilson's thoughts returned to Prince. He was *different* from the others, different from any other pilot he knew. First, Prince was a loner. Despite his good looks, he had no wife or girlfriend. Wilson realized the same could be said of the XO, but with Prince it was different. Saint could be engaging when he wanted to be, particularly with his superiors, but Prince always looked angry and impatient. He thought he knew all the answers and bristled at constructive criticism about his flying or division paperwork to the point he almost *talked back,* even to seniors. Prince was careful not to cross the line, but he went right up to that line way too often. Among the department heads and senior JOs, Prince was a "project." They needed him to pull more of his own weight, but after a year in the squadron, it seemed they had made little headway with him. Wilson tried to put the upcoming debrief out of his mind and enjoy the day, even though it had turned out to be a day in *bladeland* on Prince's wing.

They were nearing the Iranian coast, but Prince had given no indication he was about to turn away from it. After giving Prince every opportunity to monitor his own navigation, Wilson began to fear an embarrassing call from *Alpha Whiskey* and keyed the mike.

"Let's bring it west."

Prince remained silent and continued ahead.

"Now!" Wilson growled over the radio. The lead *Hornet* still did not respond. *He can't even stay out of Iran!* Wilson thought, considering this the last straw in an unsat check ride.

When Prince didn't respond, Wilson guessed Prince had switched up to another frequency on the secondary radio.

"Prince...*Prince!* You up?"

Growing concerned, Wilson added some power and nudged the stick to get closer to his flight lead. Prince wasn't moving, and as Wilson slid closer, he saw Prince's head slumped down.

The two aircraft were headed right for Iran. Over his nose Wilson saw a long, barren island. It formed a natural harbor, but Wilson saw no settlement anywhere on the deserted coastline.

"*Prince!* Bring it *west!*"

The radio crackled with a reminder that the ship, too, was watching their progress. "*Raven* four-one-two, *Strike*. Vector west for airspace."

Wilson answered, "Roger, *Strike*, standby." Wilson got into parade formation right next to Prince, who remained motionless in the cockpit. Was it hypoxia? "Prince, PRINCE!" Wilson shouted into his mask in an effort to wake him up. Prince stirred, but he remained slumped forward in his straps. "PRINCE! WAKE UP!" Wilson roared.

Wilson got as close as he could to see if Prince's mask was hooked up, but he could not be sure. He chopped power and pushed the stick down and left, then reversed the motions to come up on Prince's left. He was then able to see that the mask dangled to one side. Prince twitched again.

"Prince, NOSE DOWN, PUSH YOUR NOSE DOWN! GET YER MASK ON!"

Not knowing that one *Raven* pilot was incapacitated, the strike group air warfare commander saw the *Ravens* heading into Iran and scolded them for their poor navigation on the GUARD emergency frequency that was broadcast for all aircraft to hear. "*Raven* four-one-two, this is *Alpha Whiskey* on GUARD. You are approaching *Waterloo* red. Turn left heading two-four-zero immediately."

"NOW, PRINCE, DO IT NOW!" Wilson shouted. Prince had "altitude hold" set in his automatic pilot which was carrying him, unconscious, into Iranian airspace.

Another strike group ship called to them on GUARD. "*Raven* four-one-two, this is Mike One Kilo. You are standing into danger. Turn left *immediately* and contact *Alpha Whiskey* on two-eighty-nine-point-five."

Wilson keyed the mike and said, "*Strike*, four-zero-two... Four-*one*-two appears to be incapacitated. He may be hypoxic. We are steady, heading zero-six-five at angels twenty-eight."

"Four-zero-two, *Strike*. Say again?"

Exasperated, Wilson repeated the transmission and ignored another call on GUARD for them to turn. After several seconds, *Strike* responded, "Roger four-zero-two, standby and turn left to two-four-zero."

"*Strike*, four-*zero*-two is declaring an emergency. I *can't* turn left because my flight lead is incapacitated! I'm next to him on his wing. Get a *Raven* rep ASAP."

"Roger, four-zero-two. Emergency declared. Say your state and stand by."

As they passed over the Iranian coastline, Wilson inserted "7700," the international distress code, into his transponder. He continued to watch for signs of consciousness from Prince. Wilson maneuvered high on Prince's left side and pulled forward, flying as close as he dared, his right wing tip over Prince's fuselage. This time he saw that Prince was holding his green canteen in his right hand, a viable explanation for his mask hanging down: He had been taking a drink. Suddenly, Prince twitched.

"*Prince!*" Wilson transmitted. "WAKE UP!"

Strike came up on the radio, "*Raven* four-zero-two, we copy your emergency squawk. Squawk zero-one-four-two."

While *Strike* was talking, Wilson heard Cajun on the squadron tactical frequency. Manning up his jet for the next launch, the CO said, "Flip, Cajun, what's goin' on?"

Wilson responded, "Sir, Prince is unconscious—think he's hypoxic from taking his mask off. We're at angels twenty-eight with altitude hold on and heading into Iran. Actually we're in Iran."

As soon as he finished with the skipper, Wilson called to *Strike*. "Negative, *Strike*, I'm keeping 7700 set."

A new and strange voice with a foreign sound came up on GUARD, a detached voice with perfect English diction. "*Raven* four-one-two, this is Bushier Approach Control on GUARD. You have violated Islamic Republic airspace. Please return to international airspace at this time. Thank you."

Taken aback, Wilson selected GUARD and answered. "Bushier, *Raven* four-zero-two on GUARD is declaring an emergency. The pilot of *Raven* four-one-two is incapacitated. He appears to be unconscious."

Then Cajun broke in on tac. "Flip, shout at him. Thump him if you have to... Are you feet dry now?"

"Yes, sir, I've been shouting at him, and we've been feet dry for several minutes."

"What are you carrying?" Cajun asked.

"Nothing but a CATM, sir." And then it dawned on him. He and Prince were alone over Iran with no weapons, no expendables, no sidearm—and none of the accoutrements one would carry on a combat sortie. They weren't at *war* with Iran, but the country was by no means friendly.

"Is he moving at all?"

"He twitched a minute ago. Stand by."

Wilson slid back and crossed under to Prince's right wing. He had an idea… If he could place his left wingtip under Prince's right wingtip, the airflow over his wing could force Prince to roll slightly left. If Wilson could do that in a way that did not cause Prince's altitude hold to kick off, maybe Prince's aircraft could at least return to the Gulf. It would be a long shallow turn, but Wilson needed to try something. They were flying into Iran at a rate of over seven miles per minute.

Suddenly, GUARD frequency sprang to life and another strike group ship called out: "*Raven* four-zero-two! *Waterloo* Red! *Waterloo* Red!"

"*Shut up!*" Wilson snarled into his mask and punched off GUARD, conscious of both his anxiety and his loss of patience over the situation.

Wilson eased up next to Prince's right side and looked over this left shoulder as he placed his wingtip a few feet under his stricken squadronmate's wing. *Strike* asked him again about Prince's condition, and, as he concentrated on keeping his wings steady, Wilson responded with a terse "No change."

Holding his wingtip position under and forward of Prince, he clicked nose up trim once, then again. This did nothing but make the stick forces greater. What he was doing—looking over his shoulder as he placed his wingtip dangerously close to another aircraft travelling at 250 knots of indicated air speed—was unnatural. Every impulse ordered him to back off, and he fought these instincts to remain in position.

Wilson's slipstream caused Prince's aircraft to develop a slight left-wing-down attitude. Prince's wingtip suddenly dropped into Wilson, who had to push the stick down and away to avoid collision. He realized he was squeezing it hard, and, as he repositioned himself, he took a deep breath.

Strike inquired about his fuel state, and Wilson answered, "Five-point-one."

Prince's shoulder twitched. Wilson immediately reported this to *Strike* as he prepared for another attempt to nudge Prince to the west. At least Prince still appeared to be alive. "PRINCE! NOSE DOWN!" Wilson commanded him, in vain, on the tac frequency.

Cajun, helpless to do anything but desperate for information on his two pilots, called from his position on the flight deck. "What luck, Flip?"

"He just twitched his shoulder. I got under his wingtip and tried to lift it, but his autopilot fought me and leveled him back. It appears we gained a few degrees. I'm tryin' to get us back feet wet by nudgin' him with my slipstream. You monit'rin' *Strike?*"

"*Firm…how far in are you?*"

"About 25 miles."

Wilson looked underneath him at the desert floor, an uninhabited coastal plain that rose into a karst ridgeline to the northeast. A series of ridges and valleys were arrayed in front of him.

"What's your pressurization showing? How long has he been out?" Cajun asked.

"Twelve K, and it's been about ten minutes now. We had just finished a fight and climbed to altitude."

"Rog, must have a pressurization leak," Cajun surmised.

Wilson checked the outside temperature…-42 degrees centigrade. If Prince's cockpit was at ambient outside pressure, he was in trouble.

BOOOP.

Wilson glanced at his radar warning display. The Iranians were looking at him with an air-search radar.

Chapter 38

Are they scrambling fighters on us? Wilson wondered. Iran possessed two fighter bases in the region: Bushier, some 90 miles northwest, and Shiraz, on his nose for 100. He asked *Strike* for help from the E-2 *Hawkeye* on station. "*Strike*, are you working with a *Knight?*"

Knight 601 answered immediately. "*Raven*, *Knight*, radar contact, picture clean."

"Roger, *Knight*," Wilson replied, recognizing the voice of their XO.

"*Raven* four-zero-two, Bushier approach is trying to call you on GUARD."

"Roger," said Wilson and reselected GUARD on his up front control, wondering what they wanted, but then realized they wanted to know why and how long he would be in their airspace. Wilson keyed the mike, still in parade formation on Prince.

"Bushier Approach Control, *Raven* four-zero-two on GUARD."

"*Raven* four-zero-two, Bushier, do you require assistance?" the faceless Iranian replied.

Now what? Wilson thought. If Prince also had 5,000 pounds remaining, at this fuel flow and with the tailwind, they would remain airborne little more than an hour. That would put them well into central Iran. He also realized that, at some point, he would have to go back to the ship, almost 100 miles behind him and opening. He had to get Prince turned around and down to a lower altitude.

"Bushier, *Raven* four-one-two appears to have a cockpit pressurization leak, and the pilot is unconscious. I'm trying to use my slipstream to maneuver him out of your airspace. Request you move away traffic ahead of us and to the north."

"Thank you, *Raven* four-zero-two, Bushier has your request… Interceptors are inbound to assist escorting you out of Islamic Republic airspace."

Wilson felt a shot of adrenalin shoot through him. Iranian fighters were inbound…but what would they send? *Phantoms? Tomcats?* Those he could handle in an engagement, but with Prince incapacitated, he was worse than alone. *Fulcrums? Flankers?*

He drew closer to Prince and positioned his wingtip for another attempt, his neck muscles straining as he craned his neck left and fought through the tension of the moment. Once stabilized, he tweaked the throttles forward and added a tad of back stick pressure. The wake turbulence from his wing created a high pressure area under Prince's wingtip that pushed it up, and they started to turn left. Although he sensed the aircraft ease left, Wilson, breathing deeply and rapidly, did not dare to glance inside at the heading. *Hold it. Hoooollld it.*

Cajun's voice came over the radio again. "Flip, how's it goin'?"

Wilson was concentrating too much to answer.

All of a sudden Prince's right wingtip slammed down onto Wilson's left. *Crack!* Frantically pushing away from Prince, Wilson stabilized low and to the right. He was stunned to see Prince steady after the collision.

"Oh, that was close," he said over the radio.

"What happened?" Cajun asked.

"Just swapped a little paint, but we turned a few degrees. Surprised his altitude hold is still working," Wilson replied.

"Don't worry about touching, go ahead and hold him with your wingtip if you have to," Cajun said.

As he got back into position next to Prince, he noticed a film had developed inside Prince's canopy. Wilson studied it. It appeared to be condensation, and drawing closer, he noted small glimmers of light from the reflected sun. *Frost!* Prince was unconscious inside an icebox of a cockpit, an almost definite indication of cockpit pressurization failure.

Wilson's radar warning receiver lit up with a tone in his headset. Off his nose the fire control radar of an aircraft was tracking him. He eased away from Prince to better scan the horizon and called to the *Knight* E-2.

"*Knight*, four-zero-two is spiked at twelve o'clock. Picture!"

"Four-zero-two, single group, 330 at 60, hot… Looks like they are the bogeys out of Bushier."

"Four-zero-two, roger," Wilson replied.

Those guys are off to the northwest, he thought. *What caused the radar spike from the northeast?* The spike had disappeared, but he lifted his dark visor for a moment and scanned the eastern horizon for aircraft. Far down to the east the cold front had formed an irregular mass of white and gray clouds that could highlight an aircraft. He noticed a white nub of cloud on the horizon a bit higher than the others. He willed his 20/15 eyes to search the horizon, focusing them on one spot, then moving to another. At the same time his radar searched in AUTOACQ as he moved the elevation at intervals to search a band of airspace. Wilson stole glances to the northwest, suppressing the urge to turn in that direction to meet the bogey group…and to abandon Prince.

DEEDLE, DEEDLE, *DEEDLEDEEDLEDEEDLEDEEDLE…*

Wilson's RWR again lit up. It appeared to be a lock on from a fighter radar. With a sense of urgency, he called to *Knight* to reconcile it. *"Knight,* I'm spiked at zero-five-zero and clean. Picture!" Wilson eased away from Prince—about 200 feet. His senses were on heightened alert.

"Four-zero-two, *Knight.* Picture clean to the northeast, the E-2 answered. "Single group three-two-zero at forty-five, hot, medium."

Wilson was dumbfounded. *Knight sees* nothing *ahead of me? What's going on here?* he wondered, eyes wide with apprehension.

Flying formation on Prince, he sensed something above in his field of view. A blurred object streaked toward his wingman. Before his mind could identify it, a tremendous flash centered on the top of the Prince's *Hornet* behind the cockpit, covering the airplane with fragmentation impacts and igniting a huge, orange fireball at the fuselage and on top of the wings. The impact was accompanied by a muffled *Boom!*

Transfixed with horror, Wilson watched the *Hornet* yaw left, trailing monstrous flames and black smoke. Smoldering pieces of debris fell away to the earth, some four miles below. *Raven 412* then snapped down hard as its right wing was ripped off at the fuselage. Tearing itself apart, the aircraft became a tumbling, hurtling mass of yellow flames and charred debris. He saw a large, pointed piece fall end-over-end, trailing white smoke from the break in the fuselage.

That piece was the nose of the FA-18—and Prince was inside.

"Prince!" cried Wilson, recovering from his momentary shock. He crammed the throttles forward and pulled the jet down and away to the right. During the maneuver, his eyes picked up a single-target track lock on the radar display. Something heading at him and above him, with a high air speed, slid off the display to the left as the radar reached the gimbal limit. Rolling out, Wilson pushed the nose down in order to go weightless and increase air speed. Still floating off the seat, he strained to reach the MARK button on his display to record his current latitude and longitude—to reference the spot Prince was hit.

Returning to one g, he reached up and hit the EMERGENCY JETT, button, which blew off his empty wing tanks and caused the *Hornet* to leap forward from the sudden release of weight and drag. His mind raced to understand what he had just witnessed. Through the sounds of the RWR's *deedle* and the 450-knot rush of the airstream past the canopy, Wilson realized what had happened.

Prince was hit by a radar missile, coming from that contact on my nose!

CHAPTER 39

Wilson's training took over. Instinctively, his left thumb activated the chaff button in a vain attempt to expend chaff he didn't have. His right thumb selected *Sidewinder*, and his headset filled with the familiar growl of the seeker head—on a dummy missile. As a brown ridgeline grew larger in his windscreen, Wilson realized the contact off his nose was the fighter that had put a missile into Prince and was now targeting Wilson with an air speed and altitude advantage.

Retreating to the Gulf, some 50 miles away, was not an option. The bogey—no, the *bandit*—would just run Wilson down from behind. He looked high to the left for a sign of either the bandit or a missile in the bright blue sky—*anything*, a glint off the wing, a wingtip vortice, a missile rocket-motor plume, a dark speck… He saw nothing.

At least Wilson was no longer spiked, and the bandit, looking down toward the desert, would have greater difficulty picking him out of the backdrop. When he passed mach one, Wilson pulled the throttles out of afterburner and slid forward in the seat. Within seconds, as he passed 20,000 feet in a shallow dive, Wilson's training again formed his game plan. He would turn to engage.

Realizing he needed to get a quick report to the ship, Wilson keyed the mike. "*Knight*, they shot down four-one-two! I'm engaging a bandit to the northeast!"

"*Say again!*"

"Four-one-two is shot down. Didn't see a chute, and I'm targeted! *Turning to engage!*"

Wilson grunted through clenched teeth as he pulled his *Hornet* hard into the unknown threat. Despite his senses and mind working overtime, and despite his confusion and anxiety, he had never felt so alive.

A feeling of déjà vu came over Wilson… Everything reminded him of his *TOPGUN* graduation hop high over the Nevada desert: going into a merge with an unknown bandit, the intense pressure to succeed, even the topography below. Even his thoughts were the same. *What will I meet? Who will be flying it?* The difference? This was not a training sortie but deadly single combat—and he was unarmed.

Wilson rolled out and up into the expected threat position, pulled the throttles to idle, bumped the radar mode into WIDEACQ and searched the sky around him for the bandit. Close to hyperventilating, his mouth was bone dry and his eyes were frantic to find Prince's assailant. To the left, several miles away, he saw a dark gray cloud suspended against the blue sky. An irregular trail of smoke led to the desert floor, smaller trails of debris fanning out along the path of the main plume. Pieces of Prince's *Hornet* continued to flutter down. Still, Wilson saw no chute.

A radar spike at 10 o'clock jerked his head left. Wilson saw a large fighter pointed at the *Hornet* less than two miles away, slightly low. He yanked the stick left and put his nose on, selecting VERTACQ to place the bandit inside the two dashed lines formed on the HUD. He was rewarded with a lock at once, and the *Sidewinder* seeker tone screamed loud in his headset. With over 700 miles per hour of closure rate between them, Wilson was inside a mile in seconds and pushed the throttles into burner to regain the air speed lost in his uphill glide. By instinct he looked for a wingman …the empty sky reminded him he was alone. His eyes returned to the big fighter. Wilson feared being peppered by a high-angle snapshot from the fighter's gun, but the bandit was not pulling a great deal of lead.

"*Knight*, four-zero-two's engaged, visual!"

At first Wilson identified the bandit as a Russian-built MiG-29 *Fulcrum*, but as they drew closer, he sensed a larger, *longer* aircraft with a square intake under a huge nose and a big missile on a wing pylon. The bandit took his nose off, and the geometry on both sides dictated a left-to-left pass. Wilson pressed it inside 500 feet.

He was awestruck at what flashed past him.

The aircraft was something he had never seen before. The small nose section was stuck far forward of an enormous single intake, behind it a long fuselage with delta wings. It was painted in shades of sky-blue camouflage with a beige nose cone and the circular red, white, and green Iranian Air Force roundels on the wingtips, but it possessed characteristics of a Russian design. He saw only the one huge missile under the right wing and an unusual feature—two wing canards over the intake which signaled to him an ability to fight slow. The twin vertical stabs sat on large booms adjacent to the massive engines. He realized he was fighting something big and powerful: a fifth-generation Russian with great turning capability, top-end speed, and probably a lot more gas than he had. The fighter bowed in a graceful curve from the needle-nose cockpit down to the empennage.

What is this? he thought.

As it flashed past, Wilson inhaled and held his breath, making an audible *Hookkkkk* as he closed his windpipe. When he pulled the stick hard into his lap, the top of his aircraft turned white with condensation as the force of seven *g's* gripped the *Hornet* and inflated his G-suit. The familiar anaconda-like pressure squeezed his legs and abdomen as his horizontal stabs dug into the clear winter air and pitched his nose up. The combination of g force and his muscles resisting its pressure affected every part of Wilson's body. Wedging his head between the seat box and canopy he continued to fight against the pressure and keep sight, inhaling and exhaling—*Hookkkkk*—ah, ha, *Hookkkk*—ah, ha—keeping his lift vector on and bleeding air speed fast. *I have to get inside this guy.*

Wilson managed the presence of mind to keep a running commentary on strike frequency. *"Knight,* I'm, *Hookkkkk,* ah-ha, one-circle with a single-seat twin engine fighter," he gasped into his mask between breaths. "Never seen b'fore. *Delta wings."*

If the E-2 responded, though, Wilson did not hear it. He was completely absorbed with the unknown aircraft he was fighting. He pulled everything he had and got inside the Iranian's circle. Despite the fact Wilson was unarmed, he reasoned he could push around the mystery jet and hold him off long enough that the Iranian would have to disengage because of low fuel. Wilson then looked at *his* fuel—3,700 pounds. His F404 engines were devouring it at well over 10,000 pounds per hour. Wilson had no choice but to stay and fight.

At the second merge, Wilson guessed that both aircraft bled airspeed to around 250 knots, and he unloaded while reversing his turn to take a 30-degree bite. With looping air speed he planned to take it up at the merge. By taking advantage of his superior slow-speed controllability, he could park his nose high and flush the Iranian out in front of him. *Maybe I can spook this guy,* he thought.

As they passed, he fed top rudder, eased his angle of bank and took it up, *skates on ice,* milking the most of every knot of air speed to get above and behind the bandit. He looked inside for just a moment, a second, to check his fuel. When he returned to the bandit, he was stunned by the image of the enemy plane. Just a few hundred feet away, it went up with him and even out-zoomed him as it stood on two long pipes that belched a cone of fire visible even in the midday sun. Soon Wilson would be below and out front.

For a moment Wilson froze and looked at the white-helmeted pilot who sat high on the nose of the colossal fighter. Across the small void, he saw the pilot's eyes peer over his mask. Dark, chilling eyes…looking right at Wilson.

Holy shiiiit!

Wilson kicked right rudder to slide closer and jam any chance for a bandit gunshot. When the bandit pulled all the way over, almost on its back but in control, he cursed in frustration at what he knew was coming next. The hostile fighter reversed over the top in a negative *g* maneuver, his nose tracking down on Wilson like a falling sledgehammer in slow motion. Horrified, Wilson realized he faced an imminent snapshot. With the little air speed he had, he inverted his *Hornet* to avoid it. His aircraft still rolling, Wilson saw that the monster had another weapon at its disposal. *Thrust vectoring!*

Wilson managed to float, barely in control, in front of the bandit. Shocked at the gaping maw of the intake only 200 feet away, Wilson, upside down, looked out his left side. At that moment, the right side of the Iranian's fuselage unleashed a bright tongue of flame. Inside the flame was a nearly solid stream of what looked like flaming supersonic baseballs. Under Wilson, an earsplitting *POP-POP-POP-POP-POP* penetrated the canopy. A low guttural BORRRRP sounded in the background as the cannon rounds missed low, mere feet from his head.

Mo-*ther-FUUUCK!*" he cried into his mask.

Petrified, Wilson pulled hard and down, rolling and kicking the controls to the left. Straining to keep sight of the bandit hovering above him, Wilson saw the nose of the fighter drop to pounce once again. He let out an involuntary whimper of fear as he slammed the stick forward to unload. In the back of his mind he acknowledged his cry and recognized it as a signal of the panic that he must fight in addition to his adversary. Over the years, Wilson had known apprehension and fear. Taxiing to the bow on a pitch-black night. Caught inside a thunderstorm. Far from land trying to find a tanker at night in bad weather with low fuel. He had been afraid before and knew how to handle it through compartmentalization and preflight preparation. But this was different.

Twenty minutes earlier Prince's poor navigation had been Wilson's biggest problem. Then Prince had been blown out of the sky right next to him, and now Wilson was unarmed over a hostile country fighting an unknown aircraft with a pilot who was trying to kill him. Those flaming balls represented a stream of death that had just passed underneath him by mere feet. That stream, delivered by a thinking human, was about to reach out to him again in seconds. This realization was more than fear; it was terror.

Get down, Wilson thought.

He had two immediate and conflicting needs. First, he had to stay out of the Iranian's gunsight by maneuvering hard once he felt threatened, although that bled air speed. His second need was to get into the weeds. To do that he had to regain maneuvering air speed at the cost of providing the bandit with a predictable flight path, one that would almost surely invite a missile or a gunshot.

Wilson's senses were on fire. With his neck stretched back as far as possible to keep sight, he flew the aircraft by feel. The big fighter opened to 500 feet of separation and began to pull lead. Just seconds before the Iranian let go with a burst that missed to the right, Wilson instinctively pulled up and rolled away to avoid the shot. The rapid popping noise filled his cockpit for a second time.

Gaining confidence, Wilson thought he could hold off his pursuer. And, right now, the Iranian was about to overshoot his flight path because he had his nose buried. This gave Wilson some valuable time. Wilson chopped the throttles and popped the speed brake, stepping on right rudder to spiral into his opponent while keeping the air speed on the edge of stall. The Iranian fell underneath Wilson and pulled his nose up in an attempt to stop his downrange travel and to slide behind Wilson for another shot. Wilson's maneuver had the effect of locking horns with the strange aircraft. As heavy, white vapor poured off the tops of both fuselages, and as their wings shook violently under the deep airframe buffet, the aircraft fell, more than flew, down to the deck.

For a moment, their relative positions were unchanged. Locked in this spiral for a few turns, Wilson saw the pilot's menacing eyes stare at him again across a space less than half a football field away. Wilson warily studied the fighter's lone missile to identify it either as radar or infrared guided. *It's a radar missile,* he concluded.

Now furious at, more than fearful of, the man who had shot his helpless wingman out of the sky, Wilson's left arm swiped up *his* helmet visor to show the Iranian *his* eyes. The enemy pilot reacted with a combination upright roll aided by vectored thrust. The maneuver stopped the Iranian's downward vector, but it also immobilized him in midair for a few moments. Wilson seized the opportunity to increase their separation. He shoved the stick and throttles forward as far as he could and fed in some rudder to maintain sight as the *Hornet* rapidly picked up precious air speed. He passed through 7,000 feet in a steep dive as the enemy floated above him. As Wilson whipped his head from the HUD to the bandit, he saw the bandit's nose was now tracking down and falling off left to line up for another shot.

Wilson was still twisting his neck to keep sight when he heard *FUEL LO, FUEL LO* in his headphones. *Dammit!* he cursed through clenched teeth. Fuel was now a real factor. With only 1,800 pounds, his *Hornet* would flameout in minutes if he kept both engines in afterburner. The Iranian was at the edge of gun range as Wilson unloaded for knots.

Both aircraft were now close to the ground. They entered a narrow desert valley ridged on the east by a steeply rising mountain range of chocolate-colored karst. To the southeast Wilson noted a complex of green fields—an indication that people were nearby.

"Four-zero-two, *Knight.* Status?"

Before he answered, Wilson picked the nose up to shallow his dive. "Four-zero-two's defensive. Heading for the deck. State one-eight."

Wilson jinked into the Iranian and then pushed away in an effort to throw off any gun shot. When he sensed the ground looming below them, he flipped the radar altimeter switch into priority. He employed a maneuver that got *Hornet* pilots to the deck quickly and safely. *25 for 15...*

The desert floor rushed up to him, scarred with deep fissures that again reminded him of the badlands in Nebraska. *No people out here.* The Iranian remained above and to Wilson's 5 o'clock, inside a mile. *Why doesn't he shoot his missile?* Wilson wondered. He jinked into him again and pulled up sharply, passing 1,500 feet in gently rising terrain. Through a mixture of bunting the nose and pulling up hard, Wilson leveled at 200 feet. He continued alternately to snap his head forward to clear his flight path and aft to keep sight of the Iranian. He now had two enemies to fight: the ground and the bandit.

Wilson eased down to 100 feet above the ground, as low as he dared having to divide his scan between the ground and the threat. He sensed his pursuer holding off above him but gaining advantage. When he saw two small hills or mounds ahead, he reversed his turn in order to aim for the pass between them. He reasoned that, even for a second, the hills might shield him from a shot or cause the Iranian to lose sight. Wilson knew that, even if he avoided the enemy's gunfire, he wouldn't be able, at this fuel flow, to get back to the *coast*, much less the ship. He had little choice but to defend himself until the engines flamed out.

As he approached the pass, Wilson regained sight over his left shoulder and saw the fighter high and behind a mile, nose off but accelerating. Wilson, too, was accelerating past 400 knots, and the turbulent air caused him to bounce in his seat. Although still breathing hard from fear and adrenaline, he saw the Iranian was lagging too much which gave Wilson some lateral separation with which to maneuver. He had an idea.

With the bandit no-factor for the moment, he concentrated on putting his wingtip into the narrowest part of the pass, a few dozen feet above the rocks. He chopped power to decelerate and approached the backside of the left mound. Suddenly, he came upon a dirt trail and saw a man in a brown pajama-like outfit with a vest and turban trudging up the hill, leading a pack animal. As the *Hornet* roared past, the startled man dropped the animal's reins and jerked his head up, face frozen, wide-eyed, from a combination of awe and fear. For an instant,Wilson's eyes again met those of an Iranian. As the startled animal skittered away and the man quickly receded from view, Wilson put his plan into action. He was momentarily concealed from the bandit and pulled into the mound as close as he dared. *One-potato, two... Now!*

Tightening his muscles and throwing the throttles full forward, Wilson, almost in one motion, pushed, rolled, and pulled right and into the bandit. Again he grunted, *"Hoookkkk,"* as the g enveloped him like a vise. At this dangerous altitude he gave his full attention to staying out of the rocks, betting the Iranian would not see him reverse. A bird appeared out of nowhere, just above his flight path, and instinctively tucked its wings to avoid collision with this strange, speeding object—even before Wilson could think to evade it. *"Fuck!"* he yelled as the bird passed over his jet above his right wing.

Wilson picked up the Iranian at 5 o'clock, moving counterclockwise with his nose off. Wilson's trick had worked. The big aircraft was arcing with too much air speed to remain offensive, and Wilson's bleeding high g turn and lower air speed had put him inside the enemy circle. Wilson saw a high-deflection snapshot opportunity develop and pulled his nose up. He held the GUN trigger down as his green gunsight aiming reticle flew along the bandit's fuselage from left to right. Despite the fact he had no bullets to use in this vain attempt to shoot down the bandit, Wilson felt a sense of satisfaction.

The Iranian seemed to stop fighting—he was holding too much air speed and appeared to be as low as he was willing to go. Wilson left it in burner and with only 1,000 pounds left resisted the urge to reverse his turn behind the enemy. They passed 500 feet apart with the Iranian holding a shallow left angle of bank. Wilson watched the bandit fade away down his left wing line, without turning to engage. He kept his turn in and pulled the throttles out of burner to military. As he floated up a little to make it easier to keep sight, Wilson picked up the strange aircraft over his right shoulder, heading in the opposite direction and climbing, receding from view.

He's had enough!

CHAPTER 40

Now Wilson's biggest problem was fuel. He glanced at his moving map for the nearest heading to the blue safety of the Gulf, over 50 miles to the southwest. The *Hornet*, now light and *slick*, accelerated rapidly to 490 knots and began an emergency-fuel "bingo" climb. Getting to the ship was no longer an option. Wilson just wanted to get feet wet, and as far from the Iranian coast as possible, before he ejected.

On the way up, he searched the sky for the Bushier group *Knight* had been calling, and he took cautious glances over his shoulder to ensure his opponent had not changed his mind. He peered northwest down the valley and saw the black pall of smoke rising up from the desert floor some 10 miles away...*Prince*.

His eyes alternately scanned the cockpit instruments and outside in the familiar pattern he'd practiced since flight school. His eyes dwelled, however, on the fuel indicator, mentally noting every 10-pound drop. His engines would suck fuel until the tank was completely dry, and, the way he figured it, that was a real possibility in less than 15 minutes. The profile called for a climb to 20,000 feet at .83 mach, then an idle descent holding 250 knots at 32 miles. *Eight hundred pounds, seven hundred and ninety pounds, seven eighty, seven seventy...*

He had to get a voice report to *Knight*, and to the ship. "Knight, Raven four-zero-two."

"Go ahead, four-zero-two!"

"*Knight*, four-zero-two is passing angels twelve on a bingo profile, state seven hundred. The bandit disengaged, and I don't see any other bogeys. Didn't see a chute or get a beeper on four-twelve...There's a column of smoke on the desert floor about 10 miles north of me. Believe that's him. Get a tanker out here, now."

"Roger all, four-zero-two... Will pass to Mother," *Knight* replied.

Still concerned about the Iranian fighter threat, Wilson called, "Picture."

"Stand by, four-zero-two... Picture. Single group, BRA zero-two zero at sixty, medium, nose cold."

"Roger, declare." Wilson continued with the cadence.

"Hostile...70 miles now, no factor."

"Roger."

Wilson rolled the aircraft left and right and scanned the ground below for threats, but the landscape was barren: no twinkling AAA muzzle flashes or MANPADS missile plumes. He took a last look at Prince's crash site over his right wing. The smoke appeared less dense, as if the fire were burning itself out.

The Gulf beckoned him. Although it filled his forward view with clear blue water, he was still over 30 miles from feet wet and over 40 from international airspace. He was also fighting a headwind. Leveling at 20,000 feet, Wilson pulled the throttles to idle, which allowed the airplane to decelerate to 265 knots.

Wilson's fuel reading was just over 500 pounds, which translated into roughly five minutes of flight time. He could squeeze a few more minutes at idle power, but the ship was almost 100 miles away—over 20 minutes of flight time.

Knowing he had a chance if he acted fast, Wilson switched up to departure control frequency to back up his request for a tanker. "*Departure, Raven* four-zero-two checkin' in on Mother's one-zero-zero for ninety, angels twenty-five, low state five hundred pounds. *Texaco*, you up?"

"*Redeye* seven-zero-four's up. About 50 miles away, Flip. Comin' to ya." Wilson did not recognize the S-3 aircrew's voice, but he now knew *they* knew *he* was in *402*. The use of his personal call sign reassured him that they were apprised of his grim situation. The fact that he did not know the aircrew didn't matter. He took charge.

"Roger, seven-zero-four. *Buster*," he said, pulling the throttles all the way to idle and bunting the nose down to maintain 250 knots. He bumped them back up a bit to pucker the nozzles, which would squeeze more thrust, and precious range, from his engines.

Then he called *Knight* to shape his backup plan. He wanted them to send the SAR helo in case tanking was unsuccessful. "*Knight*, better get *Switchblade* out here."

The E-2 controller replied, "Roger, already enroute."

Wilson continued his mental calculations. His ground speed was about four miles a minute and he was descending at 1,500 feet per minute. In seven minutes, he would be at the coast passing 10,000 feet, with 300, maybe 400 pounds left. He increased his rate of descent to 2,000 feet per minute, accepting a faster air speed for a lower altitude at the coast. The FUEL LO caution remained illuminated on his left display as a constant reminder.

His radar picked up a contact 30 degrees right at 40 miles. Bumping the castle switch, he locked it, revealing a bogey with hot aspect approaching him at .7 indicated mach, 16,000 feet.

"*Knight*, four-zero-two, contact two-nine-zero, thirty-five miles, sixteen thousand, Declare."

"*Raven*, that's *Redeye* seven-zero-four to the rescue."

"Roger that – break, break – *Redeye*, four-oh-two. Descend to angels five. Turn right ten degrees to intercept. Keep your knots up."

"Roger that, *Raven*... What's your state?"

"Fumes," Wilson replied, not far off the truth.

"Roger, we're at red-line air speed."

Wilson knew the only way to affect the rendezvous with the tanker before he flamed out was for the S-3 to meet him over the coast. That would mean a third American violation of Iranian airspace during the past 30 minutes. *Screw it*, he thought. The damage is done.

But would *Redeye 704* comply? Wilson needed to know. "Seven-oh-four," he said with meaning. "I need you to help me in here."

"No worries, *Raven*," came the reply.

Wilson could not wait to find out who was in *704*. He planned to buy them a drink in the next liberty port. However, right now, he had to face the reality of a possible ejection in the next five minutes. He removed his kneeboard and placed it on the right console. He had worn that kneeboard on his right knee since flight school, and he would hate to lose it forever if he needed to blast himself out of the cockpit. However, there was just no need for it during an ejection.

"Flip, Cajun." The skipper was calling on tac frequency, which meant he was still on deck monitoring what he could from the line-of-sight radio transmissions.

"Yes, sir, on the bingo descent. Still feet dry. Less than four hun'erd pounds. *Redeye* joining."

"Roger, glad you're okay. Will let you fly the jet... Get out when you have to."

"I think Prince is gone, sir. Didn't see a chute," Wilson added.

"Roger, take care of yourself now. We'll talk about it when you're back."

Wilson thought about the CO absorbing the probable loss of one of his pilots, one of his kids. Prince was a favorite of no one, but even now, in extremis, Wilson was already mourning him. He was almost certain Prince had not survived the aircraft break-up to eject. In fact, he feared Prince had already frozen to death from the well-below-zero outside air temperature that had worked its way into the unpressurized cockpit. Wilson recalled the image of Prince slumped over in his ejection seat just before the missile impact.

He had to put Prince out of his mind when he saw the S-3 transition into the 20-mile radar scale as the *Viking* raced to meet him with its life-saving fuel.

Things were going to happen fast now, and this was his only chance. He bumped the stick to sweeten the intercept heading.

Suddenly GUARD erupted. *"Redeye seven-zero-four, this is Mike One Kilo. You are standing into danger! Turn right to two-seven-zero!"*

Damn, Wilson thought. *That small-boy* still *doesn't have the picture.* Wilson ignored the transmission and hoped *704* would do the same. He noticed, for the first time, the muscle tension that had built up in his body over the past 30 minutes. It had seemed to localize in his right shoulder and neck region, and he rubbed his shoulder through the torso harness strap.

Wilson visually picked up the *Viking* inside 15 miles, a speck against the white haze on the western horizon. Thankfully, it was descending as Wilson had instructed. He rolled the jet up to check below him and saw a dirt road meandering along the coastal plain. His inspection found nothing on it—no motion whatsoever.

Now five miles from the coast, he called to the *Redeye* tanker. "Seven-oh-four, I'm gonna call your turn. Maintain air speed. On my signal, I'll need you to break right and bleed to extend the basket. I plan to be on your left wing when you roll out."

"Roger that, *Raven*. Standing by," *Redeye* replied.

The aircraft were approaching each other fast, but once Wilson gave the order to break right, he would have no other options; he would be committed to the join up. Without extra fuel, Wilson had to plan it perfectly. He would have to direct the S-3 to roll out and to slow to the basket extension speed of 225 just as Wilson got there. The radar scale decremented to 10 miles, and the small rectangular "brick"–that signified the S-3–was now moving fast toward him. He looked outside and saw the S-3 on a collision course. The *Viking* was at five miles with lots of closure, and Wilson fought the urge to have him break well in front of him. *C'mon, c'mon...now!*

"*Redeye*, break right heading two-three-zero. *Go!*" Wilson commanded.

"Roger."

Immediately the S-3 threw his left wing up and pulled hard away from him and toward the water. Wilson watched the S-3 roll up and pull, streaming thin vapor trails from the wingtips. He checked into him a few degrees but held his rate of descent and air speed as he drew closer. Wilson's eyes were outside now assessing the closure, and he saw the *Viking* roll out a quarter-mile ahead and below him, speed brakes open and slowing to extend the basket.

"*Redeye*, check left ten," Wilson called to sweeten the rendezvous.

"Roger, Flip, checkin' left."

Wilson approached the S-3 one thousand feet above at his 7 o'clock, his fuel indicating only 250 pounds. He pushed the nose over to gain a few more knots of closure, almost directly above the tanker and practically came down on top of it. Sensing the development of an overshoot, he extended the refueling probe to slow himself, and the increased drag of the probe bled a few knots. Because he was in danger of passing the tanker, he popped the speed brake for a few seconds and then retracted it to remain co-air speed.

Wilson fed in top rudder to bleed air speed and descend, and the *Viking* extended the basket from the wing-mounted refueling store, which payed out the basket via a 40-foot hose into the airstream.

"Hold that air speed," Wilson said.

"Roger."

Wilson noticed, while holding top rudder and assessing closure, that they had passed over the coastline. *At least we are feet wet,* Wilson thought, He took another glance at the fuel—180 pounds. *This is it.*

Wilson pushed the nose down for the final 50 feet and pulled it back up to level himself as he slid behind the tanker and stabilized. Bringing the throttles up for the first time in ten minutes, he placed the probe three feet behind the basket, which was mercifully steady in the clear air. He goosed the power and gripped the stick as he maneuvered his probe inches from the basket. He was surprised one or both of the engines hadn't failed yet due to fuel starvation. He then gave it a shot of power and rammed the probe home. The impact caused the hose to make an undulating sine-wave motion back to the store. When he didn't see the green transfer light on the store, he thought, for an instant, of backing out for one more shot to seat the probe. Then it illuminated, and a sense of relief flooded over him. The fuel gauge increased to 240, 280, 350...

"*Departure*, four-oh-two's plugged and receiving," *Redeye 704* called to the ship.

"Roger *Redeye*, you are cleared to give 5,000."

The S-3 began a shallow right turn toward the ship. Wilson, still plugged in, concentrated on staying in position behind the store to receive fuel. Although he took glances at the fuel gauge—*passing 1,000 pounds!*—he did not have to think for a moment. *Let someone else navigate,* he thought. *Let someone else talk on the radio.*

At that moment the same distinctive Iranian voice came up on GUARD and jolted Wilson back to reality: "U.S. Navy warplanes, you are leaving the Tehran Flight Information Region and Islamic Republic airspace. Contact Bahrain FIR on frequency three-one-seven-point-five. We hope you enjoyed your stay. Please come again."

CHAPTER 41

CAG Tony Swoboda and Cajun greeted Wilson at the ladder as he shut down *402* along the foul line. Wilson was exhausted, and despite the piercing whine of jet engines all around him, he just wanted to sit there in the ejection seat with his head back and his eyes closed, feeling the warmth of the sun on his face. Mindful, though, of hundreds of eyes focused on him, he turned off the displays, the radios, the computer and all the other avionics components—and made sure he used the same method he always used postflight. He then gathered his nav-bag and, double-checked his seat safe, and pulled himself out and onto the left LEX and down the ladder.

Once on deck, Wilson turned first to Riley, the plane captain, and three flight deck troubleshooters. "Jet's down for overstress, guys, and the top of the left outer wing panel was impacted by four-twelve." They nodded, tight-lipped, but understood the significance of the statement. "Thanks guys, nice job." He turned to slap the young plane captain on the back and said, "Riley, thanks."

"Thank you, sir. Glad you're okay," Airman Riley replied with searching eyes, still trying to make sense of the apparent loss of Lieutenant "Prince" Howard.

Wilson then turned to CAG, who extended his hand and grabbed his arm. "*Welcome home,* Jim. You did an *outstanding* job today," he shouted over the din of the flight deck, squeezing Wilson's hand like a vise grip. "Let's talk about it below," CAG said. "The admiral wants to see you."

With a grim smile visible under the dark visor of his helmet, Cajun patted Wilson on the back. CAG led them below to the Captain's passageway and flag country. CAG Swoboda was an F-14 radar intercept officer by trade, and commanded one of the last F-14 squadrons. Short and stocky, with a weathered face and squinty eyes, he could pass for a mob boss, an impression exacerbated by his Philly street accent. In the wing, he was popular, respected as a fair leader who knew his business. As they navigated the labyrinth of passageways, Swoboda peppered Wilson with questions: *How many missiles did you see? Was there any ground fire? How many Iranian aircraft did you see? Are you sure Howard didn't get out?* Rounding the corner to the main starboard passageway Wilson looked aft and saw Psycho. She gave him a smile and a look that conveyed her thoughts: *Good to see you back, Flip.*

When they got to the admiral's in-port cabin, Wilson was led to the large, well-appointed living area, which was full of flag and air wing staff officers, including DCAG and intel officers from CVIC. Wilson, face etched with lines from his oxygen mask and his flight suit stained with perspiration, felt conspicuous in flag country. When the flag lieutenant brought him a glass of water, Wilson downed it in one gulp.

Captain Swartzmann emerged from flag plot in his navy blue sweater, glasses perched on the tip of his beak-like nose. *If he's not the oldest officer in the Navy,* Wilson thought, *he looks like it.* He resembled a dour, pasty-faced Puritan out of the Massachusetts Bay Colony—someone like Ichabod Crane. He walked up to Wilson as if to inspect him. Without even looking Wilson in the eye, he opened his notebook and asked, "So, what were you guys doing over Iran?"

Taken aback by the implication, Wilson's mouth opened and his eyes widened in shock. Before he could answer, CAG did it for him.

"Gene, his wingman was incapacitated over the Gulf and flew into Iran on autopilot. Jim stayed with him in an effort to revive him—and even tried to nudge him back to the west with his own airplane. Very dangerous. The Iranians shot Lieutenant Howard down, and Jim—with some damn good flying—fought his way out in an unarmed airplane. Barely made it back."

Swartzmann, unmoved, peered down at CAG. "I asked *him.*"

A chill filled the room, and 30 people looked at CAG to see how he would react. Swoboda, used to the cutting sarcasm of the Chief of Staff toward his aviators, was having none of it.

"This pilot is *mine,*" he exploded, "and I haven't had the chance to properly question him yet. I haven't even had the chance to review his tapes! I was ordered to bring him here directly from the jet and here he is. But I *resent* your insinuation that he or Howard were doing anything less than a by-the-book routine training mission."

Just then Admiral Smith, wearing khakis and a green flight jacket, entered from flag plot. Everyone in the room came to attention. "Flip," he said in his rich baritone as he walked up to Wilson with his hand extended. The admiral was short and wiry, with salt and pepper hair and a long, weathered face. His eyes were big and brown under bushy brows, and his booming voice did not match his slim body. "Well done today, and I'm sorry about the loss of your wingman." Turning to Cajun, he added, "Skipper, I'm afraid national assets indicate he's dead. Not *official* yet, but there doesn't appear to be much of a chance. I'm very sorry. When we're done here, I want you to call the commodore back home to prepare him for the official word when it comes. Gene, make that happen, please."

"Yes, sir," the Chief of Staff replied.

Turning to Wilson, Smith said, "Flip, let's hear it. What happened?"

"Sir, we'd just finished a 1v1 south of the ship and were on the ladder. We went up to hang on the blades at 28,000. We motored a while, and as we neared the Iranian coast, I came up on the radio for him to turn around. He didn't respond, and I got short with him to turn, but nothing. When I joined up, I saw him motionless, but I also saw his mask dangling down and his canteen in his hand. I started yelling at him to wake him up, figuring it was hypoxia. So I'm yelling at him, and then all the strike group ships and everyone else starts giving us *Waterloo* calls, so I have to deal with trying to explain to them what we've got here."

Smith nodded as Wilson continued.

"We entered Iran about 80 miles south of Bushier, a pretty deserted area, but we were tracking northeast at 450 knots ground. I figured we had to get out of Iran, so I tried to get underneath his wing to see if my jet wash could roll him up a bit. It worked a little, but his autopilot fought it. At one point we swapped paint when his wingtip slammed down on me. By then Prince was not moving, and his canopy started to freeze up. My cockpit was at 12K, and I'm thinking he's got a pressurization problem, and he's hypoxic with his mask off. I was talking to *Knight* the whole time, and he called some bogeys out of Bushier at my 9 o'clock long. At the same time, I started getting some RWR hits off the nose. My scope was clean, but something didn't feel right. I opened up a bit off Prince, and a minute later a missile came down on him. It looked like a streak—white—and I'd say it hit just behind the cockpit. No warning. No plume. Just a huge fireball, and his jet started breaking up. Never saw a chute."

Everyone in the room was focused on Wilson, and behind the crowd of officers Wilson noticed a sailor setting the admiral's dinner table. He, too, was listening.

"Go on," Smith said.

"I turned to engage—training took over—and we went to the merge. At first I thought it was a MiG, but this jet was something I've not seen before. Never seen anything like it. It had a long fuselage with a small nose, a huge intake, canards up forward, delta wings…"

"Was it *this*?" the Air Wing Intelligence Officer asked, showing him a photo of a jet. Wilson studied it…the long bowed fuselage, the huge intake, the slight "V" to the vertical stabs, the canards.

"Yes, sir, it is," he replied. "What is it?"

The "spy" answered. "It's the Mikoyan Project 1.44, also known as the MiG-35. It's a fifth-generation technology demonstrator designed and built by the Russians in the late 90s. The NATO designation is *Flatpack*. Stealth design, two big engines, 1-to-1 thrust to weight, supercruise, thrust vectoring. Russia built five of them, but rejected the design because of the poor radar in the nose and low airframe g loading. Little power out and low range—they rely too much on GCI control. And, despite the large fuselage, it's fuel limited. Hariri launched with half a fuel load anyway, like all the Iranians do."

Wilson looked puzzled. "Hariri? Who's Hariri, sir?" he asked.

"Their wing commander, a colonel," Admiral Smith said. "You fought him." Wilson absorbed the information, and recalled the pilot's eyes. The eyes had a name...*Colonel Hariri.*

The Intel Officer continued. "He's the wing commander at Shiraz. Our dossier says he flew *Tomcats* in the Iran-Iraq War and got three kills."

Smith waved his hand and cut him off. "What happened postmerge?" he asked Wilson.

"Sir, we went one-circle," Wilson said, "and I pulled inside him. I had angles at the second merge and pulled hard across his six, but he just *stopped*. Just stood on the cans and stopped in midair. He then did a cobra-like maneuver and flushed me out in front. Incredible. He took a snapshot that *just* missed low. Then we spiraled down to the deck. I had an opportunity to extend and got down into the weeds. He never took that second missile shot, and I figured it was hung. He chased me a bit down low, but I reversed. He then pitched out of the fight and headed to the northeast, probably back to Shiraz, if that's where he's from."

Wilson looked directly at the admiral to ask about Prince. "Sir, the vis was great, and I never saw a chute. But do we have *definitive* proof he's dead?"

Smith looked at Cajun and CAG, then back at Wilson. "That's what Washington says. And your eyewitness account seems to confirm it. We tend to think he didn't survive, but—for now—he's officially *missing*. We're workin' it, with Washington's help." He then changed the subject.

"Jim, again, *superb* job staying with Howard and trying to save him. And your survival against this *Flatpack* was eye-watering, not to mention your driving the join-up with *Texaco* to save your jet. The phones and e-mail are turned off now due to this ruckus, but I want you to call home to your wife. Gene, set that up, please."

"Yes, sir," Swartzmann replied, scribbling something in his notebook.

Smith drew closer to Wilson. "Lieutenant Howard is missing and we are searching for him. Tell your wife that. Tell her you are safe, and we're not going to fly tonight. She'll sleep soundly after hearing your voice."

"Thank you, sir."

"Then go to CVIC for a debrief and write your statement. Then get some food and rest. Got it?" the admiral asked with a wink.

"Aye, aye, sir." Wilson said.

"CAG? Skipper?" Smith asked each of Wilson's superiors.

"As ordered, sir," CAG Swoboda answered, and Cajun nodded in the affirmative.

"Good," Smith said with a smile, as he grabbed Wilson's arm. "*Good job, good job,*" he whispered to him before leaving.

Wilson then looked at Swartzmann who nodded for him to follow. Wilson was led into the flag staff office, and Swartzmann ordered one of the staff officers to set up a SATCOM line. Wilson wrote his number on a piece of paper for the officer, who was curious about why this pilot was receiving a special privilege. The officer dialed and handed Wilson the phone once it rang. Wilson looked at his watch – almost 0500 there. After two rings, Mary answered, still half asleep.

"*Hellooo?*"

"Mary."

"James? *James*, is that you?"

"Yeah, baby," Wilson answered self-consciously, as he looked up at Swartzmann's unsmiling face.

She exhaled. "You're calling *so early*...I need my..."

"Mary...Mary?"

"What...?"

"Mary...something's happened."

CHAPTER 42

Colonel Reza Hariri, a colonel in the Islamic Republic of Iran Air Force, lay on his back, awake in the darkness. He listened to the low tones of the muezzin from the minaret three blocks away as he summoned the people for *fard salah*, the first of five calls to prayer. Off in a different part of the city he could hear the faint sounds of another muezzin call the Shiite faithful to prayer. The mournful lines of the *Adhan* from that other minaret were broadcast across a scratchy loudspeaker.

For almost every morning of his 48 years, Hariri's brain had absorbed the message of the Holy Men chanting in Arabic…a language he little understood. He did know most of the meaning of the morning call to prayer: *I bear witness that there is no deity except God. Make haste towards prayer. There is no deity except God.*

He looked out the window at the mountain ridge to the east, outlined by a dim glow provided by a sun that would not spill over and upon the Iranian city of Shiraz for about two hours. He glanced at the alarm clock LCD display: 4:40. *He's late today,* he thought.

Hariri would have enjoyed the extra 10 minutes of sleep, but he had been awake all night, reliving yesterday morning's fight. He couldn't get the image out of his head: the American was *right there*, out of airspeed and inverted, almost hovering in the sky in front of him—less than a soccer pitch away. The F-18 had filled his windscreen as Hariri's nose tracked down to cut him in half with a cannon burst. His pipper was well above the *Hornet* when he squeezed the trigger—and nothing! Nothing for a split second until Hariri's nose fell, and he missed low. No! *He* didn't miss—it was the damned Russian aircraft and the inferior weapons system! How he wished for his beloved F-14 at that point, with a reliable gun and accurate sight.

As the Wing Commander of the IRIAF base at Shiraz, *Sarhang* Hariri happened to be inspecting the strip alert facility when the call had come in that American fighters were crossing the coast. A young *sargord* scrambled for the MiG-35, but Hariri stopped him, grabbed his helmet and ordered him to remove his g-suit, which fit Hariri to an acceptable level. Within minutes, Hariri had the MiG taxiing for the runway and his rendezvous with destiny. *I was meant to be here,* he thought.

His mind wandered to his last guns kill, an execution really. Winter of 1988, northwest of Kharg Island. A lone Iraqi *Mirage* returning to Iraq flew in front of Hariri and his wingman moments after Hariri had shot down another F-1 with a *Sidewinder,* causing the Arab to spin out of control into the white cloud layer below.

He saw the *Mirage* a few miles ahead, crossing left to right off his nose and low. The fighter was just cruising along straight and level after its own attack on a tanker, oblivious to both the destruction of his countryman seconds earlier and the presence of his assailant now coming out of the sun. With calm resolve, Hariri rolled in behind him, pulled power and popped the speedbrakes while Hariri's useless radar intercept officer cried *"God is great!"* over the intercom.

"Shut up and look for the enemy," Hariri scolded him. He lined his *Tomcat* up on the Iraqi's 6 o'clock—he still hadn't budged—and squeezed the trigger from 200 meters behind. He saw the first 20mm tracers hit the fuselage; massive yellow flames and black smoke erupted from the fuselage and wings. Hariri overtook the fighter as it slowed in its death throes—now covered in flames. He saw inside the cockpit and watched as the pilot's arms frantically reached for the ejection seat face curtain through the fire. He was being burned alive. The canopy then blew off and flames poured out of the cockpit into the slip-stream, followed in an instant by the ejection seat and pilot exploding from the inferno—completely engulfed. Hariri watched the fireball, now a flaming arc, pick up speed and rate of descent as it disappeared into the same undercast as his mate moments earlier. Despite two aerial victories inside three min-utes, Hariri could not erase the sickening image of the burning pilot from his mind. Once he crossed into a safe area south of Kharg, he wretched into his glove.

In 1979, when the Shah of Iran fell from power, Hariri was weeks away from starting flight school with the American Navy at Pensacola. Twenty years old at the time, he was identified as pilot material, and he was blessed with 20/10 vision and exceptional athletic ability. His physical stamina and hand-eye coordination as a soccer midfielder, coupled with his quick mind, caught the attention of the military representative at the University of Tehran. His father's position as the head of Tehran's electrical generating facility also was helpful in obtaining a flight school slot for young Hariri. When the revolutionaries took over, the Hariri family was spared from the purges of those bureaucrats close to the Shah...the lights still needed to work, no matter who was in charge.

Hariri was not devout growing up, but to deflect unwanted attention, he grew a beard and made the daily prayers in the mosque. His newfound religious "zeal," together with his physical and mental gifts, led to a marriage of convenience between Hariri and the revolutionaries. In order to fight Saddam's attacking air force, they needed young pilots to replenish those they had purged after the revolution. Hariri turned out to be the natural his superiors had suspected, and he soon was flying the frontline F-14 *Tomcat*, compiling an enviable combat record and moving up fast. Though he had missed his chance in Pensacola to learn from the best, Hariri was determined to prove he could succeed as a fighter pilot without U.S. training.

After his double-kill flight, Hariri was a hero of the Islamic Republic. Then, when he scored again over Kharg later that year, he thought his childhood dream of becoming a fighter ace would come true. But the Iranians had flown little during the last months of the war, and the times they did encounter Iraqi fighters, Hariri was elsewhere. The horrific ground war had ended with half a million slaughtered, and the air force had not engaged in aerial combat since.

However, Hariri's single-minded focus was to prepare himself, and then his squadron, to fight and to defeat the Gulf Sheikdoms, the Americans, the Pakistanis…. It did not matter who threw down the gauntlet, Hariri would pick it up. He eschewed women and lived like a warrior-monk until the higher-ups thought it would look better if he married. Therefore, a few years ago he had married Atosa, a beauty sixteen years his junior. She had dark almond eyes and long, flowing hair she covered with stylish Italian scarves, showing as much of it as she could at the bazaar and still keep the religious police away.

In the dawn twilight, he thought about the pilots he had defeated. *Arabs!* Arabs, who for years had proved themselves inept against the superior equipment and training of the Israelis and the Americans. Arab pilots who seemed incapable of thinking for themselves, tied as they were to strict instructions from the ground. Hariri's last Iraqi foe had at least held him off for a full-circle before Hariri's missile found its mark, but the fights were almost not fair.

Like his fourth kill yesterday—a forward quarter missile against a half-dead American in a non-maneuvering aircraft. *Nothing more than simulator training, a chalkboard exercise! A video game! What pride can one take in that?*

But his wingman….*that* was the challenge he'd waited a lifetime for, the fight he'd dreamed of. An American F-18 *Hornet*, avenging his mate's death, coming to the merge with a knife in his teeth and turning hard… *This* was a worthy opponent. Hariri was ready, knowing how he would maneuver his aircraft at the merge and bait the American to give everything away. He would then stand his MiG on its tail and let the American fly out in front. It worked to perfection, the way Hariri had dreamed it would, the way he had *planned* it. Unlike so many religious pilots who called on God to vanquish the enemy, whether they were prepared or not, Hariri had planned such a moment for years. He had studied his own aircraft, smuggled journals from Western intelligence sources, and searched out every bit of information he could on the Internet—all for that moment...

His nose tracked down.... His finger squeezed the trigger...

Damn! Blast! His weapons system let him down, and the enemy escaped, avoiding more gun shots and never having to face his remaining missile—which was *hung on the rail! Dammit!* The final insult had been running low on fuel and having to break off the engagement... all because the Iranian air force didn't trust its pilots to take off with full loads, afraid they would defect. *After I've given 29 years of faithful service, the monkeys think I, the bloody Wing Commander, will fly across the Gulf to Bahrain,* he thundered in his mind, exhaling deeply with disgust.

After landing, Hariri had exploded into a profanity-laced tirade at everyone: his crew chief, the armorers, and the avionics technicians, saving his best salvo for the Russian technical representative. During the flight debriefing, he was asked endless questions about the *Hornet*: What was it carrying? How did the American fly it? And, the question that caused his blood to boil—*Why didn't he shoot that one down, too?* While the mouthpieces in Tehran rejoiced on the BBC and CNN about downing the imperialist American fighter over Islamic Republic soil—proving to the world that the Americans are girding for a fight and that Iran would destroy anyone violating her sovereign airspace— Hariri had to hear over and over from the generals and the bastard religious officer about how *he* let down the Islamic Republic. *Swine! Imbeciles!* Despite their ignorance, it was almost too much to bear.

Then, a shock—they told him the pilot was an African! *How can an* African *fight for the Great Satan?* Hariri wondered. *If this pilot—named Wilson—is Muslim, is he devout? Do the Americans conscript Africans to fly their planes?*

When told Wilson was also a graduate of the legendary U.S. Navy Fighter Weapons School, or TOPGUN, Hariri had heard everything. He had fought, and all but defeated, an American TOPGUN, who was also an African—and possibly a brother Muslim. Hariri's initial confusion soon turned to anger and determination. *Muslim or not,* he thought, *Wilson had aligned himself with the Great Satan. If the Americans gave him a jet to fly, nothing can hold Wilson back from defecting and pledging his allegiance to the Islamic Republic.*

No matter…Hariri had proved to himself that, even without Western training, he could engage and defeat an American in a frontline F-18…a TOPGUN no less! He craved a win, he *must always* win, and prayed that the international situation would escalate so he could have another shot at the Americans. *If I am lucky, it will be this TOPGUN-trained African,* he thought. He would then become an ace and join the elite list of *Persian* aces formed during the Iran-Iraq War.

Atosa, still naked, stirred next to him. She had offered herself to him last night, but he had rebuffed her, unable to forgive the Russians, the generals, and even himself for not downing the second American. The thought of this Wilson consumed him. Exasperated, she whispered, "Why can you not sleep, azizam?"

Hariri grunted. "Too much adrenaline."

She turned to him and pressed her body close, her French perfume filling his nostrils. "You defended us from the Americans. You are a hero, *my* hero! Why can you not sleep?"

Hariri said nothing. He then took a breath, as if to talk, but only exhaled deeply. *She wouldn't understand,* he thought, but he knew she was going to rebuke him for his refusal to make love last night and to talk now.

"Let it *go*, Reza, and next time shoot them *all* down, or *don't come back.*" She rolled away and pulled the covers up over her shoulders. They remained motionless in the dark, lying in the same bed, but emotionally separated by a sea of anger, his anger.

Damn Iranian women, Hariri thought. Even though Atosa usually proved herself to be easygoing and supportive, she was an Iranian woman first, and they were *tough* on their men. Hariri let out a breath. Since the excitement of yesterday, he *had* been an ass to his young wife. Nevertheless, she was not afraid to stand up to him.

Hariri placed his hand on the warm skin of her smooth hip. She flinched, and then allowed it to remain. Hariri wondered, *Does Wilson have a wife next to him on that cursed ship three hundred kilometers away?*

CHAPTER 43

Day is done, gone the sun,
From the lake, from the hills, from the sky.
All is well, rest in peace, God is nigh.

In his service dress blue uniform, eyes locked straight ahead, Wilson saluted from his position in front of the officers and chiefs. The rest of VFA-64 stood at attention behind him in Hangar Bay Two while the bugler played taps. As he listened to the haunting notes, he thought about other times he had stood at attention in ranks and saluted other fallen comrades over the years. How many? Nine? Ten? He figured it was too many, whatever it was. Most of those comrades had been lost to pilot error...and it appeared Prince was another. Even at this moment, Wilson's mind continued to analyze the situation. Removing his mask at altitude wasn't smart, and a probable pressurization leak made the poor decision deadly. Hariri's missile destroyed Prince's *Hornet* and may have killed him outright, but if he was not dead in the cockpit before impact he was minutes from it. Hypoxia or an air-to-air missile—both can kill.

For Wilson, the past 48 hours had been a blur: debriefings, investigative queries, written statements, SATCOM calls from TOPGUN staff officers, classified email messages, well wishes from air wing friends in the wardroom and passageways, department head meetings, memorial service planning meetings, and retelling the events of the shootdown and MiG-35 engagement. Added to that mix now was the necessity to avoid the media, which had sent a dozen reporters out to the ship the day after the shootdown. He was shocked at the speed they arrived onboard, with Navy support at every level.

The swarm diligently set about finding the pilot who was with Prince and who had fought the Iranian after Prince was shot down. In a display of unity, the air wing pilots removed their identifying squadron patches from their flight suits to throw off the snoopers, but try as he might to avoid the intruders, and despite the efforts of the ship's public affairs officer to protect him, Wilson sensed they were closing in on him. Yesterday, a reporter with large glasses and a graying ponytail had stopped him on the way to the wardroom. "It's you, isn't it?"

he asked with a smirk. Wilson gave him a blank look and continued on his way, but asked Weed to bring a plate of food to the stateroom that evening to avoid another confrontation. The word was out though. Just this morning he had passed two sailors in the hangar bay and overheard one whisper to the other, "He's the guy."

Most of the air wing aviators were at the memorial service and were seated in rows of folding chairs, with the admiral, CAG, and captain sitting in the front row. A *Raven* helmet and brown boots—signifying Prince's body—had been placed on a pedestal near the speaker's lectern. A sailor with a video camera recorded the proceedings for the family, catching, through the cavernous elevator opening, the characteristic hazy sky above the mirror-flat Gulf water, the bright morning sun glinting off its surface.

As the commanding officer, it was Cajun's responsibility to preside over the ceremony. He had asked for a JO volunteer to give a eulogy of LT Ramer Howard, the person, and that task had fallen to Nttty, Prince's bunkmate in the six-man *Ranch*. Nttty did a good job of relating the "PG" version of some fun times the two had shared: their days in flight school, how Nttty had marveled at the ease with which Prince made female friends in Virginia Beach, and a story or two of their madcap adventures with cab drivers while on liberty in Dubai. Nttty also told the audience that, in college, Prince was a lead vocalist in a cover band and once auditioned for *American Idol*, getting a trip to Hollywood but no more. Standing in ranks, Wilson reflected about how he had not known that about his dead squadronmate; he regretted he had learned it too late.

Cajun returned to the lectern head down, tight-lipped and somber under the visor of his combination cover. At this point in his career, a memorial service was a familiar ritual, yet one that was always difficult, and he had hoped to never speak at another one. Wilson knew Cajun would speak without notes, from his heart, and that the message would be powerful and consoling not only to those assembled in the hangar bay but to Prince's family who would receive a videotape of the proceedings. After perfunctory acknowledgements of the senior officers present, he began:

"Ladies and gentlemen, take a moment, if you will, to look at the sea and sky though the elevator opening. This sea…flat, with its brownish tinge, sometimes with strange sea creatures on its surface…different from the familiar seas back home off our own coasts: the choppy waters of the Atlantic, the serene blue waters of the Gulf of Mexico, and the long swells of the Pacific that crash so spectacularly into the shores of our west coast. This sky…typically a milky brown haze like today that does not change for days or weeks… different from the brilliant blue skies of our homes which are often dotted with puffy cumulus clouds and accompanied by dramatic lighting displays that bring life-giving rain to our land. This sea. This sky. They look different. They *are* different.

Lieutenant Ramer Howard volunteered to leave the safety of his home and country and come *here*, to these strange and oftentimes hostile surroundings, to *defend freedom*, not only for ourselves but millions of others he never met. He was a talented and gifted young man, a man of accomplishment and promise even before he decided to volunteer. That he volunteered was enough, but he chose to pursue a career as a carrier pilot, a profession that is fraught with danger even in peacetime, and he accepted the challenge, and excelled at it. Alone over the open ocean far from shore, or high above an enemy country, carrier flying is always demanding, and often unforgiving. He met and passed the test of combat, striking blows against those who would kill and maim civilians. His loss, known to enemies of freedom around the world, gives them pause. An American volunteered to come here and risk his life to oppose tyranny. Those who use terror may now think twice about any cracks in American resolve. In his short life, he made a difference."

Wilson listened to the words of his skipper. While he knew Cajun was right, he could not grieve for Prince—and was ashamed by it. Wilson was the last person Prince had spoken to on earth, and Wilson had not felt a personal sense of loss. Had the specter of violent death so hardened him that he could no longer feel?

While Cajun finished his tribute to their fallen comrade, Wilson scanned the horizon through the open elevator door. He noticed the ship was turning, a routine occurrence in the confined waters of the Gulf. As the Chaplain closed the proceedings with the benediction, Wilson felt the ship vibrate underneath him and recognized the ship's increasing speed through the water. Once the ceremony ended and the squadron was dismissed, the sailors dispersed to their work centers and berthing spaces. Wilson ambled to the deck edge, squinting his eyes toward the western horizon. The ship was moving fast now, and he watched one large bow wave after another radiate away from the hull. Weed joined him at the edge.

"We're goin' somewhere in a hurry," he said.

"Yeah, southeast," Wilson responded, also wondering what it meant. Stepping away, he saw Lieutenant Metz approach them on his way up forward. Wilson walked over to intercept his path.

"Hey, Mike," he said, "where we goin' so fast?"

Metz stopped and looked at the two pilots. "Just got a message from NAV-CENT. We're heading out to the GOO."

CHAPTER 44

The shoot-down death of an American fighter pilot over Iranian soil was front page news all over the world. The story generated predictable glee in most African, Middle Eastern, and Asian communities, and indifferent resignation in other parts of the globe. The incident had now resulted in a diplomatic fight between Washington and Tehran, and the Iranians, masters at exploiting American misfortune, had the upper hand.

"God willing, American imperialist aggression will meet its end in the waters of the Persian Gulf!" thundered the Iranian foreign office. "The Great Satan is no match for the forces of God and has delivered to us an American angel of death who violated Islamic Republic sovereignty. Further American acts of war will be met with the full fury of Islamic Republic forces. They will guide more arrows of destruction to American planes that defile the Islamic Republic, and send their vessels of war to the bottom of the Persian Gulf to rid our waters of this wicked pestilence for all time, praise be to God."

While Washington issued a public apology for the violation of Iranian airspace, its expressions of dismay at the unprovoked downing of an incapacitated airman without warning after repeated calls to this fact on international radio distress channels was met worldwide by skepticism, if not disbelief. Many nations viewed the incident as an American probe, or as a precursor to a wider war with Iran, which in some Washington circles was viewed as inevitable. The GCC nations, always wary of their northern neighbor, quietly asked Washington to tone down their profile in the Gulf and to give assurances that this was not a sign of an American attack.

Intercepted Iranian communications, however, did show command and control confusion on part of the Islamic Republic Air Force. The Iranians were just as surprised as the Americans were at the sudden turn of events that led the two FA-18s into their airspace, and there was uncertainty in Tehran from conflicting field reports received from the south. The civil air traffic controllers correctly identified the incursion as pilot incapacity, with one aircraft in extremis accompanied by a wingman. However, airspace controllers from the military sector painted a picture of an imminent American attack. Regular saber-rattling discourse by Iranian leaders likely conditioned those on watch to default to the military analysis, and with only minutes to decide on a course of action, they scrambled strip alert fighters from Bushier and Shiraz.

Control broke down further when different military sector controllers sent out conflicting orders to the fighters. The Bushier group was ordered to intercept and escort. The Shiraz group—which consisted of Hariri alone—was ordered to engage. American analysis was that the difference in orders could be explained by the vector of the *Raven* flight path, which was almost straight at Shiraz. The intelligence community analysts in Washington surmised it was more than the proximity to Shiraz that led the local air defense sector to engage without warning and without explicit orders from Tehran. On some satellite photos Washington had found an apparent cement production facility near Shiraz, but they were unsure of its true purpose. The analysts assumed that when the Iranians saw the Americans heading right for the facility, they took preemptive action. An unanswered question about this facility in Washington may have found an answer.

Even when the story moved off the front page, it remained the number one topic of conversation in the Virginia Beach fighter community. When the Strike Fighter Wing held a memorial at the chapel, most of the Oceana community, and all the *Raven* spouses, attended the service. Prince's parents, as the guests of honor, were awash in grief, especially because they were still in the midst of a diplomatic battle to receive the remains of their son from the Iranians.

Every spouse there knew that abrupt loss could be "part of the package" in naval aviation, but it was never discussed. Even veteran wives like Mary Wilson, who were friends with more than one young woman suddenly widowed, lived in a state of denial most of the time. Mary had been the first to know her husband was involved in Ramer Howard's last flight, and though her husband downplayed it at the time of his call to her, she had learned through the Oceana grapevine that her husband had literally dodged bullets over Iran. Hearing about the danger he had been in from people other than James scared her more than anything else she had experienced in her nine years of marriage to a Navy fighter pilot.

Several days later, she e-mailed a message to him.

Dear James,

Hearing your voice when you called the other day, despite the dreadful news you told me, was a big relief. I slept soundly that night knowing you were safe aboard the ship. You've been in the news quite a bit—well, not you, but you as the "lost pilot's wingman, name withheld." So, you've been relegated to anonymous wingman. I guess that's better than nothing, huh?

The newspaper stories say you tried to save Ramer by placing your airplane close to him to get him to turn away from Iranian airspace. Then, after the missile hit and killed him, you were able to avoid the Iranians and return to the ship. I've heard rumors about what you did after Ramer was hit, that you were in a dogfight against a new type of fighter and that you almost got shot yourself. No one told me this directly, but the girls here have heard it from their husbands—the word gets out—and a friend told me. Not telling you who, it doesn't matter. And I'm glad she did. I don't blame you for not telling me yourself. You don't want me to worry, and I understand that.

You know I've seen you at parties, when you guys all gather in the corner with your beers and start talking with your hands and "shooting your watches," like you do every time. The other girls and I just roll our eyes and ignore you. But, as I watch you from across the room, you are at your most animated, doing more talking at that session than you will the rest of the evening. I used to think I knew what you do when you fly, but at times like this, I realize I don't have a clue. I can visualize you landing on the carrier and even dogfighting—but I really have no idea about the weapons you carry or the weapons you face. The complexity of what's going on around you with the thousands of little things you must monitor and consider is way beyond me. Sometimes, when you've tried to explain your flying to me, my eyes have glazed over. I want to know more, but at the same time, I really don't. In fact, I try not to even think about it until things like this make me think about it.

James, you are a good pilot, and while I understand it's dangerous out there, I'm confident in your ability, and I know you will come back to me. But I want you to know something else. The Iranian government has been causing problems and killing Americans for years. They are trying to get the bomb and they'll use it. They killed Ramer without warning and they tried to kill you. You probably wouldn't even be over there now except for them. I'm not sure what's going on, but I imagine you guys will be in the middle of it. Focus on them. If they start something with us, I want you to beat them. The kids and I are fine but America and the world must be able to live in peace. We need you and the Ravens to keep them at bay and defend freedom. Is that asking too much?

So, if the President sends you, don't worry about us, just concentrate on what you have to do, defeat them, and come back with that big shiny medal!

James, I love you so much and I am so proud of you. It's times like this—actually for the first time, during this cruise—that I realize just how important your job is, and that it's really just you guys out there on the frontline. You'll do great, too. Won't even be a fair fight!

So you've got the green light, Flip Wilson! Roger ball... Kick the fires... Hit the burner... Pull g's... Do all that pilot stuff and do it well. We're fine. We miss you tons, but lead those JOs to victory and bring everyone back soon!

Love,

Mary

Wilson smiled, and then read Mary's note a couple more times. What a woman. Alone with two little kids and bucking *him* up. He recognized her fear, but she was reassuring him, building *his* confidence and allowing *him* to compartmentalize for any eventuality in the coming weeks. He hit "Reply" and began typing:

Hey, Baby... Did you mean "light the tires?" ☺

CHAPTER 45

Where is he?

Wilson, in growing panic, searched the sky to his left. The Iranian was just there, going up in a left-to-left pass as Wilson unloaded for knots. He had been at the top of his arc and passing through the sun when Wilson had glanced inside and saw 450 knots in the HUD and the valley floor rushing up to meet him. Wilson yanked the throttles to idle and pulled on the stick as he returned his head to the top of the canopy, straining his neck and eyes back to see his foe. The g swallowed him at once, the anaconda-like squeezing of his torso and legs and the vise-grip pressure on his chest forced him to exhale. He gasped for breath as his mask slid down his nose. He heard a cockpit deedle, followed by *Tammy's* laconic warning: *Flight controls. Flight controls.* He figured he had just overstressed the airplane, but his first concern was sight, sight that had narrowed to a cone, a fuzzy gray cone—with nothing inside it! *Lose sight, lose fight.* He had just committed an error, and time—time now measured in mere seconds—would determine if the error was fatal.

As he leveled, Wilson kept the left turn in, re-engaged burner, and remained outside, looking for any moving object against the eastern horizon. He was in a large valley, karst ridges on either side about five miles away from him. *Where is he?* Wilson held his left angle of bank and searched for Hariri. He realized he was arcing and didn't know why. Wilson thought, *He's here, but where? And why am I arcing? I can't stop arcing!* His adrenaline had elevated to the point his mouth felt like it was stuffed with cotton.

Wilson's blood ran cold as he overbanked and picked up his foe. The MiG was below him at his 7 o'clock, a mile and closing—nose on. Breaking out of his funk, Wilson overbanked further and put the top of his aircraft on Hariri. With a good maneuvering air speed, Wilson continued to pull into him to throw off his shot. Hariri appeared motionless against the valley floor, and Wilson saw the speed brake open on the top of his airplane—a huge panel that made the *Flatpack* appear even bigger. Wilson was fascinated by the scene. He looked down into the gaping intake of the big Russian fighter, those powerful engines delivering 80,000 pounds of thrust. He saw white missiles on the pylons—pointing right at him.

189

Wilson had a sense of being "frozen," flying but unable to move through the sky. The Iranian seemed to be holding him in place—holding him by the throat before striking. Even in full afterburner, Wilson couldn't escape. It was as if he were running on sand in heavy boots, his antagonist drawing closer, showing more of the bottom of his aircraft. *He's pulling lead to shoot me,* Wilson thought, transfixed.

A bright, flickering light flashed over the right intake. Time compressed. Smaller lights floated off the fighter, then accelerated toward him. Wilson saw several whiz past, sounding a loud *pop* under his left wing. He wondered what they were…23 mm? 30 mm? He knew he needed to roll down and into the threat, make his jet skinny, gain more time, throw him off…but he couldn't. He was cornered, held in place as if the wily Iranian had pasted him against the sky like a cloud, a soft puffy cloud. Wilson was giving up, and he knew it.

Wilson watched the first round strike dead center on the left outer wing with a loud *crack.* The airplane shuddered as the black composite material splintered. He kept the pull in, into the threat over his left shoulder. For an instant the flashing stopped, but when it resumed, a great tongue of fire leapt from the Iranian's gun muzzle, and Wilson thought he could see the shell casings ejected into the air stream. The hits were almost instantaneous on his left wing, and he heard and felt another *crack* on the leading edge flap, followed by two impacts that sounded like a pencil punching through aluminum foil stretched across a tin can. These impacts caused small explosions on the top of the wing and fuselage. The alarms followed. A cacophony of warnings burst into his earphones in rapid succession: *Flight controls. Engine fire left. Engine left. Engine fire right.* More aluminum punches were accompanied by a chorus of pops as the rounds whizzed past at supersonic speed. The *Hornet* shook with each hit. More cockpit warning lights illuminated in unison, led by *both* engine fire lights.

The airplane *felt* different.

When Wilson snapped his head back over his left shoulder to find Hariri, fuel-fed flames filled his entire field of view. The bright orange fire, fanned by his 200-knot indicated air speed, covered the top of the aircraft and licked at the canopy. A sudden, loud *clank* threw Wilson hard against the left side of the cockpit, and his helmet slammed into the canopy with such force he thought he cracked the Plexiglas shell. The negative g caused his arms to fly up, and the force pinned him against the canopy. He couldn't reach the controls! His mask was pushed up against his eyes, and when he managed to open one of them, he saw nothing but orange fire and black smoke…then blue sky…brown earth…orange…black…blue… brown…. He was tumbling, and through the sounds of aluminum and composite tearing into pieces, he noted that the aural warning tones had stopped.

Then a sickening sight flashed in front of him. The flaming fuselage of a *Hornet,* missing one wing and throwing off burning debris, corkscrewed through the air. When the *Raven* emblem on the tail emerged from the thick smoke, he realized in horror he was trapped in the tumbling and disintegrating cockpit now separated from the fuselage. His mind called out, *Eject! Eject!* but his arms would not, could not reach for the handle, pinned as they were against the canopy.

At that moment, the MiG flashed into view. It was Hariri! Then, a crushing explosion of pressure from rapid decompression pushed down on Wilson from all sides as the canopy was wrenched off the cockpit. A simultaneous roar of wind ripped at his helmet and pulled it off his head with the mask still attached. Wilson couldn't feel his left arm, and his feet and legs took blows from debris as the cockpit disintegrated around him. His mind again said, *Eject!* but he couldn't reach the handle. He wasn't sure if he was strapped in the seat anymore, and sensed a passing burst of heat in front of him. He heard a succession of loud pops with no idea of the source. *Reach for the handle! The handle!*

But he couldn't…his arms would not respond. With eyes closed against the cold wind lashing his body and whistling in his ears, he hurtled through space. Falling…. Waiting….

Wilson opened his eyes wide and realized he was inhaling and exhaling long and deep through his nose, his neck bathed in sweat. He rolled over and looked at the time on the digital clock: 4:37. Light streamed through small openings in the passageway bulkhead, and he heard footsteps walking past his stateroom door. Weed snored in his rack. The air conditioning blower thrummed as normal.

A nightmare. He had fought Hariri and lost—again. *Gunned! A tracking guns kill!* But worse than that, worse than the image of tumbling to his death, was the fact that he had *given up.* Jim Wilson did not give up, had never quit anything in his life. It was part of the fighter pilot creed: *Never give up.* You never give up on the count, never give up on a putt, *never* give up in a guns defense situation. That he gave up in his dreams scared Wilson, and as he lay in bed slowing his breathing, he thought about the implications. Was he afraid? The OPSO of VFA-64? The Strike Fighter Tactics Instructor who taught half the guys in the air wing about basic fighter maneuvers, about the importance of keeping sight, about last-ditch maneuvers to defeat a guns attack? Who was better than Flip Wilson in a 1v1? Hariri? The combat-proven Iranian flying a monster jet that had power and an ability to point the nose unlike anything Wilson had ever seen before?

Was he afraid?

Wilson lay on his back in the darkness and looked up at the bottom of Weed's rack for the next hour.

Chapter 46

Approaching midnight, the guided missile frigate USS *Richard Best* cut through the murky waters of Hormuz on an outbound transit, her gas turbine engine emitting a steady high-pitched whine as she proceeded at 15 knots. In her darkened bridge, soft red lights used to preserve night vision and the green symbols displayed on the radar repeater, illuminated a group of shadowy figures. The watch team peered into the gloom—the haze reducing visibility to three miles—and plotted the course through the strait using radar and GPS navigation. Oman was 10 miles to the south, and the barren coastline offered few sharp objects or known lights from which to shoot bearings for fixes, even if the night had offered one of those rare moments of clear visibility.

The fracas between the *Valley Forge* FA-18s and the Iranian jet was several weeks past, and things appeared to be settling down between the two countries, now that the carrier was operating in the Gulf of Oman. However, what the *Airedales* did mattered little to the crew of *Richard Best*. After four long months in the North Arabian Gulf guarding the damned Iraqi oil platforms and dodging the lumbering tankers that seemed to have no one on the bridge, they were one month away from San Diego and home. The crew was more than ready to say good-bye to this hellhole.

Ready, but only after they passed one more challenge—a night transit of Hormuz. Following the shoot-down incident, NAVCENT had directed night transits of Hormuz in an effort both to minimize and to conceal the American presence among the north/south traffic on the waterway, much of it potentially hostile. *Best's* captain, Commander Mark Albright, blond and athletic at 39 years old, sat up straight in his chair, trying to discern the faint lights off his port bow. His left hand nervously stroked his chin. His helicopter was down with a transmission-line leak, and he wanted it airborne, scouting for contacts ahead of him in the outbound lane. He wanted, and needed, it *now*. He picked up the sound-powered phone to the flight deck.

"Yes, sir," answered one of his aviation lieutenants.

"What's the story, Eric?"

"Sir, we found the leak, and the chief is patching it up. We're going to run it to make sure it holds pressure…10 minutes, sir."

"*Expedite!* I need it airborne right away."

"Yes, sir."

Albright cradled the receiver, and queried the watch team. "Range to the *skunk?*"

"Eight thousand yards, sir," the officer of the deck replied.

"CPA?" Albright could just make out a white light on a masthead, stationary on the black horizon, as he waited for a reply.

"One thousand yards. He's tracking south at 3 knots," the OOD responded.

Dammit, Albright thought. From the other side of the bridge the young conning officer under training gave a command to the helm to maintain their track in the outbound lane. "Come right, steer course zero-seven-seven."

"Come right, steer course zero-seven-seven, aye," the 20-year-old helmsman answered. Moments later, he added, "Ma'am, my rudder is right five degrees…coming to new course zero-seven-seven."

"Very well."

Albright assessed the situation. The unidentified surface contact was tracking left to right and closing his ship. Not knowing what it was and with no airborne aircraft to tell him, he wanted to give it a wider berth. The only problem was that shoal water ahead on his right allowed him only so much sea room.

He spoke in a low voice to his officer of the deck who was standing next to him. "John, let's give this guy some more room. What's the CPA if you put us on the southern border of the lane?"

After consulting the radar repeater, Lieutenant John Reynolds answered, "Three thousand yards, sir."

Albright grunted. "All right, give me that and some change—as much as you can. Call him bridge-to-bridge."

"Aye, aye, sir," the officer of the deck replied, as he charted a course to comply. Within 10 seconds, he turned to the conning officer. "Conning officer, come right to new course one-one-zero."

"Aye, aye, sir. *Helm*, right standard rudder, steady course one-one-zero."

The helmsman turned the wheel while watching the rudder position indicator and repeated verbatim, "Right standard rudder, steady course one-one-zero, aye."

Just then the phone talker piped up. "Sir, signal bridge lookout reports surface contact bearing three-three-five relative, range 7,000 yards as a dhow, sir."

"Very well," Albright said. *A dhow,* he thought as he studied the solitary light in the distance. *But who's in it? And what are they doing?*

"Are they inside the lane, John?" he asked.

"Just outside, sir, but should cross into it in a few minutes."

"Rog," Albright replied.

He was tired, tired of four months in these restricted waters with obstacles everywhere, unidentified threats all around: above...and below the surface...sometimes even on his bridge in the form of junior officers who were for the most part competent, but who could suffer, without warning, a momentary lapse of judgment. Albright was on edge, and had to control himself so as not to alarm the crew.

Six hours to sunup, where we'll be pointing south and steaming fair into the Indian Ocean, Albright thought. He looked forward to opening her up to flank speed and leaving a wake behind him pointing aft at this god-forsaken patch of water he'd spent years of his life operating in. Never got a summer Med cruise, never got a Caribbean swing. Every single deployment of his 18-year career had taken him *here.*

"I hate this fucking place," Albright muttered under his breath, staring ahead into the black night. Again, he rubbed the stubble on his chin.

"Sir?" the OOD inquired.

"What?" Albright answered, surprised he had spoken out loud. "Oh, nothing."

In the pilothouse of the dhow, the master walked to the port bridge wing and stepped outside. He looked down at a cluster of eight speedboats, each crewed by three or four Revolutionary Guard irregulars. The motley fleet of *boghammars,* as they were known to the Americans, consisted of everything from small, open-cockpit cigarette boats to a glorified skiff with an outboard motor. The boats were armed with RPGs, recoilless rifles, and sometimes frame-mounted mortars, with other light infantry weapons aboard. He motioned them to cast off their lines from the dhow and from one another, but warned them to keep close and out of sight of the American frigate. He then went inside and bumped the diesel throttles forward with his open palm. The engines growled deeper as the dhow increased speed on a course to intercept.

"Cap'n, the dhow's pick'n' up speed and appears to be heading southeast."

Albright snapped his head to the port bow. Because the dhow showed only a single light, it was nearly impossible to discern aspect in the darkness. Other lights on the horizon signified strait traffic, but this vessel, instead of falling off to port as per the rules of the road, had increased speed and had set a course to intercept or to cross in front. *Why is this guy screwing with me?* Albright wondered.

"Range to the contact?" Albright barked.

"Five thousand yards, sir. CPA one thousand."

"Increase speed to full," he responded.

"*Increase speed to full,* aye sir. Helm, engine ahead full. Indicate one four two revolutions for 20 knots," the conning officer commanded.

Once the lee helmsman repeated the order, Albright calmly said in the hushed darkness, "Sound general quarters."

"Sound general quarters, aye, sir!" the bosun acknowledged and reached up and hit the Klaxon.

BONG, BONG, BONG, BONG... "General quarters! General quarters! All hands, man your battle stations! Now set Material Condition Zebra throughout the ship!" *BONG, BONG, BONG, BONG...*

The bridge watch could hear the scramble of sailors running to their stations and closing watertight doors and hatches. Like the others, Albright broke out the gas mask stowed under his chair and pulled his socks up over his blue coveralls. All the while, he kept an eye on the dhow. Others in the bridge already had their flash gear and helmets on. Albright smiled at how much faster his people could do it for the real thing vice scheduled exercise. The whine of the LM 2500 gas turbine increased in intensity and permeated the bridge as the ship increased speed.

Albright shouted across the bridge, "Mister Reynolds, keep us outside 10 fathoms, but give me as much room as you can between me and this idiot."

"Aye, aye, Captain!" the OOD responded.

Richard Best was now hugging the southern border of the outbound shipping lane in order to run past this unidentified dhow that was getting dangerously close. Some three miles to starboard was shoal water and Omani territorial waters. Ahead was clear, with radar showing a very large crude carrier making the southbound turn in the lane at eight miles.

"*Range?*" Albright barked the question.

"Twenty-five hundred yards and closing, sir!"

"Five short blasts."

"Five short blasts, aye, sir!"

The ship delivered five blasts from the ship's horn, a deep resonating *hmmm* that carried across the water. The blasts, a message common to mariners, signified danger or disagreement. "Battle stations manned and ready, sir!" the bosun bellowed from his station amidships.

"Very well," the OOD answered.

Just then the phone talker sang out.

"Officer of the Deck, signal bridge lookout reports multiple contacts bearing three-three-zero relative at 2,000 yards. Identified as possible *boghammars,* sir!"

Albright snapped his head to the left and shouted, "Put a light on him! *Now!*"

A few seconds later a searchlight illuminated the water off the port bow, and the watch team saw several small bow waves cutting through the serene water a mile away—and pointed at *Richard Best.*

Boghammars!

"This is the Captain. I have the conn!" Albright shouted for all to hear. "Right standard rudder!"

"Right standard rudder, aye…. Sir, my rudder is right standard. No new course given!"

"Increase your rudder to right full," Albright said in a sharp tone, and grabbed the sound-powered phone. He snarled into the receiver. "We are under attack! Get that helo airborne *right now!*" Turning to his OOD, he added, "Mister Reynolds, give me a course between the sandbar and the coast. I want to scrape these guys off before we reverse to the east." The ship heeled to the left.

"Aye, aye, sir. We're going into Omani waters though," Reynolds replied.

"They'll get over it…*Rudder amidships,* mark your head!"

"Rudder amidships, aye, sir. Sir, my head is one-four-eight!"

"That should work for now, sir," Reynolds chimed in.

"Very well, steady as she goes. *Engine ahead flank,*" Albright added.

As the helmsmen shouted over each other responding to the Captain's orders, the ship's *Seahawk* helicopter, *Talon 42* took off and flew past the port bridge wing. *Finally,* Albright thought.

The bridge was a flurry of activity, with Albright issuing orders to the helm and to his XO in combat concerning weapons status. He also sent a report to the task force commander with a call for assistance. His officers shouted navigation bearings and depth soundings to the team, and lookouts reported range and bearing to the lead *boghammar.* The Iranians were engaged in a tail chase with Albright, who planned to use the sand bar to port to prevent the Iranians from cutting the corner once he turned east. Maybe he could even cause them to run aground in the darkness, despite the fact the shoal was well marked with a light. The lead boats were inside 1,500 yards and gaining as *Richard Best* sped through the water at 27 knots. Albright did the math in his head. They would be in effective RPG range in less than five minutes. The aft lookout had already reported sporadic small-arms fire from two of the boats.

"XO, any guidance from Fifth Fleet?" Albright shouted into the sound-powered phone.

"None yet."

That was all the captain of *Richard Best* needed. He was not going to subject his ship and crew to any more risk from these clear acts of war. "XO, this is the captain. Weapons free on the *boghammars* in trail approximately 1,000 yards."

"Aye, aye, sir," he replied.

Okay, Albright thought. *The wheels are in motion.*

"Sir, we're approaching shoal water in two minutes on this heading. Recommend come left to zero-nine-five."

Just then the CIWS 20mm cannon mounted above the helo hangar sprang to life with a loud guttural *BORRRRRRRPPP* as it targeted the first *boghammar*. Albright shouted over the din. "Mister Reynolds, you have the conn. Take us close aboard the sandbar, but stay outside 10 fathoms!"

"Aye, aye, sir. On the bridge, this is Lieutenant Reynolds and I have the conn. *Belay your reports!*"

Before Albright headed to combat one deck below, he stepped out on the port bridge wing and looked aft, covering his ears at the din. Another angry burst from the CIWS sent a streak of yellow tracers aft. They lit up the back of the ship and appeared to float toward the *boghammars*, almost hovering in space before hitting its target. He observed numerous ricochets and, for a moment, was awestruck at the display. At least one boat was now out of action, but Albright counted muzzle flashes from five or six other boats nearby. The ship heeled to starboard as Reynolds initiated his turn, unmasking the 76mm mount. The gun immediately unleashed a series of deafening metallic *BOOMs*, accompanied by a bright muzzle flash every second as it worked over a target. *Talon 42* got involved as it rained down a sudden band of machine-gun fire on the easternmost boat. Albright had pulled himself away to go below when a splash close aboard surprised him: then another splash slid past him as high as the bridge wing. *This isn't small arms*, he thought, and as he stepped back inside the pilothouse, he heard the lookout report. *"Boghammars* at three-one-zero relative going to three-two-zero. Five hundred yards!"

Recoilless rifle fire tore into *Richard Best's* superstructure and against her bridge windows, causing the watch team to duck down and scramble for cover in order to avoid the shattered glass and flying debris. The .50 cal mount opened up on their swarming attackers, contributing to the confusing racket. The scene became a kaleidoscope of flashing light, screaming and shouting, heat, concussion…and blood. Just as Albright grabbed the sound-powered phone, a tremendous explosion blew through the bridge overhead, knocking everyone down. Once Albright regained his senses, the first thing he saw was an arc of sparks from a severed electrical cable. Then light from a battle lantern allowed him to see that several men were down on the starboard side of the bridge. His OOD Reynolds looked at him from under his helmet in wide-eyed shock. "Are you okay?" Albright shouted.

"Yes, sir!" Reynolds answered, touching his ears to indicate he could not hear Albright well.

"Let's get out of here!" Albright shouted as he picked himself up.

The OOD worked the helm on a course to get them back into open water. The port side of the frigate delivered a broadside of withering fire into the nimble Iranians, even as additional RPGs arced over the ship. Some hit the rigging and sprayed shrapnel on exposed personnel. Three members of the bridge watch team were down, and one wasn't moving. Cries of "Corpsman!" and "Get the Doc!" pierced the air.

The running gun battle lasted 10 minutes before *Richard Best* could speed away from her attackers, re-enter the outbound lane, and turn south. A line of impact marks marred her port side, and some rounds penetrated into the ship, killing one man in a damage control station. One "lucky" RPG found its way into the open helo hangar. Topside personnel took severe casualties, with one lookout and one gunner dead.

The Iranians took heavy losses: Eleven of nineteen *boghammars* were put out of action; few survived the well-aimed 20mm and 76mm fire. The .50 caliber gunners claimed two, and *Talon 42* was a key force multiplier with their 7.62mm gun. Once the Iranian boats had turned around in retreat, *Talon* had also seen mortar positions on the sandbar and silenced them.

Albright walked across the bridge and knelt over the conning officer where she had fallen. He held her cool hand, fighting the urge to recoil at the ghastly scene. She struggled to breathe, her breaths coming in gurgling fits that wracked her small body. Her lower jaw was gone, and her neck and khaki shirt were covered in blood. *What is she? Twenty-two years old?* he thought. A sailor with a battle lantern shined it near her face. Her eyes reacted, following the light, and then settled on her CO. Skin the color of porcelain surrounded her pretty blue eyes, all that was left of her face. Albright held back sobs.

"Molly," he said, just loud enough to be heard over the whine of the engine and the wind whipping through the bridge. She studied him for a moment as her body heaved and struggled. Then she looked ahead…and stopped struggling.

The corpsman began CPR immediately; "One, two, three… C'mon, Ensign O'Hara! *C'mon!* …six, seven… C'mon ma'am! Please don't! *Please!*" With each compression, blood oozed out of an opening in her neck, and Albright placed his hand on the sailor's arm, a signal for him to stop. Tears streaked down the young man's face and his shoulders heaved. He opened his mouth and cried out to anyone who was listening. "She was e-mailing my little sister with tips on baton twirling. *She did that for me.*" Albright put his arm around the young sailor and knew that he, too, would miss the energy Ensign Molly O'Hara had brought to his wardroom.

Looking up to the dark sky, the corpsman wiped away a tear and streaked his face with the blood of an officer, now dead, who had cared about him as a person.

Part III

That he which hath no stomach to this fight,
Let him depart; his passport shall be made,
And crowns for convoy put into his purse;
We would not die in that man's company
That fears his fellowship to die with us.

from Shakespeare's *Henry V*

CHAPTER 47

Wilson stepped into his stateroom and flicked on the overhead light. "Wake up, sunshine, we've got tasking," he said.

His roommate was still under the covers in the top bunk. Groaning, Weed rolled over and said, "What now?"

"The Iranians hit a frigate in Hormuz last night, swarmed 'em with *boghammars*. USS *Richard Best* was transiting alone. Five dead, a bunch wounded."

Pulling himself up on his elbows, Weed looked at his roommate in shock. "*Holy shit!*" and sensing the increased vibration of the ship, asked, "Where are we going?"

"Southwest at 30 knots. Heard something about Masirah. Should be in the vicinity by sundown."

Weed climbed down from his bunk, went to the sink, and drew some water. "Are we meeting in CVIC?" he asked as he opened the medicine cabinet to retrieve his razor.

"Yep, zero-seven-thirty for all strike leads. CAG's kicking it off and Intel's going to give us the run down." Wilson answered as he ripped the Velcro patches off his flight suit and tossed them on his desk.

"And to think I was just getting used to seven-hour hops over Afghanistan with an oh-ridiculous-thirty recovery," Weed deadpanned, applying shaving cream to his cheek. "Oh, well. Care to grab a bowl of fruit loops with me before we join CAG?"

"No thanks, my brother. What time did you get in last night?"

"Zero-three."

For a few moments they were silent, Weed at the sink shaving and Wilson at his desk busy with some routine paperwork. They both thought about the Iranian targets they could be hitting, very soon. Wilson's mind wandered. It was incredible. The Iranians had taken on an American warship with no provocation. Did they want to start World War Three? Surely this was the big news in every capital across the globe. Wilson imagined world leaders calling Washington and imploring the Americans not to send waves of nuclear bombers to obliterate Iran...which Washington could do. *Why do world leaders defend Iran every time*

Iran kills or acts out some way? He further imagined there were some politicians in Washington calling for that. *Tehran, a city of millions—wiped out.* Or would they nuke Bandar Abbas? *Five sailors dead and we are spinning up. Rightfully so! But the frickin' Iranians kill that many soldiers* each week *in Diyala with IEDs and booby traps, and we look the other way.* Wilson wanted revenge, wanted to pop off a nuke and end the nearly 30 years of Iranian-sponsored terror and instability they exported around the world. *We'd be doing the whole world a favor.* He then remembered the Bible verse: *"For the sake of even ten good people, I will not destroy the city."*

Wilson broke the silence. "Gonna be a long day in CVIC."

"Yea, verily."

Thirty minutes later in the Carrier Intel Center, Wilson and Weed sat together in the third row. They waited, with other department heads from the *Buccaneers* and *Spartans*, for CAG Swoboda to address them with the tasking from above. Sitting in front of them were the air wing COs and XOs, and behind were assorted JOs, as well as officers from the flag and air wing staffs. Cajun sat in the front row next to the E-2 skipper, while Saint was at the opposite end of the row chatting up the Big Unit. Before them on the bulkhead were charts depicting Iran, with smaller charts and satellite imagery of the areas around Bandar Abbas, Jask, and Chah Bahar. Across the room the aircrew studied the charts, murmured about threat concentrations, and imprinted the surface-to-air threat rings on their brains. In the corner, Wilson noticed the SINS readout that confirmed the steady vibration of the deck below his feet. *Valley Forge* was on a southwest heading at 30 knots.

"'tenshun on deck!"

Chairs shifted and conversation stopped as the room sprung to attention, eyes locked forward. CAG's purposeful footsteps broke the silence, and halfway into the room, he grunted, "Seats." Everyone relaxed and sat back in their chairs. DCAG followed, and to Wilson it looked as if neither had slept during the night. The bare Velcro of CAG's flight suit, devoid of any patches but ready for imminent combat, was somewhat disconcerting. It indicated a *mindset.* Swoboda's face was set in a taciturn frown as he prepared to address his aircrew. Weed noted it, too, and whispered to his roommate, *"That's a game face."*

Swoboda wasted no time getting started:

"All right. You guys know the Iranians hit *Richard Best* last night as she was transiting Hormuz. Ambushed by a double-pince of *boghammars.* Five dead, seventeen wounded. The ship took heavy damage to the bridge and topside spaces from RPG's and recoilless rifles on the boats and from *mortars* they staged on a sand bar in the narrowest part of the strait. You gotta hand it to them. Although I'm told the ship was alert for trouble and the captain did a great job, the Iranians waited till the last moment to show their hand. Their timing could not have been better. *Richard Best* did good work though…eleven *boghammars* sunk, several damaged and some 30 Iranians dead.

"The Revolutionary Guard conducted this attack. Iran has two navies, the Islamic Republic of Iran Navy and the Revolutionary Guard, or *Pasdaran*. They can work in concert or independently. This appears to be the Revolutionary Guard working solo. Since last night, commercial shipping through the strait has stopped. As a result, oil futures have shot up over thirty dollars per barrel, and the Asian markets are down five percent from their opening yesterday. You've seen CNN. Hormuz is the focus of the world right now as the Iranian action is a clear act of war. In Washington last night, the first question was *"Where's the nearest carrier?"*

Wilson's eyes wandered to the chart of Iran, figuring the distance from Shiraz to Bandar Abbas. *Three hundred miles? Two fifty?*

CAG continued:

"National command authority has tasked NAVCENT with the following objectives: severely degrade Iran's ability to harass shipping in the strait, hit the *Pasdaran* bases of operations, and eliminate the Iranians' *Kilo* subs wherever they are found. Imagery shows one of those subs in dry dock at Bandar Abbas. That's the first one to go away. The others will be found and *sunk*, at their moorings or on the high seas. If the Iranian surface navy stays in port, we'll leave them alone. But, if they come out, they are fair game and we'll put them on the bottom. The friggin' *boghammars* are what we're after, and we're going to hit them in their nests and degrade their ability to operate by destroying their fuel supply or maintenance facilities. Any *boghammar* we find underway? Gone."

The room was silent, every aircrew focused on the air wing commander. He was clearly incensed at the Revolutionary Guard. Behind him, Wilson overheard a shipmate whisper, "CAG's *pissed*." Swoboda pointed to the chart.

"Our tasking is to hit targets in Bandar Abbas, Jask, and Chah Bahar. We will also conduct SUCAPs in the GOO and Hormuz to find any *Pasdaran* or Iranian navy assets underway. The coastal targets will take a couple of nights, and we'll be flying a dozen or so strike packages to accomplish it. The international waters stuff will take as long as it takes, and the priority is to locate and to neutralize the *Kilos*.

"We're going to have help, too. In the Gulf, SEALS are going to raid *Pasdaran* facilities on the Tunb Islands and Kisk. The *Tinian* ARG is coming up from the Horn of Africa with *Harriers* and *Cobras* to augment our SUCAP posture; they should get here by tomorrow. Air Force *Buffs* and B-1's from Diego Garcia will fly with you on several strikes. P-3's out of Masirah, with another four inbound, will help with the ASW picture. AWACS and more are coming. We are also going to have *Tomahawk* shooters from our own strike group and some more TLAM from one of the ARG small boys coming up. We've got lots of assets, and they are at *our disposal*. Right now *we* are the focus of national command authority."

Wilson glanced at Cajun, who remained focused on CAG. As Cajun's assistant strike leader, Wilson wondered what target they would receive, and surmised CAG would assign the skipper a tough one—probably in and around Bandar Abbas.

"Iran isn't a pushover like Iraq was five years ago. *Two hundred and fifty* combat aircraft, many of them fourth-generation, and as we found out last month, *fifth*-generation jets. Double-digit SAMs. Effective triple-A ranging from light to 100 millimeter. Modern, sea-skimming antiship missiles. And hundreds of *boghammars* using swarm tactics. These guys don't have what we have, but they present us with a formidable military problem. They are *smart* and they have *will*. They know we are heading back to the GOO, and they are dispersing their forces and getting their defenses ready. Again, our goal is not to invade Iran or even destroy the Iranian Navy, but to degrade their ability to conduct these raids in and around Hormuz and the GOO. This response option is limited and proportional, and it needs to be timely. That's why we are doing this now, because we don't have time to wait for help, and these guys need to know that we can smack them down with just a portion of the forces we have in theater. We need to make them think twice before they engage in another act of war, against us or anybody.

"Our first strike is tomorrow night in Bandar Abbas, followed by packages going to Jask and Chah Bahar. So as not to tip them off using any land-based activity, these strikes will be Navy and Marine only, from us and *Tinian*, and lots of TLAM in a coordinated manner. This could run just one night, probably two, with the Air Force bombers joining us then."

Wilson studied the known SAM rings along the Iranian coastline, as well as the fighter bases at Bandar Abbas and Chah Bahar, defenses which offered little in the way of sanctuary and reached well into the Gulf of Oman. Coordination, timing, and contingency planning, from launch to recovery, were going to be extensive. His mind raced through what they needed to plan within the next 36 hours: the weapons plan, the launch sequence plan, the tanking plan, the defense suppression plan, the strike plan, and the search and rescue plan. Each had myriad requirements and considerations, and each carried its own set of variables that required detailed answers.

For the air wing strike leaders—senior squadron aircrew such as himself—striking anywhere along this heavily defended coastline would become a monumental challenge of coordination and execution. They had to accomplish the mission and keep losses to an absolute minimum. He knew the air wing would be up all night planning it, and up the following night flying it. *And* the next night, according to CAG. Air Wing Four and *Valley Forge* were up to the task, but CAG was right: by no means would this be *easy*. And by the looks of the huge black circles on the chart that signified the SAM threat rings, it was damn dangerous. CAG finished his message to his aviators.

"Ladies and gentlemen, we have frontline aircraft with *stand-off* weapons, accurate cruise missiles, superior sensors, and state-of-the-art electronic warfare capability—both active and passive. And we have you, the most highly trained and combat-experienced aircrew in the world, all purchased at great expense by our country. We will prevail, but we've gotta be smart and keep mistakes to a minimum. Keep it simple, and maximize the effectiveness of your blows. USS *Richard Best*, our sovereign U.S. territory in the Gulf, was there to defend the economic lifeline of an allied country. While conducting innocent passage through a vital international waterway, she was attacked by the forces of Iran, an attack which killed Americans and has thrown the world into economic turmoil. The Iranians miscalculated, and whether it was on a national or local level doesn't matter. Washington is tasking us with significantly degrading Iran's short-term ability to attack again, and to keep Hormuz open for commerce. Maybe the diplomats will de-escalate this, but you and I are going to be ready to go tomorrow night with fused ordnance on our aircraft and a detailed plan to use it. After the *spy* briefs you on the order of battle, each strike planning team will be assigned a target…and a secondary target for night two, if we get to that. Strike leaders, today at 1500 I want you and your assistant strike leads to brief me or DCAG on your thoughts and plans regarding your primary target. Later tonight, once we approve your choices, you'll visit the admiral's staff and brief him. Just give an overview, and we'll provide any rudder you need at that time. Obviously, this is all classified, and the crew can see we are transiting west at high speed, but we are to discuss this only in cleared spaces—not the wardroom, not in the passageways."

Once CAG finished, the air wing Intel officer provided an order-of-battle briefing, and the aviators listened in tight-lipped silence. Iran possessed the latest in high-tech military equipment, purchased from Russia, China, North Korea and even Europe. And the United States had sold Imperial Iran the F-14 *Tomcat*, which the Islamist regime had used to great success in skirmishes with the Iraqi Air Force during the 1980s. Even the venerable F-4 *Phantom II*, also provided to the Shah by the United States, was a serious airborne threat.

The SAMs were numerous and also modern, led by the Russian-built S-300, and had a range of over 100 miles. The Iranians had lots of tactical SAMs and modern MANPADS, some developed indigenously. While all of *Valley Forge's* fighter aircrew were combat experienced, very few had experience dodging a radar-guided SAM, or even seen one fired in their careers. It was common knowledge that CAG Swoboda and Admiral Smith had seen several of them during Desert Storm, and Wilson knew of Cajun's close encounter with a SA-6 over Kosovo, but that was it. With his talk, the CAG had done his job. Although they already knew the facts, everyone in a flight suit had been reminded that Iran possessed a major league defense. CAG had also reassured them, just by his demeanor, their leadership was not asking them to face anything they had not.

When the meeting broke up, groups of aircrew gathered around the chart and discussed the defenses and targets. Rows of long tables allowed planning teams to pore over the charts and weapons manuals in order to devise the best plan for success. Banks of computer terminals along the bulkheads were manned by JOs inserting target coordinates for closer review. Cajun's eyes met Wilson's, and Wilson walked over to join him.

"Yes, sir."

"Let's you and I look over this folder. It's the first strike—Bandar Abbas. Have the ready room pass the word for our strike planning team to join us here at 0900. Also, *Raven* AOM in the ready room at 1300. No, make it 1230."

"Aye, aye, sir."

"This is a big one," Cajun added as he leafed through the contents of the folder. He then gave Wilson an intense, direct look to ensure his meaning.

"Yes, sir," Wilson responded, expecting nothing less from the man CAG tasked to lead the first strike.

CHAPTER 48

Wilson and his CO reviewed the tasking for Strike 1A: fourteen designated mean points of impact, or DMPIs. The two pilots studied the target imagery, all in and around the harbor area of Bandar Abbas. A nest of *boghammars* along the wharf. A SAM site. A storage and repair facility. The fuel farm. Located at the top of the Strait of Hormuz, Bandar Abbas was essentially surrounded on three sides by land, with the restricted waters of the strait to the south. To the east, on the other side of the city, was an Iranian tactical air base with MiG-29s and F-4s. Assigned time on target was the next night at 2315 local. Coincident with this strike were two smaller strikes down the coast at Jask and Chah Bahar.

Once the strike planning team, consisting of an aircrew from each air wing squadron, got together, Cajun briefed them on the overall plan and assigned various tasks: the launch sequence plan, the electronic warfare plan, the combat search and rescue plan, and the weapons delivery plan. He assigned the last to Wilson. All around them in CVIC were dozens of other aircrew in flight suits, working on their assigned targets, the room an orderly hum of activity.

After about 45 minutes, while the team worked quietly, several of them studying charts, others building the aircraft load out on the computer, Smoke leaned over to Wilson. "Sir, can we talk for a minute outside, please?" Smoke spun to leave before his department head could answer, and Wilson, puzzled, watched him for a few seconds before he got up to follow him, grateful for a break. Cajun and the others continued, lost in their concentration.

Smoke entered the passageway and went forward, and Wilson followed, thinking, *What's this about?* Over his shoulder, Smoke gave him a clue. "We have to go see Psycho," he said, continuing forward toward the stateroom Psycho shared with Olive on the O-2 level.

"What about her?" Wilson asked. "Why doesn't she contact me herself?" Smoke stopped and turned. "She asked me to bring you to her room. You can hear it directly from her, sir."

"Hear what?" Wilson asked, and wondered why Smoke was *sir*-ing him so much. As Smoke left Wilson's question hanging in the air and continued forward, a feeling of dread came over the VFA-64 Operations Officer. *Oh shit*, Wilson thought.

When they arrived at her stateroom, Smoke knocked twice. "Come in," Psycho responded.

Lieutenant Melanie Hinton sat on her bunk in her flight suit, dabbing at her puffy eyes. She came to her feet as Wilson stepped inside. Smoke closed the door behind them.

"Please, be seated," Wilson said to Psycho. "What's goin' on?"

Psycho drew in a breath. "I'm pregnant."

Wilson looked at her and let it sink in. Turning his head to Smoke, he lifted an eyebrow.

"Yes…sir," Smoke nodded.

Wilson took a deep breath and exhaled through his nose.

"I didn't know until today! This morning. I had my flight physical yesterday, and Doc Laskopf called me back in this morning to tell me."

"Who else knows?" Wilson asked.

"Just us," Psycho answered, taking a seat on her bunk.

Wilson needed more. "Who *exactly*?"

"Us and Doc Laskopf," Psycho answered. "I *just* found out an hour ago!" she added, exasperated and looking away.

Wilson continued to pull the string. "Doc, or the corpsman who did the test? They haven't told anyone?"

"Sir, I *pleaded* with Doc not to tell, to let me handle it inside the squadron first. He said he would. I know we are planning to hit Iran tomorrow night, and I want to be a part of it. And you'll need me as a pilot for the flight schedule."

"Why didn't you keep quiet then?"

"Because Zach…Smoke… said I needed to tell you to schedule me in the best manner. But I feel fine! I'm ready to go tomorrow night."

"Morning sickness?"

"No, not counting when I threw up after Doc told me."

Wilson smiled, and then thought for a moment. Pregnancy was a grounding condition. Psycho could not fly anything while pregnant, and the news was a serious blow to his ability to schedule pilots for the upcoming operation. "Smoke is right. You did need to tell me, and you need to tell the Skipper."

"*No!*" Psycho exploded. Looking at Smoke with fire in her eyes, she added, "See, I *told* you this would happen! I could have flown these hops…!"

Wilson cut her off. "Psycho, it's *his* squadron. He makes the call. That's why he's paid the big bucks."

"He's gonna *shit* when he finds out, and he's going to shit on me…and Zach." Psycho was shaking her head. She began to tremble.

"Psycho…"

Seething with rage, Psycho lashed out. *"You don't know what it's like!"* she cried. "I'm a *Hornet* pilot with combat experience, but to the rest of this ship I'm just a piece of ass! Half the guys in the air wing have tried to get in my pants: JOs, *chiefs,* even officers senior to *you.* I'm doing my job and doing it well, but I have to deal with this crap *all the time.* Zach protects me from you guys, and if we've fallen in love and gone too far, then *guilty.* We can *handle* it!"

Smoke, horrified, watched as his department head absorbed the outburst from the petulant junior officer. Wilson glared at Psycho, his blood boiling. The look on her face indicated that she knew she had crossed the line.

Rubbing his hands together in an effort to control himself, Wilson began. "I would tend to accept what you've just told me better if you put a 'sir' on the end of that, *Lieutenant,* and I resent being lumped in as 'you guys.'"

"Yes, sir," she replied, her eyes downcast.

He's going to rip her spine out, Smoke thought to himself, his heart pounding.

"And I would add that, yes, I *do* know what it is like to be judged by appearance, and I do know the resentment that can bring. And I know that I must outperform white officers in every aspect of my job."

"Yes, sir, I'm sorry."

"What separates us, Lieutenant Hinton, is that instead of feeling sorry for myself, because I cannot control the color of my skin or what people *may* think any more than you can control your sex, I channel any resentment I may have into building qualifications and learning more about the airplane and displaying the best officer-like behavior I can for my people. And I've found, over the years, that that behavior leads to success for any officer—no matter the skin color, whether male *or* female. Yes, I must work a bit harder. But I can hack it, and I take great satisfaction in that. And I've been richly rewarded by the great meritocracy of naval aviation."

Psycho, eyes still downcast, answered, "I have to outperform 90 percent of the pilots in the air wing to be taken seriously."

"At this point I'd say a 100 percent! You aren't going to *win this,* Psycho," Wilson replied. Again on the verge of losing his temper, he let his words hang for effect. "In the air and with your ground job, you can outperform all the aviators in the Navy, but if you don't stop the valley girl act in the wardroom—and if you don't stop treating this whole cruise as a high school musical—you *won't* be taken seriously, ever. You are a beautiful woman, a talented aviator, and you, as you say, have half the players in the air wing after you. From what I see, any other woman on this ship, any of them, would love to be you for a day. But the difference is most all of them would eliminate 90 percent of the unwanted attention up front by carrying themselves as *adults*. But here you are expecting me to deal with this for you when you are closer to 30 than 20, face combat tomorrow, and are pregnant with child. Time to grow up!" Wilson saw Psycho's lip quiver.

"Where's your roommate?" Wilson asked, referring to Olive.

"Down in CVIC, strike planning," Psycho replied, eyes still down. She was barely able to keep her composure.

"That's right, where the three of *us* should be right now, instead of dealing with *this*. What I need, and what the skipper needs, is for you, both of you, to be on your game because, for the next 72 hours, we need every ounce of ability from everyone in the squadron." Motioning to Psycho he added, "You represent a significant portion of the combat power of this squadron. Are *you* ready to go? Can *you* compartmentalize?"

Springing to her feet she responded, "Yes, sir!"

"Don't *bullshit* me, Psycho! A few minutes ago you were whining to me about your lot in life!"

"Yes, sir, whatever you need me to do. I can do it. I *can,* sir." Their eyes locked, and Wilson knew she meant it. He turned to Smoke.

"And you?"

"*Yessir,*" Smoke answered, jaw set.

Holding Smoke's gaze, Wilson nodded his understanding, and turned back to Psycho. "Okay. *After* the 1230 AOM, you and I will have a private meeting with the CO. You will tell him the situation, *including* who the father is. I don't know what the Skipper's gonna do, but I'll recommend we fly you because we'll need everyone tomorrow night. If you can convince him that you can compartmentalize this and not cause harm to yourself or others in formation, that would be good. After that, it's *his* call. Copy?"

"Yes, sir," she replied. "I'm ready."

"All right. Let's get back down there and help."

CHAPTER 49

The *Raven* officers took their seats while Cajun stood resolute at the front of the ready room, leaning against the white board tracks with arms folded. The mood of the room was pensive, with all eyes on their commanding officer in anticipation of his message. The 1MC sounded a single *Ding* signifying 1230. Wilson turned in his seat and surveyed the silent room behind him, sensing the eyes shift on him.

"Everyone's here, sir," Sponge Bob said from his duty desk perch.

Wilson turned back to the front, nodded to his CO, and said in a hushed voice, "Skipper," the signal for Cajun to begin. All hands knew that Cajun would be the only one to speak at this AOM.

"If you've watched CNN and Sky News, checked the SINS screen, or been topside and seen the huge wake behind us, you know we're heading west in a hurry. And you don't have to be a pilot who spent the morning in CVIC to know why. Iran attacked one of our small boys last night, killing our sailors. This is an act of war. National Command Authority tasked NAVCENT with a response, and we are now planning to carry out that tasking sometime tomorrow, probably after sundown. We should arrive at our station late this afternoon, and we're gonna fly maintenance test hops and get some air wing guys in night qual. Our SUCAP alert posture begins later this afternoon, and the ordies are loading the jets now.

"We'll be facing the Iranians, who have a modern air force and navy, with sophisticated weapons and a formidable integrated air defense system. They have a history of innovation, and they want to surprise us and *hurt* us, as they did last night, *and* with Prince last month. Remember, he was unarmed and incapacitated when they shot him down with no warning. They should *not* be underestimated, and we have a tough job to suppress their defenses and hit the assigned targets. However, they aren't 10 feet tall, and if anyone should be afraid about any upcoming action, it should be *them*, afraid of what this strike group, and you guys in particular, can do to them. We will prevail, but we have to be smart. *Pilots,* until further notice, your schedule consists of flying, eating, sleeping, and planning. No mindless video games or movies, no division paperwork, no spending hours in the gym. Part of flying consists of briefing and debriefing, and standing watches in CATCC or Pri-Fly."

Cajun pointed to the duty officer, Sponge, and said, "Or this duty here... Want to make sure you frickin' *sea lawyers* don't use my words to get out of it." The comment elicited smirks from the JOs and served to ease some tension.

He continued:

"Ground pounders, we need you guys to run the squadron. If routine paperwork can wait for the department heads or me and the XO to review once this is finished, then let it. Or, if you can handle it at the Assistant Admin or Maintenance Material Control Officer level, then do it. Now, if you deem that there's something I or the XO or the department heads must deal with immediately, bring it to our attention. Whatever call you make will be the right one; I'll support you. Don't worry about how much sleep I get.

"Now Weed here, he's a different story. *I* worry about how much sleep *he* gets." The room snickered, and Wilson heard his roommate chuckle at the needling from the CO. Cajun returned to business.

"We are four months into this deployment. We're experienced operating in this part of the world, we've been in combat in two theaters, we're looking good around the ship, and the jets are flying great. We are on the step.... We are *ready* for this. If we just follow the *basics* of solid preflight planning, comm discipline, section integrity, combat checklists and flying smart tactics with our superior weapons and sensors, we'll do fine. Plan for contingencies. Take a good look at your wingmen's aimpoints, and be ready to flex if you have to. Know the geography. If you are hit and can still fly, get feet wet. If you can't do that, get away from populated areas. If your wingman punches out, mark the position, sing out immediately, identify an on-scene commander and call away the CSAR. Your priorities for ejection are over water followed by any country but Iran, and if you can find a deserted area you may be able to evade before we pick you up. That's what I mean by knowing the geography. Have a plan up front, such as 'Safety is 10 miles east, or west, or whatever.'"

Raven One paced a few steps and exhaled, gathering his thoughts. Wilson and the others remained riveted.

"Once again, our friends and enemies around the world are calling for *us* to restrain ourselves. Europe reminds me of the cowardly lion, and Canada, who we protect like our own country, is AWOL. The GCC sheikdoms are petrified that we'll do something to ruin their holiday plans in Switzerland. Russia warns against American military adventurism, and China denounces our movement as reckless saber-rattling that only increases tensions in the strait. Japan, who gets almost all its oil from the Gulf, and much of that from Iran, is silent. Only Australia has spoken out against the Iranians and is expressing regret at the loss of American lives.

"That's always the case, isn't it? When the victims are American service personnel, at a Khobar Towers or aboard a USS *Cole* or even at the Pentagon, nobody in the international community, including many in our own country, much cares about it except for the fact they can get a few days coverage for their news media. But the world community, with the exception of the North Koreas and Venezuelas, secretly wishes that we *do* respond to the Iranians. They *want* us to swat them down, so they'll stop causing problems. They also know that we will continue to guard against flare ups, and that will allow the world to go back to living what passes for normal.

"Therefore, it has become the responsibility of this strike group, and you and me in particular, to handle this for them, and to do the dirty work. Myself, if I can strike a blow that allows my family and your families and millions of families around the world to live in *real* peace and harmony, I welcome the opportunity. These Revolutionary Guard assholes are causing my wife to worry and my kids to cry—and have been for years. In my small way I want to prevent them from doing so any more. They are smart. We must be smarter. They fight dirty. Within the limits of the rules of engagement, we'll fight dirtier and hit where and when they don't expect. *They shot down our shipmate* experiencing an airborne emergency. For me, this is personal, this is payback, *they* overreached, and any action we take will be proportional and justified and professionally carried out. If Washington decides to throttle this back, then aye, aye, it's their call. But for now, I plan to go up there tomorrow night, and you're coming with me."

Wilson and the others sat in their seats with backs straight, soaking in Cajun's intensity and purpose, ready to burst out of the room and man the jets. The pilots shared his grim determination to prevent the *Pasdaran* from causing any further loss of life or any further disruption of international commerce. With the opportunity the *Richard Best* attack had afforded them, they would literally follow Cajun through fire to do it *now*, despite the fearsome Iranian defenses.

"Anything for me?" Cajun asked, as he met the eyes of each officer in the room. When no one spoke, he said, "Then let's do it. Ready, break," Cajun finished, as he clapped his hands together.

"QUOTH THE RAVEN!" boomed from Ready Seven, rattling the photos on the *Spartan* and *Moonshadow* ready room bulkheads.

Sponge hit play on the stereo and cranked up the volume to George Thorogood's *"Bad to the Bone"* as the pilots broke up into smaller groups. Some headed back to CVIC and others moved to the front to study the Iranian coastline on the pullout chart.

In the midst of the activity Wilson approached Cajun, who was now head down searching for something in his seat storage drawer. "Skipper, can we talk for a moment, in private?"

Cajun looked up and into Wilson's grim face. He noticed that Psycho hovered behind him in an apparent state of distress. Knowing Wilson's request indicated some kind of problem, he stared for a moment at both of them. "Yeah, let's go," he said.

Chapter 50

"Dismissed," Cajun whispered. As she got up to leave, a shaken Psycho glanced at Wilson and stepped outside.

After she closed the door, Cajun gave Wilson a disappointed look. "When did you know this?"

"Four hours ago, sir. I wanted to wait until after the AOM."

"Right before my brief to CAG?"

"It was a trade-off, sir. I made a call."

"What's your recommendation?" Cajun asked, still not convinced.

"Sir, she's five weeks, and says she feels okay. This is combat, and we need her. We don't have enough pilots as it is to cover all the strike packages, SUCAP, and alerts. Recommend a waiver."

"And Doc Laskopf? You think he's going to agree to remain quiet when he sees Psycho on the flight schedule? He works for CAG, too."

"Recommend we ask him for two days, sir. Both of you can tell CAG that you kept it from him because he has more pressing issues now. Just like you asked the ground pounders to handle the routine stuff and leave you out of it during this operation."

"This isn't small stuff."

"No, sir—but in the context of the next 48 hours, it actually is."

They were interrupted by two raps at the door. "Come in," Cajun answered.

XO Patrick entered, and appeared surprised to see Wilson.

"Yeah, what'cha got, Saint?" Cajun was irritable, leaning back in his chair with his hands folded behind his head.

"While in the passageway, I saw Lieutenant Hinton leaving here, so I thought I'd catch you and ask for a quick ruling on AD2 Moran's request for MEDEVAC due to his rotator cuff. He says it hurts, but Doc Laskopf thinks he can handle light duty."

Cajun looked at him for a few moments, and then looked away. He tried and failed to hide his disgust. "Light duty... Is there anyone in the squadron Doc Laskopf hasn't seen today?"

"What do you mean?" Saint replied.

Wilson's heart beat faster. *Don't do it, Skipper!*

"Psycho was just in here. She's med down. Pregnant."

Damn! Wilson thought.

"Are you going to tell CAG? He'll need to know," Saint responded, incredulous.

"No, I'm not. We need her for the flight schedule. We've got 15 pilots, and after they are scheduled for strikes, spares, CAPs and everything else, we're tapped out. She's not bleeding, is in possession of her faculties, and wants to fly. So she's flying. Flip, keep her off the overland stuff—just SUCAP, alerts, Iron Hand escort...relatively easy stuff and away from the threat to the max extent. It's two days; then we can proceed."

Saint protested. "You *can't* do that. It's cut and dried. We have to tell CAG, and..."

"No, we, *don't!*" Cajun shot back, glowering at Saint through clenched teeth. The two commanders locked eyes on each other, refusing to blink, both conscious of the fact their subordinate department head was observing them. Cajun was enraged at having his authority questioned in public. When Saint's countenance remained defiant, Cajun detected what he was thinking and lowered his voice to an icy growl.

"XO, I swear, if you go to CAG, you will *never* command this or any squadron. *Is that clear?*"

"*Yes*, Skipper." Saint's eyes narrowed as he stared at Cajun, and both men breathed deep while Wilson held his breath. This display among seniors was shocking, and, for a moment, Wilson thought Cajun was going to choke the XO.

His hands balled into fists, Cajun continued to fume with rage. "I'll go right to CAG and the Commodore and tell them how you've usurped my authority and suppressed morale in my ready room. *I* am the CO of VFA-64, *not you. I* make policy. *I* decide on waivers. And *I* ground my pilots or *unground* them. *Do you...?*"

Cajun caught himself before he went too far. For a moment he looked for something nearby to throw, but then he slumped in his chair and looked away, face red and muscles taut. During their years together, Wilson had had several opportunities to observe Cajun's volcanic temper, and he now watched as Cajun struggled to keep it in check.

After a few moments Saint spoke. "Will that be all, sir?"

Cajun lifted his head and folded his hands in his lap, eyes again burning into Saint. "*Yes*," he answered. Saint left without making eye contact, closing the door behind him.

The two pilots listened to Saint's footsteps recede down the passageway. "Sorry you had to see that," Cajun said, closing his eyes and rubbing his temple.

"It's okay, sir."

Cajun looked up at Wilson. "Tell Psycho—and Smoke—I need them to get their minds right and I need them to fly. We are in combat. I'll contact Doc Laskopf and ask him to give us 48 hours. He'll work with us. And if those two *can't* get their minds right, then I need to know ASAP. No more secrets."

"Yes, sir," Wilson replied. He noticed a single gray hair in Cajun's moustache.

"Tell her I'll talk to her tonight, after the flag brief."

"Yes, sir. How about *you*, Skipper?"

"I'm fine. Just give me 10 minutes, Flip. I'll meet you in CVIC," Cajun added.

"Take 20, sir. We've got well over an hour before we give CAG our game plan, and it's pretty much set already."

"Roger that. Thanks," Cajun answered, his weary fingers again rubbing his temple.

CHAPTER 51

While the world nervously watched the Strait of Hormuz and wondered if the United States was going to send a nuclear missile into Tehran, Cajun looked at his watch. "Okay, time to go."

He then stood to leave and gathered up all the pages and put them in his strike planning folder while Wilson rolled up the chart of Bandar Abbas. Wilson followed him out of CVIC, where the bright fluorescent lights illuminated the activity of dozens of aviators in various stages of strike planning for *their* assigned targets. Admiral Smith and his staff expected Cajun and CAG Swoboda to brief them in 10 minutes. The so-called "lap-brief" would consist of big-picture items—such as strike composition, other assets assigned, and enemy order of battle—interspersed with myriad details concerning timing, tanking, target area tactics, and of critical importance, the aimpoints for the strike aircraft. CAG had approved Cajun's thumbnail sketch of the plan earlier, which had allowed Cajun and his team to refine the plan and add detail for this brief with the strike group commander.

Cajun and his team had been assigned several aimpoints and a time on target from NAVCENT, with recommended weapons load outs and available intelligence and support assets at his disposal. However, the strike leader had the responsibility to orchestrate the plan and to obtain flag-level validation prior to execution. Cajun left CVIC confident of the plan his team worked on all day. Soon after turning right on the starboard passageway, he and Wilson entered the blue tile area and arrived at CAG's stateroom door. Cajun knocked twice.

"Come in," CAG said from inside.

Cajun opened the door and saw CAG and DCAG sitting at the table. "Ready to go sir?" Cajun asked.

"Yep, let's do it," CAG replied. Both of the seated officers rose to lead the way to the flag briefing spaces, eight frames aft. As the junior in the group, Wilson brought up the rear. In this meeting he would remain silent, but he would watch the proceedings carefully and take detailed notes of any of the admiral's concerns.

CAG led them to the conference table in the empty briefing room. The admiral's chair was at the head of the table, and Cajun staked out a position to its right, with Wilson next to him. CAG and DCAG sat down as their mirror images on the other side of the table.

Soon Captain Swartzmann entered wearing his blue, pullover sweater and carrying his ubiquitous notebook and coffee cup. He was followed by the Air Ops officer in a green flight jacket and another sweatered surface warrior. CAG Swoboda greeted Swartzmann with a cordial *"Gene."* The chief of staff made a face but otherwise ignored him, and Wilson saw that CAG's informal greeting got under Swartzmann's skin. He, no doubt, preferred the formal *Captain Swartzmann* to his given name. Wilson suppressed a grin. Even the heavies found ways to bug each other.

Moments later the admiral arrived wearing his flight jacket and also carrying a cup of coffee. The room came to attention and Smith responded, "Seats. Seats, please." Placing his coffee on the table, he surveyed the room and nodded at each of his air wing guests, greeting them by name and with a smile. "All right, Skipper, you are the first out of the block. What'cha got here?"

"Package 1A, sir, Bandar Abbas," Cajun answered.

"Yeah, yeah…okay, go ahead," Smith said, focused on the imagery slide Cajun placed in front of him.

Cajun began:

"Sir, this package is going after several aimpoints in and around the naval base at Bandar Abbas to interdict *Pasdaran* and Iranian Navy ability to harass shipping in Hormuz. As a premier naval base, you can see it's heavily defended—with long range SAMs here, here, and here and with tactical weapons in and around the harbor areas. These islands in the strait are inhabited with triple-A of all calibers, and we can expect MANPADS everywhere. Bandar Abbas is also a fighter base, and we've imaged *Phantoms, Tomcats,* and MiG's at the airfield. If they come up tomorrow night, we have a dedicated sweep to deal with them. And the strikers will be loaded out to deal with any leakers."

"*Phantoms* and *Tomcats,*" Smith grumbled, shaking his head at the irony his pilots would have to face American-built aircraft.

Cajun described the aimpoints, the weapons load out and the delivery profile for the strike aircraft. Each of the senior officers leaned in to capture his every word and ensure their understanding—and Cajun's complete mastery—of the reason for this strike. Because errant bombs were unacceptable, the strikers needed to be 100 per cent certain of their aimpoints and release parameters.

Smith looked at the satellite imagery, puzzled. "What are these?" he asked.

Cajun looked at the aimpoint. *"Boghammars* in a nest, sir."

"Then what are *these?"* Smith added.

"Dhows, sir, also in a nest." Cajun saw where the admiral was going.

"Well, they look a lot like *boghammars* to me."

"Yes, sir, but the dhows are larger and pretty much uniform. *Boghammars* are smaller and have irregular shapes, as you can see."

"Yeah, I can. But tomorrow night, will one of your tired and stressed JOs, or even you, be able to positively ID it on a targeting FLIR before you release? We can't have the media bastards beat us over the head because we blew some fishing boats out of the water."

Wilson noticed that Swartzmann gave Cajun a sanctimonious look, and CAG did not appear to want to help in this situation. Wilson's CO was on his own.

Cajun frowned at the imagery photo and looked up at Smith. "Sir, I can't *guarantee* you the strikers, or even myself, can discern a dhow or a *boghammar* in every instance, but we can put a bomb in the middle of any nest along that wharf. The target is *boghammars,* but if a dhow is in among them, then they picked the wrong night to go alongside. They used dhows in the *Richard Best* operation."

"That's another question," Smith added. "What if there's nothing there? How old is this imagery? Hell, it doesn't matter. It could have been taken today, and it wouldn't matter. The Revolutionary Guard can move these boats in hours…less."

Wilson watched as Swartzmann's eyes burned holes into Cajun, then shifted to Wilson, who held his gaze for a moment. *Screw you, sir*, he thought, and returned his attention to the admiral.

Cajun didn't flinch. "Yes, sir, and the answer is a radar-to-FLIR-to-visual delivery. We can see on the radar if anything is along the wharf, sweeten it on the FLIR, and then roll in visually on goggles to refine the aimpoints. Wherever they moor these guys, we can hit them. And if nobody is home, we have alternate targets. There's a boat crane here and a gasoline pipeline pump here connected to the fuel tank that services everything on the wharf."

Smith studied the targets again. Bandar Abbas was a tough nut, and his A-team had to get in there. With an element of surprise, and led by Cajun Lassiter, they could suppress the defenses *and* take a toll on the *Pasdaran* before they could even react. Follow-on strikes along the coast would attrite *Pasdaran* assets to prevent further raids in Hormuz, of that he was certain, but could they destroy *boghammars* in numbers? *Damn things could hide in every cove and along every breakwater, or in some shack along the beach.*

Smith motioned for Cajun to continue and followed him through discussions of the expected weather, DMPIs, contingencies, show stoppers, command and control nets, rules of engagement…. The list was exhaustive, and Smith let him move along, knowing they could anchor down on any of these subjects—and be here all night discussing the nuances and contingencies. *Damned media!* Smith surmised the Iranians could blow up a dozen of their dhows anywhere and blame America. He knew CNN and the BBC would run with it without questioning the source. Smith looked at the threat rings: big and lethal. *How many of my aircraft and aviators will I lose?*

"Any questions, sir?" Cajun was finished. Jolted from his daydream, Smith rapped his pen on the table and spoke in his low baritone.

"Skipper, I'm confident in your plan and in your ability to lead this strike. But go back and take a look at the suppression plan. If you need more assets, ask. Much can still be done in the next 24 hours. This is the first strike, and it needs to be effective. We all want to provide you with what you need."

"Yes, sir, Admiral. We'll give it another look with that in mind. Thank you," Cajun replied.

"How about you, Flip?" Smith changed the subject with his wry smile. "Ready to meet up with that MiG-35 again?"

Sensing the approving nods from all but Swartzmann, Wilson answered with a confident smile of his own. "I'll be armed this time, sir. Let's do it."

The admiral's word touched a nerve; tomorrow night he would be shot off the bow with a full load of ordnance. Headed for Iran.

Smith smiled, his eyes lingering on Wilson for a second. Turning his head to CAG, he then signaled the meeting was over. "Okay, guys, thanks for coming. Press on."

Cajun and Wilson took their cue and left, but CAG stayed behind. Smith caught his eye. "Whada'ya think, Tony?"

Swoboda answered with assurance. "Sir, Cajun has a sixth sense tactically, and Flip Wilson is the finest pilot in the wing. They are my go-to warfighters. They'll get everyone in and out and bring back video of their hits. Color these aimpoints gone."

Smith nodded, and looked up to see that the next strike leader had arrived for his lap brief. *CAG's right,* he thought. *Package 1A will deliver the initial hammer blow we need to set these guys back on their heels.*

CHAPTER 52

Back in CVIC, surrounded by his strike planning team poring over charts and entering info into the computer for kneeboard cards, Wilson looked at his watch. Almost 2200…14 hours since CAG had gathered them there. Psycho's announcement, Cajun's pep talk, the scene with the XO, briefing Admiral Smith. It all seemed like days ago. Wilson rubbed the stubble on his face, then reached over his shoulder to massage the kink out of his neck. Two more hours…then sleep. He thought of tomorrow night—24 hours until launch.

Thinking out loud and hoping for guidance, Dutch worked on the tanking plan. "If we join up overhead in high holding, it's easier, but we may tip off the Iranians if we break the radar horizon. If we join up on a radial toward Bandar Abbas, we can save transit time and gas."

One of the *Moonshadow* captains countered. "What if that radial is clobbered by the marshal stack?"

Wilson turned to join the conversation. "I'm not sure we'll have an event up when we launch. If we can get away with joining low the guys on the beach won't see us until we climb up, giving us time to close the target. Anyway, let's check with Strike Ops on the schedule.

"JD, how about it?" Wilson asked one of the marines at the table.

Just then the 1MC sounded a whistling *taa-weet,* followed by the bosun's message: "Now stand by for the evening prayer."

Dutch, oblivious to the 1MC announcement, continued. "We have two packages of aircraft, the strikers and…"

With his head down and straining to listen, Wilson raised a hand to stop the conversation. Dutch and the others looked at him, and then bowed their heads when they realized what he meant. While much of the room continued to work, Wilson and his team listened to Chaplain Dolan's prayer. His familiar voice was rich and soothing.

"*Heavenly Father, as this day comes to an end, we, Your servants, thank You for our many blessings: a letter or e-mail from home, the friendship of shipmates, a kind word from a superior, a moment of solitude, good food to eat, and a warm bed. Lord, many of us are busy with the serious tasks our nation has assigned us. We ask You to give us strength as we prepare for the challenges of tomorrow and each day, so that each of us may better serve You and one another. In Your name we pray. Amen."*

Wilson reflected on Father Dolan's words. With day-to-day duties and distractions, Wilson often forgot that, in this life, we are here to serve one another. Caught up as they were with whatever duty was assigned and their own self-important roles in it, the need to fulfill that obligation was regularly lost on Wilson and many of the 5,000 sailors aboard *Valley Forge.*

The evening prayer complete, the conversation about the tanking plan resumed where it left off. A few minutes later, the 1MC sounded four bells, followed by an announcement: "Taps, taps. Lights out. Maintain silence about the decks. Now taps."

For the most part, activity throughout the ship continued unabated, especially in CVIC. Wilson continued his study of the chart, the bells serving as another reminder that time was passing quickly.

Cajun leaned back in his chair and stifled a big yawn. As he stretched one arm behind his head, he looked at the bulkhead clock: 0115. His strike planning team was exhausted. After considering and answering hundreds of variables, they had produced a PowerPoint briefing and kneeboard cards for strike 1A. Although it seemed they had reached the point of diminishing returns over an hour ago, five of his team were still at work. The remnants of several other planning teams were scattered about, but they also looked as if they were going to soon call it a night.

Cajun then spoke up, stifling another yawn.

"Guys, let's knock this off for now and hit the rack. How about we meet tomorrow—today—at 1400 and wrap up the kneeboard packages and briefing slides? We're looking to brief at 1900 in Ready 7."

The team responded with enthusiastic *yes sir's* all around, gathered their planning materials, and put them in folders to be placed in the safe by the intelligence officers. Wilson was more than ready to shut down for the night. He gave his CO a casual "See you tomorrow, Skipper," and departed CVIC.

The darkened passageways were illuminated by red lights. Exhausted, Wilson made his way forward toward his stateroom, pushing off a bulkhead at one point to steady himself. Many frames forward he saw the shadow of a sailor walking aft toward him, then disappearing as he turned into a starboard passageway. He heard the engine of an FA-18 howling one level above on the flight deck; apparently, night-check maintenance was doing a high-power turn to check some component. *Valley Forge* never slept completely, but most of the crew was asleep now, and Wilson's body craved it.

He trundled down the ladder and aft, shielding his eyes from an area of bright fluorescent lights. Entering officer's country, he navigated the dim maze to his stateroom on autopilot. Opening the door, he switched on his desk light to minimize the disturbance to Weed, asleep in his rack. Or so he thought.

"Hey, you guys done?" Weed mumbled. Facing the bulkhead, he was a motionless lump in the top bunk.

"Nah, still have some element brief stuff…kneeboard cards. How about you?" Wilson replied, unfastening the laces on his boots.

"Pretty much the same."

Wilson was wiped out, and neither pilot was in the mood to talk. He removed his boots, hung his flight suit on a hook, and crawled into bed, pulling the covers up around him. *Rest, finally. What a day!* The news about *Richard Best.* Psycho. Strike planning all day and night. *Hitting Iran tomorrow. No, tonight!*

Wilson put all of it out of his mind. He had to sleep, knowing it would be the only uninterrupted rest he got in the next 36-48 hours.

"G'night, man," he mumbled to his roommate.

"G'night."

Wilson woke and looked at the numerals of the LCD clock: 4:30. *Oh-ridiculous thirty.* He had been asleep only three hours and had popped awake now because of adrenaline and stress. *Calm down,* he thought. *Go back to sleep.*

Over the next hour, Wilson tried to sleep, but he couldn't shake the image of a *Hornet* in formation next to him, ghostly green under the illumination of night vision goggles. The cultural lighting of Bandar Abbas slid closer and soon the AAA appeared as a reverse waterfall of small lights rising into the air in a graceful arc. The heavier stuff followed, which to Wilson looked like flashbulbs popping in a cluster. It seemed much closer when viewed through the NVG light intensifiers.

Wilson marveled at the serene background of aerial combat. It was for the most part silent. He recalled how, in 2003, the armada of American and Brit aircraft had approached Baghdad in waves. The floating waves of aluminum pummeled the Iraqi capital with precise violence while the defenders fired barrage AAA into the air in a desperate attempt to hit something, anything… but still unsuccessful after 12 years of trying since the truce in 1991. He remembered the muffled flashes as *Tomahawks* hit their targets around the brightly lit city from many miles away. He also watched the tentacles of AAA rising into the air like fingers of a rotating hand looking for something to grasp. The sight was fascinating to watch, and both the *beauty* of the light show and the *silence* of the scene held him spellbound as he approached the target at transonic speeds. His only interruption might be a terse *"Ramrods check right twenty"* from an element leader on the strike common frequency. Dozens of aircrew experienced this incongruity from inside their warm cocoons, the rumble of the engines behind them and the hum of the cockpit their only company, as they are drawn by their mission plan into this hornet's nest of defenses. In contrast, it must have been hellish on the ground as numerous AAA pieces fired their ear-splitting staccato bursts into the air, frantic crews reloaded, and soldiers shouted angry orders or cried out in fear. It was not silence that permeated the background of these scenes but the haunting sounds of air raid sirens and the thumps and booms of ordnance hitting its targets.

Would it be like that over Bandar Abbas? *Probably so, and worse,* Wilson surmised. Would he be able to pick up a SAM amid all the cultural lighting? Would the Iranian gunners be better than their Arab counterparts? Was there a lucky BB up there with his name on it? He thought of Hariri. Would he, or other pilots in MiG-35s, rise up to meet him? As the fear built up inside, Wilson focused on the rise and fall of his chest in an effort to control his breathing. *Please God, let us all come back.*

He looked at the clock: 5:40. *Damn.* He needed to sleep but was wide awake. He thought about checking the computer to see if Mary had sent anything during the night but decided against it. He needed to stay here and get rest.

Weed stirred above him, and Wilson heard him mutter under his breath. "Fuck."

"Can't sleep either?" Wilson asked.

Weed rolled over and exhaled. "No."

"Where are you going tonight?"

"Jask—Skipper Sanderson is leading it," Weed answered, referring to the *Spartan* CO. "You guys going to Bandar Abbas?"

"Yep."

Lost in their thoughts and fears, they didn't speak for a while. They knew they were the finest tactical aviators flying the finest aircraft with the finest weapons in the world—their "blade" honed sharp during months of combat in *Iraqi Freedom* and *Enduring Freedom*— but they also knew the Iranians were *serious* opponents. Wilson recalled the Skipper's words: While the Iranians were not their equal in the air, they definitely had a way of hurting Americans in the past.

"You afraid?" Weed asked in the darkness.

Wilson contemplated the question as he continued to stare ahead into the shadows of the frame of his roommate's rack. He admitted to himself he was afraid of dying and of getting himself captured, but he was even more afraid of hitting the wrong target or making a mistake in the planning that could render strike 1A unsuccessful. While confident of his ability and training, he was not infallible. What was he missing? Why the anxiety? Did he and the others have to be *perfect*? Was it Hariri?

"Yeah. But I'm ready to go up there and strike those dickheads. If not now, when? If not me, who?"

Silence returned to the stateroom, both men still thinking about what the next 24 hours would bring. Wilson returned the question. "How 'bout you? Ready to go, big guy?"

"Yeah, I'm ready. Just apprehensive, like the night before the high school district championship game. And I'm not sure how this story ends, either. Do we knock this off after a few nights? Do the Iranians escalate? What happens to traffic in Hormuz, oil prices, all that?"

"So, you're worried about your portfolio?" joked Wilson.

"You know, we've been in combat every cruise since we were nuggets in the 90s. Yet it gets harder, not easier. Like night traps. Guess a little apprehension comes with age."

"Yeah. Sometimes I think about the World War II guys. They flew out hundreds of miles from their ship using heading, airspeed, and time on a damn *plotting board* to fight their way through the Zeros and roll in on a carrier in a near vertical dive. Imagine diving into that ring of fire, every gun on the ship pointing at you. Then they had to use dead reckoning to get themselves back to their ship. Or the Vietnam guys—*two or three times a day*—dodging SAMs and going to the merge with MiGs that could out-turn them. We won't have to face what they faced."

Weed grunted. "Um, hmm. Yeah, we *are* fortunate. You know, I hate it when you're right and make me feel like shit."

Wilson chuckled, but knew they needed sleep. "Let's sleep 'til 10, get cleaned up, get some food, and press on."

"Sounds like a plan," Weed replied, and they both rolled over and closed their eyes in an effort to will themselves to sleep.

After several minutes four bells sounded over the 1MC: "Reveille, reveille, all hands heave to and trice up. The smoking lamp is lighted in all designated spaces. *Now reveille.*" Wilson pulled the covers up to shield his eyes from the white light that, when switched on in the passageway, leaked under the door. Aboard *Valley Forge* a new day was beginning. He thought about the time: 0600. Sixteen hours to go.

CHAPTER 53

While her department heads conversed in their racks, Olive, 40 frames aft, had no one to talk to.

Unable to sleep, she had pulled herself into a fetal position and wrapped her arms around her long legs. She figured other Air Wing Four aviators were struggling for sleep, but the reality of this night had hit her in the deep recesses of her mind.

Tonight, as a senior JO, she would be flying on Cajun's wing in the first strike going against an alerted and capable enemy. *Combat.* This was not an Iraqi close-air-support bomb toss. Tonight they would face SAMs and AAA, and maybe even Iranian fighters. *Downtown* Bandar Abbas with multicolored and interlocking threat rings. She knew their defenses would be effective. Determined. And only hours away.

Like everyone else, she had long ago come to grips with the knowledge that death could come any day with no warning. A routine cat shot suddenly transformed into a crash. A shipboard fire. An unexpected and lethal jet of scalding water in the shower. Electrocution. The list was almost endless both aboard ship and in the air, and the fact that it hardly ever occurred was little solace. Sometimes it *did* occur, and putting oneself over Bandar Abbas tonight raised the odds significantly.

As a warrior she would go. There was no doubt of that.

Her worst nightmare was capture, which would soon be followed by rape. Repeated and vicious. And, if there were a captured American male in the next cell to hear her screams, the enemy would continue the brutality to get *him* to talk. She would be alone, and she would be singled out night after night. While she had long realized and accepted that fearful reality, it was now a much greater possibility…a possibility she may have to experience within the next 24 hours.

Compared to rape, death—fast and painless in an exploding *Hornet*—would be welcome. But what if she were conscious in a spinning, burning jet? Would she pull the handle, be it consciously or reflexively, at the chance to live? Even if that meant consigning herself to the living hell that would await her in captivity? She shuddered when she realized that, yes, she would.

Olive knew all about loneliness, but she had never felt more alone than she did at that moment. Twenty-eight years old. Had any man, even her father, ever loved her? Olive's only sexual experience had come two weeks before she entered the academy, and the boy's drunken premature finish had left her ashamed and confused. That was it? Where were the supposed fireworks? There were certainly no bells or singing birds. She didn't even remember his name anymore, and she knew he had forgotten hers within days.

The only real remnant of the experience was anger...which revealed itself in her cold and always professional demeanor. Both her anger and her loneliness had become a burden. When was the last time she had laughed as a carefree girl?

During the past 10 years, as she had entered adulthood and become a capable woman, Olive had been *surrounded* by men in this testosterone-drenched, male-dominated culture. Many were still *boys*, for sure, but they were technically men. Legal, adult men who could pursue Olive if they wanted—but chose not to. Who was she kidding? Even the "boyfriends" of her youth had taken her on a few unexciting dates before they moved on. Her athletic body and mysterious way had gained their initial interest, but they dropped her with no explanation.

In the darkness, she felt her face, felt the skin around her jawline. The only fat on her body was *right there*. With her fingers, she measured the close distance between her dark eyes, touched the high forehead, glided over the acne scars, felt the coarse hair. She had followed this routine every time she had moments like this—ever since she was in seventh grade. That was when the image of Camille's disappointed and disapproving expression was seared into her memory. Her mother had touched Olive's face in the same way, and then with hands on hips, said to her the words that had set the course of her life: *"How did I end up with a plain Jane like you?"*

Not now! Olive thought as she rolled over and hugged her pillow. She fought mentally to keep her finely constructed emotional barriers from sagging under the stress of impending combat. Her thoughts, though, soon turned dark again.

As a student of history, she knew that on the eve of combat men of every culture traditionally found women—*any* women they could find—and deposited their seed in an instinctive human desire to spread their genes and leave as many offspring as they could before they died. Doughboys on their way to the trenches of France. Bomber crews out in London before a mission. Japanese soldiers with "comfort women" sex slaves before their banzai charges. The examples were many over the millennia. Men could find a woman for release, could spread their genes, and it was all accepted.

But a female warrior on the frontline was relatively new to human history. And, as a woman, Olive had to be selective. Sure, she could remove her clothes and get any number of sailors within a thousand feet to screw her in a fan room or dark alcove, right now or practically anytime she wanted. The problem was she had to carry *his* genes with hers, and she had to deliver and care for a child—forever. Her instinctive need for love included a need for a strong father to support a baby, and that could not be met unless a man was committed to her and *loved* her. For Kristin Teel, that was not going to happen tonight. No one had ever offered.

Resentment began to build when she realized that Psycho, sleeping so peacefully above her, *did* have all this. The thick, silky hair, the high cheekbones, the blue eyes, the creamy skin, the fun personality—and a killer body. And inside that killer body was a growing baby, *Smoke's* baby, spreading *his* genes, a fact that would keep Psycho from the heavy overland stuff tonight. While Olive was risking everything over the Bandar Abbas meat grinder, "poor Psycho" would be flying quick-reaction surface combat air patrol high over the North Arabian Sea with a near-zero threat. She would then go back home for maternity leave with her Air Medal while baby-daddy Smoke passed out cigars. Later they would get to move into the house with the picket fence.

Olive suddenly hated Psycho, her admiral father, Smoke, and the whole Navy. Psycho was just like the rest of the party girls in high school and at Bancroft Hall in Annapolis. They were loyal to Olive—until their guys came by and picked them up. She thought of the dozen bridesmaid dresses she had worn to their weddings.

Bitches.

Stop this! Olive hissed into her pillow. When Psycho stirred above her, she froze. After a moment, though, Psycho settled back down into silence, sleeping as peacefully and as carefree as a *Hornet* pilot could be on the eve of combat—and loved by a man.

Olive rarely allowed herself to wallow in this much self-pity. She resolved that the timing of this episode would not deter her from walking to the jet tonight. She would launch, fly into the maw of Bandar Abbas, and deliver her JDAM with cold precision. Lieutenant Teel didn't need either a baby or a man. Or want one. Maybe she never would.

Maybe she would.

CHAPTER 54

Wilson and Weed awoke midmorning and were among the first in line for lunch. They joined most of the Carrier Air Wing Four aircrew, many of whom they recognized from the previous long day's planning in CVIC. The mood was quiet, if not a little tense. Most of the aviators were still tired after a fitful night's sleep, and each one was preoccupied with thoughts of the Iranian coast. Wilson remembered a similar feeling just before launch time on the first night of *Iraqi Freedom*, and all the aircrew knew that tonight would be much hotter than "routine" patrols over Iraq. After lunch, the aircrew spent time checking gear and studying their procedures. Many of them also tried to catch a few moments to write a note home, some writing "the letter" to their families in case they did not return. Wilson already had such a letter for Mary stashed in his desk drawer in a sealed envelope.

Wilson was always amused, if not a little put off, by the disposition of the sailors before major combat. To the majority of them, many of them teenagers, it was just another day at sea. Their major goal, from the time they rolled out of the rack, was to survive the day, mentally if not physically. They thought of the pilots as the guys who flew the planes over the horizon and returned hours later. Who knew what they did, and if knowing was not going to make the job any easier, then who cared? Over four months into the deployment, fatigue and tension wore on everyone, and sailors bore the brunt of it.

While the aviators were well aware of the historic significance and geopolitical consequences of the missions they flew, the sailors, for the most part, were oblivious. Wilson smiled at the idea that, despite what they may think, the aviators were not the center of the universe to thousands of kids just trying to make it through the regimentation of another day at sea. The young sailors were proud of their roles and welcomed opportunities to learn more about the aviators' missions, but not all of their leaders took the time to visit them in their shops and explain. Time, after all, was a precious commodity at sea for everybody.

For Wilson and his team the afternoon went fast as they folded updates on the tactical situation, the weather, and expected ship's position into the strike plan. When Wilson joined Olive and Dutch afterwards for dinner, he sensed the disposition of the air wing had picked up and ranged from quiet confidence to eager anticipation. Wilson was familiar with those feelings, too. *Let's get this show on the road.*

After he finished dinner, Wilson went below, for no particular reason other than he wanted to be alone for a few moments. He stepped inside his stateroom and flicked on his desk lamp.

He looked at Mary's framed picture on his desk, his favorite of her at the strike fighter ball. She had looked stunning that night. He leaned in toward her image and stared at her beauty, drinking her in, trying to seek comfort.

Wilson fought against the empty feeling in his stomach, the foreboding tension always felt prior to combat in a high-threat environment. *What will Iran throw at us? What are they preparing up there?* He answered his own question. *Bandar Abbas is going to be hot. Compartmentalize, dammit!*

Wilson stood to head aft to the ready room for the Skipper's strike brief, but paused to pray instead. Holding his folded hands against his chin, he closed his eyes and whispered, *"Please, God, bring us all back. Let us do well. Give us strength. And your will be done, not ours."*

Before he flicked off the light, Wilson took another long look at Mary's photo, and said, "I'll come back to you, baby." He glanced at his watch: four-and-a-half hours until launch.

On a whim, Wilson decided to take the long way to the ready room—via the hangar bay. Sunset was in 15 minutes, and sunsets on the open ocean were often breathtaking in their beauty. Going this way he could look out to the horizon through the open elevator doors.

He walked aft, through a hatch, and down two ladders to the hangar bay. Winding his way through the parked yellow tractors, drop tanks on dollies, hydraulic jacks and various other pieces of hangar bay equipment, Wilson walked past a *Raven* aircraft, *401*. Wearing a respirator, a young, female petty officer maneuvered an orbital sander on a piece of wing in preparation for some routine touch-up paint. He looked at the name on the cockpit:

CDR STEVE LASSITER
CAJUN

Wilson realized the skipper wasn't going to be flying "his" aircraft that night. While *401* had a reputation as a solid flyer, maintenance would put Cajun, and the rest of the pilots, in full mission-ready aircraft, right now being loaded and fueled topside.

Wilson walked under a *Prowler* tail and over to the Elevator 1 opening. The sea was a deep blue, and where it met the sky, he saw the white superstructure of a tanker, brilliant from the reflected sunlight, peeking over the horizon. Realizing the carrier was pointing north, he scanned for other ships and noted another tanker, this one less than 10 miles away, and heading east. Several miles away to the southeast, he recognized the familiar outline of a guided missile destroyer in escort, paralleling the carrier's course. Further east, dramatic cumulus buildups, illuminated by sunlight, formed a sharp line in the sky, all the way to the horizon. Great visibility.

Wilson savored moments like this, alone with his thoughts in the vastness of the Indian Ocean. But he couldn't help thinking of what was in store after the sun set: the tension of the man-up, taxiing among dozens of loaded strike aircraft, joining up in the darkness and pushing toward Bandar Abbas, the radar cursor sweeping like a metronome as it searched for contacts, with terse, clipped radio transmissions interrupting the electronic hum of the cockpit. *SAMs.* They would see SAMs tonight, probably in numbers. Wilson imagined his RWR lighting up, accompanied by loud *deedles* in the headset, if his aircraft were caught in the electronic snare of a missile-tracking radar. His head would snap in the direction of arrival in a frantic search to pick it up visually and maneuver to defeat it. Known AAA sites surrounded the target area. It was also likely the American formations would be ragged and confused once they reached the release points. He visualized more arcs of AAA rising up to meet them, giant rapiers swinging through a swarm of bees in a desperate effort to hit one, just one. Would it be him?

And MiGs. Would the Iranians launch their fighters tonight? All of the fighter aircrew actually welcomed a fight, and prayed for the chance to down a MiG or *Tomcat* or *Phantom.* So did Wilson, but in the back of his mind, he knew more than the others how formidable the MiG-35 could be: invisible to radar, possessing an incredible thrust-to-weight ratio, slow-speed maneuverability. He wondered if the IRIAF would deploy them down here? *What is Hariri thinking right now?*

Enough! Wilson scolded himself, still trying to scan the horizon out to 1,000 miles. He was the operations officer in a deployed *Hornet* squadron and a TOP-GUN instructor with as much green ink as anyone in the air wing. *You can do this*, he thought. *If anything, it should be the* Iranians *who are worried right now, knowing we are just over the horizon.* And if there was a golden BB out there for him, then so be it. He could not be more prepared for this moment.

Wilson said another prayer. *God, please take this anxiety from my shoulders. Please allow me to do Your will now and always. And please bring us all back. Your will be done. Amen.*

The apprehension left him at once, replaced by quiet confidence and assurance. There was no need to dread this mission; he would prosecute the assigned targets with aggressive energy. He was ready.

Wilson ambled along the length of the hangar bay and took in the scene: sailors and marines working on airplanes, yellow shirt directors talking in a group by Elevator 2, two young sailors in dungarees walking forward and nodding to him with respect as they would on any other day. Yep, to most everyone aboard, this was just another late afternoon at sea.

Hoping to view the sunset through the Elevator 4 opening, Wilson continued aft through the jumble of parked aircraft, each separated by mere inches from its neighbor. The tight spacing sometimes required him to lower his head or contort his body to squeeze past. Coming around the tail of an S-3, Wilson froze. Ahead of him, about 20 yards away, he saw a lone aviator in a flight suit. Standing motionless at the edge of El 4 and looking out to sea, with arms folded, was his CO...Cajun Lassiter.

He did not want to disturb Cajun, but decided to observe him for a few moments. Redness from the sunset reflected off Cajun's pensive face as he looked to the west, eyes squinting from the light. Wilson walked to the starboard side of the bay well behind Cajun, who was now silhouetted against the radiant setting of a red sun over a gray mountain range of clouds. Beautiful streaks of light broke through the clouds and illuminated distant patches of ocean. Though Wilson rejected an impulse to join Cajun—because he especially wanted to stay and take in the beautiful scene—Wilson realized that he himself could be discovered. Knowing Cajun would be embarrassed if caught in a quiet moment, even by Wilson, he headed aft to a starboard-side hatch by the jet shop. Wilson had to stop, though, to take one more look at the *Raven* skipper—who remained a statue—before he proceeded to the ready room where Cajun himself would arrive shortly.

CHAPTER 55

Ready Seven was standing room only as the aircrew assigned to strike package 1A met to brief. The aviators, most from other air wing squadrons, studied a stapled "kneeboard package" of briefing cards that contained the aircraft lineup, frequency plan, navigation plan, drawings of target area tactics and aimpoint photos. Some talked among themselves as they sat in the high-backed chairs. Others clicked open their ballpoint pens to write notes in the margins.

Cajun stood at the front of the room with a projector screen behind him. He looked at the clock: one minute to go.

"A'tenshun on *deck!*" one of the lieutenants sang out, and all rose as CAG Swoboda entered from the back.

"Seats," said CAG as he strode to the front of the ready room, nodded a greeting to Cajun, and took his seat in the front row next to Wilson. Cajun handed Swoboda a kneeboard package and asked the room if anyone else needed one. With 20 seconds to go, he reminded all to synchronize watches with the SINS clock.

At 1900, six bells sounded over the 1MC, and Cajun began:

"CAG, welcome to strike 1A, a strike designed to degrade and attrite the IRGC maritime forces in support of national tasking. We've got two groups of strikers—accompanied by dedicated sweep, defense suppression and jamming packages—going into Bandar Abbas. Launch time is 2200. We'll tank overhead from two dedicated *Redeyes.* We will push out along this route, with my flight, *Hammer* one-one, in the lead." As Cajun spoke, Dutch advanced slides on the projector. The "snapshots" of key events during the strike gave the aircrew a sense of the plan.

After the overview, Cajun turned the brief over to the Aerographer's Mate from the ship's meteorology office for the weather forecast. The clear weather Wilson had seen from the hangar bay was to hold, with probable low-scattered clouds in the vicinity of Hormuz, and a partial moon rising just before recovery time. Next, the Intel officer, the *spy*, gave the rundown on the Iranian order of battle. It appeared the MiG-35s could not be found in Shiraz and may have been dispersed nearby. Wilson again thought of Hariri. *Those eyes.*

Once the spy finished, Cajun resumed his brief and, for the next hour, led the aviators through the step-by-step details of the roll call, the launch sequence plan, the tanking plan, navigation, target area formations, off target egress and return-to-force procedures. And contingencies: dozens of them from unexpected weather conditions to communication backups, from search and rescue procedures for a down plane to go/no-go criteria. Cajun reinforced the "snapshots" from earlier so each aircrew would have a good idea of where their formation was supposed to be at a given time and in relation to the others. The cadence of the brief was familiar to the aviators and offered no surprises. They had practiced power-projection strikes many times during stateside work-up training off the Virginia Capes, and after months of flying from the ship, things like in-flight refueling, formations, and weapons carriage were easy. Even night operations around the ship, which were particularly dangerous, were also routine. However, a large power-projection strike package into a well-defended target area was *not* routine, and the aviators paid close attention as Cajun led them through the actions to take if they confronted their worst nightmares. After answering a few questions, Cajun offered CAG a chance to address the group.

CAG Swoboda stood and turned to the group.

"Skipper, good brief, thanks. Ladies and gentlemen, Bandar Abbas is the first of several heavily defended targets we're going to hit tonight along the Iranian coast, and because it's the *Pasdaran* HQ, we want to ensure we hit hard and with precision. Any element of surprise will be expended on this strike. We've got a smart suppression plan with exposed DMPIs and standoff precision weapons. In your element brief, talk contingencies: your backup delivery, comm degrades, the jamming plan if you get a pop-up emitter you didn't expect. We have to do some serious damage on this strike because the others build on it. So, continue to brief it in detail, fly the brief, and use those blocking and tackling skills we've practiced all cruise. Fly solid formations, know and use the code words, do combat checklists early and double check 'em. And study the targets and how you'll use funneling features to find them. If they send up fighters, shoot them down. *But* if you accept a commit, know what you are flying over. Be aggressive and be smart. That's all I've got. See you out there."

The room jumped to attention as CAG walked down the aisle to the door. "Seats," he said as he left, his Ops Officer "Bucket" following him out. The room then broke up into groups. Some talked in a corner and others left for other ready rooms where they would go over their formation tasking in detail in their element briefs. A few flight leads sought Cajun to clarify a point. Within five minutes only the *Hammer* and *Iron* formations remained. Cajun took the floor again to brief the target areas and how they would attack them.

The *Hammer* division, also led by Cajun, consisted of Olive, Wilson, and Dutch, and would hit several aimpoints around the harbor. A wharf, where imagery showed the *Pasdaran* berthing and servicing their *boghammars,* was the primary target. Each pilot was assigned a particular aimpoint in order to deliver their GPS precision-guided weapons. To get to the release points, they had to fly past two inhabited islands, one of which they figured to have a SAM site. They knew for sure both islands housed AAA in all calibers. The *Sweeps* would clear the skies ahead of them of any airborne threat. Then the suppression aircraft, call signs *Tron* and *Zap*, would take out the surface-to-air missile sites allowing the four *Hammers* and the *Irons* unencumbered access to the target area. After release, both formations would flow south and away from the threat.

At that point, the *Iron* pilots, made up of marines from the *Moonshadows*, departed and Cajun spent another 10 minutes going over standard launch and recovery procedures, formation lighting, and aircraft emergency procedures. One hour and 15 minutes to go.

Wilson spent a few minutes alone in his chair with his eyes closed. He imagined himself as he taxied to the cat, climbed away from the ship, joined on the tanker, pushed out in formation, adjusted his goggles, set up his switches, and funneled his eyes to the target on his radar and FLIR displays. He saw the silent streams of AAA, graceful white lights climbing single file into the black sky, and he saw a SAM blast off its launcher with city lights in the background. He reviewed the procedures to deal with each. He saw his weapon, signified by a white infrared dash, fly into the FLIR display and explode. The blast covered his aimpoint in fire and smoke as it hit. All the while, Wilson kept sight of the others in formation and followed Cajun out of the target area. He imagined a push out of marshal on time and flying a centered-ball pass all the way to touchdown.

Wilson routinely used this personal preflight ritual to *visualize* his success in every phase of the flight; it had become part of his habit pattern. The *Raven* pilots knew not to disturb Flip prior to launch whenever he got into his "zone."

Wilson looked at his watch. Ten minutes to walk time. He went up to the duty desk and was the first to pick up a personal sidearm, a clip, and a "blood-chit" guarantee from the United States Government. Written in dozens of languages, it offered a reward if this pilot—Wilson—was returned safely to friendly forces. He also signed for a pair of night vision goggles.

Ensign Anita Jackson, one of the maintenance "ground pounders" was at the duty desk and offered him a log and a pen to sign for the items. A former airframe chief who came up from the deckplates, Jackson was soft-spoken and sweet in demeanor, but could be a ball of fire if pushed.

She smiled at Wilson as he finished signing his name. "Kick their ass, sir," she whispered so only he could hear.

Wilson smiled and said, "Will do, Anita."

He then stepped outside into a passageway that ran along maintenance control and picked up the book for *Raven 403*, the aircraft with his name stenciled on the side. He reviewed the aircraft discrepancies, or gripes, and the actions taken over the last several flights, but *403* was a familiar bird and a good flyer. While reviewing the book, he sensed the maintenance master chief and Ted Randall, both in their green flight deck jerseys, were watching him with interest. He glanced up at Ted and back to the book.

"Any problem, OPSO?" Ted asked.

"Nope, looks great, Ted. As usual!" Wilson replied with a smile.

He returned the book to a young female airman who took it with a look of concern in her eyes. Wilson smiled at her, understanding and appreciating her unease. He realized she did not know what the pilots would do tonight or the threats they would face. She just knew it was serious and hoped that Lieutenant Commander Wilson and all the pilots would return in three hours.

As Wilson grabbed his helmet bag, a burly chief slapped him on the back and said, "Blow 'em away, sir."

"We will, Chief," responded Wilson.

He grasped, in that instant, that it was here, and in squadron spaces throughout the ship, where personnel showed their appreciation for the human risks their pilots were taking. Such moments also allowed them, through their comments to pilots like Wilson, to strike a vicarious blow against the enemy. He knew he was representing them, and could not let them down.

CHAPTER 56

Wilson entered the ready room and noted that the skipper, Olive, and Dutch were at the duty desk signing for their gear. He walked through the room and stepped into the passageway where he saw Gunner Humphries coming into the ready room from the flight deck.

"Hey, Gunner, all loaded up there?"

"Yep, which one are you?"

"Four-oh-three."

"Four-oh-three… Yeah, you're on the bow, one row."

"Great, thanks." Wilson turned toward the paraloft to suit up. Before he could walk away, the gunner stopped him. "Wait, I've got a joke for you."

Wilson stopped and chuckled. "Go ahead."

Humphries was in his element. "What's the fastest thing known to man?"

"What?"

"The water that shoots up your ass after you take a shit. What's the second fastest thing known to man?"

Still chuckling, Wilson took the bait. "What?"

"Your asshole when it slams shut to catch it," he replied with an expectant look, suppressing a grin.

Wilson smiled and laughed, shaking his head at the absurdity of Gunner's joke. With his years of experience, Gunner knew how to keep pilots calm.

"Have a good one, OPSO. Hit 'em hard," he added with a knowing smile and a squeeze to Wilson's arm.

"Thanks, Gunner, will do." Wilson replied as he turned for the paraloft, still smiling and shaking his head.

Wilson entered the paraloft, or "PR shop," and greeted Petty Officer Zembower, the shop supervisor. Pulling the first item of flight gear from his hook, Wilson donned it in his same superstitious manner: g-suit around the waist, zip it up, followed by right leg, then left. The butterflies returned as he anticipated what lay ahead, not the least of which was a night cat shot. Cajun, Olive and Dutch entered together and went to their own hooks from which their flight gear hung.

241

Cajun, apparently, was also thinking about the dark night. "Flip, when did he say the moon was coming up?"

"About 2330 or thereabouts, sir. Just in time for the recovery."

"It's actually 2334, Skipper," Dutch chimed in.

Cajun looked at Dutch. "Next thing you're gonna tell me is the percent illumination, aren't you?"

"Actually, sir…"

"Yeah, *I know* you know, Dutch!" Cajun replied, feigning mock disgust. "JOs know these things, like days between duty, so you guys can wheedle your way out of it with some BS excuse. Seniority among JOs is like virtue among whores."

Wilson and the others smiled at the CO's rambling. After a few moments Cajun looked at Olive. "Do *you* know the illumination?"

"Yes, sir, 72 percent," she answered with a smug smile, working her straps.

Vindicated, Dutch puffed out his chest. "See sir, the JOs have you covered!"

The aviators were all aware of Petty Officer Zembower on the bench, polishing a helmet visor and enjoying the pilot's banter without appearing too interested.

Cajun shook his head. "All right then, *Dutch*, tell me this: Is the moon *waxing* or *waning*?"

"Ah, sir, so long as I have a night light for the trap and know the percent illumination, even at only 72 percent, I'm good."

"And you call yourself a naval officer," Cajun replied in retort as he worked his g-suit zippers, shaking his head. While the skipper was pulling Dutch's chain, Wilson knew he was halfway serious.

The four aviators finished dressing in silence as their thoughts returned to the bow catapults, or Bandar Abbas, or the recovery. On the PLAT Wilson noticed an E-2 hooking up to Cat 3, the deep hum of the *Hawkeye* engines reverberating as background noise in the shop.

Wilson was the first one done, and as he stepped to the door, Cajun raised his voice. "Good hunting up there, OPSO."

"You too, Skipper. See you guys out there," Wilson replied.

He noticed that Zembower looked up at him as he walked past to the door. "Have a good flight, sir," he said with a smile.

"Will do, PR1. Thanks," Wilson answered and exited the space with a confident grin.

Wilson stepped into the starboard passageway and began his familiar trek to the bow, trudging over knee-knockers and through open hatches to the "point" area of the flight deck some 700 feet away. *I wonder if they're going to turn this off,*

Wilson thought, imagining the mixture of disappointment *and* relief he would feel should Washington decide not to launch the operation.

While lost in his thoughts, a sailor traveling aft passed him and muttered, "Good flight, sir."

Startled for a moment, Wilson turned and responded, "Thanks!" The nameless sailor was one of hundreds of teenagers aboard.

When he had almost reached the wardroom, he turned outboard, passed underneath the Catapult 1 trough, and stopped in front of a hatch leading to the catwalk. He lowered his visor and pulled his gooseneck flashlight from his survival vest. Opening the door, he stepped into a black vestibule and flicked on the flashlight. His watch read 2110. Fifty minutes to go. Wilson reached down and grasped the bar to undog the hatch, and yanked it up.

A torrent of salt air, wind, and turboprop noise bombarded his senses as he stepped outside onto a small steel platform and dogged the hatch behind him. Lightening holes in the deckplate allowed him a view of the froth generated by the bow wave on the dark water 50 feet below.

Wilson grabbed the railing and stepped up the ladder and into the catwalk. He kept his head down and swept his flashlight ahead to locate any fuel hoses or electrical cables that might snake along his path. As he crouched low and steadied himself against the wind, he stepped up another small ladder onto the flight deck. The illumination provided by sodium vapor lights high on the island gave everything an eerie yellow tint. He directed his light on the tail of the *Hornet* next to him and read the side number: *403*.

Airman Muriel Rodriguez greeted him at the ladder with a salute, her big eyes visible through the cranial goggles even in the low light. A slight girl of only 19, she had entered the country from Mexico at age 10. Without any knowledge of English, she worked hard to learn the language and graduated from high school with honors. She had joined the Navy last year, and this was her first deployment.

Wilson returned her salute and ascended the ladder to stow his gear inside the cockpit while maintaining a precarious balance on the LEX with one hand, holding the flashlight as he did so. He returned to the deck and did his usual preflight inspection. Working his way around the nose and aft, he inspected the aircraft panels and circuit breakers and then ducked into a wheel well and checked the tires and struts. He paid particular attention to the JDAM on the parent stations.

Two of the red-shirted aviation ordnancemen lingered near the JDAM hanging on the right wing. "Sir, do you have a message for those fucks that killed our guys?" one of them asked, handing Wilson a black magic marker.

Wilson smiled, took the pen, and thought for a moment. *Hmmm.* The Navy's politically correct leadership frowned on such messages, but they looked the other way as long as one of the media's cameras didn't pick it up. Not wanting to disappoint the young sailors, Wilson asked one of them to point his flashlight on the weapon as he wrote:

LIGHTS OUT, ASSHOLES – YOU PICKED THE WRONG NAVY

"There you go, guys," Wilson said as he finished.

"All right, sir!" The *ordies* nodded in approval.

"Thanks for loading these up for us. Don't expect you'll have to download," Wilson replied.

"Thanks, sir, have a good flight," the sailors answered and moved to the next bird in line. Wilson continued with his preflight, the familiar nerves returning. He wondered if they were due to Bandar Abbas or the cat shot. He could see some stars overhead through the broken clouds. Although he'd seen blacker nights than this, it was still very dark. On the horizon he noted the running lights of a ship, one of the escorts. He forced his mind to concentrate as he folded himself under a wheel-well door to check the APU accumulator pressure, strut pressures, and landing gear links.

Wilson ascended the ladder with nimble steps and, after checking the ejection seat, slid in and began to hook up his fittings. Airman Rodriguez was right behind him, hooking up the oxygen and comm cords and helping Wilson with his Koch fittings. "Sir, are you going to attack Iran?"

Wilson nodded as he slammed a fitting home. "Yep, looks like. They attacked our ship in international waters and killed sailors. We're going to prevent them from doing that again."

"Sir, look!" Rodriguez called out, pointing to port.

On the distant horizon a slow-moving light lifted off the water like a faraway sparkler. It then picked up speed and moved in a northerly direction. Another missile burst from its vertical launch tube amid the fiery smoke generated by its rocket booster and lit up the superstructure of the guided missile cruiser on the horizon. It followed the path of the first missile north to an unknown target.

"Are we under attack, sir?"

"No, those are *Tomahawk* cruise missiles. We're attacking *them.*" As he watched the two small lights climb away and pick up speed, Wilson realized that the United States had just crossed the Rubicon. There was no turning back.

Valley Forge aircraft would soon deliver the main strike power against Iran. *Holy shit. We're really doing it,* Wilson thought. He looked directly at the young plane captain. "Rodriguez, you are part of history tonight."

She returned his look, slightly uneasy. "Have a good flight, sir," she said as she descended the ladder.

"Thanks, Rodriguez! See you soon!" Wilson said. With a reassuring smile over his left shoulder, he added, "We'll be okay."

The plane captain lifted her head, and Wilson could detect a faint smile through the darkness before she disappeared under the LEX.

CHAPTER 57

Wilson's thoughts returned to Bandar Abbas, and as he set up the cockpit for launch, he noted a third *Tomahawk* arc away from its launch vessel. He noticed his deep breathing as he checked that the circuit breakers were stowed and the rudder pedals were set to his liking, only two among the dozens of little cockpit checks he had to perform. Then, with a start, he froze as he looked at his left knee. His kneeboard was attached to it. With his mind on autopilot, he had attached his kneeboard around his *left* leg, something he had never done before in nearly 13 years of flying. It shocked Wilson to see it there, and after a moment, he unhooked it and placed it on his right knee where it belonged. The nerves were returning, and Wilson fought them as he continued the rest of his checks. *Calm down, buddy. Step by step.*

The E-2 was now in tension on Cat 3, its big turboprops digging into the air with a deep hum heard throughout the ship. The pilot illuminated the aircraft's external lights, signifying readiness for launch. Moments after the catapult officer touched the deck, the aircraft shot forward as the shuttle hurtled it down the angle to obtain precious flying speed. *Knight 600* whizzed past the bow with a *WHOOOOMM* as the pilot set the climb attitude.

With the E-2 gone, the flight deck became quiet again, save for the wind that whipped through the aircraft stacked on the bow. Finished with his checks, Wilson savored the quiet, but his eyes scanned through the cockpit again and again. *Nerves*, he thought. He sat in the cockpit and glanced at Cajun finishing his checks in the *Hornet* next to him. Olive, in her cockpit on the other side, sat motionless with her head back, as if asleep. Rodriguez stood at parade rest and watched him from her position on deck. *He* watched dozens of ordies and maintenance technicians behind her as they milled about in preparation for engine starts. He looked up at the stars and sensed the ship in a turn. Thirty minutes to go.

Just then the Boss came over the 5MC. "On the flight deck, aircrews have manned for the 2200 launch. Time for all personnel to get in the proper flight deck uniform." As the boss continued with the standard prestartup litany, the tempo on deck picked up as plane captains and troubleshooters moved into position in anticipation of his finish: "Let's start the 'go' aircraft. *Start 'em up!*"

Over a dozen *Hornets* scattered over the flight deck reacted to the command as the mournful sound of auxiliary power units cranked to life in order to provide starting air to the jet engines. With his APU online, Wilson gave the two-finger start signal to Rodriguez. She then approved and authorized him to start the right engine. As soon the generator kicked on and the *Hornet* sprang to life, Wilson's hands flew through the cockpit and turned on displays and radios in another ingrained routine. Within minutes, the flight deck had become an ear-splitting cacophony of jet engines, and once Wilson got the other engine started, he lowered the canopy to drown out the din. He wanted to concentrate on the navigation and weapons displays he would soon need.

In a businesslike manner, after 36 hours of thorough preparation, *Valley Forge* was in the final stages of thrusting the "tip of the spear" into an enemy of the United States. At command and control operations centers in Manama, Tampa, and Washington, staff officers and their commanders monitored the status of Air Wing Four's Strike 1A and counted the *Tomahawk* launches and tracked their progress. They also relayed the latest intelligence regarding the surface picture and enemy readiness to Admiral Smith and his staff who would pass it on to the pilots once they were airborne. National intelligence, surveillance and reconnaissance assets all had their sensors focused on this part of the world in support of both the *Valley Forge* strike group and the *Tinian* amphibious ready group. Inside the great carrier, the next wave of pilots were already signing out their maintenance books and getting dressed in squadron paralofts for Strike 1B—even while others gathered in a ready room to brief Strike 1C, a strike package that would launch and recover in the wee hours.

Ten minutes after engine starts, observers on the bridge and in pri-fly watched as the first *Hornets* pulled out of their bow parking spots. The directors used yellow light wands to funnel them aft and guide them, with only inches to spare, down the narrow opening between two rows of fueled and loaded strike-fighters. Hundreds of officers and sailors, each with a vital job, were scattered about the flight deck. Each sailor, depending on his or her job, wore a cranial helmet and float-coat of a certain color, marked with reflective tape that showed as bright gold when illuminated by the island spotlights.

One by one the aircraft moved either aft, or forward from the fantail, to feed the catapults. By design, two *Viking* tankers moved into position on the waist cats. They would be shot early to take station and top off the *Hornets* after they launched. In the blackness, the stars rotated overhead and the running lights of the escort ship moved steadily along the invisible horizon, clues that the carrier was turning to a launch heading. The flight deck was a screaming whine of jet engines as waves of kerosene exhaust and sea air cascaded down the length of it. The aircraft began to form patterns familiar to the crew as the yellow shirts arranged the deck to launch one jet every minute off the four catapults.

Wilson's eyes were locked on his yellow shirt director as he moved past the island and aft to a spot behind a *Super Hornet*. Once stopped, he checked his FLIR operational and finished his comm checks.

Cajun came up on strike common for the roll call: "Ninety-Nine *Tomahawk*, stand by for check-in. *Hammer* one-one."

"*Hammer* one-two," Olive replied next.

Wilson keyed the mike. "*Hammer* one-three."

"*Hammer* one-four," Dutch responded, followed by the other air wing strikers answering in order until all were accounted for.

With everyone up, Cajun switched back to departure frequency and waited with the rest of them. Wilson sensed the ship steady out and looked over his shoulder as the *Viking* on Cat 3 hooked up to the shuttle. Seven minutes until launch. He looked over his left shoulder toward "Vultures Row" and saw that the galleries were full of off-duty sailors wanting to witness history. If Wilson could have been, he would have been pacing to settle his nerves. Buckled as he was into his little cocoon, he had to be satisfied with drumming his fingers on the canopy bow and waiting his turn. He did the combat checklist again.

The *Vikings* whizzed down the cat tracks in order and launched, position lights slowly receding into the black as they climbed away. Led by two *Prowlers* on the waist cats, this allowed the conga line of aircraft to move up. He looked over his right shoulder and saw *400*, Cajun's jet, behind him, painted in a colorful scheme with the *Raven* emblem taking up the entire vertical tail. Even under these conditions, Wilson admired the sharp manifestation of squadron pride. *One more minute*, Wilson thought. He saw the sailors on the waist look at the island for the signal to begin.

"Green deck."

On signal, and with a metallic shriek, the first *Prowler* roared to life. The pilot cycled the controls and, once ready to launch, flicked on the external lights. Seconds later, the big jet thundered down the track and into the Indian Ocean air. Almost immediately, Wilson heard another aircraft go into tension up on the bow so that, one minute after the *Prowler* was airborne, a *Rhino* followed it into the night sky. Strike 1A was on its way. The yellow shirts continued to feed airplanes to the hungry catapult crewmen who hooked them up and shot them in a practiced sequence, as if it were any other night on deployment. The airborne aircraft climbed out and began to form a jagged string of blinking lights ahead of the ship.

With eyes locked on his yellow shirt, Wilson maneuvered behind the waist catapult aircraft in a familiar succession. He saw he was being led to Cat 4, and as he taxied behind Cat 3, *Raven 403* was buffeted by the jet blast from a *Rhino* in tension. Once the *Rhino* was airborne, the *Hornet* on Cat 4 went into tension, and this time Wilson's jet bounced and rocked in place. Shielded only by the steel jet blast deflector mere feet from his nose, Wilson was bombarded by waves of exhaust from the white hot burner plume of the jet. At maximum power, it produced a deafening sound of deep, continuous thunder. Finally, the jet roared down the track, the fire and thunder tearing at the deck as it accelerated to flying speed in less than three seconds. When it reached the deck edge, a loud *THUNK* was felt throughout the ship. As the jet rose into the darkness, the pulsing heartbeat of its anticollision lights receded in the distance.

A yellow shirt straddling the catapult motioned Wilson to inch forward with yellow light wands and signaled slight turns that Wilson responded to with a gentle push of a rudder pedal, causing his aircraft to lurch this way and that. Wilson's eyes remained fixed on the yellow shirt, dutifully following his orders. Billowing steam clouds swirled about the director and nearly obscured him from view even while the lighted wands called Wilson forward. On signal, Wilson stopped and turned the handle to spread his wings.

Cajun was next to him on Cat 3 and would be shot first. Once Cajun went into tension, Wilson watched him wipe out the controls and then, on signal, select afterburner. Wilson shielded his eyes from the dazzling twin 20-foot cones of white hot fire to his right and watched as two *Raven* troubleshooters crouched low. They lifted their arms high, with a thumbs up, to signal ready. Suddenly, the strike leader shot down the angle and into the sky, afterburners blazing. The observers in the tower saw the glow reflect off the water below and move away from the ship.

With *400* clear of Cat 3, attention turned to *Raven 403*. With his heart beating faster, Wilson lifted his arms above the canopy rail as the ordies armed the gun and the *Sidewinder* missiles on the wingtips. Once complete, he inched forward on signal until he felt the holdback catch him, and pulled the throttles to idle. A *Hornet* roared off the bow, and Wilson knew he would be next to launch. His eyes darted across the cockpit for a last-minute check. His breathing deep and body tight, the adrenaline began to flow.

The cat officer turned and signaled to the sailor tending the launch bar underneath Wilson. The yellow shirt director then looked up and down the cat track and spread his arms in the take-tension signal. Wilson slammed both throttles to military power, and the engines roared to life. He felt the catapult assembly "grab" his aircraft, and looked at each engine instrument as he cycled the control stick and rudder pedals with his right arm and feet. Engine and flight controls good. One last check of the cockpit displays.

Wilson's machine strained hard against the catapult, begging to be released. He glanced at the catapult officer who signaled him for afterburner. Wilson shoved the throttles all the way forward, locking his arm in place. He felt the power behind him and saw it reflected in his rearview mirrors. Satisfied, he grabbed the towel rack and placed his head on the headrest. His little finger flicked on the external lights, and the flight deck around him seemed to pulse as the red strobes flashed on and off.

It will come any second now. Wilson's eyes scanned the instruments. Arm muscles locked in place. Heels on the deck. Braced. Waiting. In tension.

Walking to his airplane, Weed popped his head over the catwalk aft of El 3, and saw a *Hornet* in burner on Cat 4. He noted the side number: *403.* With a little jump, the jet shot forward and accelerated down the track, on its way to join the rest of Strike 1A forming up overhead.

"*Vaya con Dios, roomie.*"

CHAPTER 58

The tanker pilot extinguished the green light on the refueling store, which was Wilson's signal to back out of the basket. It also signified that he had received all he was going to get from this *Viking*. *Two thousand pounds*. An extra thousand would top him off, but Olive was next in line and needed her share for the long drive to Bandar Abbas.

Wilson tweaked the throttles and slid back as the basket popped off the probe and stabilized in the relative wind. He retracted the probe and slid to the right to join Cajun and Dutch information on the *Viking's* right wing as Olive took her turn in the basket. Once stabilized next to Dutch, he glanced up and saw the light clusters of the *Iron* division aircraft on their *Viking* 1,000 feet above. The three of them waited for Olive to plug, and once fueled, she backed out of the basket and slid over to Wilson's right. The *Viking* retracted the basket and illuminated its anticollision light, banking away from the *Hornets*. Cajun led his three wingmen in an easy right-hand turn—away from the tanker and toward the initial point some 30 minutes away.

The strike aircraft were assigned exact target times, which allowed the sweep, suppression and jamming aircraft, all coordinated by the E-2, to know where each formation was at a given time. As they pressed out, Wilson took a position abeam Cajun, and the two wingmen got into formation on their respective section leads without a voice call. All four pilots clicked their night vision goggles into place on their helmets and, while maintaining their place in formation, made the necessary adjustments. To the west Wilson saw the desolate coastal plain of Oman rising to rugged mountains, with the glow from the metropolis of Dubai dominating the horizon beyond them. On this side, the town of Fujairah was the major settlement and shone brightly off their left nose.

The radio crackled. "*Sweeps* pushing, no alibis."

Looking north, Wilson found the *Sweeps*, four dots of light moving among the stars, each one representing a *Super Hornet*. At his 4 o'clock was the *Iron* division, moving fast to catch up. At his left seven, well aft, he picked up the suppression aircraft, the *Zaps* and *Trons*. He noted Dutch in position and then

251

looked north again at the long coastline of Iran, punctuated by the cultural lighting of the scattered settlements along its length.

A moment later Cajun keyed the mike. His "*Hammers* pushing" was quickly followed by "*Irons* pushing" from the *Iron* lead.

Though flying at hundreds of miles per hour, the formation glided as one unit high over the Gulf of Oman. The radio stayed silent except for an occasional "picture clean" call from *Knight*. The route they took funneled them into Hormuz, closer and closer to the Iranian coast. Their green radar cursors bounced back and forth across the displays while the pilots scanned the horizon through their goggles to pick up any movement. Below him, Wilson saw the scattered lights of the Gulf's merchant shipping, and noted one very large crude carrier stopped dead in the water. *Maybe they're waiting for this operation to complete before entering the Gulf*, he thought. *Maybe they know something.*

Looking toward Hormuz, Wilson saw a muffled flash in the vicinity of the target. A *Tomahawk* impact, he guessed. *They know we're coming now.* A minute later, he noted a second flash, then two more in rapid succession. His radar warning receiver was clean. No enemy radars were painting his aircraft. Wilson looked over at Cajun and Olive, then over his right shoulder at Dutch. They were all flying perfect form, and the *Irons* were where they should be. They glided on in silence, scanning their radar and FLIR displays and trying to keep busy without spending too much time looking at the Iranian coastline as they edged closer. Fifteen minutes to go. Wilson took another look at the target imagery on his kneeboard card and, following ingrained habit, checked his fuel.

Suddenly, Wilson got a *boop* in his headset and his eyes flashed to the RWR display. Now someone out there *was* painting them, and before long, they would enter several threat envelopes. Up ahead, the *Sweeps* committed on an airborne contact north of the target. Though the contact was not "hot," any unknown airborne aircraft ratcheted up the level of excitement for everyone. The *Sweeps* were there to shield the strikers, and this unknown aircraft could turn and become a threat to the Americans at any moment. The *Super Hornets* tracked the contact while searching for others, ready to blow the bogey out of the sky should it be identified as hostile. The *Hammer* and *Iron* divisions had almost reached the initial point—where they would split to go after their respective targets.

"Ninety-nine, *armstrong*." Cajun's firm tone was evident as he called on strike common.

His second message came over *Hammer* tac: "Let's bump it up. Check right twenty. *Go.*"

In unison, the *Raven* pilots rolled right to the new heading and accelerated to their run-in speed, each one lifting the MASTER ARM knob to ARM.

An *Iron* pilot called out. *"Iron two-three, SAM launch zero-two-zero!"*

Wilson and the others looked right and saw a plume rising fast from the coast but falling aft as they continued north. "Doesn't appear to be tracking— ballistic," the *Iron* lead responded, with each *Iron* pilot reporting "clean."

Nevertheless, all the pilots tracked the missile's bright, elongated tail. It looked much closer when intensified by NVGs, but it soon fell aft. Wilson figured it to be a tactical SAM.

One of the *Zaps* called, *"Magnum* from *Zap* two-five."

Looking high out his right side, Wilson saw a supersonic HARM missile fired by one of the *Zaps* climb high into its profile, searching for a threat emitter to home in on.

As they neared the target area, they began to pick up some AAA off to the left from one of the islands south of the harbor. Unguided barrage fire, this heavy stuff resembled popping fireworks. It was no factor as the *Hammers* pressed on without reacting.

Cajun came up on aux. "Anyone having trouble with their weapon?"

Wilson punched up his weapons display and selected both JDAMs that were to be dropped on separate DMPIs near the harbor. At first all looked normal, then NO GPS flashed up on the screen. A chill of foreboding came over him as he deselected and reselected the weapons.

Dutch came up and said, "Mine are degraded."

"Hammer one-two concur," Olive added.

Dammit, Wilson thought. *We're less than two minutes from release!*

Cajun came up again. *"Irons* from *Hammer.* How are your weapons?"

"Good so far," the *Iron* lead replied.

"Roger, *Iron,* continue as fragged. Break, break, any luck, *Hammers?* Check BIT status." Cajun asked his pilots, who each answered *negative.*

Why are our *weapons bad?* Wilson wondered. *When the* Irons *only a few miles away are receiving good guidance?* Localized GPS jamming? Were they tracking his division and spoofing the JDAM somehow?

Wilson looked at his display in disbelief. The target area was passing under their nose! And the RWR was suddenly cluttered up with threats, sending distracting *deedles* into his headset.

Cajun Lassiter had a decision to make and, at their transonic run-in speed, less than a minute to make it. Without GPS guidance the JDAM accuracy decreased, and near misses on the assigned aimpoints were unacceptable. JDAMs could be delivered with a tolerable degree of accuracy from a visual dive, but that would bring the *Hammers* down into greater concentrations of AAA and would significantly increase each pilot's risk. Lugging the bombs out of the target area meant degraded maneuvering off target and not accomplishing the mission. Simply dumping the JDAMs in the ocean before recovery was a non-starter for Cajun.

With 40 seconds to the roll-in point, Cajun keyed the mike. "Okay, *Hammers,* we're gonna put 'em all on the wharf. One run. Standard visual division roll-in to the left. I'll take the southernmost boats...Olive and Flip the middle...and Dutch the northern *boghammars*. Egress left and south. Check right twenty. *Go!* Olive, cross under."

Now alarmed, Cajun's anxious wingmen responded in order. They set up their switches, found the wharf on their FLIRs in the remaining seconds before rolling in on their targets, and designated where Cajun wanted them to aim.

Wilson eased closer to Cajun and took a look over his LEX at the harbor. He noted several blinking AAA guns, some sending near solid streams of fire into the sky. It was into that image he and his squadronmates would soon dive. Through the goggles he could make out the clusters of *boghammars* moored along the wharf.

"Don't ferget yer chaff program," Cajun reminded them. "Four miles to go," he added. *"Tapes on! FLIR!"*

Wilson's mouth felt like the desert below. He fought to control the quick breaths through his mouth that seemed to suck in his oxygen mask. Between the *Sweeps* and *Knight* clobbering strike common about the will-o'-the-wisp contact to the north and the *Irons* calling in and off on their aimpoints, his mind neared sensory overload. Even more insistent, though, was his own RWR screaming threat indications in all quadrants with near incessant threat tones in his headset. It was all Wilson could do to ensure his switches ready and to maintain position in formation. Adrenaline coursed through his body.

What Wilson could not hear was the AAA below his aircraft, but he sensed the muffled flashes of shells going off underneath him. He moved his head constantly to keep situational awareness inside and outside the cockpit. With too much closure, Olive slid into her new position between Wilson and Cajun and had to throw a wing up in a desperate move to stop her overshoot. Dutch was high and even with Wilson's wingline. *Ready to go.*

Was that another SAM to the east? Wilson ignored it and focused on the next 15 seconds...the reason they were there.

"*Hammer* one's in hot," Cajun called in a calm voice. He pulled his jet across the horizon then overbanked and pulled down into the target area—a move he had performed hundreds of times during his long career.

Once Cajun's nose was down, Olive followed in the same manner. Through his goggles, Wilson observed the hot exhaust gas that shot from her tailpipes as she selected military and pulled the airplane around. Bright explosions of chaff expelled behind her from buckets on the bottom of her jet. Once her nose committed, Wilson said, *One potato,* and pushed the throttles to military, rolling left and pulling his nose across the horizon.

For an instant, Wilson looked out his left canopy at the wharf below him. He observed muzzle flashes from several guns, including one big one with a slow rate of fire north of the wharf. He then rolled further left, pulled the stick in his lap so his g-suit inflated, and then sucked the throttles to idle. When he banged out a chaff program and craned his neck to full extension to keep the target in sight, his goggles picked up multiple rows of tracers crisscrossing his view. Some moved fast and some slow against the stationary lights of the harbor and the dark water in the background.

Holy shit! he said to himself. They were diving into a confused buzz saw of AAA, heavier than he had ever seen.

CHAPTER 59

Pulling his nose down to the target, Wilson unloaded and rolled out wings level in a steep dive. As his *Hornet* accelerated and raced downhill carrying a heavy load of ordnance, his years of training took over. Wilson noted Olive still in her dive, but he didn't see Cajun. He shot a glance at Dutch, who was behind him with adequate separation, and brought his attention back to the HUD to track his target. Wilson struggled to line his aircraft up on the green HUD aiming cues, which required a lightning quick scan to ensure proper weapons delivery. He made crisp corrections with the stick while slewing the aiming diamond on his exact aimpoint —the middle group of *boghammars*.

With release altitude fast approaching, he heard Cajun call, "Lead's off." Wilson made a last-second azimuth correction, pressed the red "pickle" button on the stick with his thumb, and held it down hard. His HUD release cue "flew" through the velocity vector and signaled the computer to eject the bombs. The airplane shuddered as hundreds of pounds of ordnance was suddenly released from each wing.

Wilson heard *Boom! Boom! Boom!* in rapid succession off his right side. He pushed the throttles to military and hauled back on the stick to stop his dive. He sensed a bright flash to his left, banged out another chaff program, and jinked hard right into Dutch for a count. He then rolled back to wing's level in order to catch his bombs' impact on the FLIR.

He then heard an alarmed Olive call out. *"Skipper!"*

Wilson looked left and saw a wild, gyrating fireball. The dazzling, white-hot light almost washed out his goggles, but he saw the unmistakable planform of a *Hornet* wing poking through the flames before it, too, became engulfed. Horrified, he looked under the goggles and saw the yellow and orange flames of the fireball spinning in a steepening dive. Flaming pieces of debris ejected from it and trailing black smoke could be seen against the radiance of the city lighting.

Two huge flashes underneath him caught Wilson's attention, and he over-banked to see concentric circles emanating from tall geysers of water and smoke. Flaming pieces of debris cartwheeled through the air from where the skipper had laid his bombs, bullseye hits. Two more flashes erupted next to them, one on the wharf pier and another one on an adjacent warehouse. They produced circular supersonic shock waves as more debris floated into the air in slow motion.

Wilson pulled hard up to the left and watched the flaming wreckage continue to gyrate out of control. "Get out!" he cried on strike common, and then repeated, "*Hammer* one-one, get out!"

Receiving no response, Wilson called to Olive, "Olive, keep your knots up, egress southeast! Dutch, you with us?"

"Affirm, visual two, coming out your left seven high. No chute yet!"

"Roger, bug southeast!"

Wilson noted AAA fire above with more streams in front of him as he kept his turn in to egress. His fist banged out more chaff, as he violently maneuvered the jet in order to keep sight of Olive above him. He then overbanked to see *Raven 400* in its final plunge. The aircraft had now disintegrated into several flaming pieces, with the largest one falling toward the mouth of the harbor. He checked his airspeed—a slow 300 knots—*Dammit!*—and crammed the throttles to burner as he punched off his drop tanks. Looking down, he saw only splash circles on the water south of the wharf—all that remained of his skipper's aircraft.

Wilson keyed the mike on aux frequency and shouted in vain. "*Cajun! You up?*"

As he jinked left, a bright flash burst to his right. *Fuck!* The flash was followed by a rapid *bap, plink, plink* off to his right. *Did they hit me?*

Wilson bunted the nose to regain precious airspeed while his threat receiver was going off—the aural warnings in his headset were constant. He could barely think. Instinctively, he continued to jink in three dimensions to throw off the gunners aim and ran away from the threat on brain stem power and a very human will to survive. He spotted Olive and Dutch several thousand feet above as all three aircraft clawed their way toward safety.

A transmission from the *Iron* lead broke through Wilson's fog. "*Hammers,* you guys okay?"

Still jinking and searching the ground for threats, Wilson recognized the voice of the *Moonshadow* XO and answered between breaths. "*Hammer* one-one could be down. Any *Hammers* see a chute?"

"*Hammer* one-two negative."

"One-four negative."

"*Hammers* from *Iron*, we have the impact marked."

"Roger," replied Wilson.

Now running to the briefed get-well point, with the threat from the AAA appearing to subside, Wilson almost allowed himself to relax. But he couldn't. No chute. No emergency beeper. Instead, the horrific image of Cajun's jet being torn to pieces by both an antiaircraft shell and the forces of nature. His skipper, Cajun, *gone*. Yet, if anyone could survive, it would be Cajun.

The familiar voice of CAG Swoboda broke the short silence. *"Hammer* lead, this is *Sweep* zero-three. I've got the on-scene command with *Sweep* flight. *Hammers* and *Iron*, RTB. *Tron* three-one and *Zaps*, remain at your orbit, max conserve. *Knight*, pass to mother...*Hammer* one-one is missing and appears to be down. Launch the Alert CSAR and send bucket brigade *Texaco* to the briefed get-well point."

Still jinking south of the target and looking for any AAA batteries on the islands, Wilson remained beneath Olive and Dutch who were in formation above him. He fought the urge to disagree with CAG, but impulsively keyed the mike. *"Sweep,* from *Hammer* one-three, request remain behind to help, have the posit marked." He got the answer he expected.

"Negative, one-three. I *understand*, but get your people home and send your post-strike report."

Embarrassed, Wilson replied, *"Hammer* one-three wilco." He banged the top of his instrument panel in frustration at his inability to help. At this distance from the ship, CAG knew that the *Hornet* strikers were marginal on fuel even after they topped off from the *Viking* tankers and pushed out.

Once out of the AAA envelopes, the *Hammers* transited over the strait and into the GOO. They hugged the Omani airspace to put as much distance between them and the Iranian coastline as possible. This allowed Wilson to flick off a bayonet fitting and take in lungfuls of air. His *Hornet* was flying fine—no flight control anomalies or engine problems—so, if he *had* been hit, it was superficial. Still thousands of feet underneath his wingmen, Wilson pulled the canteen from his g-suit pocket for a long drink, taking wary glances north and east for SAM launches. He then stowed the canteen, reset his mask, and climbed up to their altitude on the left.

"Flip has the lead on the left. Check in with state," Wilson transmitted.

"You've got the lead on the left. Two's five-point-eight," Olive replied.

"Three's six-point-one," Dutch added.

Wilson responded, "Lead's five-point-three. Everyone get their hits?"

"Affirm," Olive said.

"Got everybody's," Dutch answered. His FLIR tape had picked up the impacts from all four *Hammers*, invaluable intel once the analysts in CVIC could review it.

With this information, Wilson made his report through the *Knight* to relay to the ship. He also added the aircraft status and a request for a tanker once they got to *Valley Forge*.

Transiting to the southeast, Wilson looked at the port of Jask to their left and saw faint streams of AAA, then two bright flashes on the waterfront, followed by two more. On the goggles he strained his eyes to see the 1B strikers overhead, but could not discern them, lights out, among the stars. Nevertheless, something was hitting Jask, and Wilson figured Weed was involved. It was fascinating to watch, live, from over 40 miles away.

"Check out the action to the east," Dutch transmitted on aux. Wilson acknowledged him with two mike clicks.

As they continued in glum silence, Wilson's thoughts soon returned to Cajun. *No way was Cajun going to bring those bombs back.* But why were *their* GPS receivers bad when the *Irons* had no problem? Was the AAA too hot? Should they have aborted? Was that level of intensity the go/no-go standard now?

Wilson thought again of the World War II aviators diving into the ring of fire, and the Korean War and Vietnam aircrews facing sophisticated integrated air defenses. They had set the standard his generation had to uphold. Cajun, too, was on government time—and he had delivered. *Did he get out?*

Wilson thought of Billie Lassiter in Virginia Beach. *What is she doing now? Welcoming the kids home from school, figuring out what to feed them?* Maybe turning on the TV to learn right now that American aircraft are attacking Iran in response to the *Richard Best* attack. Billie has been around this business long enough to know that the *Ravens* would be involved, with her husband leading from the front. In less than two hours, the Commodore and the chaplain could be knocking on her door with bad news, or uncertain news... Either way, it would be devastating.

To the east, the moon peeked above the jagged cloud-lined horizon. On its slow journey across the black sky, its glow created a welcome line that helped the pilots distinguish up from down at a glance. Though the pilots could see the moon from four miles up, far below on the surface it was still well below the horizon, and, to the left, the dark Omani coastal plain was almost indistinguishable from the sea. This region was one of the most desolate and inhospitable places on earth. Its desolation, however, possessed a beauty of its own, and Wilson had observed it many times during his deployments here. The ugliness, in contrast, was pronounced: the cruel heat of midday; the wind-blasted and sun-scorched wasteland; and a strange, unfriendly people whose ways were so foreign and views so absolute—yet accommodating, if it suited them.

Wilson had been forged a warrior here, and the region held a special place in his heart. At the same time, he hated it, hated coming back…but could he *walk away* after this cruise? Wilson looked over at Olive and Dutch, dutifully following their flight leader. At the moment, they were mere position lights in the darkness.

The radio crackled, and Wilson returned to the task at hand: Get everyone home.

Then it hit him, pent up and long suppressed emotion welling up from inside, the tectonic plates of service before self and the desire to live a normal life with Mary and the kids that ground away at each other for months and years suddenly shifting at this time and place, alone in the cockpit of a low-fuel-state warplane high over a dark and hostile sea on the other side of the world, surrounded by strange combinations of numbers and letters on his night-dimmed cockpit displays, hearing and comprehending short and clipped radio transmissions that are all but indecipherable to only a few thousand people on earth.

A question, a cry rose up from a place he did not know he possessed. *What am I doing here?*

As he looked up at the Milky Way, as if asking someone, anyone, for an answer, he let the question hang and then repeated it in his mind. What made him come *here*, again and again, fighting the Iraqi's, Al Qaeda, the Taliban, and now the Iranians? Going back home to recharge, retrain, and reload? And repeating the cycle for *another* deployment? And another? And if successful in his career path, he'd have *many* more deployments, all of them here in this literal hellhole of a region. And was that it? Promotion? Advancement? The all-consuming obsession with *command?* Was he thinking only of himself on the way up, willing to miss vast swaths of his children's lives in the process and even to risk making Mary a widow at worst? He thought of what she was doing now—at home watching the kids during the midafternoon doldrums. Soon the phone would ring and someone would tell her to turn on the news, and she would start wondering and worrying and praying. Then, she would receive another call with the shocking news that Steve Lassiter is missing, and she would rush over to Billie's house with the other girls to support her. They would each begin living their own personal hells while they watched one of their own experience it for real. His career choice was going to do that to her in mere hours.

"Damn you!" he shouted at himself in guilt and frustration.

"*Raven* four-zero-three, Strike?"

Wilson snapped out of it and keyed the mike to answer the ship over 100 miles away. "Go ahead."

"Check in with flight number and state."

He took a deep breath and responded. *"Ravens* checking in with three, low state four point one, requesting *Texaco."*

"Raven four-zero-three roger, vectors for *Redeye* seven-zero-two is one-five-zero at sixty, angels fourteen, switch up departure on button two."

"Strike, four-oh-three copies. *Ravens* go, button two," Wilson said as he punched in the tanker frequency and prepared for another night tanker rendezvous in a thirsty jet over a dark ocean.

Almost an hour later he climbed down from *403* on the foul line, emotionally and physically spent. Airman Rodriguez met him at the bottom of the ladder with a salute, but Ted Randall and the troubleshooters were there with some news. "You took some dings on your right wing, two in the aileron and one in the trailing edge flap. One of the aileron hits went clean through, a hole about the size of a quarter. Did it give you problems?"

"No, no problems," Wilson said, walking past the group to see for himself, while Ted and two of the troubleshooters following. He looked up at the folded right wing and saw the top of the aileron with its composite fibers exposed. Then he inspected the trailing edge flap with his flashlight, running his fingers over a one-inch exposed shard of metal embedded in the skin.

They hit me, he thought. If he had been a little closer, or if the frag had hit him in a vital area, he, too, would be in the dark waters of Hormuz—or worse.

"Can you patch them?" he shouted over the whine of nearby jets. Before Ted could answer, a *Prowler* trapped and rolled out some 60 feet away, and they waited for the deafening roar to subside to continue the conversation.

"Yeah, won't make the last go, but tomorrow for sure. What happened to the drops?"

"Had to punch 'em off, needed the airspeed," Wilson answered, still fascinated by the damage, albeit light, to his aircraft.

They hit me.

"Is the Skipper okay? Is he going to be late?" Ted shouted. The troubleshooters leaned in to hear the answer.

Wilson sensed they already knew what it would be. He looked at Ted with a pained expression. "I don't know. Doesn't look good, Ted. What have you heard here?"

Ted shook his head and said, "Nothing. Just that he didn't check in."

The troubleshooters drifted away in grim silence, but Wilson stopped one of them and shouted close to his ear. "Petty Officer Mansfield. I want that frag, please."

"You got it, sir," the metalsmith replied with a solemn nod. "I'll deliver it myself."

"Thanks."

Wilson turned to complete his post flight and saw that Airman Rodriguez stood in his path. She looked up at him in confusion and disbelief. "Mister Wilson, is Commander Lassiter coming back tonight?" She had to shout in her accented English to be heard over the din.

"Don't know, Rodriguez. We're looking for him." Wilson didn't know what else to say.

The girl refused to believe it.

"Sir, you said everyone would be okay." She looked at him as if he had deceived her.

CHAPTER 60

Wilson sat bone tired in his ready room chair, head back, legs stretched out in front. He tried—and failed—to nap while waiting for Saint to show up from his early morning strike. Shortly after his own return, Wilson had answered endless questions from the CVIC *spies* about the enemy defenses, the hits, Cajun's last known position, the JDAM indications, and routine coordination procedures. He was then led to flag plot to relay the story, again from the top, while Admiral Smith, with his staff looking over his shoulders, studied target photos and charts of Bandar Abbas. He learned from the admiral that CAG and the *Sweeps* could not raise Cajun on his survival radio. Neither could they remain in the area where he went in due to the heavy concentration of AAA and a tactical SAM launched at them. Their assessment was that *400* went in several hundred yards off a jetty near the harbor entrance with no indication that Cajun made it out; but there was no proof he was dead, either, so the search and rescue effort was ongoing. Nobody wanted to turn it off and declare him missing—or killed—too soon.

Smith had dark circles under his eyes. Every person in the room did.

Wilson then went on to the strike debrief, which he held in place of his CO. With Cajun's hits on a nest of *boghammars* included, Strike 1A had done significant damage to the *Pasdaran*, and the *Irons* were four for four with no JDAM problems. The suppression plan was also a bright spot. But to the aviators gathered in the somber ready room the strike was a failure: One of them, the strike lead himself, had not returned.

Air Wing Four had hit the other coastal targets with good results and no additional losses. The last of the early morning strikers were returning. This included the XO, who was now the de facto commanding officer of VFA-64.

Wilson raised his head and looked around at everyone in the silent ready room, which continued to function as a fighting force, even wrapped as they were in the pall of loss. Anita remained at the duty desk, and behind Wilson were several JOs. Among them were Olive, trying to nap; Nttty, in his alert flight gear; and Smoke, taking a sip of water.

Wilson got up and spoke to the group as a whole. "Guys, if you aren't brief-ing or debriefing, standing an alert or eating, go and get some rest. We have another big day and night coming up."

Smoke put down his cup and left without saying anything, and others filed out in glum silence. They didn't know what to do and were too keyed up to sleep. Wilson felt the same way. Nttty, however, settled in to doze, and exhausted from the flight and her restless sleep from the previous night, Olive remained in her chair with her eyes closed. Wilson sat down next to her and waited for her to respond. Sensing a presence, Olive opened her eyes and turned to Wilson.

"What did you see?" he asked.

Olive looked at the back of the chair in front of her as she formulated her an-swer. "Just as he pulled off, his right side exploded, as if a round went down the intake. The wing was blown off, and the jet became a tumbling fireball, flaming pieces thrown out. No chute...just...*fire*... just a shower of fluttering, flaming debris."

"Yeah...I was releasing when you made your call."

"What call?"

"You called '*Skipper!*'"

Olive looked away. "I don't remember," she said. Wilson studied her and noted lines on her face he had never noticed before.

"You okay?"

"Just whipped. I'll be fine."

"I need you to go back up there tomorrow night. Can you do it?" Wilson asked.

"Yeah, I'm good," Olive replied as she again closed her eyes.

Thirty minutes later, Saint came into the ready room still in his flight gear. Wil-son rose to his feet as the XO asked, "What happened to the skipper?"

"Just as we passed the IP, the four of us had NO GPS indications, and the skipper flexed to a visual roll-in, standard high-dive, one run and off. Skipper took a triple-A hit on the pull off. Olive watched him explode right next to her. No chute, no indication of ejection. We marked the wreckage in the water south of the harbor, and CAG relieved me as on-scene commander. However, he couldn't stay in the vicinity because it was too hot."

"Yes, I heard you took a few rounds yourself."

"Yes, sir, superficial damage."

Saint handed his weapon and blood chit to Anita, and then continued with Wilson. "What do you think?"

Wilson looked away, then back to Saint. "I *hope* he's captured, sir."

"Concur, but is that what you think?"

"No, sir...don't think he got out." Nttty and Anita didn't dare move.

Saint wriggled out of his torso harness and nodded. "I tend to agree with you from everything I've heard. I'm going to visit CAG and report as the acting commanding officer of this squadron. You are now acting XO. CAG Ops says he has new strike tasking from above—that's coming to Skipper Lassiter's strike planning team—that I will now lead. Meanwhile, we've got another day and night of CAPs and strikes coming up. You need to schedule your people smart."

"Yes, sir."

Saint grabbed up his flight gear in one arm and headed toward the door. Halfway down the aisle, he turned and said over his shoulder, "Oh, yes, about Hinton. She is now grounded, effective immediately." He then craned his neck fully to lock eyes with Wilson and ensure his message was received.

"Yes, sir," Wilson answered and stood still as the new commanding officer of the *Ravens* exited the ready room.

Nttty and Anita exchanged looks and wondered what they had just witnessed.

Chapter 61

Valley Forge had completed her interdiction strikes for the night, except for the helicopters and S-3's monitoring the surface picture. Two hours earlier, a formation of *Tinian* AV-8's had come across two *boghammars* well south of Chah Bahar that were transiting at a high speed into the Indian Ocean—on an apparent suicide mission to find and attack anything they came across. Each *Harrier* shot a *Maverick* guided missile into the boats, blowing one apart and setting the other on fire. After reporting the action on GUARD, the Americans had given the Iranian search and rescue helicopter plenty of sea room to affect the rescue of survivors, which appeared to be small in number.

Just after *reveille*, Wilson followed Saint along the passageway of blue tiles that led to CAG's stateroom. Arriving at a blue door emblazoned with a large CVW-4 emblem, Saint knocked twice.

"Come in," CAG answered, and Saint opened the door.

CAG and DCAG were seated at a table in the middle of a living area. The room was spacious and plush by modern warship standards, yet spartan for a man responsible for more assets and people than the CEOs of many Fortune 500 companies. It featured a desk in one corner, with a squawk box and built-in shelves in another corner, where CAG displayed several personal and professional mementos. Two couches were arrayed against the wall, and another door opened to a bedroom that was little more than a closet.

CAG motioned them to take a seat at the table. "How you guys doing?" he asked.

"We're making it, sir, but still in shock," Saint answered. "Any more news?"

"We've got some assets in the vicinity of Bandar Abbas watching. The Iranians know where he went in and were observed trolling the area with something like a johnboat to pick up anything they can. Still no contact from Cajun. We have to figure that if he's not dead, he's captured. You saw him go in, Flip?"

"Yes, sir, but it was lots of flaming pieces and debris heading for the water, last I saw of him."

"How many would you say?"

"A handful, sir. Three? Five? Lots of smaller pieces."

CAG looked up and rubbed the stubble on his chin. Wilson figured he, like all the others, had not slept well, if at all, during the past 48 hours. "Okay—Saint, you are obviously leading the *Ravens* now until we get Cajun back, and we need you guys. We are going to continue with strikes against the *Pasdaran* tonight as planned, but we've got pop-up tasking for one more.

"The GCC countries are wringing their hands that Iran is going to strike them with a ballistic missile, and they're leaning on Washington hard to prevent it. We've got several Aegis ships in the Gulf, but they can't be everywhere. And Iran is threatening anyone and everyone who provides sanctuary to the Great Satan. These missiles aren't Saddam's SCUDs either, these guys can target and hit what they aim for. They rattle their sabers and test these things, and the GCC Arabs are deathly afraid they'll strike them. GCC mouthpieces are already condemning our strikes to placate the street, but their front offices all know they need us here in the region or Iran takes over everything."

CAG pulled some imagery from a folder and placed the photos on the table. Saint picked them up and studied them for several moments.

"Saint, your target is a missile final assembly facility in south central Iran called Yaz Kernoum. You can see it's a hike from here, and it looks like some kind of cement plant or mine out in the middle of nowhere. According to DIA, though, it's the one place in Iran that can fuel the rockets and install the guidance section and warheads. The GCC thinks their counties are targeted next because who knows who is controlling the IRGC these days. Frankly, they have a point. We know Iran has been working on nukes for a long time, and although the experts say they are years away, the *experts* have been wrong before."

Wilson noticed a sudden look of disdain on DCAG's face as he stared at Saint's khaki uniform shirt. Wilson glanced at it himself and saw why. Saint had affixed a command-at-sea pin, which signified an officer in active command of a sea-going unit, over his right pocket.

Bastard couldn't wait to put it there, Wilson thought.

CAG pointed out the targets on imagery. "You have eight aimpoints, and I'm going to give you two divisions of strikers—plus a dedicated *Iron Hand* package. We'll be in this vicinity for the next 24 hours. Time on target is 0530 local, just after sunup. And this strike has to be covert from the get-go, with perfect comm discipline. We must show our hand only at the last moment. We'll have made an announcement that the current operation is over, then hit 'em with this a few hours later…part of the "fighting dirty" I mentioned a few days ago. You'll have AWACS for target area control and the dedicated mission tankers you need from Air Wing Four. This is an add-on—after we finish the scheduled strikes tonight. I want a brief at 1600 with your plan. Then we go to the boss for his blessing."

CAG paused for effect, then added, "This strike *has* to go. Losses are acceptable."

Saint looked up at CAG, then back at the imagery. Wilson noticed Saint's discomfort and the minute shift of his body. "What weapons do you want us to use, sir?"

"You tell me, but give me as much heads up as you can so the ship can break 'em out and build 'em up. Given our GPS hiccup or spoofing from last night, I want a solid backup plan."

Wilson looked at the chart. One hundred miles northwest of the target was Shiraz. "CAG," he asked, "any indications the MiG-35s flew last night?"

"Thought you would recognize this place. And the answer is no, not as far as we know. But Yaz Kernoum is just down the street from Shiraz. Plan for it."

CAG signaled it was time to leave. "Lots of work to do, and my staff is here to support. See you back here in 10 hours."

DCAG spoke up as Saint rose to leave. "I see you wasted no time pinning that 'sheriff's badge' on your uniform." He was not smiling.

Saint, eyes downcast, said nothing as he gathered up the folder. CAG noticed the pin and then looked away, embarrassed. The two *Hornet* pilots turned to leave.

"I spoke to Billie," CAG said, just as they reached the door. They both turned back to face him, waiting for more.

"She's holding up well, knows Steve is a fighter, and, even now, is a rock of strength to the other wives. She said the outpouring of support is overwhelming. I imagine all the squadron wives are with her right now."

Wilson knew he was right, and noted the time...approaching midnight in Virginia Beach. It was going to be another very long day and night for all the *Ravens*.

CHAPTER 62

After breakfast Wilson and Saint met in CVIC, in a small room set off from the main planning spaces to review the target folder CAG had given them. Wilson looked at the overland navigation chart first and plotted the distance: over 500 miles on a direct line and right over Hormuz, a place Wilson did not want to see again with its layered defenses. However, as with any layered defense, there were seams to exploit, and areas that would provide concealment from radar detection, allowing the strike package to expose itself at the last possible moment…if they stayed low on the ingress. At some point, though, they would have to climb to stay out of any local defenses and give themselves the best chance of acquiring their targets. The time on target was troubling, too, just after dawn, which degraded night vision goggle and infrared sensors. It also required a daylight egress, which increased the threat of scrambled interceptors from any number of fighter bases in the region, which to Wilson meant Shiraz—and Hariri.

While Saint stepped out for a moment, Blade joined Wilson in planning. Within 10 minutes, they both knew what they needed, and they had determined the "A" team to fly it. Wilson called down to his stateroom and summoned Weed to join them. The *Raven* division would be Saint, Blade, Flip and Weed, with Saint as the strike lead and Wilson backing him up.

Saint returned and spent a few moments looking at the chart while Wilson and Blade worked in silence. After a few moments, Saint took a straight edge and drew a line from the ship's position to the target. "Hmm…" he said, "if the ship can launch us in order, we might be able to do this without tanking up front. Mister Cutter, give me a max-range profile to the target area, high all the way, and the fuel when we return feet wet. Maybe we won't need to ask CAG for so many tankers."

Blade, incredulous, looked at Wilson and back at Saint. "*Sir?*"

Commander Patrick looked up and coldly assessed the senior lieutenant. Pointing with his finger on the chart, he repeated himself. "Here to *here*, max range, with this bomb load, two tanks, standard self-escort load out. We brief our plan in eight hours. I need the answer in five minutes. *Am I clear?*"

Blade swallowed hard and said, "Sir, that takes us right over Bandar Abbas, with double-digit…"

"I see exactly where it *takes* us, Mister Cutter," Saint shot back. "We'll surprise them off the cat with our audacity and high speed. Thinking we are already done for the night, they won't be able to react until we've passed over them."

Blade chuckled and shook his head in disbelief. "Those guys are going to see us coming for miles, and their gunners will still be at their posts from our previous strikes!"

"I am leading this strike, not you!" Saint fired at Blade, now visibly upset.

Wilson spoke in a low tone. "Blade, *leave us.*"

"This is *bullshit!* You can't…" Blade said through clenched teeth before Wilson interrupted him.

"*Lieutenant Cutter!* I said, *leave us!*" Wilson's words thundered at Blade and shocked him into silence. Regaining his composure, Wilson added in a low voice, "Now. *Go!*"

Blade abruptly pushed away from the table and stepped out. Wilson and Saint looked at each other. Saint spoke first.

"He's off the strike. Why did you even select him?"

"Because he's the TOPGUN trained squadron tactical expert—and a damn good pilot. He stays."

Saint's eyes narrowed as he stared at Wilson. *"What did you just say?"*

"He *stays*, sir, because *I* need him." Gesturing at the chart, he added, "And we aren't going to fly this profile, either."

Incensed at Wilson's insubordination, Saint fired back. "Let me warn you now that *you* can be replaced, Mister Wilson. I will forget I heard this mutinous talk coming from a senior department head and *subordinate*, obviously affected by the stress of combat, once we complete this strike as fragged."

Wilson was prepared for this confrontation and decided, at this point, he was unwilling to needlessly risk his life and the lives of the others.

"Commander Patrick, when we launch tonight, we are two individuals trying to do the job, and we're also trying to give ourselves the best chance of survival. We aren't going to highlight ourselves and motor straight up there like flying pincushions for their missiles. We are going to stay low and tank enroute, under the radar until we get into the Persian Gulf. We will then ramp up over a less heavily defended area, hit the target, and egress to safety the way we came. I am going to plan this, and you are going to brief it and lead it and *take the fucking credit*. But if you deviate from my black line by so much as a mile, I'm gonna take it back. You'll know when you hear me transmit on strike common,

'Flips, go alternate tac.' We will then wheel away from you *en masse,* and you will be *alone,* sir."

Saint leaned in and whispered, "You're fired."

"As you wish, sir, but who are you going to get to help you? Weed? Blade? They aren't stupid. Clam? He's not a qualified strike leader. And CAG thinks the lineup is already set. Tell him that the *Raven* department heads are off the strike, and then brief him and the admiral on your flawed plan. He's right down there in his stateroom just 10 frames away, probably trying to nap." Wilson pointed to the starboard side of the ship for effect. "Go ahead, sir. Wake him up, and get this news to him early so he has time to flex." Pausing for a moment, he then said, "You *need* us, sir, and we'll come through with a plan that's tactically smart and meets CAGs objectives and gives us *all* a chance at survival. Now, *commander,* shall we proceed? Or am I still fired?"

Wilson watched a crimson flush of color race across Saint's face, still locked in its piercing stare. Wilson knew Saint didn't have the guts to follow through on his threat.

After several seconds, Saint pushed back from the table and looked at his watch. "When I come back at noon, I want the plan and the weapons load out, in detail. CAG needs the load out ASAP."

"Aye, aye, sir. You'll have it." Wilson nodded slowly with determined eyes.

CHAPTER 63

Fifteen minutes before launch time, Wilson released the parking brake and tax-ied, under the skillful control of the yellow shirt, from his spot on El 3. In the 20 hours since their confrontation in CVIC, he and Saint had managed to plan the add-on strike to Yaz Kernoum with a minimum of friction. When disagree-ments did occur in front of the others, a raised eyebrow from Wilson was all it had taken to get Saint to defer.

The plan was to launch the package after a routine "dawn patrol" launch of two S-3s and two *Hornets* to monitor the surface picture around the strike group and deal with any threats. *Valley Forge's* two nights of retaliatory strikes against IRGC and Iranian Navy units was complete. There had been no addi-tional American losses, and the last of the strikers had recovered the previous hour. Just before walk time, Wilson had stolen a glance at CNN and heard a Pentagon reporter say the strikes were over. The report was accompanied by an Iranian-manufactured propaganda videotape of burning residential areas and frenzied crowds chanting "Death to America."

Wilson had shrugged it off, too tired to care anymore. Messaging was not his job.

He *was* tired. During the past 48 hours, he may have slept three hours, maybe four, grabbing fitful catnaps whenever he could. He had forced himself to re-main alert during the strike brief, which Saint delivered to the equally exhausted aircrew in his flat monotone.

Now, in the early morning darkness, the typical nadir of human perfor-mance, he and the others had to perform at their peak to make this strike a success.

An E-2 and two *Vikings* were soon launched into a clear night, half-moon almost overhead. They were followed by two *Buccaneers* off the waist. On rou-tine patrol, these aircraft would make themselves known to the Iranians, and keep their attention, while the strikers worked their way, unseen, into position low on the water. The deception plan was beginning to come together.

In line behind the waist catapults, Wilson fidgeted in the cockpit of *405*, his familiar nighttime butterflies returning. Weed was behind him in the queue in *407*, hands resting on the canopy bow, and Blade was going through final checks on El 4 in *411*. Dutch was the airborne spare, turning on the fantail in *413* with his canopy down, ready to go. Saint was starting up in *404* someplace on the bow. The *Raven* division call sign on this raid was *Anvil*, and the *Spartan* division was designated *Sledge*. The two divisions would be joined by the *Tron* self-escort suppression element of one EA-6B and two *Moonshadows*. Tonight there would be no check-in on strike common, no post launch voice calls from the strikers. To a great degree, the strike's success hinged on their ability to maintain communications discipline, waiting to expose themselves at the last possible moment.

The *Rhino* tankers were next off, as a *Prowler* taxied down from the bow to feed the cats with airplanes. Wilson looked at his kneeboard card: just a few minutes behind schedule, time Saint could make up.

Off to his right, Wilson sensed motion, and looked down to see Chief Grant waving to get his attention. Pointing to the bow, Grant raised four fingers, then a fist, then four again, followed by a thumbs down. Wilson immediately grasped the meaning: Saint's jet was down and, as alternate strike leader, this would now be his mission to lead.

Yes! Wilson thought, as he returned a thumbs up in vigorous acknowledgment. He caught Weed's attention and, through hand signals, passed on the news. His roommate shook a thumbs up in return, followed by two raised fists of encouragement. In the last moments before the launch, Wilson shook his head with contempt. He *knew* Saint would find some reason not to go, but at the same time he was relieved he would not have to deal with Saint's airborne leadership.

In short order, the *Sledge* and *Tron* elements launched. Then, Wilson, a mix of adrenalin and rage coursing through his bloodstream, impatiently waited for his turn at the catapult to do what he trained a career for: lead a long-range power projection strike deep into enemy territory, which would *make everyone happy*. Make Washington happy, make the GCC happy, and make the admiral's staff happy. *Just hook me up, dammit!* and put Yaz Kernoum out of action *now* and bring everyone back and everything will be okay. Saint, Cajun, Psycho, CAG, the admiral…even Mary and the kids… *all* was blocked out when he was finally hooked up to the catapult, checking the cockpit, cycling the controls, watching for the burner signal, and then shoving the throttles to max, locking his left arm hard against the stops, like a caged animal, impatient to be set free, furious to get off the friggin' ship, breathing deeply as he scanned the blackness off the cat track ahead of him, full of resolve to do his duty and *make everyone happy*.

With a familiar jolt, Wilson was shoved back in his seat. The deck edge rushed up and under as he accelerated into the void, fiery thrust lifting him into the night, a free man.

Saint exploded, in a barely suppressed rage, into the ready room, followed by Ted asking for more detail on *404*. Saint threw his helmet into his chair, but it bounced onto the deck with a crack. At the duty desk, Psycho rose to her feet in shock, and Nicky froze in his back-row chair.

Saint turned and let loose a salvo at Ted. "Is it too much to ask to have a fully mission capable jet for the biggest strike of the year? I'm the damn strike lead and you put me in *that?*"

"Sir, four-zero-four flew last night, no problem. It's a good flyer. We had no indication the TACAN was bad until now. We're swapping it out."

"Too late, Mister Randall. Launch complete! My strike is going up there without me, and I have to explain to CAG why I'm not leading it." Beads of sweat dotted Saint's forehead as he placed his sidearm on the counter. He then removed his blood chit and flung it at Psycho.

"XO, we could have made it, but you downed the jet just as they began to taxi you, and the deck wouldn't let us work on it until you were respotted." After the hectic maintenance pace of the previous two days, Ted's own patience was wearing thin.

Saint's jaw remained set as he continued to remove his gear. "The TACAN is a vital piece of equipment—*every* component of the jet is vital—and when it's down, especially in combat, the jet is *down!*"

"Yes, sir, no argument. We had a small window to make and we couldn't. At least you and the jet are safe on deck."

"*Fuck! Fuck! Fuck!*" Saint muttered audibly to himself. Nicky was sure he was witnessing a breakdown, and everyone in the ready room was embarrassed by the display.

Psycho broke the silence. "Excuse me, sir, but you should have another pistol clip…"

Saint reached into his survival vest pocket and answered, "Yes, another clip for the combat mission I'm *not* going on because of the unsat jet I was assigned." He tugged on the clip once, and when it didn't come free, he yanked on it hard.

With a loud *hiss,* an orange smoke, tinged in pink, shot from his vest and formed a billowing cloud in the front of the ready room. While others scrambled away, Saint dropped the vest to the floor in disbelief.

"Cut it!" somebody cried.

That call propelled Nicky forward. He took his XO's shroud cutter from the pile at his feet and cut the lanyard to the still-firing flare. Gunner Humphries appeared beside him and reached over Nicky to grab the flare and get it out of the ready room. *"Make a hole!"* Gunner shouted as he opened the door and walked briskly past astonished onlookers in maintenance control. He turned aft and then outboard to toss the flare over the side from a hatch under the LSO platform. The high-visibility smoke, however, lingered in the passageway and compartments as sailors fanned it away from their faces.

The ready room was still in shock, when Psycho yelled, *"Attention on deck!"* The room popped to attention, and Saint's face fell, and then turned white, as he looked through the wafting smoke.

Swoboda stood, stunned and incredulous, at the back of the *Raven* ready room.

"CAG...yes...sir."

CHAPTER 64

This would be no "ordinary" power projection strike.

The strike package stayed low on the water under strict radar emissions control and veered northwest in a running rendezvous with *Super Hornet* and *Viking* tankers. Each pilot judged range, bearing, and closure by means of the sight picture provided by a cluster of lights from the tanker and the aircraft that may have already joined on it. The pilots had rarely used this method since flight school. Flying without the aid of their radars, especially when they could not even use the radio for a dark night *"comin' left"* sugar call or to check everyone in on the proper frequency, was disconcerting. The key, though, was to remain as covert as possible.

Wilson eased up next to Weed's darkened jet while Blade was in the basket. The airborne *Anvil* spare, Dutch, appeared on his bearing line. To the north several miles and 1,000 feet above were the *Sledges* on their tanker, and he hoped the *Tron* division was somewhere nearby. The aircrew in these aircraft was the best A-team Air Wing Four could put together on such short notice after the previous night's schedule.

Once Blade and Weed completed their refueling, Wilson extended his probe and slid behind the basket as the formation motored northwest in silence, still over an hour from the target. While in the basket, he noted a small light on the water, maybe a merchant—or a dhow—just off their nose with no chance to avoid. They would hear the jet engines and maybe even see a position light.

Damn. Who was on that vessel and what would they make of it? Would they radio someone about what they observed? After the recent action, he surmised it was unlikely to be an Iranian vessel way out here, but not knowing gnawed at him as it always did.

Wilson finished refueling and crossed under Blade and Weed as they waited for Dutch. Donning his goggles, he scanned the surface of the water and saw some lights well north—not a factor. He found the *Tron* division behind them and to the south, but at least they were there. *Good, we're all aboard and on timeline,* he thought.

Wilson checked his fuel: two hundred pounds low. Despite needing every drop to hit the target and escape with a reserve, two hundred low was not bad. Now the strike package would accelerate ahead, staying low, while the tankers joined on another tanker to top off and meet the strikers at the get-well point in the Arabian Gulf for post-strike tanking.

Dutch finished refueling and crossed under. A minute later, the *Super Hornet* retracted the refueling store basket and veered away left in a shallow angle of bank. The *Anvils* were alone on their track.

In silence, they shuffled the formation, Blade and Dutch flying cruise on Wilson's left wing, Weed on his right. Wilson completed his combat checklist for the second time since launch and popped out a bundle of chaff. To the others it looked like a flashbulb under Wilson's jet and served as the signal for them to complete their checklist and check their systems. Wilson noted each pilot expend a bundle in order. *Even at 0445, we are on our game tonight,* he thought.

In the distance, Wilson saw the mountains of Oman rise out of the northwest horizon, and aided by his NVGs, he could see the glow of cultural lighting from the Iranian coastline. Scanning the sky, he saw no aircraft lights over Iran, but he did see a few over the GOO. He surmised they were American, and those he saw over the Persian Gulf could be American or civilian. On his moving-map, the distance to the coastline was 45 miles, but it looked much closer on goggles as the moon backlit the rising terrain. To his right, he sensed a muted flash and noted Weed's *Hornet* was now without its drop tanks. When he looked left, he saw Blade punch off his tanks and watched them tumble away. Wilson noted he had only a few hundred pounds remaining in each of his tanks and prepared to jettison them once they were dry. This would reduce both his weight and drag and would increase maneuverability.

As the little formation continued through the darkness in silence, each pilot busied himself in the cockpit monitoring the navigation and thinking about their individual weapon deliveries and the enemy threats they might face.

As they approached the coast, Wilson hit SELECT JETT, and, as he felt his tanks leave the aircraft, he cracked the throttle back to compensate for the increased airspeed. He veered the formation left to lead them into a fissure in the rising Omani wilderness, which offered a place of concealment from visual or electronic detection. He looked back to see Dutch clean off his tanks, just in time, as the coastline loomed ahead.

Low-altitude on NVGs in mountainous terrain—in the wee hours—was varsity flying, and each of the *Ravens* worked hard to accomplish three things: to keep position on Wilson, keep themselves out of the rocks, and look for threats.

The half-moon bathed the terrain in all the light they needed as they turned their heads right and left to scan through the green-tinted spotlight their goggles provided. Wilson led them up the illuminated side of the ridge face, and the wingmen held tight positions above their leader, which allowed them to maintain formation and monitor ground clearance as well. The nearby *Sledge* and *Tron* formations did likewise over a moonscape of rugged, uninhabited land. As they transited over the ridgelines, they maintained radio silence, avoided the shadows and stayed as far away as possible from scattered settlements that would be alarmed at the sudden thunderous rumble from the jet formations breaking the stillness of the desert night.

The *Anvils* made an easy left turn on a westerly course. Wilson led them down the backside of the Omani range to the sea as he increased his ground-speed for the next leg, which led into the Persian Gulf. He noted that the cultural lighting from Dubai dominated the southwest horizon and bounced off a high overcast that bathed everything in a greenish NVG glow. Numerous lights from shipping and oil platforms dotted the Gulf ahead of them.

He checked the clock… Inside 30 minutes to go.

Losses are acceptable. He remembered CAG's words and the punch they sent to his stomach. Air Wing Four was going to take no chances. The strikers were loaded with laser-guided bombs each pilot would manually guide into their assigned aimpoint with a laser beam…all while flying formation and monitoring the threat. Because they still didn't know why the *Raven* division had NO GPS indications over Bandar Abbas, the strikers needed a weapon that didn't depend on GPS guidance. Laser deliveries, however, required clear line-of-sight, so if a cloud deck got in the way over the target, the *Anvils* and *Sledges* would be forced to get underneath it. That would mean exposing themselves to the threat to a much greater degree deep inside a hostile country. Looking in the direction of Yaz Kernoum, Wilson couldn't see any weather. They were on time and Wilson's fuel was as planned. Things were looking good.

Now on the water, Wilson took them down as low as he dared, his obedient wingmen still in loose cruise as the eastern sky began to lighten behind them. He looked under his goggles to assess the ambient light and decided to keep them on as long as he could before the rising sun compelled him to remove them.

Wilson reached down to find the fuel dump switch and held it for a second before he secured it. He then switched on his radar. The others saw a shot of fuel burst from Wilson's fuel dump masts: a welcome sight, their briefed signal to energize their own emitters. Now led by the radar, it was as if they had been blind and could suddenly see. Each of the pilots immediately devoured the tactical information the electronic eye provided them about the surface and the air contacts ahead. They avoided the islands in the Gulf, some Iranian and some Arab, as they continued west just above the tranquil waters. Wilson was struck by the lack of tanker traffic—there wasn't any.

A new voice filled his radio headset. *"Thor, picture clean."*

Wilson transmitted, *"Anvil"* to answer the AWACS controller orbiting high over the Gulf in an E-3 *Sentry*, the Air Force aircraft providing early warning and tactical control for the strike package with an aircrew he had communicated the strike plan to the day prior. In succession, he heard the others.

"Sledge."

"Tron."

All were up strike common and another potential disconnect appeared to be solved. *Thor* responded with "Houseboat," the code-word to continue. No last-minute reprieve from Washington; the strike was going to go.

Wilson got to the end of the navigation leg and turned northwest on the established route. When he could see Weed's helmet next to him with his un-aided eye, he decided it was time for his goggles to come off. The first warm rays of sunlight creeped up from the eastern horizon and silhouetted the sharp shadows of *Hornets* next to him. The formation sped closer to a remote area of the Iranian coastline where they would enter the Islamic Republic to begin their final run-in for Yaz Kernoum.

CHAPTER 65

In his alert facility bed, Reza Hariri had finally gone to sleep after another restless night of waiting in vain for the Americans to come to him. It had been a long and frustrating two nights at the Shiraz alert strip, his armed and fueled MiG-35 parked in a shelter off the end of the runway, just beyond the wall of his small sleeping area. The setup allowed him and the other alert pilots to be in their aircraft and taxiing for takeoff within minutes.

The action around Hormuz had been disappointing, with IRIAF fighters recording no kills and maintaining CAPs far from the American strike groups in an effort to distract them and lure them away from the targeted areas—and into the teeth of the defenses. To Hariri it was all foolishness. *No, idiocy.* Iran possessed *dozens* of modern fighters with beyond visual range weapons, including the MiG-35!

Let me get down there, at night, and every one of my missiles will have a target, he thought, railing against the Iranian leadership that kept the MiGs *here* on strip alert, hundreds of miles from the action—while his F-14s and *Phantoms* were given worthless CAPs well inland. It was like a bullfighter waving a red cape at a charging bull from the safety of the grandstands. *No, we need to get down there, take some losses, but bloody their nose—much more than we did two nights ago.*

One (*one!*) *Hornet* had been shot down by antiaircraft guns over Bandar Abbas. He was surprised the Americans even *continued* their strikes after that loss, so risk averse and pampered a people. The intelligence collectors said the dead pilot was the commander of Wilson's squadron, and Hariri reflected that Wilson may have been inspired by the example of this man, a commander who *led from the front.* Pity that more in the IRIAF did not lead that way. They were worried, instead, about currying favor in Tehran!

Wilson. Surely he was involved with the actions to the south, and Hariri chafed to get another shot at him. He realized, though, it would be most coincidental if fate put them together again. He was certain he would have at least gotten a chance last night, the reason he spent the night here, hoping for a scramble in his *fully fueled* monster that would have covered the distance to

Hormuz in minutes at Mach 2. But the Klaxon had never sounded, and his excited junior pilots had returned hours ago with their weapons still attached to their aircraft and bogus stories of "standing up to the Americans." Knowing the pilots had been safe on CAP stations miles away from the *Hornets* while the enemy attacked his homeland with impunity, the stories had filled Hariri with contempt. At least the *Pasdaran,* and even the Islamic Republic Navy, was willing to shed blood against the Great Satan. Hariri would have sacrificed himself, and a squadron of his pilots, to down just *one* American fighter last night.

Indications were that the Americans had accomplished whatever goal they had after two nights of limited retaliatory strikes along the coast: an example of their clumsy and predictable military-stick-followed-by-diplomatic-carrot approach. Exhausted and unable to believe he and the IRIAF had missed the opportunity of a lifetime, he fell into his alert bed with his boots on, thinking of fat generals in Tehran, and fighting a TOPGUN, and squeezing the trigger one last time.

Vehicle headlights moved east on a desolate stretch of the two-lane coastal road—just as the *Anvils* approached from the south at low level. *"Damn!"* Wilson muttered to himself. Too late to avoid them, he led the *Hornets* feet dry into Iran as the vehicles passed underneath. Wilson imagined their startled drivers reaching for their cell phones to warn authorities of a sudden roar of jets crossing the beach in the twilight. He rolled up on a wing for a second to ascertain the vehicle types, which looked like sedans in the early morning murk. Wilson whispered more than transmitted, *"Fly ball,"* on strike common. The code word commanded the strikers to arm up and signified to *Thor* they were feet dry, a fact that was soon transmitted to eager staff officers monitoring their progress at command centers in the region, in Tampa, and in Washington.

If they had not been spotted until now, Wilson liked their chances. That meant they had avoided detection from sailors on "innocent" vessels in the GOO and Gulf and Iran's own early warning net…a combination of luck and solid planning. He noted 10 miles to the "pop" point. Within minutes, the Iranians would be alerted to their presence, and if Wilson's plan worked, they would be powerless to counter the Americans with anything like defense in depth.

Because of the rugged terrain, he elevated the division a bit but remained under the radar horizon and out of the shadowy darkness of the desert floor. The desert was now a dim, gray-blue surface, but the growing radiance from the east was beginning to highlight the ridgeline off to his right. This low-light situation *at low altitude* was dangerous, and once they crossed the coastline, the strikers moved out into combat spread formation. In 15 seconds, they could climb.

Wilson brought the throttles up, eased back on the stick, and commanded his *Hornet* to enter a shallow energy-sustaining climb; his wingmen followed in mirror image. Off to the east a few miles, he saw the *Sledges,* four dark *Super Hornets,* outlined against the pink sky as they, too, started up. The radar cursors in every cockpit swept back and forth in search of any airborne threat on their nose. With their senses sharpened by fear and adrenaline, the pilots scanned the horizon for threats, monitored their navigation, checked their fuel state, and fiddled with their weapons programs. Throughout, they kept their knots up in a steady climb as they pressed further into Iran.

About halfway up, Wilson looked over his right shoulder and saw the orange sun burst above the eastern horizon and spread its warm rays of light from north to south. While observing this tranquil scene, he noted his first RWR hit—an early warning radar at 4 o'clock. *Not bad,* he thought. They had avoided Iranian radar detection until now, exposing themselves only when they had gotten behind the lines, minutes from the target. The strikers continued their transonic climb, knowing they were now drawing the attention of a hostile and surprised integrated air defense system.

In his semicomatose state, Hariri's mind attempted to grasp the meaning of the first sounding of the alert Klaxon. With open eyes, he heard it again accompanied by rapid footsteps and excited shouting outside. He bolted out of bed as a junior pilot, running to his own alert fighter, flung the door open and shouted, "*Sarhang* Hariri, the Americans are coming!"

Knowing every second counted, Hariri whipped his g-suit on with swift tugs on the zippers, grabbed his helmet and dashed to his jet. His mind raced. *Where? What are they doing? How many?* He bounded up the ladder and dropped himself into the cockpit in the same manner he had 20 years ago defending his homeland from the Iraqis. Sergeants shouted commands and linemen pushed open the shelter doors as Hariri, with help from his crew chief, hooked himself into his parachute harness. With a loud *whoosh,* a giant hose connected to the MiG became rigid and forced air through the turbines as Hariri initiated the fuel and spark required to begin the continuous cycle of jet propulsion.

Hariri taxied out from under the fluorescent lights and into the dawn twilight, cleared for immediate takeoff. He was given an initial vector of southeast, following a section of F-4 *Phantoms* that were already thundering down the runway ahead of him. He looked over his shoulder into the adjacent shelter and saw that the other alert MiG-35 had its canopy up and was surrounded by maintenance technicians. *Russian morons!* he shouted to himself before ignoring his wingman's plight.

The alert shelters were located adjacent to the runway, and Hariri didn't even stop as he taxied onto it. He brought the throttles up to afterburner, and his jet roared over the concrete behind two giant pillars of white-hot fire: a horizontal rocket ship accelerating to flying speed within 2,000 feet. Hariri picked the nose up and rolled right on course, in his single-minded focus to find and kill the enemy.

CHAPTER 66

The strike package leveled off high over a stark desert landscape of erosion-scarred ridges. The predawn light showed deep crags and fissures on every surface. During the planning, Wilson had picked this area for the ingress because it was devoid of surface threats but, as he looked at the dim surface from high above, he thought it the most uninviting terrain he'd ever seen. Harsh. Foreboding. The land below was *ugly*, and Wilson wanted to minimize his time over it, if for no other reason than to get to the target before the Iranians could mount a threat.

With fewer than 10 minutes to go, the pilots took last-minute glances at their assigned aimpoint imagery and double-checked their weapons switches set. Yaz Kernoum was located in a small valley separated from a village to the west by several miles. Nearby, and typical of this region of the world, were long green agricultural fields that reminded Wilson of Balad Ruz. The topography was also reminiscent of the Fallon training complex in the high desert of Nevada. Wilson's aimpoint was a rectangular building that looked like an abandoned industrial facility. It was located between two identical buildings on a road that bisected the complex. Weed's target, a missile final assembly tower, was nearby. Blade and Dutch were to hit fuel storage magazines set apart from the complex to the northwest, and the *Sledge's* target was the missile component storage warehouses on the eastern perimeter.

The idea was for all eight strikers to release on their aimpoints, guide the laser weapons from their cockpits while flying formation and scanning for threats, and then egress with mutual support while the *Tron* division behind them provided defense suppression. All the aircraft, except the EA-6B, were loaded with air-to-air missiles to defend themselves from enemy fighters. Wilson and the others knew the Iranians were now watching them on radar as they raced to the target with their heads on a swivel.

At the initial point, no one was reporting any radar contacts. Wilson selected AIR-TO-GROUND and transmitted, "Tapes on!"

Just then the radio crackled as *Thor* provided the strikers with their first contact report, a God's-eye radar view of the situation around Yaz Kernoum. "*Thor* picture–single group, bullseye, three-four-zero at sixty, medium, hot."

"*Anvils,* roger, *declare,*" Wilson responded, asking the AWACS controller if the airborne contact was hostile, already knowing the answer.

"Hostile," *Thor* replied.

"*Anvil* one-one."

Though separated from the enemy by 80 miles, the Americans now faced a problem that called for a decision from Wilson. The two groups of aircraft were approaching one another at well over 1,000 knots of closure and would merge in minutes. Knowing the strike package would be at their release points in about half that time, and the target must be hit—*Losses are acceptable*—pressing to the target was required. But if they were shot down by fighter-launched, forward-quarter missiles before the bombs impacted, all was for nothing. It was going to be close.

Wilson keyed the mike. "*Sledges,* send a section and take the bandit group. Everyone else continue as fragged."

"*Sledge* two-one, wilco... Break: *Sledge* two-three flight, target bandit group, bullseye three-four-zero at sixty, medium, hot."

"*Sledge* two-three. *Thor, Sledge,* two-three committing group three-four-zero, sixty, declare."

"*Thor,* group three-four-zero, sixty, hostile."

"*Sledge* two-three, hostile."

Wilson's decision effectively cut the American firepower against Yaz Kernoum by 25 percent, but it was a contingency they had planned for as the *Sledges* were all going against the missile storage warehouses and could spare some overlap. The *Rhino* weapons system operators worked the intercept with the two AMRAAM missiles the larger aircraft carried. Wilson's *Anvil* division each carried only one AMRAAM for self-protection. All the fighters were loaded with two *Sidewinder* heatseekers.

On time line, Wilson commanded his radar and FLIR to find his assigned aimpoint. His targeted building came into view on his FLIR, as if viewed through a soda straw. In a deft motion, he slewed his aiming diamond over it. He checked that his wingmen were in position and noted the trajectory of a HARM missile fired by one of the *Trons.*

"*Thor,* new picture. Bandit group bullseye, three-three-five at fifty, medium, hot. *Second* group bullseye, two-niner-zero at sixty, low, hot!"

Damn, Wilson thought. Another bogey group to complicate the picture. He queried *Thor.* "Declare!"

"*Hostile!*"

The fact the Iranians had sent two groups of interceptors, separated laterally by some 40 miles, posed an even more difficult problem for the Americans, who were already limited by available fighters to counter this new threat. Wilson could picture the geometry in his mind—these guys could pose a problem for their egress to the get-well point in the Gulf.

Weed came up on the radio. *"Anvil* one-two is spiked, zero-two-zero, chaff, defending."

Wilson saw Weed pull away and down in order to free himself from the electronic grasp of a SAM missile radar. He also noted the two green bombs on Weed's wings and realized he needed them, and all the remaining bombs, to hit their assigned aimpoints. Wilson searched the ground ahead for a launch plume and found it: a bright flare trailing a white plume that rose in the distance. The missile picked up speed as it ascended but was not tracking Weed, who, still in his defensive maneuver, was now 90 degrees off and descending. Wilson called out to his friend.

"Anvil one-two, tally on the *light post,* out your left nine o'clock long. No factor! Resume!"

"One-two, ah, *visual,* roger."

Wilson saw Weed reverse his turn to come back to his place in formation. Ahead and to his left, Wilson noted some black AAA puffs suspended in air, then some flashes from fresh air bursts underneath them. On his HUD, the seconds counted down to release. Switches set. The aimpoint grew larger in the FLIR display. A glance at Blade and Dutch confirmed they were in perfect position abeam.

A call from *Tron* filled his headset: *"Magnum* from *Tron* five-two."

Things *were* happening fast. Another picture call from *Thor* reminded him of the new threat to the west and the need to counter it.

"Trons, can you take the group to the west?" he asked.

"Affirm!" one of the marines answered.

"Roger, inside 30 seconds to release," Wilson acknowledged, just as his RWR lit off.

DEEDLE, DEEDLE, *DEEDLEDEEDLEDEEDLEDEEDLE!*

Wilson snapped his head to the spot from which Weed's SAM had launched and saw another missile lifting from the shadows of the ridge to the east. Weed saw it, too.

"Light post lifting at the *Anvil's* one-thirty!"

"Anvil one-one is spiked with a tally," Wilson replied, knowing he couldn't defend himself without throwing off his delivery. With five seconds until release, he kept his thumb pressed down on the pickle switch and held steady on the steering cue. At the same time, he kept one eye on the SAM that was now passing above the horizon and tracking toward him. Three...two...one...

The bombs left his jet with a lurch, and Wilson whipped the aircraft left and pulled hard, spitting out chaff to evade the missile. Looking straight down, he saw his bombs begin their earthward journey, a trip that would take over 30 seconds to complete—time he would need.

***

The confused predawn sky over Yaz Kernoum was dotted with black clouds of AAA fire, SAM plumes arcing here and there, and laser-guided bombs en-route to their aimpoints. Waves of RF energy filled the air performing diverse tasks in the service of each adversary. The cockpits were populated by highly trained professionals in their 20's and 30's, their minds trying to grasp what they saw and heard, identifying who made terse, nervous radio transmissions to build a mental picture for themselves and their wingmen. The men struggled to maintain as much situational awareness as they could while maneuvering hard in three dimensions to survive and guide their weapons to impact. It was the culmination of years of training from habitual drill to replicating this type of power projection strike in a permissive environment, and in the low morning light over the central desert of Iran, the intensity of this mission was the most they had ever experienced.

***

Wilson picked up "his" missile, but it was drifting aft on his canopy and going ballistic as he pulled back to the target. He rolled out to unmask his FLIR and reacquire the aimpoint. His mind absorbed a transmission from *Thor*—the northern group was 20 miles away—as he found the middle building and held the aiming diamond on it, while taking peeks at his wingmen who were also heads-down in their cockpits. He heard a "Fox-3" call and looked right to see *Sledge 23* and *24* launch AMRAAMs at the lead bandit group. Slender fingers of white smoke produced by the bright "lights" of the missile rocket motors moved away from the fighters at high speed and began a graceful climb to intercept the enemy aircraft the Americans could only see with their radars.

Ten seconds till impact. Wilson corrected some aiming diamond drift with a deft slew to the middle of the building. His ears picked up the voice calls of his wingmen and the *deedles* from his RWR, but they did not register now, lost as he was in the concentration needed to hold his aiming diamond on target. The seconds counted down and the FLIR view shifted as the *Hornets* flew over the target, the countdown always too slow for the impatient aviators who just wanted to get out of *Indian Country* as soon as they could.

On the FLIR he saw his bombs, two white dashes, enter the screen and hit the building, the infrared image turning white from heat and smoke generated from the impact. Selecting WIDE, he saw Weeds' bombs explode on his aiming point with two concentric shock waves flying out from the middle of his target. Returning to NARROW, Wilson noticed a strong surface wind had blown away most of the smoke, and he could now see that a majority of his building was destroyed. A steady flame, resembling a blowtorch, shot from the target.

"*Anvil's* Miller Time!" Wilson broadcast on the radio. He overbanked left to begin their direct route to the Gulf.

"*Sledge* two-one and two-two clear, visual on *Anvil.*"

"*Sledge* two-three, timeout on the lead bandit. Tally smoke! Splash one!"

"*Sledge* two-four, timeout on the trailer. Tally ho! Splash two! Visual, six clear!"

In the northern twilight the pilots saw two black puffs with fiery trails falling to the desert floor. Two down.

"*Sledge* two-three, flight visual, six clear, egressing."

Having dispatched the lead group of bandits, their type still unknown to the Americans, *Sledge 23* and *24* jinked through the target area to join the lead section who were now trailing the *Anvils*—with all aircraft heading southwest, the shortest direction to the coast. On the surface, the muzzle flashes of over a dozen guns sent familiar arcs of deadly tracers skyward. Though the AAA was heavy, it was ineffective, and the SAMs were still lifting off their rails. With the extent of the defenses, they now had no doubt this area was more than just a cement plant next to a rural village.

Wilson's RWR lit off again. A SAM was tracking him from his 8 o'clock, and he picked it up visually. Breaking into it, he bunted the nose—and saw the missile mimic his move. *Oh shit!*

"*Anvil* one-one spiked, defending!"

Straining to keep sight of the missile against the dawn sky, Wilson bunted the nose again to pick up knots, and realized that he was surrounded by AAA puffs. He lit the burner and jinked into the missile, this one tracking his movements, watching it draw near from above the horizon, waiting for the right time...*Damn, it's fast! Now!*

Wilson rolled and pulled into it, crushed by instantaneous g that made it difficult to keep sight. Trailing a residual plume, the missile flew underneath him. He flinched when it exploded close to his jet with a sharp *BOOM* heard through the Plexiglas canopy, the warhead making a blooming circle of flame and frag.

"*You okay?*" Weed called with concern.

Wilson rolled through the horizon and was relieved that he saw no cautions in the cockpit.

"Yeah, can you bug southwest?"

"Affirm, I'm at your right five, comin' to four."

"Visual, six clear. *Let's bug two-three-zero,*" Wilson directed.

The strike package was now sprinting southwest to the coast and safety, leaving the heavily defended caldron of Yaz Kernoum behind, columns of smoke from burning aimpoints rising into the sky. The *Tron* escort was off a few miles to the northwest, prosecuting the western group of bandits, acting as a blocking force for the rest of the package. After defending from the SAM, the two *Raven* department heads were now supersonic, several miles behind the others, as they all ran to the safety of the Gulf.

Wilson noticed a contact on his radar inside 10 miles, crossing left to right. Alarmed, he locked it, and soon identified it as the *Tron* EA-6B, alone, and going in the wrong direction.

"*Tron* five-one, *Anvil* one-one is at your right two o'clock long. Bring it southwest!"

"*Tron* five-one, roger," the *Prowler* answered, immediately turning southwest. The AWACS controller then called to inform them of a new threat.

"*Thor*, new group, bullseye, three-four-zero, fifteen, medium, heading one-eight-zero."

From this call, Wilson knew the bandits were nearby and probably gaining. "*Thor, Anvils* on the egress. BRA from *Anvil* one-one. Declare!"

"Standby, *Anvil*...*Anvil, Thor*, hostile BRA zero-one-zero at twenty-three, medium, hot."

"*Heading?*"

"Two-zero-zero."

With his arm locked against the throttle stops and the airframe moaning from the supersonic airspeed, Wilson did some mental calculations. The Iranians were 20 miles aft and on an intercept course, with the Gulf sanctuary over 50 miles away. However, the *Tron* EA-6B was up ahead with Wilson and his roommate set to pass them soon. A heading change would buy a bit of time.

"*Tron* five-one, check left twenty! Gate—*everything you've got! Unload for knots!*"

"Five-one, roger!" Wilson saw the *Prowler* bank left a few miles ahead.

"*Thor,* picture. *Tron* five-two, hostile BRA, three-one-zero at twenty-five, medium, hot."

"*Tron* five-two, sorted left."

"Five-three sorted right!"

By listening to the comms Wilson formed a picture in his mind. The *Tron* escort fighters were running on the bandit group to the northwest, their right flank. The other bandit group was running them down from behind, and, with its limited top-end speed, the *Prowler* would be easy prey. Well ahead, the other strikers were egressing hard with the coast in sight.

"*Tron* five-two, Fox-three on the western bandit!"

"*Tron* five-three, Fox-three on the eastern bandit." Wilson saw two more AMRAAM plumes appear in the distant sky, about 10 miles away. They headed toward the still unseen bandits to the northwest.

"*Anvil, Thor,* threat BRA three-six-zero at seventeen, medium, hot."

DEEDLE, DEEDLE, *DEEDLEDEEDLEDEEDLEDEEDLE!*

Wilson was locked up by a fighter radar behind him.

"*Anvil* one-one is spiked at six. Spike range?"

"*Thor,* fifteen miles."

"One-two's spiked, six o'clock!" Weed added.

CHAPTER 67

Although Wilson and Weed were gaining on the *Prowler* less than two miles ahead of them, the bandits at their six were gaining on all three American aircraft due to the airspeed limitations of the EA-6B. At their current speed, Wilson and Weed would pass the *Prowler* in a minute and leave it exposed to the gaining threat—an unacceptable condition for their impromptu high-value escort mission. Wilson guessed the Iranians had radar missiles that could catch them from behind, and due to the speed differential, the Iranians could easily run down the Americans and employ short-range weapons in minutes.

Looking over his shoulder to the north, Wilson tried to find the bandits but could not discern them in the dawn light. Then, his heart skipped a beat when he saw an object, a thin shadow, cutting through the eastern horizon. It passed 100 feet behind Weed from high to low as a white mist trailed in its wake. The missile had been fired from the bandit group just outside the range that would have turned Weed into a fireball. Wilson knew what they had to do, fast, to avoid the next enemy missile from finding its quarry.

"Weed, we've gotta engage now. Short-range set, I'm high, out of burner. *Go.*"

"Two," his wingman responded as both aircraft reduced power. The pilots were held in place by their straps as the aircraft slowed through the invisible barrier that separated supersonic and transonic flight.

"*Tron, Anvil,* lean right, descend for knots," Wilson directed the *Prowler,* still running for its life. "We're going to engage with these guys."

"Roger, *Tron* five-one leaning right. You can only push a barn door so fast!"

Wilson got another quick transmission in before they turned. "*Thor,* you copy? *Anvils* one and two engaging to the north."

"*Thor,* roger. Bandits now twelve miles, hot."

"Roger! One-two, you ready?"

"Affirm!"

In measured cadence, Wilson keyed the mike. "Roger, in-place-left, *go!*"

"*Two!*"

In unison, the two *Raven* pilots slammed their throttles to afterburner and yanked the jets left. Still not sure what type of aircraft they would encounter, they pulled hard in a nose-low, energy-sustaining turn back to their pursuers to the north. With his head all the way back and straining against the pressure, Wilson struggled to look out the top of the canopy and pick up the bandits at the same time his fingers selected the radar mode and a *Sidewinder* missile. What they were doing was a dangerous last-ditch defense of the *Prowler*, running as fast as it could to the coast in a desperate attempt to escape the closing Iranian fighters.

Rolling out of his turn, Wilson got a lock at his 11 o'clock, 10 miles slightly high. He noted the distinctive planform of an F-4 *Phantom* closing the distance. Despite the screaming *Sidewinder* launch acceptability tone in his headset, but not wanting to take a chance, he selected the more powerful AMRAAM and pulled the trigger hard, holding it down. After what seemed like a long pause, the missile fell from its fuselage station. The rocket motor then ignited and shot the missile forward with a loud WHOOOM, trailing a big white plume as it sped away from under Wilson's jet.

Before his radar-guided AMRAAM impacted, Wilson saw it was tracking the "eastern" of *two* fighters, now crossing over the companion *Phantom* to engage Wilson. Just then Weed got a call out before he pulled his own trigger. "*Anvil* one-two, Fox-2 on the eastern bandit!" Wilson saw Weed's *Sidewinder* zoom away and twitch twice before tracking one of the two enemy aircraft. Wilson's AMRAAM impacted the "eastern" *Phantom* first and instantly turned the aircraft into a bright torch, tumbling through the sky and shedding flaming pieces as it tore itself apart. "Hey!" Weed cried out after Wilson's missile hit what Weed thought was *his* bandit. Weed's *Sidewinder* obediently tracked and exploded inside the plummeting inferno with no added effect.

The surviving *Phantom* was now coming straight for Weed, who quickly recovered. "*Anvil* one-two engaged with a *Phantom*. Chaff! Flares!"

Wilson was three miles away and headed to his roommate's rescue. He made a hard right turn, watching the two aircraft come to the merge on his nose, the *Phantom* turning his tail toward Wilson and inviting another shot. As Weed turned hard to go one-circle, Wilson's sixth sense caused him to do a belly check to the left. A few miles in the distance, Wilson instantly saw the dark planform of a big fighter, nose on, with a huge intake crowned by a high nose fuselage section. Seconds after he spotted it, a bright light erupted from underneath the fighter—and headed straight for him, trailing heavy white smoke.

Sonofabitch!

Wilson snap rolled left and pulled nose-down to sustain energy. He also went to idle and spit out expendables as he watched the missile arc up and then down toward him.

Time slowed. Placing the missile on the top of his canopy generated the maximum angles off for a potential overshoot if Wilson could anticipate the right opportunity to give away everything and break into it. The fiery dot seemed to lunge toward him, and he snatched the stick back in a break turn into it, banking for the second time that morning on a last-ditch maneuver to make a missile go stupid. Though straining hard, he was mesmerized as he watched the missile go horizontal as it tried to turn the corner—*right next to him.* Instead, it fell off with a twitch and shot past him, the rocket motor still burning brightly, on its way to land on the desert floor. Wilson looked up and saw his assailant high and to the west, ready to pounce. At that angle, he at once recognized the strange planform of a MiG-35. *Is that Hariri?*

"*Anvil* one-one engaged defensive!"

"Roger, I'm engaged offensive," answered Weed, "Should have a shot in 20 seconds!"

Wilson saw the MiG overbank and pull down toward him. He pushed the nose down to regain valuable knots and, reselecting burner, floated in his seat while he kept sight high behind him and slightly left. With the bandit's nose buried, Wilson pulled his lift vector up and into the MiG in an effort to force it into an overshoot. Awestruck, he watched the aircraft, cloaked in a white cloud of condensation, rotate from nose-down to nose-on as if it were stationary in the sky. He was certain another missile—or tracking guns shot—was imminent.

Wilson stood his *Hornet* on its tail to close the distance and, maybe, generate an overshoot. *Just hold him off until Weed comes to the rescue.* He felt the *Hornet* shudder and saw the flight control surfaces behind him move in computer-generated spasms in response to his efforts to keep the aircraft on the edge of controlled flight while his airspeed bled to 100 knots. Feeding in rudder, he veered left and watched the MiG slide behind him as both aircraft held their noses high.

The *Flatpack*, painted in a light blue air-superiority camouflage, with the IRIAF roundels visible on the fuselage and wings, was still behind him. The bandit now pulled his nose even higher to flush Wilson out in front, the canards working hard to keep the big Russian in controlled flight. Wilson craned his neck to the right to keep sight and watched the Iranian slide his nose back left and pull lead for a gun shot. Just before the enemy nose came to bear, Wilson pushed forward on the stick to foil the shot, which missed high. The all too familiar sound of large-caliber bullets snapped the air outside and penetrated his canopy. Once the MiG fell off to reposition, Wilson pulled up again, stood on the cans in full blower and fed in right rudder to force another overshoot. As he threw out chaff and flares, he also squeezed every bit of energy he could from his aircraft to throw off his attacker. The MiG then countered as the *Hornet* redefined the fight once more.

Wilson heard an exuberant Weed call on the radio. "Splash the *Phantom!*"

"Roger, man, get over here! I'm engaged defensive!" Wilson cried.

"Looking!" Weed answered.

"In a flat scissors…I'm high, angels eleven!"

In heavy buffet, Wilson held his nose up as high as he could, ruddering his jet into a weave to hold off the MiG. He was using every pound of thrust his twin engines could deliver in an effort to fly *slower* than his opponent. The *Flatpack* recovered and pulled up next to him. Wilson froze as he looked into the cockpit.

Those eyes. Hariri! He was fighting Hariri for a second time!

For a moment, both aircraft were suspended 100 feet from each other, each pilot looking at his opponent from across the void, oxygen masks covering all but their eyes. Hariri with enough excess power to cut his opponent in half with a multi-barrel buzz saw and Wilson on the edge of stall knowing he could be blasted out of the sky in seconds. The dawn sun glinted off Hariri's canopy; it was definitely him. Cunning, dark eyes, determined to kill.

"Flip, tally, visual. Break left!"

"I can't, man!"

Hariri lifted the MiG up and over on its back, the hooded cobra ready to strike again and deliver the coup de grâce. Wilson knew he could not stay with Hariri and watched in helpless horror as the *Flatpack* drifted back on his canopy. Unable to run, unable to maneuver away—and with Weed unable to help—Wilson squeezed every knot he could from his jet to hold off the Iranian. He was trapped. With his heart pounding almost in time to the shake of the airframe in the heavy buffet, Wilson knew he was unable to avoid another shot. Breathing heavy with fear, he sensed he was about to die.

"C'mon, man! *C'mon!*" he shouted into his mask, coaxing his jet to give him more power.

Then, Hariri's jet began to shake.

With the MiG's nose parked high, it fell off right from its own heavy weight and began to backslide. Finally, out of power to bring his nose to bear on the American or to outzoom him, the huge fighter fell straight down under Wilson.

"Yes!" shouted Wilson and, with rudder, slid his aircraft right as he watched the light blue aircraft fall away. *Turning room!* Wilson took just enough separation to gun him and rocked back on the weapon select switch. Hariri sensed he was becoming defensive and pushed his nose down to gain knots and reposition. Wilson had to make his move—*now.*

Selecting GUN, Wilson slammed the stick forward hard to the stops and pulled the throttles back. The airplane pivoted nose-down in one g flight. When he pulled the stick to neutral, his HUD was filled with MiG-35, the green gun reticle positioned just in front of it.

Hariri saw the shot coming and tried to roll left underneath Wilson, but, at his speed, the *Flatpack's* roll rate was too slow. Wilson squeezed the trigger from less than 500 feet above and riddled the right wing of the MiG. The impact explosions were followed by an eruption of fire from the right side of the aircraft, a huge fuel-air explosion that buffeted Wilson's *Hornet* and reached right out to him. The wall of bright yellow-orange flame, mixed with black smoke, enveloped him for an instant before he flew through the edge of it. Wilson snapped his head left to watch the MiG roll right, belching huge quantities of flame and smoke. Finished.

"Shit hot!" Weed crowed from a mile away. "I'm at your right four high!"

"Roger, bug southwest! Check six. Lead's three point one."

"Three point five...comin' out your left seven."

"Visual, six clear."

"Visual, six clear."

The MiG rolled out of control toward the desert floor, flame consuming the right wing root. Wilson continued to watch its descent and soon noted a white parachute bloom next to the smoke trail that marked its path. *Hariri got out to fight another day.* In the distance, Wilson saw two other chutes, which he figured were the aircrew from Weed's *Phantom* kill.

The *Raven* pilots climbed up in combat spread, searching the sky and surface for additional threats as they brought up the rear on the strike package egress out of Iran. Going feet wet over the Gulf, they descended for their tanker rendezvous, with low fuel states as usual. Above them a CAP of Air Force F-15 *Eagles* was present to discourage any Iranian fighters from pursuing them into international airspace. Weed, mask dangling down to show his wide smile of joy and exhilaration, joined up in cruise position on Wilson's left. Wilson flicked off his bayonet fitting and smiled back. Pumping both fists, gulping big lungfuls of air, the two veteran pilots were as excited as little kids at Christmas. Relieved—and alive. Wilson then made a gun-cocking motion with his left hand, followed by a slashing motion across his throat to safe the switches. They had done it.

Hariri grimaced in pain as he looked up at the canopy of white nylon above him. The seat-slap from the ejection had caused something to snap in his lower back, and the shock of the parachute opening seemed to have pulled a muscle in his groin. Floating above the desert wasteland, he saw his burning aircraft pointed straight down in a tight corkscrew just before it slammed into a fissure and exploded into a fireball. The flames soon became a black mushroom cloud rising into the morning sky, the sharp *boom* of the impact reaching his ears after several seconds. To the southeast, he could see two other palls of smoke rise from the surface. He was then conscious of the low rumble of jet engines to the southwest but unable to see them. *Probably the bloody Americans.* And then it was quiet, save for the gentle wind whistling through the nylon shrouds above him.

As Hariri descended from 3,000 feet above the desert floor, his mind tried to comprehend what had just happened. The *Hornet* he had tried to shoot down had a black bird on the tail, like Wilson's aircraft from last month. He wondered if it was Wilson. Regardless, the American was lucky, defeating his missile by doing a belly check at the last minute—and then engaging him in a slow-speed scissors. Once again, Hariri's equipment had failed him: the stupid missile didn't guide, his gun pipper was *right on him* yet the aircraft missed high.

Damn you! Hariri shouted into the still desert air—at everyone but himself.

When he had flushed the American out in front, his MiG couldn't stay with it. The tons of fuel in the wings and fuselage had caused it to fall under its own heavy weight. He knew what was happening and cursed his jet as he fell below the *Hornet*, pushing the throttles forward with all his strength, almost bending them, in a vain effort to get more power out of the burner cans. When the American had pivoted down in midair, Hariri knew he was trapped.

The bullet impacts on the wing sounded like a string of holiday firecrackers, but they were followed by the roar of fuel-fed flames mere feet away. Time slowed as he pulled the handles by instinct, watched the canopy fly off, and winced in pain as the initial impulse of the seat motor slammed into his butt and rocketed him out of the aircraft. Hariri saw the canopy rail fall below him followed by the flames and smoke of his doomed jet.

He immediately regretted ejecting. *It would have been better to ride it in.* Now he would have to face the scrutiny he would receive from Tehran and his pilots, even from Atosa.

The sun that rested on the eastern ridgeline fell below it as he continued his descent. He knew there was a settlement on the other side of the ridge, but he saw nothing here but a dry stream bed among the shadowy limestone fissures.

Maybe he would die out here: of dehydration, of a broken back when he landed, or by wild animals. *A just fate*, he thought.

He heard shouting and scanned the surface for its source. He determined the language he heard was Farsi, and soon saw a village man with two boys and a pack mule on a dusty trail. *"We are coming to you,"* the man bellowed, and the excited boys ran ahead to the spot where he was about to land.

I can't believe there are people out here! Right under me! Hariri then realized he would probably live, a fact that filled him with a deep sadness.

CHAPTER 68

After Yaz Kernoum, *Valley Forge* and the other strike group ships stood down from further combat. Remaining vigilant, they flew only routine sea surface search hops in the GOO and made single-ship transits of Hormuz to ensure freedom of navigation, but otherwise kept a low profile. The Iranian maritime forces did as well, not only due to attrition from the American attack but from a practical sense, so as not to invite a further and possibly more damaging response from U.S. forces.

Reaction from world capitols was characterized by predictable expressions of regret at the American action, with little condemnation of the Iranian recklessness that had precipitated the use of force. The statements of American condemnation were accompanied by demonstrations in several European population centers, as well as damaging comments from some American left-wing politicians. However, the Arab world was silent for the most part, save for government expressions of shock at the American action and a few chanting mobs for local media consumption. Privately, the GCC governments thanked Washington for the prompt action at Yaz Kernoum that placed Iranian missile forces in check, if only in the short term. The United States also received quiet congratulations from many of the same governments that publicly expressed regret or worse. Even the Chinese remained officially silent but conveyed their approval behind the scenes.

Tehran loudly claimed victory over the Great Satan, feeling triumphant in the fact they had absorbed the best blow the United States could deliver and still had their blue-water maritime capability intact. They also sent out ominous warnings of devastating retaliation against American and GCC installations at a time and place of their choosing. Surviving *Pasdaran* assets were back at sea for the benefit of cameras, but they stayed inside the 12-mile territorial limit and went nowhere near the international safe passage lanes of Hormuz. Crude prices began their slow decline from the previous week's spike, and the Iranians communicated through the Swiss embassy the identity of the pilot the Americans had lost on the first strike over Bandar Abbas: Commander Stephen J. Lassiter.

The great majority of Iranian people, however, were unnerved at the military action their government had initiated with the world's only superpower. They saw through the pompous indignation of the Revolutionary Guard leaders who were acting independently of the central government that itself raised regional and world tensions on a routine basis. In essence, the Iranian people were in the back of a vehicle careening down a mountain road with a wild man driving, or in this case, two wild men—Guard and Government—fighting for control of the wheel. They were tired of Iran's international pariah status, and the daily hardships it placed on them, and wished only for what the West had, what the *United States* had…a representative government and a free-market economy that could unleash the vast untapped potential of the Persian people.

The current situation began, as it so often does, with young people, students unwilling to accept the lifetime of misery their parents had endured. They re-joiced at the fall of the brutal Pahlavi government, but their joy was short-lived when they found a brutal kleptocracy, cloaked in Islamic fundamentalism, had taken its place. They protested with nonviolent sit-ins, marched with placards, staged strikes in factories and questioned the legitimacy of the regime. The smuggled video of the vicious government crackdown was difficult to watch, but Iran's youth stood firm as the protests spread to Shiraz and Bushier, and even to Bandar Abbas. The people there envied the bright free-market light that gleamed from the Emirates cites on the southern horizon each night. Claims by the government that the Americans and Israelis wanted to conquer Iran fell flat—the people knew who caused trouble for the region and for themselves in their daily lives. The Islamic Republic government found itself with a more pressing problem than the regional proximity of the American military or the existence of Israel. The loud demands of their own people were at the moment a serious threat to the regime.

Life changed little for the sailors aboard *Happy Valley* as they watched the news from Iran. Their job was to orbit a piece of water in the North Arabian Sea in order to provide an American presence that sent a message to the Iranians and reassured others in the region. Days drifted by, and when the news that *Harry S. Truman* had gotten underway from Norfolk to relieve them was announced over the 1MC, a cheer went up throughout the ship. With tensions in the region lowered to a simmer, *Valley Forge* could soon point her bow southwest and transit the coastline of the Arabian Peninsula on the first leg of her 8,000-mile journey home.

In CAG's stateroom, however, a sensitive conversation was taking place, a conversation that had a great bearing on the future of the *Ravens* of VFA-64.

CHAPTER 69

"So, I come out of the admiral's office, and Bucket tells me Saint's jet is down and he's out of the airplane. What the hell for? His *TACAN*, for crying out loud! His people are launching on the biggest strike of the year, and he's not leading it for what I would consider an "up" gripe. An irritant, yes, but for a strike of this magnitude, and considering he's the lead with jets taxiing to the cat, you take it."

DCAG Allen listened, nodding his head in understanding and approval. Swoboda continued.

"I'm like, *what the fuck*, and walk direct to Ready 7. I open the starboard-side door and see Saint up there ripping his people, just having a cow about the airplane with his MMCO. I thought he was having a nervous breakdown. The duty officer asks him for his extra ammo clip, and Saint's still out of control, screaming. He reaches into his vest, rooting around in there and friggin' *heaves* on the clip to free it, and sets off the day end of his flare! Smoke goes everywhere, but his people swing into action. And Saint…he's just standing there…deer-in-the-headlights. They yell 'Attention on deck.' Then, he's looking at me—with real fear. I mean, his lip was quivering. Darth, I think he's lost it."

"The Human Factors Board said it was the stress of combat."

Swoboda grimaced and shook his head. "Not buying it. He had a strike against Chah Bahar, lots of standoff, low threat. No, he was in over his head going to Yaz Kernoum."

"Maybe he knew it."

"Maybe he did."

"You think he effectively turned back under fire?"

Swoboda paused and looked ahead in thought. After a long silence he lifted his head. "Yeah, I do."

Allen watched him, but said nothing. Swoboda exhaled deeply.

"You know, as a nugget I had this CO who flew *Phantoms* in Vietnam. He was a fire-breathing dragon and kicked our ass. He said turning back under fire was unforgivable. I think you have to temper that—especially as a CO. You don't want to lead guys into a meat grinder and lose half the strike group. But on the other hand, you go. You take the jet and make a call on scene because *you* have the experience, or at least the seniority, to know what's acceptable. Saint abdicated that to his subordinate because of fear—of either screwing up the lead or getting shot down. It doesn't matter. He couldn't handle it. I mean, he's an administrative wizard, but he's hard on his people. When the pressure was on, he went to pieces. I'm sorry, but he's just not ready for command of that strike-fighter squadron. Maybe he slipped through the cracks to get here, but I've gotta make a call here and now."

"*Devil's advocate*," DCAG said, raising a hand, "but I've got to touch on this. Cajun took his division into that meat grinder and paid for it with his life. Not excusing Saint, but couldn't Cajun have pumped once to troubleshoot the friggin bombs or dropped them in a level delivery using his radar and FLIR? He and the jet would still be here."

"Sure, on Monday morning that's a reasonable call, but Cajun made the call then on the first strike of the operation, with one minute to go. And he got the job done—he was *committed* to it. He stepped into the arena." Swoboda took a breath and his voice trailed off. "We need more Cajuns."

"You flew into that shit as the on-scene commander—after they were stirred up down there."

The CAG nodded. "Cajun would have done the same for any of us."

The two men sat in silence and stared into space, each pondering the next move that they knew would lead to the "firing" of a senior officer. It was the same agonizing decision they had watched others make during their 20 plus years in the military. CAG broke the silence.

"I'm going to relieve him."

The Deputy Wing Commander looked up and held his gaze for a moment. "You really sure you want to do that? The board says otherwise. It's his first day as CO after Cajun's shootdown. You can make a case that a TACAN is a downing gripe. He developed a plan, and the strike package executed it successfully. They are going to second-guess you in Norfolk. Besides, we're leaving here and heading home soon."

"*He* didn't develop that plan. Flip Wilson did, and Flip took the lead for him and did an *outstanding* job. After witnessing Saint's display, *I* should be relieved for assigning him the strike lead."

"You were out of strike leads; he was next in the rotation."

"Yeah, but for the same reasons you stated, I should have thought it through better—should have assigned it to you."

DCAG smiled.

Leaning forward with his elbows on the table, CAG made a pyramid with his fingers and brought them to his lips in contemplation. "Can we agree that Saint is a project?"

"No doubt."

"You'll be CAG next year. Do you want one of your squadron COs to be a project?"

DCAG looked at his shoes and exhaled, then lifted his eyes. "No," he said quietly.

Swoboda nodded in agreement.

"Who will you get to take over?" Darth asked. "The Big Unit?"

"Jim Wilson."

"*Flip?* He's too junior."

"He's the right choice. Who knows the squadron better? Who has proven himself under fire, time after time? Who has more credibility in the air wing? If anyone, it's Flip. I'm adamant about that. He'll take the *Ravens* home as acting CO, and the Commodore can get a short-term relief in another month or so. Flip will then go on shore duty, and he'll screen for his own squadron in a few years."

"I hear rumblings about him resigning."

"Doesn't matter. He's still the guy I want."

"Are you going to talk to the admiral?"

"After the fact…not gonna ask. When in command, *command*, right?"

They again sat in silence, thinking about the next difficult step.

"How are you going to do it?"

"Not going to humiliate or shame him. I'll bring him in tonight at 2100. Want you here, too. Let him pack his trash and manifest him on the COD tomorrow. If he wants to address the squadron, fine. In the meantime, we will keep it quiet that he's leaving so he can do so with as much dignity as he can. *Forgive* him…but he's done."

"Roger," Allen said. As he rose to leave, he added, "Tough business."

"Yeah…but there are tougher things. Oh, by the way, call Flip yourself, and have him report here at 2130."

"Yes, sir."

CHAPTER 70

At reveille, Wilson rolled out of the rack after a night of fitful sleep. Saint Patrick had been relieved for cause—and CAG had informed him that he would be the acting CO. He was sworn to secrecy until tonight after the humiliated officer was off the ship.

For months he had hated Saint: hated the dressing downs, the incivility to the troops, the bullshit busywork, the incompetence masquerading as effective leadership. Saint was an anomaly. *Nobody* liked him, and he had no friends among his peers. Not long after returning from the Yaz Kernoum strike, Wilson had learned about the flare going off in the ready room. How that scene had played out in front of CAG was amazing, even for Saint. Since then, the JOs had treated Saint with thinly veiled contempt—*Coward*—and Wilson had known it would be just a matter of time before CAG acted.

How had Saint gotten this far? The Navy that had promoted warriors like Cajun, CAG, and the Big Unit had also promoted Saint. How could the system have gotten this one so wrong? Somebody along the way had liked his abilities, but was Cajun—and now CAG—the first to see through him?

Restless, and knowing he would be alone at this early hour, Wilson donned his flight suit and went up to the wardroom for breakfast. He grabbed a tray, poured himself some coffee, and went through the speed line for bacon and eggs, oatmeal and juice. Sitting down at the deserted *Raven* table, Wilson picked up the ship's "newspaper" and began reading a wire story about the NCAA Final Four. Someone placed a tray down opposite him. When he looked up from his reading, he jolted back in surprise. Saint, impeccable in his khaki uniform, stood in front of him.

"May I join you, *Skipper?*"

Wilson didn't move.

Saint waited for an answer and, when none came, proceeded to take a seat. Wilson kept his eyes on Saint as he arranged his silverware, poured cream in his coffee, and stirred it in silence, eyes down. After a long pause, Saint poked at his eggs, looked up, and spoke.

"You know, *Skipper*—or are you the CO yet? I'm told there's a big change of command ceremony in the ready room tonight."

Wilson held his gaze. A sailor was wiping down an adjacent table, but they were essentially alone.

"I won't be attending, of course, since I'm on the COD this afternoon. But congratulations just the same," Saint said between mouthfuls of eggs. He stopped and looked at Wilson as a question formed on his mouth. "Jim...may I call you Jim? Did you ever see reruns of the show *Branded*? If you haven't, it was a show in the 60s about an Old West cavalry officer unjustly accused of cowardice. His reputation precedes him wherever he goes, and he has to prove himself at every stop. You may be familiar with the opening...the accused humiliated in public, epaulets ripped off, buttons pulled off, sword broken in two, then drummed out of the fort, never to return. Are you familiar with that show?"

Wilson nodded. "Yes, sir."

"Thought you might be," Saint replied, and started humming the theme song. "*Branded... scorned as the one who ran. What do you do when you're branded, and you know you're a man?*"

Wilson pushed back from the table.

"Won't you *stay*, Lieutenant Commander Wilson? Or are you, yourself, a coward?"

Baited by Saint's insinuation, Wilson remained seated. He watched Saint closely, certain he was witnessing a breakdown.

Patrick took another bite of his food.

"That will be me this afternoon...walking down the passageway in my civilian slacks and collared shirt, carrying my sea-bag, 5,000 pairs of eyes judging me, condemning me, banished from this ship forever, but, unlike the guy in the TV show, without a word. *What do you do when you're branded?*"

"Sir, when you get home, I hope you get..."

"Oh, *spare me*, please! You don't give a *fuck* about me, Jim. I hear they are putting you in for a medal for leading *my* strike. Bravo Zulu, Commander! Here, take my command, while you're at it."

"You would have failed. You know it. I know it."

"Perhaps so. Flying was never my strongest suit, you know. But one thing I *am* good at is *working the system*. Yes, and I cannot wait to *work it*, Mister Wilson. I mean, *Skipper*, sir, to put doubt in a promotion board's mind about *you*, your crybaby whining and insubordination, how *you* left Howard to the wolves, how *you* undercut me, ignoring regulations and essentially lying to CAG because *you* had a sexual relationship with Hinton, Mister '*Family Man.*'"

With that, Wilson stood up, eyes narrowed. Saint began to laugh.

"My, the dramatics, and look at that balled fist! A fistfight in the wardroom, Mister Wilson, on your first day in command? The other side of the story *will* be told when I get home, professionally, of course, not to besmirch the sterling reputation of a *war hero* such as yourself. Despite what I say, you'll probably do fine. After all, you do have your skin color to hide behind."

"You pathetic racist sonofabitch."

"Do I get under your *skin*, Jim? Hey, no pun intended. Play that race card, Jim. Press charges! You see I have nothing to lose. I'll deny it of course; it's basically us here, alone at this early hour, *hours* before your precious lieutenants wake up. Did anyone ever tell you that when you wrestle with a pig, both get dirty—and the pig likes it! I will *like* getting dirt on you, Mister TOPGUN Golden Boy."

"You are going *down*, Commander, and I will lead the witnesses at your mast hearing."

"Are you going to take me to *mast*, Skipper? Can I go *down* anymore than I already am? Heh. You know I always wanted to tell a CO to go to hell. Fuck you, Wilson. Fuck you. *Fuck you*." Saint spit the words out under his breath, seething as he also rose to his feet. From across the room, two shocked sailors watched, wondering what was going on between the pilots.

Wilson kept his eyes on Saint as he walked around the table toward him, wondering what he would do when he got there. Saint stood his ground, smiling at him and whispering, "C'mon and hit me, Jim. Hit me. You've been waiting for this moment. *Do it*." Wilson stopped, nose to nose with Saint, fury barely in check, hating him. Saint smirked back at him with satisfaction.

"*You pussy*," Saint spewed, his face suddenly contorted in contempt.

Wilson inhaled deeply through his nose. He could go to CAG immediately and make several charges: threats, racist comments, conduct unbecoming. How he wanted to shove Saint through the bulkhead, to *show him*, to exact *revenge* for the months of public humiliation and derision. Flashbacks of the knotholes Saint had dragged everyone through, the pain and embarrassment he had caused the squadron, exploded in his memory as he stared him down.

A smile slowly spread across Saint's face, a wide beaming grin that showed his perfect white teeth. Wilson couldn't let Saint *win*. Leaning in toward him with narrow eyes, Wilson simply whispered, "*Go*." He let the word hang there between them, and turned to leave.

Saint chuckled. "Turning your back on a senior officer? More ammo."

Wilson stopped and faced him. "There's only one officer in this room, and it's not you."

Chapter 71

Ready 7 was standing room only except for the two empty chairs in the front row that had belonged to Cajun and Saint. The officers were in their seats, the chiefs standing in the back or filling a few empty seats. The *Ravens'* Command Master Chief opened the door to the ready room and barked, "Attention on *deck!*"

All hands jumped to their feet as CAG Swoboda strode to the front in his khaki uniform, DCAG behind him. "Seats, please, relax," CAG commanded, and the assembled personnel complied. DCAG took Saint's chair, but, out of respect, no one sat in Cajun's seat.

Swoboda clasped his arms across his chest and began. "Ladies and gentlemen, I've called you here this evening to convey to you my admiration of and appreciation for your performance on this deployment, and particularly these past few weeks. During our recent combat operation, VFA-64 led the wing in sorties flown, ordnance expended and enemy aircraft shot down. That's no surprise to me as the *Ravens* have always been my go-to warfighting squadron, a winning team I can depend on to deliver fused ordnance on target, on time. You in this room have lived up to the high standards set by your ancestors in Korea and Vietnam.

"You've had some tough breaks on this deployment, not the least of which is the loss of your fine CO, Cajun Lassiter, to enemy fire. Even after that devastating blow, you compartmentalized and never missed a beat during your subsequent combat hops over the beach. I thank you, your Navy thanks you, and our nation owes you a debt of gratitude.

"By your performance, from you guys in flight suits, the maintainers and admin personnel, all led by a superb chiefs' mess, you've earned the best leadership the Navy can provide. As your immediate senior in command, I did not feel you had the leadership you deserve. No doubt you've heard that I relieved Commander Patrick of his duties, and he left the ship this afternoon for Oceana and reassignment. I offered him the opportunity to address you, and my understanding is he did not take it. This is a decision I did not come to hastily, and it was not one incident that caused me to act. I didn't ask for 'approval' either. It is my decision who remains in command of my squadrons. Commander Patrick is to be afforded every courtesy befitting an officer of his rank, and I encourage you to reach out to him should you desire to do so."

Wilson thought of the morning's wardroom exchange, and found it ironic that CAG had just bestowed honor upon a wretched man who deserved none. Swoboda then motioned with his hand. "Lieutenant Commander Wilson, come on up here."

Wilson rose, and standing next to CAG, faced his squadronmates. Swoboda put his hand on Wilson's shoulder and said, "This is your new skipper."

The room was now energized, but the muffled cheers and scattered applause showed that the *Ravens* were not sure if it was appropriate to unleash their joy in front of CAG. Wilson noted, though, big toothy grins from Dutch and Sponge, and Pyscho nodded with an approving smile. CAG continued.

"Flip Wilson is a proven warrior, and he has my complete trust and confidence. During our remaining time in this AOR, he's the guy I want leading you, and he'll bring you home in the coming weeks. The Commodore will get you a new CO, but, until then, Lieutenant Commander Wilson is your acting CO. *Congratulations, Flip!*"

As the room erupted into applause and cheering, Wilson accepted the small gold pin that signified command at sea. "Thanks, CAG," he replied, shaking hands with a humble smile, still not knowing what to make of it.

"You're the right man for the job, Skipper," CAG said. "Well done."

A call for *"Attention on deck"* rang out, and the Air Wing commander departed the way he had come. DCAG offered Wilson a handshake of congratulations, with a wink, before he followed CAG out of the ready room.

Wilson was mobbed as his squadronmates shook his hand and slapped his back. He was touched by the sincere well wishes from the chiefs. After the commotion died down, Dutch asked, "Skipper, what's your first command?"

Wilson looked around. "Let's get some music going in here."

"QUOTH THE RAVEN!" boomed from inside Ready Room 7.

Before he left the ship, Saint Patrick took a last look at his empty stateroom. Not the sentimental type, he nevertheless knew he would never see the inside of another one, much less set foot on a warship again. His meticulously planned career had come to an end—here.

Wearing his grey slacks and blue polo shirt, Saint hoisted his bag and walked aft on the starboard passageway toward the Air Transport Office. He felt the stares at once...dozens of nameless sailors noticed he was out of uniform, in civilian clothes. Silently, they braced up against the bulkhead so he could pass, blank faces watching him leave while they stayed. Bitter bile formed in his mouth—in essence, they were tearing off his epaulets, seizing his sword and breaking it over a knee. *These idiot sailors who know nothing, judging me,* he thought. He then saw The Big Unit coming in the opposite direction, both uncomfortable to see each other. Averting his eyes until the last minute, Saint looked up in time to see the *Buccaneer* XO slow down to say something with an anguished face.

"Bill, I'm sor-"

Saint silenced him with a look as he trudged past. *He's one of them,* he thought.

In the ATO shack, alone in his bitterness, he was surrounded by sailors and junior officers waiting, like him, to board the COD and return to staffs in Manama or Doha or travel home to the states. During the hour-long wait, his silent anger and sullenness was noted by everyone, and some sailors stood rather than sit next to him. After the scheduled event launch was complete, he heard the COD trap and listened to the hum of its engines as it taxied to its spot abeam the island.

Suddenly, the Air Transport Officer entered and said, "Okay, everyone, put on your cranials and float-coats." Like a condemned man being led to the gallows, Saint stood and donned his cranial and life vest, and, befitting one so senior in rank, was the last person to board the aircraft. The ATO Chief cheerfully offered him one of two window seats, which he took without a word, ignoring the crewman's brief as he cinched down the straps to his four-point release.

With the engines started, the cargo ramp slowly closed, swallowing up the flight deck scene in front of him. Saint then looked out the small window, only to see a *Raven* jet outside, prolonging the agony. He looked at the pilot, face covered by the visor and mask, elbows on the canopy sill and hands on the towel racks. He noticed the pilot looking in the small C-2 window, staring at him, as the *Hornet* waited for the next yellow-shirt command. Saint wondered who was in that cockpit, motionless, eerily judging him from across the flight deck. *They never gave me a chance,* he thought. His resolve stiffened. He would have his revenge.

Once in Bahrain, he bought some groceries at the commissary and went to his transient quarters for what became a five-day wait for his flight to the states, during which time he did not bathe or shave or step outside, but instead stared silently at the walls. He thought of his father, Vice Admiral William S.

Patrick: Vietnam MiG-killer; carrier CO, fleet commander; life-of-the-party with a broad smile and deep laugh; a work-hard, play-hard flag officer. His father had been distant to William Jr. as a boy; being on deployment, putting in the extra hours to advance his career and cheating on his wife left little time for games of catch or helping his only child with homework.

In spite of all that, like most sons, Saint wanted to please his father and gain his approval. An appointment to Annapolis was the first step, the first of *hundreds* of steps to get this far. Then *command at sea*...a middle management rung on the career ladder to four stars. He had worn the pin on his uniform! But CAG had taken it away because of the moron Randall and the stupid TACAN. And the sonofabitch had given it to the insubordinate Wilson.

Saint cleaned up in time to board the charter flight for Philadelphia in the wee hours, with stops in Sigonella and Lajes, sitting silently and staring out the window between bouts of fitful sleep. Over 30,000 feet below were clouds and water and, in the distance, North Africa and more miserable brown sand. Over the long day of flight, he ignored the Air Force sergeant sitting next to him, not saying a word to anyone, just staring at the endless water below.

Landing in Philadelphia, Saint had an overnight layover for the flight to Norfolk. However, being wide awake, he rented a car and drove down the Del-Mar-Va Peninsula to his home near Virginia Beach, arriving at his Sandbridge beach house as the eastern horizon was lightening. The long drive had given him plenty of time to think. For years, Saint had considered wives "distracters," so there was no family to greet him, no food in the refrigerator. He was not expected by his neighbors. *He was not supposed to be here.*

He entered his bedroom and opened the top drawer of his dresser to retrieve the large command-at-sea pin given to him 20 years ago by his father. His full-dress white uniform was ready in the closet where he had left it in November, and to it he affixed the pin above the ribbons on the right breast pocket, its rightful place. He thought of his father's words: "Get your reports in on time and stay out of trouble in the air, and you'll do fine."

Thanks for the great fucking advice, Dad.

The red sky to the east brightened as he buttoned the last gold button and placed the hook from his sword belt through the opening in his uniform. Annapolis. Noon formation at Bancroft Hall. *Pre-seeennnnt!...Hoh!* Hundreds of mids in his regiment, standing in orderly ranks of navy blue uniforms on a crisp autumn day, entering Bancroft for the noon meal in sharp formations under *his* command. At 21 he knew he was on his way, and no matter how many stars Dad had received, he would have one more.

Medals clanking, he walked out to the beach and into a stiff Atlantic wind that kicked up angry surf. Looking left toward Dam Neck, he saw a couple in the distance. To the south, he saw nothing but white mist along the shore. He thought again of his father, who, a few hours from now would join his retired flag cronies for their early tee time at the North Island course. The golf course was in sight of the Third Fleet Commander's home where, as a boy, he had spent so many lonely and troubled hours looking at the blue Pacific.

Saint pulled the .45 from his belt and looked at the eastern horizon: red, menacing, *angry.*

Red sky at morning, sailors take warning, he thought as he placed the muzzle inside his mouth.

CHAPTER 72

Nine *Raven* FA-18s, flying as one, descended in a shallow left-hand turn just east of Cape Henry. Now less than 10 miles from home, they would make up that distance in little over a minute. As Wilson lined the formation up on Runway 23, he glanced left at Little Nicky who maintained parade position, with Clam on his wing in the background. Both concentrated on flying sharp formation as Wilson rolled out in a measured rate. On his right side, Guido and Weed followed his moves as they remained welded to his wing line. Even though their faces were covered by helmet visors and oxygen masks, Wilson could recognize them, after months of flying together, by their body types and how they sat in the cockpit.

The pilots had been airborne just over an hour, launched 470 miles east into a gorgeous spring morning scattered with columns of cumulus clouds that hovered over a blue ocean. Wilson and the fly-off pilots had found it hard to sleep the night before, so excited were they at the prospect of seeing, in mere hours, the families they had said good-bye to six months earlier. For the first half of their flight, the pilots saw only water and clouds. From their vantage point at 28,000 feet, though, it wasn't too long before they could see the thin beige strand of the Outer Banks leading north from Cape Hatteras to Virginia Beach and Cape Henry. When they checked in with controlling agencies that had familiar names like GIANT KILLER and Oceana Approach, their excitement grew. Wilson looked over his shoulder at his wingmen and chuckled to himself when he noted they had all eased into parade formation, even though they were well out to sea and no one four miles below could admire their skill.

While the others concentrated on him, Wilson stole quick looks at the scenery. Dozens of sport fishing boats and motorized yachts poured out of Rudee Inlet leaving sharp white wakes behind them. The sun-washed, high-rise hotels along the strip boasted beaches covered with sunbathers, and the cars jammed Atlantic Boulevard as usual. To the north, beyond the green space of Fort Story, he saw the merchant ships lined up on their way past the north and south entrances of the Chesapeake Bay Bridge-Tunnel. Various containerships, bulk carriers, and crude oil tankers headed for the ports of Norfolk, Baltimore, or Philadelphia, on the final leg of their long journeys from Rotterdam or San Juan…or Hormuz.

Wilson keyed the mike. "Oceana Tower, Navy Alpha Hotel four-zero-zero, flight of nine, seven miles northeast for a flyby."

"Navy Alpha Hotel four-zero-zero, Oceana Tower, winds one-niner-zero at five. You are cleared for a flyby. Welcome home, *Ravens*."

"Four-zero-zero, roger. Thanks, great to be back."

Raven One eased them down to 350 knots over Virginia Beach Boulevard and lined them up on the squadron hangar. From three miles away, he could make out a faint cluster of colors in front of the hangar bay doors and allowed himself a small smile. Mary, Derrick and Brittany were in that cluster with the rest of the *Raven* families, and he put them in the middle of his HUD as he signaled the others to level off.

In a tight wedge, they thundered over the crowd and disappeared behind the hangar, leaving behind a group of giddy women, hugging each other in their tight dresses and sunglasses. The children jumped up and down, and a few startled babies cried from the sudden noise.

South of the air station Wilson detached Weed and Clam to lead their own formations back to the field. He took his three-plane echelon into the break, whipped his jet over to the left and pulled power to idle, waving at the crowd below. Wilson then dropped the gear and flaps and called the tower for permission to land, the first time in six months he would land on a runway.

Once they were all on the ground, Ensign Jackson, who had left the ship early with members of the advance party, drove out to meet them in the flight line truck. As they taxied up to their hangar in order, Anita delivered a bouquet of roses to each of the pilots. Wilson's heart soared when he spied Mary in a black and white dress, new to him, with one kid clinging to each of her hands. As the pilots had briefed it in the ready room, they shut down 18 engines on signal and popped their canopies in unison. Wilson grabbed the roses and a few other items, bounded down the ladder, and removed his helmet.

"Welcome home, Skipper!" Senior Chief Nowlin said as he took Wilson's helmet.

"Thanks, Senior Chief. You doing good?"

"Doin' good, sir," Nowlin answered, smiling. "Now go to your family."

"Roger that, Senior!"

Wilson donned his squadron ball cap and had taken only a few steps before Derrick broke loose from his mother and ran at him full speed. In one motion, he gathered his son up and squeezed him tight. "Oh, I missed you!" he said.

"Me, too, Daddy!" said Derrick, his voice muffled by the flotation collar of Wilson's survival vest.

As other families squealed with joy around them, a beaming Mary walked up with little Brittany in her arms. Wilson deposited Derrick on the concrete and looked at Mary. "Hi, baby!" he said before he wrapped his arms around his wife. As he kissed her lips and held her tight, the bottled-up tension of the past six months ran right out of him. He then took his daughter from Mary and smiled at the three year old, who was still not quite sure what was happening.

Thank you, God.

The *Buccaneers* had returned for their homecoming before the *Ravens* and were gathered in the hangar space next door. A small party followed. With smiles all around, the *Raven* and *Buc* families put aside their competitive spirit in their adjacent hangar spaces to enjoy an abundance of food and drink with excited kids showing their fathers missing teeth or new toys and with the relieved women clinging to their men. Wilson shook hands with his pilots and hugged their wives or girlfriends. He spied Olive smiling with an attractive middle-aged woman dressed as if she were at Churchill Downs for the Kentucky Derby, a woman he learned later was Olive's mother. The rest of the squadron personnel would come home the following day when *Happy Valley* shifted colors at Pier 12 in Norfolk.

But Jim Wilson had one more task to perform before this cruise was over.

CHAPTER 73

That evening, Mary got a sitter for the kids and the Wilsons paid a visit to a suburban residence several miles south of the naval air station. Mary drove them into the familiar driveway of a brick colonial, grass neatly trimmed, porch light on.

"You ready for this?" she asked him.

"Yeah. Let's do it."

They walked to the porch in nervous silence, and Mary pressed the doorbell. After a few seconds, Billie Lassiter opened the door.

"Jim," she said with a warm smile and threw her arms around him. "Welcome home."

Wilson didn't know what to say as he hugged her back, but knew he needed to be there. Billie invited them inside and poured everyone a cup of coffee. Her oldest son, Drew, a strapping, dark-featured high school junior, came downstairs to join them. He sat close to his mother, both surrounded by the memorabilia from Cajun's career on every wall of the family room. A middle-school daughter was out with friends, and their 10-year-old boy played video games in a nearby room.

After a few moments of awkward small talk, Wilson asked, "How are you?"

Billie sighed and looked at her son. "We're doing okay. My parents just left, and Mary and the girls have been wonderful. The support from the whole Oceana community has been great. The President called…and we had a nice conversation. The governor of Louisiana called, too, as well as the Chief of Naval Operations. Everyone is supportive and has said to call if I need anything."

"They mean it."

"I know, but we have what we need now. My family has some money, and we're okay. Jim, how was the ceremony on the ship?"

"Very nice. We did it topside on a beautiful day in the Indian Ocean in our white uniforms. The admiral said Skipper Lassiter was a gentle soul with an iron will. We then did a missing man flyby. As the missing man pulled up into the sky, the aircraft went into a cloud and 'disappeared.' That symbolism was moving to all of us who saw it. It was a solemn, very beautiful ceremony. The squadron took his loss hard. He was a popular CO."

"Who flew the missing man plane?"

"Olive… Kristin Teel."

"Ha! Missing woman! Steve would have found that funny!"

Mary giggled to release her nervous tension, and Wilson smiled. For the first time, though, Wilson noted Drew was not listening. He looked sullen and detached. *Angry.*

"I was shocked about Bill, so sad. The poor man. Why did he do it? Did he think Steve's death was his fault?"

Wilson's pained expression revealed he didn't know how to answer. "I don't know. We were shocked, too. He was… *different.*"

Billie then asked the question Wilson had known was coming. "Jim, what happened?"

Drew now looked at him, eyes cold, waiting for his answer. Wilson looked down and swallowed.

"After the Iranians made the initial attack on our frigate, we were tasked with a series of strikes along the Iranian coast to degrade their ability to close the Strait of Hormuz. The skipper was assigned to lead the first strike into their main naval base at Bandar Abbas. We launched and formed up, but, close to the target, we noted our weapon guidance system was degraded. Skipper immediately made the call to roll in, to deliver the weapons in a dive, which exposed us to greater threat. All of us got our bombs off, including the skipper, but, as he pulled up, his jet was hit by antiaircraft fire and exploded. He had no chance of survival."

"Did you see it?" Billie asked him.

"I saw the wreckage as it fell to the surface."

"You didn't see it blow up?" Drew asked, with definite hostility in his voice. Billie looked at him.

"No, Olive—that is, Lieutenant Teel—did. She was right next to him."

"He didn't eject? Are you sure? The Iranians didn't capture and murder him after you guys abandoned him?"

"*Drew!* You will treat Commander Wilson with respect!" Billie scolded.

Wilson raised his hand. "It's okay, Billie." He looked at the teenager's fierce, accusing eyes and knew he had to try and reach out to him with compassion and understanding. "I saw your father's jet tumble out of the sky, burning and breaking up until it impacted the water. None of us saw a parachute, and a parachute would have been obvious on our night-vision goggles. There was no emergency beeper, no radio call, no flares, no raft in the water, no reflection from your father's helmet. We would have seen that, too.

"We stayed until Captain Swoboda directed us to leave because we were low on fuel. After we left, he directed the pilot of his *Super Hornet* to make runs over the crash site. They took heavy fire the whole time and saw no sign of your father, no evidence he was alive. Over the next two days, we continued with the operation, but we also searched for your dad, until the Iranians identified him. We have some national assets that verify he was never alive on the surface. He probably died instantly and never knew what hit him."

"That's what you think," Drew replied, looking at Wilson with contempt.

"That's my professional opinion, as an eyewitness to your father's final moments."

"So Tony Swoboda's dad sent my dad to his death."

"*DREW!*" Billie was mortified.

Wilson remained calm and answered, "Your father was the finest strike leader on that ship, and CAG Swoboda knew it. The target your father was given was a tough one, and he devised a plan to get the job done at a minimum of danger to us. Captain Swoboda was devastated by the loss of his trusted friend and shipmate. He'll be here to visit with you tomorrow because I asked him to let me come over tonight."

"But the stupid weapons didn't work!"

"The Iranians did something to upset their guidance. We still don't know what they did or why the other aircraft weren't affected like we were. But your dad knew we had to succeed right then to take advantage of the element of surprise we had, before the Iranians could disperse their assets or hide 'em. He was a man of conviction and accountability—and courage. If he didn't do his job at that moment, then someone else would need to do it the next night—and it would have been a lot tougher for them. He reacted immediately, exposing himself to danger so others wouldn't have to."

At that moment, Drew Lassiter broke down in heaving sobs. Tears had already lined his cheeks before he could cover his face in embarrassment. He choked on the words he forced out of his mouth. *"But I don't have a dad!"*

Mary's hand flew to her lips to hold back sobs, and Drew slumped into his mother's arms. His six-foot body was wracked by waves of pent-up emotion as Billie patted his back with stoic resolve. Wilson struggled to remain in control, and remembered one last image of his fallen commanding officer.

"Just before your father briefed us that night, I spied him on the hangar deck. It was sundown, and he stood by himself, looking west, the pink glow reflected on his face. It was a beautiful scene and, as he stood there taking it in, I have no doubt he was thinking of his handsome family far over that horizon. He had much to live for, and I'm sure that one of them was the pride he felt in having a young man like you as his son."

Her stoicism gone, Billie's lip quivered as she looked at Wilson. She mouthed the words, *"Thank you,"* and continued to comfort her son. She tried to fight back her own tears but failed. With a start, Drew bolted into the next room.

The Wilsons took that as a cue to leave. Billie wiped her tears and fanned her face before Mary surrounded her with a hug.

"Thanks for coming. I'm so sorry you had to experience this on your homecoming night," Billie said with a nervous laugh. "Drew didn't mean it."

Wilson hugged her. "We know, Billie, and we are here for you now and always. Whatever you need, you call us."

She pulled away and held him at arm's length. "He loved you, you know."

"And I him. He was the greatest CO I'll ever have."

CHAPTER 74

A brisk November wind churned the fallen leaves into a small cyclone outside the Pentagon Metro Entrance. Mary Wilson led her two children toward the metal detectors, her parents and Wilson's parents behind her. Mindful of the growing line of businessmen waiting to get through the security checkpoint, she tore the jackets off the children, and then realized she needed to go through first. As she removed her overcoat, it caught on her brooch. Her mother helped her free it while she became increasingly frazzled. Finally free of her coat, she walked through the detector and set it off—the brooch! She removed it before trying again and avoided eye contact with the impatient businessmen who looked at their watches and with the disapproving security personnel who monitored the checkpoint.

Once inside the building, they were met by Wilson in his service dress blue uniform, a loop of gold braid high on his left arm, and Weed in his khakis. Both men were there to escort them to the E-ring for the ceremony. Once up the escalator and into the open hallways, the children broke free and dashed ahead, dodging the endless stream of adults in business suits and harried action officers of every rank and service carrying folders of paper. An amused general watched Mary scurry after the children in her heels as they weaved through the crowd, first in one direction and then another. Mary looked over her shoulder at her husband, and Wilson got the message. "Excuse me, Mom, Dad. I think I need to lend a hand here."

After navigating corridors and escalators for several minutes, they found themselves in *Navy Country*, a command-suite corridor on the fourth deck with a décor characterized by wood paneling, paintings of former Navy Secretaries, and glass-encased ship models that showed the evolution of U.S. naval vessels through the years. The reduction in foot traffic allowed them to see people nearly a football field away as they walked down the corridor. The group peeked in at the furniture and paintings of some well-appointed offices and passed by others that had certain signs above the doors: "Secretary of the Navy" and "Chief of Naval Operations."

Wilson led them into a wood-paneled conference room. Empty of furniture, a ceiling-to-floor navy blue curtain at one end of the room served as a backdrop to the "Stars and Stripes" and the Navy flag. Through the windows they could see people working in the offices of D-ring.

Many guests were already assembled, including several *Ravens:* Dutch, Blade, Psycho and Smoke had driven up from Oceana, and Olive had taken the afternoon off from Test Pilot School at NAS Patuxent River. The former squadronmates caught up with each other in the back of the room, and Wilson found a moment alone with Olive.

"How you doing?" he asked.

"Good. Okay. Studying hard."

"Great. Flying a lot?"

"Yeah," she said and smiled. "Flew a *Seahawk* the other day. Pretty cool. I mean, you are right in the weeds, and you have to *fly* that thing."

"I'll bet. Thanks for coming."

"Wouldn't miss it."

"It was an honor to be in the same squadron with you. You are a hell of a naval officer."

Touched, Olive nodded her thanks. "Thank you. If I stay, it will be to serve with you again."

As Wilson smiled, another lieutenant commander wearing a gold braid loop walked up to him and whispered, "The boss is on the way."

Wilson excused himself from his squadronmates to greet his boss. The Chief of Naval Operations was a surface warfare officer in his late fifties, tall, with thinning dark hair accented by a touch of gray around his temples. His engaging smile, a smile especially suited for ceremonies like this, lit up the room as he walked in. Wilson introduced him to his family, and the CNO shook each person's hand warmly and gave special attention to the children, both of whom were taken by this gregarious stranger. The sleeves on his blue uniform were weighted down by bands of braid that signified his four-star rank. The junior officers, who had never met a four-star, much less a CNO, were dazzled. After he worked the room, the CNO stepped with Wilson to the front and welcomed the crowd, recognizing everyone he had just met by name.

"Those of us in the Navy know it is a *family*, and we especially see that today. Retired Chief Warrant Officer Raymond Wilson, with whom I served over 20 years ago, stands here as the proud father of Jim. You may not remember, Warrant Officer Wilson, but I was the XO of *Sampson,* and your SURFLANT inspection team found a few discrepancies with our damage control equipment, discrepancies that you laid out to me in no uncertain terms—with a few 'sirs' thrown in there to keep everything professional."

The audience chuckled, and Wilson's father beamed. "*Sampson* was a good ship, CNO."

"Well, *yes, she was*, and she was made better by the great job you did inspecting us and pulling no punches, and I mean *no punches*, in your debrief to me. So thanks, Warrant—I think—and welcome!"

After laughter and polite applause, the CNO turned serious.

"Again, everyone, thanks for coming today. It's an honor for me to preside over this ceremony, the first presentation of this prestigious combat award to a naval aviator since the Vietnam War. When I met Jim Wilson, and interviewed him to be my aide, I was immediately impressed by his professional demeanor, his attention to detail, and, of course, his quick, friendly smile.

"While I was aware of his combat record during his recent deployment aboard *Valley Forge*, it wasn't until I read the justification statement for this award that I realized just how *eye-watering*, to use an aviation term, his aerial performance was over the skies of Iran. A close-in dogfight, twice, the first time completely unarmed, with one of Iran's most experienced pilots, who flew a secret fifth-generation fighter.

"Jim also planned and led a key strike on a vital facility that we needed to neutralize. With minimum time to plan and a small number of aircraft to accomplish the mission, this was an awe-inspiring performance. Jim Wilson's feats are already legend throughout the aviation community.

"Jim, I think you will agree that, to a great extent, the awards we receive are a reflection of the outstanding job done by our subordinates. This award, however, is truly a reflection of your superb flying ability and preflight preparation. *You* took the aircraft and training our country provided you, and with your own aggressive spirit and a resolute commitment to excellence, you contributed to a big win for our nation. This award Jim, is *yours*, and your Navy and your country thank you."

The CNO picked up the Navy Cross and motioned to his flag writer. "Linda, go ahead..."

As the military members in the room came to attention and the award citation was read, the CNO placed the Navy Cross, second to the Medal of Honor in precedence, on Wilson's chest, speaking in a low tone only Wilson could hear.

"Jim, I can't tell you how honored I am to present this distinguished award to you and to have you on my staff. Well done, sailor. My very best wishes to you and your family." With a smile, the admiral then added, "We'll go downtown to celebrate a bit. After that, take the rest of the night off, and I'll see you tomorrow at zero-six-hundred!"

Remaining at attention, Wilson smiled slightly and said, "Thanks, sir."

The ceremony concluded, and Weed walked Wilson's family back to their cars in south parking. The CNO offered Wilson and Mary a ride in his staff car to the reception, and they walked down to the River Entrance to wait for it. While standing next to the heavy columns, they looked north toward Rosslyn, and watched as a 757 airliner weaved along the river on final approach to Reagan National Airport.

"You wish I was flying that?" Wilson asked Mary.

"You want to?"

"Well, I'm flying a desk here. That looks kind'a fun right now."

Mary studied the airliner. "No."

"No?"

"No, that kind of life isn't for people like us. Gone half the time. Chaotic schedule. Low pay. Inexperienced pilots who barely shave. No, not for us. Who needs that kind of stress?"

Wilson smiled, put his arm around her, and looked at the next jet in line.

Navy Cross Citation

The President of the United States of America takes pleasure in presenting the Navy Cross to Lieutenant Commander James Daniel Wilson, United States Navy, for extraordinary heroism in action against the enemy on 17 February 2008 and 20 March 2008 as a Pilot in Strike Fighter Squadron SIXTY-FOUR (VFA-64) embarked in U.S.S. VALLEY FORGE. During a routine training mission over the Northern Arabian Gulf, his incapacitated wingman drifted into Iranian territory. Demonstrating exceptional aeronautical skill, Lieutenant Commander Wilson used his own aircraft in an attempt to return his wingman to international airspace. After Iranian alert fighters destroyed his wingman without warning, he engaged, completely unarmed, a heretofore unknown fifth-generation fighter, successfully evading fire and safely returning to force. On 20 March Lieutenant Commander Wilson displayed exceptional professional skill and sound judgment in planning and leading an extremely dangerous, low-level night, power projection strike on the strategic and heavily defended Yaz Kernoum missile assembly facility in Iran. Seconds before bomb release, an enemy surface-to-air missile was observed to be tracking his plane. Undaunted by this threat to his personal safety, Lieutenant Commander Wilson avoided the missile and then proceeded to complete his attack, releasing all weapons with extreme accuracy and dealing a significant blow to Iranian ballistic missile delivery capability. After release, he guided his plane through intense antiaircraft artillery fire and on the egress defended a valuable strike asset by turning back to the threat and pressing his attack, engaging and downing two enemy interceptors including one confirmed fifth-generation aircraft. His superb airmanship and courage reflected great credit upon himself and were in keeping with the highest traditions of the United States Naval Service.

ABOUT THE AUTHOR

Captain Kevin Miller, a 24-year veteran of the U.S. Navy, is a former tactical naval aviator and has flown the A-7E *Corsair II* and FA-18C *Hornet* operationally. He commanded a carrier-based strike-fighter squadron, and, during his career, logged over 1,000 carrier-arrested landings, made possible as he served alongside outstanding men and women as part of a winning team. Captain Miller lives and writes in Pensacola, Florida.

RAVEN ONE is his first novel.

I hope you enjoyed reading *Raven One* as much as I enjoyed writing it. Whether you found it good or "other," I'd sincerely appreciate your feedback. Please take a moment to leave a review on Amazon or Goodreads.

Thanks and V/R,
Kevin

IT HAD ALL GONE TO HELL SO QUICKLY...

KEVIN MILLER

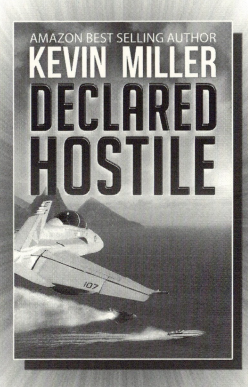

AMAZON BEST SELLING AUTHOR
KEVIN MILLER
DECLARED
HOSTILE

107

When does a covert mission become
an undeclared war?

www.braveshipbooks.com

DECLARED HOSTILE

PROLOGUE

(OVER THE YUCATAN CHANNEL)

Doctor Leighton Wheeler suppressed a yawn as he arched his back and stretched his arms. With nearly two hours to go in the cockpit of the Beech *King Air*, he fought the urge to sleep. A half-moon high above kept him company and provided a horizon out in the middle of the Gulf of Mexico, but he slapped his face to stay awake. He knew he was now, at this 1:00 am hour, in the trough of human performance, and he had to concentrate on his gyro horizon and altimeter. Five hundred feet—even with altitude hold engaged, it was unnerving to be so low over the black water underneath. He figured it didn't make much of a difference. One hundred feet or one thousand feet; it looked the same over a dark ocean. He was tired, and the energy drink he had downed before take-off was now wearing off. He considered another one, but the physician in him rejected the idea. He twisted off the top of a plastic water bottle instead and took a long swig. He replaced the top, and as he put the bottle back in the cup holder, glanced at his fuel...a little over 2,200 pounds with 453 miles to go and fifteen knots of wind in his face. He would make it, but barely.

Wheeler twisted the heading select switch to 324, and the aircraft rolled gently right as it steadied up on course. *Nothing out here,* he thought, unlike the Yucatan Channel some forty minutes earlier. He had not been able to avoid flying right over a half-dozen lights below him. Not knowing what they were had bothered him, but they were most likely fishing boats, Cuban and Mexican. He knew it was too early for the motor and sailing yachts, most of which spent the winters in and around the Virgin Islands, and the Belize yacht traffic was another month away at least.

The moon illuminated the low scattered clouds, so typical above Caribbean waters. They cast splotchy shadows on the surface below. Wheeler knew the next hour would be boring, so to pass the time, he thought of his favorite subject...himself.

A youthful forty-seven years old, Wheeler owned, with three partners, the Women's Cosmetic Center, the top plastic surgery clinic in Birmingham, Alabama. They offered everything from rhinoplasty to Botox...the whole gamut of services, many on an outpatient basis. The overwhelming majority of the procedures were boob jobs, with augmentation surgeries leading the way. For nearly two decades the Women's Cosmetic Center had offered hope and delivered results, with the ladies (and their men) gladly paying top dollar for their services. It was a gold mine.

Just last month two of Wheeler's clients had brought in their teenage daughters for consults. Cullen, his own teenage daughter, wanted him to perform an augmentation for her 16th birthday—to a tasteful C-cup that would "allow her clothes to fit better," an argument that was part of the tried and true cover story. He certainly wasn't about to let his lecherous partners touch her. Cullen would go to Atlanta with her mother, Tammy, for the procedure, allowing time to recuperate before her birthday party next month.

Tammy. A former homecoming queen at Alabama, Tammy had never allowed anyone to augment *her*—not even her husband, despite how much he had wanted to add some strategic curves to her tall and leggy figure. She was all for her husband performing plastic surgery for *other* women, and Wheeler had done work on several of her girlfriends. He had even had an affair with one of them that Tammy probably knew about but didn't press him on. No, all was perfect with Tammy: hair, makeup, body, clothes, house, kid, husband…in that order. Between the Garden Club, the Tri-Delt national vice-presidency and innumerable shopping trips to Atlanta and Nashville, Tammy had little time for her husband. That was all the excuse he needed.

Ten years ago he had taken up flying and now was the instrument-rated owner of a *King Air* twin. He used the plane for trips to South America to perform *pro bono* reconstructive surgery on cleft palates for Doctors Without Borders, giving deformed kids a chance for a normal life. Yes, the guys at the Club admired him for it, *giving back* to underprivileged third-world kids and all that.

He accepted their kind words with aw-shucks modesty, never letting on for a minute about his *other* motive: holding heavenly bodies in Bogotá and Cartagena and watching what the owners of those bodies *could do* with them. The coke, the money, the nightlife, and the girls—always the girls. *I'm an American surgeon, here to help children.* He would say it with a shy smile, looking down at his drink. And the girls crumbled before his eyes; leaning in, grateful, fawning, *buying it,* cooing in English or Spanish. It didn't matter. Within the hour, they would lead him out of the hotel lounge and to their rooms or apartments—rich European girls on holiday, local gold-diggers, sophisticated American businesswomen, Asian flight attendants on layover, ages ranging from 22 to 50. A citizen of the world like Doctor Leighton Wheeler believed in diversity.

The first year he flew to South America twice, and now he was on his fourth trip in the past 12 months. Surely Tammy suspected something, but his altruistic alibi provided cover for both of them. She took advantage of his absences with shopping outings with her girlfriends to Atlanta or New York. Both felt entitled.

Yes, the coke! How it felt when it entered his nostrils, the euphoric explosion of his senses. The girls fed it to him! They carried it in their purses and formed neat lines for him on their creamy thighs. And the guys at the airport loved to look at the plane, crawl around inside, talk flying. *Señor Doctor, want a blow before you take off?* And he would take a hit and fly hundreds of miles to the Caymans in what seemed like minutes, alert like he had never been before, feeling like he could fly on to Alaska if he had the fuel. Cocaine just didn't seem to be a big deal south of the U.S. border.

One day a guy he had befriended during a previous trip was at the airport and asked if he could take a package of "product" with him back to Birmingham. "C'mon, man. No one is going to suspect you, Mister Save-the-Children Surgeon!"

The guy tossed a worn duffel bag in back with his other luggage and handed him a black zipped-up folder. Wheeler glanced inside and quickly closed it, but once he got airborne with the autopilot engaged, he laid the contents out on the seat next to him and counted: *five hundred* Ben Franklins and one typed note.

"Mike" met him at the FBO in Birmingham to park him and to service the aircraft, just like the note said. He smiled as he pulled the bags from the compartment, placed the duffel in his tractor, and helped Wheeler button up the airplane. Chatting away, he was a really friendly guy, one of the nicest guys Wheeler had ever met. When they were finished, Mike offered his hand, just as a golf partner would coming off the 18th green. "Enjoyed it!" he said.

Wheeler had found yet *another* double life to lead, one that paid very, very well, more than enough to cover any of Tammy's activities. *Sure, Honey, go to Lenox Square Mall in Buckhead. Take Cullen. Anything you want. Have fun!*

Tonight Wheeler was on his fourth "mission," and it was a big one. He had told Tammy he was going to spend a couple of nights in the Caymans and rest—and get something nice for Cullen—before he took off for home. Once he arrived at George Town and parked his plane, "Luis" met him and led him to a different *King Air*, one loaded with product worth over $100 million on the street. With a box lunch and a five-hour energy drink, he set off in the aircraft for a dirt strip along the Mississippi coast called Goombay Smash Field. He would abandon the airplane there—the cost of doing business—and "Rich" would pick him up, drive him to Diamond Head, and put him in a G5 for a sprint back to the Caymans. The morning sun would still be low in the sky by the time they landed back at George Town.

After a day of rest at the hotel, maybe a little *senorita* overnight, he would fly his own plane to Birmingham the next day for another hero's welcome—and a $5 million payday. A yacht. Yes, a yacht would look good parked next to their condo in Orange Beach. He would go to Miami next week and make a down payment on a 53-footer. Once the purchase was sealed, he would make a house call on a former augmentation client—to perform an important post-op examination, of course. That client, and many, many others, inspired the name with which he would christen his new yacht: *Two For the Show.*

A sudden *whoomm* on his right startled him. He studied the eastern horizon but saw nothing but ghostly clouds overhead—no lighting flash. He held his gaze and strained his eyes for several seconds. Nothing. He wished this airplane, expendable or not, had weather radar in it and cursed the cheap-screw *narcotraf-ficales* for not getting him a suitable plane for a long, overwater flight. Instead they had put him in this rattle-trap to save overhead dollars. He checked the INS and noted he was making 265 knots ground. The wind must have shifted to the east. And, for the umpteenth time tonight, he checked the fuel, doing a mental time-distance calculation.

What was that? he thought. *A bird? Did I hit a bird?* The airplane hadn't twitched, so he reasoned it may have been an engine surge...but all seemed normal. There were no indicator lights. He shifted in his seat uncomfortably, wishing he had a blow right now, and turned his thoughts back to Miami.

As if jolted by electricity he flinched by the loud *pops* coming from the right engine. Wheeler let out an involuntary *Fuck me!* as the airplane rolled hard right and the engine, mere feet away, exploded into flame. *Oh, God, please!* he cried, instinctively pulling the airplane left and up, away from the water below. Red and yellow lights flared on the instrument panel, and the annunciator bleated shrill warnings of danger. He pushed the throttles forward and felt heavy vi-bration from the right side, so he retarded the right throttle to idle and fed left rudder to stay balanced. He was already passing 1,000 feet, hyperventilating, and was nearly paralyzed with fear at the persistent flames coming from the right engine nacelle. Whimpering in confusion, he noted airspeed decelerate through 120 knots. *Don't stall the damn thing!* He let out another involuntary sound as he pushed the yoke down.

His heart pounded as his hand lifted the right throttle around the detent to shut down the engine. *Mayday!* he cried without thinking, then realized he was truly alone over the invisible sea, the nearest land over 100 miles away. Should he turn right to Cuba? Left to Mexico? He hit the right engine fire light which doused the flames, and turned the yoke easy left. *What the fuck?* Still breathing hard through his mouth, his eyes went to the RPM gauge in an attempt to identify why the right engine had burst into flame. He was in a positive climb—even a shallow 100 foot per minute rate of climb was welcome—and he calmed down enough to think about a divert into Cancun. As he rifled through the maps to find the low altitude chart and dial up Cancun's VOR/DME, he made a decision. This was it, no more trips to South America, *ever.*

With a deafening series of staccato hammer blows, the right side of the cockpit erupted into fragments. As the instrument panel exploded in front of him, Wheeler drew his hands and arms in by reflex to defend himself from the flying debris. The windscreen shattered, then caved in from the airspeed. Wheeler was conscious of only three things: the rubbish and forced air swirling about him, the loud roar of the left engine permeating the cockpit, and the fact he was crying out in terrified shock.

Bullets? Is someone shooting at me? Why? Who? Mexicans? Cubans? Out here, at this hour? Then, without warning Wheeler was slammed against the left side of the cockpit with more force than he had ever experienced. A metallic wrenching sound accompanied a violent roll right, and he realized he was upside down and still rolling. *An aileron roll in a* King Air! His control inputs were powerless to stop it, and sensing flames again, he began to scream, *Please, God, no! This can't be happening!* Watching the altimeter unwind, not knowing what caused it, not knowing what to do, Wheeler feared the unspeakable. *Not now! Not here!*

Pinned as he was amid the churning chaos, Wheeler's charmed life flashed before his eyes. Brian, his childhood best friend, smiling at him, hair flowing behind as they rode their sting-ray bikes down a steep hill. Tammy's loving brown eyes looking up as they walked hand-in-hand to her dorm. A group of med school classmates laughing as he told a joke at the pub near the hospital. A beaming five-year-old Cullen running up to him as he got out of his car after a day at the clinic. Sitting in the church pew during Easter Sunday services, looking up at his mother—his beautiful young mother in a smart suit, her smooth skin and dark hair in its sixties flip highlighted under a pillbox hat. Her red lips forming a tender smile as she took his hand. *"God loves you, Leighton."*

The *King Air,* one wing gone, corkscrewed through the darkness in a near vertical dive. Trapped by the force of it, Doctor Leighton Wheeler, tears pushed *back* toward his temples, was filled with regret.

"I'm sorry, God," he shouted with eyes closed. *"I'm sorry."* He cracked open his eyes in time to see the yellow light from his burning plane reflected on the surface of the Caribbean as it rushed up to meet him.

Follow Flip Wilson on his next deployment and order *Declared Hostile* today!
https://www.amazon.com/dp/B01KNGFCAS

SUPERSONIC CARRIER AVIATION FICTION FROM

KEVIN MILLER

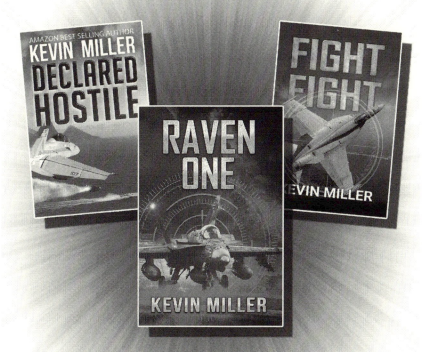

The Unforgettable Raven One Trilogy

www.braveshipbooks.com

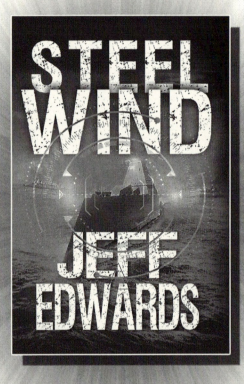

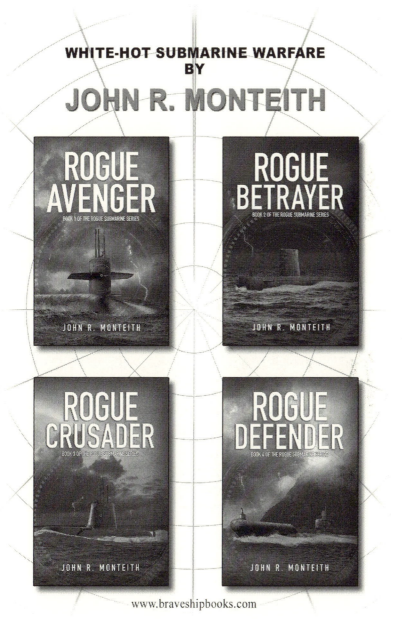

WHITE-HOT SUBMARINE WARFARE
BY

JOHN R. MONTEITH

ROGUE
AVENGER
BOOK 1 OF THE ROGUE SUBMARINE SERIES

JOHN R. MONTEITH

ROGUE
BETRAYER
BOOK 2 OF THE ROGUE SUBMARINE SERIES

JOHN R. MONTEITH

ROGUE
CRUSADER
BOOK 3 OF THE ROGUE SUBMARINE SERIES

JOHN R. MONTEITH

ROGUE
DEFENDER
BOOK 4 OF THE ROGUE SUBMARINE SERIES

JOHN R. MONTEITH

www.braveshipbooks.com

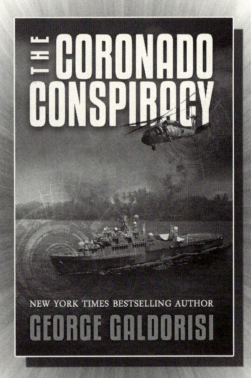

Made in the USA
Monee, IL
15 July 2021

73681453R00206